BORDER STORM

Amanda Scott

ZEBRA BOOKS
Kensington Publishing Corp.
http://www.zebrabooks.com

To Nancy and Charles Williams,
who proved that
Tea and Sympathy
is good for everyone.
Thank you!

One

Shrill was the bugle's note,
Dreadful the warrior shout . . .

The Scottish Borders, August 1596

A drizzling, early morning rain had cast a dark, gray gloom over Liddesdale when, without warning, shortly before sunrise, the English army struck.

No beacon flamed. No voice cried out. The enemy had crept up during the night with—for the English—uncustomary stealth.

A single horn sounded the charge, and after that, pandemonium roared. Two thousand heavily armed soldiers under the command of Thomas, Lord Scrope, Queen Elizabeth's warden of the west march, descended on the unsuspecting citizens of Liddesdale.

Most had little chance to defend themselves when soldiers in steel bonnets and plate crashed through their cottage doors, slashing men, women, and children without mercy. Men or lads who would have run to warn their neighbors were cut down before they could escape.

As the army swarmed over the hills and swept inexorably up the dale, gunshots rang out and steel clashed against steel wherever a Liddesdale man managed to lay hand to pistol, sword, or dagger before meeting his Maker. Women and children screamed, and injured, dying men and horses screamed, too.

At first, the attackers did not bother with livestock. Bent only on punishment, they fired cottages and killed without compunction, most caring little whether the victim was male or female, child or septuagenarian.

Halfway along the dale, on Watch Hill, the grassy ridge between the Liddel and Tarras Burn, a lad of ten summers herded a flock of sheep. His father had said the sheep would not mind the rain, and he did not care if his son minded it or not. Wee Sym would drive them to pasture, willy-nilly.

Sym did not mind the rain, although he had complained about it for form's sake. He enjoyed the solitude of his days with the flock, and although he and his two canine companions had to keep a cautious eye on their charges, they had time now and again for more interesting activities as well.

The first hint of trouble came from the dogs, unimaginatively named Lass and Laddie. Both abruptly stopped dashing and darting to turn heads as one toward the southeast, their softly folded ears lifting alertly. Attuned to these signals, the little shepherd stopped to listen. At first, he heard only the patter of the rain and the bawling of lambs, but his senses were nearly as well honed as the dogs', and the horn's call, distant though it was, was enough.

"Tak' 'em, Lad! Tak' 'em, Lass!"

Shouting the orders over one skinny shoulder, he took to his heels, certain that the well-trained Border collies would guard the flock and not wasting one precious second to make sure they obeyed. His toughened bare feet flew down the wet, grassy slope toward Tarras Burn, and when he slipped on a patch of mud, he slid downhill for a bit on his backside but picked himself up again without losing more than a moment's time. Sharp pebbles did not slow him, or anything else. He knew every bog and obstacle that lay in his path, and his feet were quick and sure.

At the bottom, leaping from stone to stone, he crossed the burn. Now, at the height of summer, it was safe enough, although it was known in spring flood to run with such speed that men said it was impossible to drown in it. The burn was so wild then that it would dash out a man's brains before his head went under.

Most of the area around the burn was boggy, part of the infamous Tarras Moss that, along with the great primeval forest known as Tarras Wood, generally protected the inhabitants on that side of the ridge from English invaders. But, here and there, cottages occupied higher, dryer bits of land.

At the first one, Sym shoved open the unbarred cowhide door without ceremony and shouted for the woman and three children gathered round the fireplace to flee. "Raiders comin'!"

Without awaiting a response, he was off again, finding two men next in a sheep pen, marking lambs despite the drizzle. "Horns!" he shouted at them. "Raiders in the dale!"

"To horse, Will," the elder snapped to the younger. "Ride for Hermitage!"

"But the laird's clapped up at Blackness!" the younger protested.

"His captain will ken wha' to do. I'm for Broadhaugh, m'self."

Paying scant heed to the exchange, Sym was off again, having known before the men spoke what they would do and where each would go. It was not the first time in his short life that the English had attacked Liddesdale and its neighbors.

More cottages hove into sight, clumped around a small common near one of the many peel towers that dotted the Scottish Borders, this one a dilapidated square tower perched on a rocky outcropping above the burn. Sym saw men, women, and children on the common.

"Raiders," he cried. "Trumpets!"

In well-practiced actions, the people of the hamlet reacted, women calling to the children and darting into the cottages to grab the various household goods they called "insight," while the men snatched up arms and fetched ponies.

Sym raced on.

He could see others now on the opposite bank of Tarras Burn, running to spread the alarm. Beacons soon took fire on hilltops despite the drizzle, for the wood was soaked in sheep fat and the beacon woodpiles kept covered until needed.

The lad's breath came in heaving gasps, but he could not stop. He had farther to go. At the next hamlet he found breath enough to shout, " 'Ware raiders!"

Doors opened. People gaped out at him and then darted back inside, reappearing with children and precious possessions, ready to make for the hills and nearby Tarras Wood. The shadowy gloom of the dense forest loomed ahead of him now in the gray mist.

As Sym darted into the forest, he heard a low, thunderous rumble behind him in the dale. He also heard screaming. The raiders had swarmed over the ridge.

His chest ached, but he dared not pause to catch his breath. Hoping the trees would provide cover enough for him to reach the cottages near the center without being run down by mounted soldiers, he ran on. With the slightest luck, any who tried to follow him would find themselves trapped in one of the many bogs that turned Tarras Moss and the forest floor into a treacherous maze. Sym had known them all since his toddler days and easily found his way.

He emerged at last from woodland into a clearing and flew over its grassy slope to the first of three stone cottages, shouting, "Dad! Dougald! Raiders!"

The cottage door opened, and to his relief his father's tall, lanky figure filled the opening. Even before Sym could gather wind enough to shout again, he saw Davy Elliot cock his head to listen in much the same way that the two dogs had.

Sym stopped running at last and bent over, hands to his knees, gasping to catch his breath. He heard voices and scrambling movement from his parents' cottage and by the time he looked up again, his father was already emerging from the second cot, where his uncle lived, and heading for the third, which housed his granny and gramp.

His cousin, yellow-haired Anna, ran to help catch the ponies.

When Sym went toward his parents' cottage to help his mother with the bairns, he saw a familiar dark-haired young woman standing in the doorway. "Laurie," he shouted, "dinna stand like a post. There be raiders comin'. Tak' yer pony and gang home!"

"Your mam's got the baby, Sym," she replied calmly. "Come and pick up Wee Fergus for her, will you?"

Without argument, he hurried to do her bidding, although it was still a struggle to catch his breath.

Laurie was a special friend. Not only was she merry enough, most days, to enjoy a prank as much as he did, but he liked that she called him plain Sym and not Wee Sym the way his folks did. Around other people she called him Davy's Sym, the way others called his dad Sym's Davy. Sym was named for his gramp, and since so many Elliots and Halliots bore the same first names, it was easier to tell them apart by using their to-names. His was Sym's Davy's Sym to anyone who took long enough to say such a mouthful. Mostly, though, folks other than Laurie called him Wee Sym and would do so until he did something distinctive enough to make them call him by a more impressive name.

Breaking into his train of thought, Laurie Halliot said thoughtfully, "Do you think you can hold Wee Fergus if I put you on my pony, Sym?"

"Aye, o' course I can," he said, still trying to catch his breath. "But what will ye do then, yourself? That pony willna tak' three."

"Your father will help me. Come now, be quick!"

But when they went outside again, although Laurie's pony stood waiting, when she moved to help Sym mount it, Davy Elliot stopped her.

Hurrying toward her with his brother Dougald at his heels, he said, "We canna tak' your pony. Ye'll be needin' it."

"Not if we've still got time enough for you to put me up a tree in the wood," Laurie said firmly.

"Aye, well, I can do that right enow, but if you're no goin' to need the pony, then I'll put my Lucy and the bairn up. We've ponies enough for the old folks, Dougald's Anna, and ourselves, but the lad there will ha' to scamper."

"Nay then, Davy," she protested. "You can see that he's purely winded. He'll bide with me to protect me from the raiders. Can you do that, Sym?"

Sym nodded, fiercely determined to see that no harm befell her.

"Send the others on to the cave, Davy," Laurie continued in a matter-of-fact way. "Then, once you've put us up the tree, you must go after them—and watch well. They will need you when the raiders leave."

"Ye might fit into the cave along wi' the rest of us," Davy said, but his tone was doubtful.

"Nay, you've barely enough room for yourselves," she said. "Quick now, the others are ready. Sym, give Fergus to your Uncle Dougald and come with me."

Kilting up her long skirts as she ran, as barefoot as Sym, Laurie dashed ahead of them up the wet slope of the clearing to the woods.

Sym did not think that he could run another step, but to his relief, when he had handed Wee Fergus to his uncle, Davy swung him up onto his shoulders. With Sym clinging to his long, dark hair, Davy loped after Laurie.

She had not gone far into the woods before she stopped beneath a tall beech tree and looked back. "This one will do," she said in a low but carrying voice. "The lower branches are too high for anyone to reach unaided. No one will seek us here."

From his perch on Davy's shoulders, Sym looked down at her with a frown and said, "But what if they fire the trees?"

"They are too green and wet from the rain," she replied. "If the raiders fire aught, they'll fire the cots. Oh, be quick, Davy! I think I heard a man shout."

Quick as thought, the tall man swung the boy down and clasped his hands together to make a stirrup. When she put her right foot into it, he hoisted her high, and she climbed like a cat, clearly not caring that both males could catch glimpses of all that she had beneath her skirts.

When she was safe on the lowest sturdy branch, she lay lengthwise along it and reached a hand down for the boy. His father practically tossed him to her, and after she had dragged him up, the two of them climbed higher.

"Go back now, Davy," she called down to him urgently.

"I can still see ye," he said.

"Then we'll climb higher. Now, by the blessed Mary, go!"

Without further protest, he ran off to look after the rest of his family.

"You climb higher, Sym," Laurie said. "Climb as high as you can, but take care that you do not fall. I shall be right behind you."

Sym began climbing, but he had not gone much higher when he stopped and whispered over one shoulder, "Some'un's comin' close."

His words barely reached Laurie's ears, but she understood them, for just then she too heard the soft splat-splat of a horse's hooves on the wet leaves of the forest floor. A moment later, she realized that two horses approached.

She could not climb higher without forcing Sym to do likewise, and not only were the branches above him slender and thus less safe, but the two of them could not risk noise or movement. Taking comfort from the fact that dense leaves almost completely concealed him, she decided that no one would see him from the ground. But she knew that they might see her if they looked up at the right moment.

Not daring to speak, she hugged the thick trunk of the tree and tucked her skirts beneath her, trying to make herself small. Her overskirt was a soft green, close enough to the leaves' color to go unnoticed, but her underskirt was the usual red flannel, and she prayed that none of it was showing. On such a gray day, even a wee patch of red would stand out like a spark in Davy's black cave.

The horsemen drew nearer. She was surprised that they had

managed to get so far without encountering difficulties in one of the bogs.

The two men did not converse, and she realized that they were probably listening for sounds of flight or alarm. If they knew about the three cottages in the clearing, doubtless they were hoping to surprise the inhabitants.

A moment later, she saw them in their gleaming steel bonnets and plate. One was tall and broad-shouldered, riding a dun-colored pony with black points that was larger than most she had seen. The other man rode a chestnut roan. He was shorter and square of shape, his waist and hips nearly as wide as his shoulders. He carried a bill, an English weapon, part spear and part ax. His companion wore a sword at his side and a longbow strung across his back where he could easily reach it. In one ungloved hand, he carried an ominous looking pistol at the ready.

Scarcely daring to breathe, knowing that the boy above her would keep still, she sent a prayer heavenward. Although it was not unheard of for the English to kill women, even women of her rank, she did not fear for her own life as much as for Sym's. English raiders were not noted for asking questions or for encouraging conversation of any sort before putting their victims to the sword. Nevertheless, she felt oddly calm. Had Tarras Wood suddenly swarmed with horsemen, she told herself, she might have felt more fear, but the two silent men seemed harmless—unless, of course, one of them looked up.

In any event, if they caught her, she would do whatever she had to do to save the lad.

When the pair drew rein almost directly beneath the tree where she and Sym hid, she stopped breathing. A chill of pure terror shot up her spine. Quaking, she realized that she had grossly underestimated her composure.

The man carrying the bill said in a gruff voice, "There be two or three cottages ahead. Like as not, they've heard nowt, so we should take 'em easy."

The other man wiped a leather-clad arm across his face and brow, and then, resting his pistol on a muscular thigh, he took off his steel bonnet, revealing a shock of red curls a shade or two darker than his neatly trimmed, reddish-blond beard. As he thrust long fingers through his hair, he tilted his head back.

For one horrible, frozen moment, Laurie's gaze locked with his.

"Brackengill?" The man with the bill spoke sharply, and the red-haired man turned to look at him.

"Aye?"

"If ye've finished combing your pretty locks, we've work yet to do."

"Let's get to it then." His expression did not alter.

When he replaced his helmet, raised his pistol again, and rode on, Laurie decided with a surge of relief that the dark foliage surrounding her had prevented him from seeing her after all.

TWO

He rang'd all around down by the woodside,
Till in the top of a tree, a lady he spy'd.

Sir Hugh Graham, Lord Scrope's deputy warden, had seen the girl in the tree. Indeed, he had seen her clearly enough to know that her eyes were large for her face and so dark as to look black. But he had seen little more than those dark eyes and the small, pale, heart-shaped face framed in a halo of dark, damp curls.

It was the face, he thought, of a child. Doubtless, her eyes had seemed enormous because of her terror.

As he followed Martin Loder, Scrope's chief land sergeant, Sir Hugh was not certain why he did not mention seeing her. He knew as well as anyone—perhaps better than most—that a female could be as dangerous as any man. For all he knew, the girl in the tree held a pistol cocked and ready to shoot.

A nerve between his shoulder blades twitched.

The girl had seemed young, though, and more terrified than terrifying. At all events, despite the nervous twitch, every fiber of him rebelled at the thought of telling Loder about her.

Martin Loder was a villainous creature, envious of his betters and overeager to prove himself to Scrope. Moreover, given a choice in the matter, Hugh did not make war on women or children. What he had seen that day had already been enough to turn his stomach, though his reputation was that of a hardened soldier.

The last straw was seeing armed men forcing women and children to remove their clothing, then leashing them in pairs like dogs and driving them naked through the dale. That sight had stirred his impulse to follow Loder into Tarras Wood.

Loder's courage—or foolhardiness—had surprised him, for the man was not aware until Sir Hugh had shouted that he was following him. Sir Hugh considered himself a brave man, but he would not have ridden alone into that infamous bog-ridden area.

He understood Scrope better than he understood Loder. Scrope was determined to teach Liddesdale a lesson, and Hugh understood his fury, for Liddesdale was a notorious reivers' nest. The whole, wide valley was a grim, forbidding place dotted with robber towers. Shut in by bleak fells, it consisted largely of quaking morass and vast primeval forest. Reivers flourished in every march, but in Liddesdale, every able-bodied man was one.

Just months before, a small army of Liddesdale men and other ruffians—doubtless under the direction of their powerful leader, Sir Walter Scott of Buccleuch—had raided Carlisle Castle to free one of their own. Carlisle was Scrope's stronghold.

Having made the English warden look foolish, they had to pay. Sir Hugh had understood that from the outset. He had supported Scrope when, immediately after the Carlisle raid, determined to punish the raiders, Scrope had organized several forays against them with the official blessing of the Queen and her Privy Council.

Those forays accomplished little of note, however. Buccleuch had retaliated each time, with the result that livestock moved back and forth across the line so frequently that men said the poor beasts were losing weight as fast as they gained it. As a result, many would likely be too weak to survive the winter.

Elizabeth of England was as offended as her warden over the high-handed way the Scots had freed his prisoner and royally indignant at Buccleuch's continued forays into her realm.

She had written angrily to King James of Scotland, demanding the Borderer's immediate surrender to her authority.

So far, the King had refused to comply with that demand, and Hugh was certain that if James enjoyed the same freedom that some of his predecessors had, he would have continued to repel all her demands. But James hoped to succeed to the English throne on Elizabeth's death. Knowing that she could squash those hopes with a word, he feared her anger and thus bowed to the inevitable.

James did not prostrate himself, however. He merely ordered Buccleuch into ward at Blackness Castle, which overlooked the Firth of Forth a few miles outside Edinburgh. If he had hoped to placate Elizabeth with the compromise, however, he had failed.

The English Queen, like nearly everyone else in England and Scotland, soon began to hear tales of Blackness luxury and of James and his favorite out hunting together. She heard tales of dicing and playing chess and, worse, tales of the two of them laughing together at Scrope's fury. Her demands became more imperious. James, she insisted, must hand Buccleuch over to English authorities.

In the meantime, with Buccleuch safely out of the way in Edinburgh, Scrope had stepped up his activities until, in Hugh's mind, the present one overstepped the bounds of what was fair and reasonable. He had dutifully supported the warden's earlier raids, understanding as all Borderers did the need for immediate retaliation. But it was not long before he began to suspect that Scrope was not acting out of a sense of duty but out of plain vengeance against Buccleuch. The rescue of the prisoner had deeply wounded Scrope's pride, and now he was extracting a far heavier toll than even blackguard-ridden Liddesdale deserved to pay.

In truth, Hugh reminded himself, Buccleuch had taken Carlisle by stealth and cunning with less than a hundred men. Many were not even Liddesdale men but were followers of Rabbie Redcloak, the man Scrope still pretended to believe he had captured.

And to be fair, they had had reason for the raid. Scrope's erstwhile prisoner was actually Sir Quinton Scott, Buccleuch's cousin and deputy warden, and Sir Hugh's cousin, Francis Musgrave, had seized him unlawfully during a truce.

Scrope had ignored these details, however. He had also ignored the fact that no one had suffered in the raid (since he had mounted no resistance), and as time passed, he developed a veritable passion for revenge, culminating in the Liddesdale raid. Hugh knew that Scrope had acted out of pique and thought less of him for it.

"Looks like the cowards have fled," Loder said, snapping Hugh's thoughts back to the present.

Realizing that they had reached the clearing Loder had mentioned and that the three cottages showed no sign of life, Hugh felt a wave of relief. Was he growing soft? Surely Scrope would say that he was if he ever learned about the girl in the tree.

Loder said, "We'd best fire these cots."

"Leave them," Hugh said curtly. "Only the thatch and doors will burn, and the smoke is likely to draw our men nearer. This deep in the woods, we'd lose any number of them to bogs, if not to armed Scots perched in those damned trees. I don't know what drew you here, Loder, or how you found this place without miring us in a swamp, but I'll be happy just to get out of here alive."

"I know the way," Loder said. Shooting a look at Hugh, then looking away again, he muttered, "Had cousins hereabouts when I were young."

Since he said no more, Hugh assumed that the cousins were not friendly now. Such was the way of life in the Borders.

He expected an argument over whether to leave the cots or burn them, but Loder offered none. He merely suggested that they look inside each cottage to be certain that the occupants had gone and had left nothing worth the taking.

"You check," Hugh said. "I'll keep watch out here in case of ambush. At least the rain seems to have stopped."

Nodding, Loder walked his horse to the first cottage and dismounted.

Hugh kept his pistol at hand. The presence of the girl in the tree meant that there were folks about, but instincts honed over years of service told him that no danger threatened him. He watched alertly while Loder took his time to search the first cottage but relaxed when he entered the second without incident.

They had made little noise, but there were still only two of them. If armed men waited in the trees, they would likely have seen or heard some sign of them by now. Indeed, they would likely be dead. Although he and Loder were both skilled at defending themselves, the odds were not in their favor. He wondered again why Loder had seemed so willing to enter the woods alone.

Loder was not a friend. Having made no secret of his belief that Hugh served as deputy warden only because he had a powerful kinsman in London, he also made it plain that he thought he, Loder, would make a better deputy. If he laid eyes on the girl, he would surely tell Scrope that Hugh had seen her and tried to protect her. He would do that just to make trouble, and Hugh knew that Scrope would listen.

He did not trust any of Scrope's men. Most were mercenaries who, for a price, would do whatever Scrope told them to do. They cared little for folks on either side of the line. On the other hand, Hugh believed that his own men generally felt as he did about the attack, especially with regard to the burning of so many crops and cottages, and the terrorizing of women and children.

The burned cat-and-clay cottages did not matter much, because their owners could rebuild them quickly—usually in a day. Stone towers were easily patched, and doubtless many people had managed to remove their belongings, just as those in the clearing had.

As for cattle and other livestock, Hugh told himself sardonically that any loss would be a temporary annoyance at best, because the Liddesdale men would just steal others to replace them. Crops were a different matter, though, for without them people could starve, which was why Scrope was so bent on destroying them.

Borderers on both sides of the line disapproved of burning crops and had since the beginning of the violence a century before. When the Earl of Hertford had served as a march warden, he had once had to hire Irishmen to burn the Scots' standing corn. His English Borderers had refused to burn their neighbors' crop.

The size of Scrope's army precluded such refusal, and Hugh's men dared not disobey Scrope's orders, in any case. They knew that many Grahams were already at risk, because Scrope suspected that members of the tribe had helped Buccleuch with the raid on Carlisle. He blamed them as fiercely as he blamed Buccleuch, and he was bent on punishing as many as he could catch and convict.

Still, Hugh thought, it was one thing to order men to pursue someone who had just stolen one's cattle, or to help carry out a righteous act of vengeance. But Grahams, like other clans with members on both sides of the line, disliked setting off in cold blood to harry folks who might be allied in marriage or otherwise to them or their kinsmen. Their way of life, after all, was much the same.

Even Scrope's mercenaries had displayed certain wariness upon entering Liddesdale. They had obeyed Scrope's command, but Hugh knew that they hated and feared the area.

Liddesdale fairly teemed with scoundrels, but the forests and bogs that protected their hideouts terrified most invaders. Even the mercenaries knew that any safe paths—if the reivers had not blocked them with tree trunks or the like—were imperceptible to untrained eyes. Added to the ever-present risk of ambush, therefore, invaders risked floundering, even drowning, in a stinking swamp.

With these thoughts stirring his unease again, and reminding him again that one girl in a tree might mean many men in other trees, Hugh was glad to see Loder emerge from the third cottage, shake his head, and go to mount his horse. Watching him, hearing nothing more menacing than water still dripping from the leaves of the trees, Hugh wondered if the massive raid would accomplish anything positive.

Many—Scrope's men and Hugh's as well—had commented quietly on Scrope's weak justification for so great an invasion. The usual excuse for a warden's raid was that he had goods to pursue. That was not so today.

A warden could also pursue a man he wished to bring to justice, but that required him to declare a "hot trod," and such a pursuit had to take place within six days of the offense. One could hardly argue that a military invasion taking place months after the offense fit that definition.

However, Scrope had offered the third excuse, declaring that the activities of a particular surname—to wit, the heathenish Scotts—had become so obnoxious that they warranted the laying waste of Liddesdale with fire and sword. Even that excuse was feeble, though, considering that their leader lay in ward at Blackness.

"I still think we should fire the cots," Loder said as he joined Hugh. "There's still smoldering peat on the hearth in each one, and only the outer thatch will be wet. You saw how easily the ones in the dale caught fire despite the rain."

"Leave them," Hugh said again.

Shrugging, Loder turned his horse back up the slope the way they had come.

Hugh nearly suggested that he take another route, one that would not pass near the tree where the girl was hiding. He dared not, though. Not only would any other route likely prove more dangerous but he did not want to take even a chance of stirring Loder's curiosity.

They entered the shadowy gloom of the woods.

"Look at that," Loder said abruptly.

Although the shadows were dense, Hugh thought at first that Loder had seen the girl in the tree. He was looking that way.

Even as that thought crossed his mind, however, he heard

a snarl and saw a wild black boar angrily pawing ground near the base of a tall beech.

Almost certain it was the tree where he had seen the girl, Hugh grabbed his longbow and swung it into position to shoot. Quickly nocking an arrow, he let fly, aiming to wound the boar rather than kill it.

"Bad shot," Loder said when the animal dove screeching into underbrush.

Hugh quickly sent a second arrow after the first and was nocking a third when the screeching stopped.

"You got him!" Loder exclaimed. "We can take boar steaks to his lordship."

"Let's see if we can fetch him without falling into a bog," Hugh said.

"I never thought you could hit him," Loder said, clearly impressed.

"It wasn't as hard as you might think," Hugh said. "I shot too quickly the first time; that's all."

His eyes still alight at the thought of roasted boar meat, Loder urged his horse to a trot and rode on ahead.

Hugh followed at a more leisurely pace. Glancing up as he passed beneath the tall beech, he could see no one.

Three

Say thou, lady, and tell thou me
How long thou wilt sit in that tree.

Laurie felt as if she might tumble from the tree out of sheer relief when the two men rode away. She heard them stop to truss up the boar, and for a few moments her terror returned, but then they were gone. For a long while, the only sounds were the faint gurgling of a nearby burn and the soft drip-drip of rainwater falling from leaves to the forest floor.

Not until she heard the chatter of a squirrel and an exchange of birdcalls did she say quietly, "Are you all right, Sym?"

"Aye, sure," the lad muttered from his precarious perch above her on a branch that strained even under his slight weight. " 'Tis odd he missed the creature when it were standing and then hit it when it were running. Me dad says that's the hardest bowshot to make, 'specially through shrubs like that."

"You heard what he said. He shot too quickly the first time. Likely, his nerves were twitching a bit here in our woods."

"Aye, he did say that, too," the boy agreed, adding with disdain, "English."

"They found their way to your clearing, Sym. Few on this side of the line know where it is. It is never wise to underestimate the English, laddie."

"Well, at least they didna fire our cots," Sym said practically. "Can we get down now, Laurie, d'ye think?"

"Aye, I doubt they'll come back here today."

"Can ye get out o' the tree wi'out help?"

She grinned. "Can you?"

"Aye, sure, I can," he retorted indignantly.

"Well, I'm going to get down first," she said.

"Ye'll ha' to," he agreed. "I canna very easily get by ye."

Not until she moved did she realize how stiff she had become, sitting there tightly tucked against the tree's stout trunk. When the two men had ridden into the clearing, she and Sym had crept precariously upward until she could no longer see the forest floor through the leaves and branches of the beech. Then, when the boar had rushed the tree, either stirred by their scent or simply by its own cantankerous nature, she had thought they were spent. Surely, the two men would come straight to their tree to see what the boar was after.

What good fortune it was that the Englishman had missed his first shot and had sent the beast charging off away from them!

"Watch well," Sym muttered from above her as she carefully made her way to the low, stout branch onto which Davy had first hoisted her.

"Aye," she said, thinking the distance to the ground looked farther now than it had when Davy had stood below them. Then it had not looked nearly far enough.

Taking a deep breath, and using her bare feet against the rough trunk to steady herself, she slipped from the branch until she was hanging by her hands. Swinging just enough to miss the thick root ball at the foot of the tree, she let go.

She felt her overskirt snag as she dropped but was too intent on landing without hurting herself to pay much heed to it. Flexing her knees, she landed inelegantly on all fours but stood upright at once, feeling pleased with herself.

"You next," she said.

"Aye," he muttered, looking down at her with a doubtful grimace. " 'Tis a wee bit farther for me t' fall, ye ken."

"You'll make it," Laurie told him confidently. "I'll help you as much as I can, but you're too big for me to catch, you know, so be sure you land lightly."

"Aye, sure, like a wee feather," Sym growled.

He did not hesitate, though, swinging himself over in the same way that she had. Then, as if he dared not give himself a moment longer to think about the danger, he dropped at once.

Laurie caught him by his slim waist, intending only to slow him, but when his weight hit her, the pair of them tumbled together to the ground with Sym landing on top of her.

Chuckling, she pushed him off and stood, holding out a hand to him.

Sym lay on the ground, looking up at her, grinning. "Ye're a sight, Laurie."

"I'll warrant I am," she agreed, wrinkling her nose at a stench she had noted when they fell and realizing now what it must be. "I'm afraid that first arrow had a purgative affect on the boar's bowels and I landed in the result," she said. "Are you getting up, or are you hurt?"

"I'm up," he said, suiting action to words, then stepping hastily away from her and from the mess between them on the ground. "Och, aye, 'tis nasty," he agreed. "We'd best not linger, anyhow. We should find me dad and the others."

"You should find them," she said. "I should go home. I'm sure I'll find trouble awaiting me when I get there, as it is."

"Aye, ye will that," he said as his critical gaze moved from her head to her dirty bare feet. "But ye canna go till ye've got your pony back, and I think ye'd best clean your skirt some afore her ladyship sees ye—or smells ye."

She could not deny the worth of that advice. Not only did she reek of boar scat but also her feet were filthy, and neither the rain nor the trip up the tree had done her overskirt any good before she landed in the mess. Even the front was mud stained and torn.

"I'll do what I can, but I do not think that I can repair things to Lady Halliot's satisfaction," she said as she gathered a handful of moss and wet leaves and tried to remove the worst of the feculent mess on the back of her skirt. "At least this time I can throw a portion of the blame onto the English."

"Aye, tell her ye had to hide from 'em under a privy," Sym recommended.

By the time that Laurie and Sym had met the rest of his family at the cave in which they were hiding, persuaded them that the forest was safe again, returned with them to the cottages in the clearing, and Laurie was able at last to return home, more than two more hours had flown by.

The rain had stopped, but although she assured Davy Elliot that she did not need an escort, he and his brother Dougald insisted upon seeing her safely home, and Sym begged to accompany them, as well. By the time the four approached the foot of Aylewood Fell on the west bank of upper Tarras Burn, the gloom of the morning's rain had given way to a sunny noontime sky dotted with scudding white clouds and a rainbow arced behind the square tower dominating the crest of the hill.

"Ye'll be safe enough riding alone from here, mistress," Davy said. "I'll warrant they've seen us, any road."

"You need not have come this far," Laurie said. "We saw no English, after all. Doubtless, they had no interest in coming this far up Tarras Burn. Mayhap they have even gone back where they came from."

"I doubt they've left Liddesdale yet, but they'll leave muckle destruction and misery in their wake when they do," he said curtly. "Aye, well, Himself will mak' them pay dearly enough for their devilry when he comes home from Blackness."

"Who knows when that may be?" Laurie said with a sigh, knowing that Davy was talking about Sir Walter Scott of Buccleuch, Keeper of Liddesdale and of its great royal stronghold, Hermitage Castle.

"They say he's enjoying himself, for all he's in ward," Dougald muttered. "He's been out hunting wi' our Jamie, they say, and dicing and playing chess, too."

"Aye," Davy agreed, "and they've had a good laugh till now over Scroop's fury, the pair o' them. What's more, Himself wields as much power from Edinburgh as he does when he's right here in Liddesdale. We all ken that. I'll wager his captain at Hermitage be raising an army even now to ride after them villains."

"Rabbie Redcloak will make them pay, too," Laurie said. "Surely he and his Bairns will not let Lord Scrope get away with what he and his army did today."

"The less said o' Rab the better," Davy said, hastily looking around as if he expected to see ears popping out of the shrubbery. "He's no shown his face abroad since the raid on Carlisle, ye ken."

"He will show it now," Laurie said confidently. "You'll see."

"Mayhap, he will, but ye'd best go now, Mistress Laurie. Sir William's like t' be displeased with ye as it is."

Laurie shrugged, concealing the apprehension Davy's words stirred. "My father is rarely pleased with me, Davy. You know that as well as I do."

"Aye, but shaking straw at a boar will no ease his temper much," Davy said. "Off ye go now."

Thanking the three Elliots again for their escort, Laurie obeyed him, urging her pony to a trot and not looking back. She held her head high, knowing that guardsmen were watching her from the eight-foot-high wall of the barmekin that surrounded Aylewood Tower.

In the course of telling Davy and the others about the two men who had nearly caught them in the tree, Laurie had also told them about the boar—not that she had had to, since despite her efforts, they could still smell its leavings. Her pony had not liked the smell either. But although Davy's parting words had stirred a mental vision of the red-haired man's handsome enemy face beneath his steel bonnet, that vision soon vanished, replaced by that of her father. Davy had not overstated the matter. Sir William would not be pleased.

The gates swung open at her approach. Nodding at the two

men-at-arms holding them, she rode through into the cobbled forecourt, which revealed no sign of disturbance. As she and the others had deduced on their way to Aylewood, the English had not penetrated so far up Tarras Burn. Liddesdale proper—the wide part of it that actually bordered Liddel Water—had suffered the brunt of the attack.

A lackey came running to help her dismount. "Your father would see you straightaway, Mistress Laura," he said, his countenance carefully wooden.

"Thank you, Willie. Must I truly go to him at once, or have I time to make myself tidy? There was a raid, you see, and—"

"Aye, we ken well about the raid, mistress. Were ye . . . That is—"

"I barely saw them," Laurie said, cutting in to allay his embarrassment. "One of the shepherd lads brought warning, and we hid. That's why I look such a fright."

"Well, he did say ye should come to him straightaway, but I wager he'll no mind if ye brush your hair and . . . and mayhap change your gown first."

"Where is he?"

"In the hall, I expect. That's where he said to send ye."

"Then I shall go in through the kitchen," Laurie said.

Hurrying across the forecourt, away from the main entrance in the tall, square tower that housed the great hall and two floors of bedchambers, she approached the newer section, housing the kitchens and a ladies' parlor above them.

The door into the kitchen and bakehouse stood ajar, but she slipped silently along the stone passageway between them to the narrow, circular service stair that led to the upper floors.

Her bedchamber and the one that her two younger sisters shared were two floors above the great hall, but to reach them, she had to pass by the southeast corner of the ladies' parlor. Although she knew that she could rely on the servants not to tell her father she had returned unless he asked them, she hurried, her bare feet nearly silent on the stone steps.

As she approached the servants' entrance to the ladies' parlor, she slowed, straining her ears to hear the slightest sound from within.

She could not see directly into the parlor, for an angled wall blocked her view. That wall separated the parlor from the ladies' closet and the servants' stair.

On tiptoe now, holding up her skirts with one hand, she used the thick, oiled-rope banister with the other as she went up. She had taken but three steps beyond the parlor entry, however, when an all-too-familiar voice stopped her in her tracks.

"So, you come sneaking in like a thief in the night, do you? You've been up to mischief again, I'll warrant. Turn around and show yourself properly, girl."

Obeying reluctantly, Laurie faced her stepmother.

Blanche, Lady Halliot, stood with her hands primly folded at her waist, looking, as always, precise to a pin. Taller than Laurie by a head, she bore herself with natural elegance.

She wore a simple, crescent-shaped French hood tilted away from her face, with a semicircular white veil sewn at the back. Her dove-gray, pearl-trimmed bodice fit her trim figure flatly and smoothly without bulge or wrinkle, and her corset was laced so tightly above her wide farthingale that when she moved, she seemed to do so only from the waist down.

Like most Border women of rank, Lady Halliot wore a great deal of jewelry—several gold chains and bracelets, a long string of pearls, two brooches, rings on every finger, earrings, and gold tips to her lace points.

From gold chains attached to the girdle at her waist hung a jeweled black pomander ball, a black feather fan, and her gilded hand mirror, scissors, and needle case. Thanks to the pomander, a veritable cloud of ambergris and cloves accompanied her everywhere she went.

Laurie had often wondered how Blanche moved under so much weight, but Blanche seemed supremely oblivious of it.

Certainly, Blanche was not thinking of baubles now.

"Just look at you," she said scornfully. "You should be ashamed of yourself, Laura. Up to your pranks again, and on such a day as this one! Here," she added, stepping back, "come into the light where I can see you properly."

Laurie obeyed, dismally conscious of her unkempt hair, filthy skirts, and an odor that even Blanche's pomander would not hide. To her relief, except for themselves, the ladies' parlor was empty.

Since her stepmother clearly meant to berate her, she took some small comfort in the fact that her sisters would not be present to hear what she said.

"Disgusting," Blanche said. Raising her chin sharply and wrinkling her nose as Laurie stepped into the sunlit room, she said, "Whatever is that dreadful smell?"

"We had to hide from the raiders," Laurie said quietly. "There was a boar, and when someone shot it—"

"One does not wish to hear the sordid details," Blanche said. "Nonetheless, why did you have to hide? One would presume that even murderous English invaders would not dare lay a hand on a daughter of Sir William Halliot."

"I do not know if they would have dared or not," Laurie said. "I did not think I would be wise to test them."

"Wise? You think yourself wise, Laura? Such a notion is utterly laughable."

But Blanche did not laugh. Instead, she regarded Laurie with much the same expression of distaste as she might have assumed upon discovering a toad in her wardrobe.

The silence lengthened until Laurie shivered.

"If you are cold, you have only yourself to blame," Blanche said unsympathetically. "You deserve beating."

Laurie did not reply.

"If your father is sensible, this time he will take a good stout switch or a strap to you. He certainly will have much to say to you."

"Yes, madam. He is awaiting me even now in the hall."

"Then you must go to him at once."

"I . . . I would prefer to change my dress first and tidy my hair."

"One should be gratified to learn that for once you care

about your appearance, I expect, but it is more important that your father see exactly how his daughter comports herself. I shall take you to him myself, as you are."

Swallowing hard, Laurie followed Blanche to the far end of the parlor, where a gallery led to the great hall and the main stairway. Determined to behave as though nothing were out of the ordinary, she strove to keep her head high.

Ahead of her, Blanche passed gracefully through the arched entry to the hall. Ignoring members of the household and men-at-arms who attended to various duties there, she approached burly, richly attired Sir William Halliot, who sat in a carved wooden armchair, hunched over the high table.

Surrounded by ledgers and numerous, important looking documents, he was carefully reading one of them and did not look up. A slender scribe perched on a stool beside him dipped his quill into the inkpot and wrote steadily on, clearly oblivious, as his master was, of Blanche's approach.

"Sir William," she said in a clear, sharp voice that brought both men's heads up, "you will be gratified to learn that your daughter has returned at last from her illicit morning ramble. Although she attempted to disobey your command that she present herself at once, I soon put a stop to that."

"So I see," Sir William said gruffly, frowning at Laurie. "What the devil have you done to yourself, daughter? You look as if you'd been dragged through a swamp and half-drowned."

"I was caught in the rain, sir."

"Did you not have a cloak?"

She had forgotten about her cloak. "I did have one, but I left it in Davy's cottage when the raiders came. I don't know what became of it after that."

"And your shoes?"

Laurie looked down at the dirty bare toes peeping out from beneath her skirts. "I forgot them, too," she said.

"At Davy Elliot's?"

"No, sir, here," she admitted with a sigh. "I do not like wearing shoes."

The hall had become uncommonly quiet—and extraordinarily so, considering the number of people there.

Imperiously indifferent to the fascinated audience, Blanche said, "Such behavior must cease, Sir William. This unnatural girl has grown as wild as a gypsy and is a sad disgrace to the Halliot name."

"Now, madam, surely—"

"You have allowed her to defy you for too long, sir," Blanche went on without a pause. "She defies you in every way, even refusing every effort that you have made to see her properly married. Surely, you see now that she must be tamed before anyone will have her. Having flouted your orders yet again by running off to consort with low persons, this time endangering even her own life, she surely deserves a sound beating. Moreover, although perhaps you cannot smell her, apparently she rolled in dung of some sort before presenting herself to you."

Hearing muted, hastily stifled chuckles from some of the observers and feeling heat flame in her cheeks, Laurie did not dare meet her father's gaze.

Curtly, Sir William said, "Clear these people out of here, Samuel."

The scribe got up at once and cleared the hall, taking himself out with the others. Other than a couple of hounds stretched on the hearth before the roaring fire, only Blanche, Sir William, and Laurie remained.

Sir William said grimly, "You do deserve beating, daughter."

Laurie, saying nothing, heard Blanche's sigh of satisfaction.

Sir William went on, "This is no example to be setting for your younger sisters. You must do better, lass."

"Yes, sir.

Haughtily Blanche said, "One need not fear that *my* daughters would ever be so foolish as to follow Laura's bad example, Sir William. God in His mercy has seen fit to give you two children whose behavior is faultless."

Sir William smiled faintly at her. "You have done well with May and Isabel, Blanche. I'll not debate that with you."

"One hopes that no debate will arise betwixt husband and wife on any point, sir," Blanche said, bowing her head with apparent submissiveness.

"I could wish, however," he added gently, "that you had done as well with my eldest daughter."

" 'Twas yourself who ordained that she should not be properly disciplined," she reminded him, lifting her chin. "Perhaps now you will admit that you erred in taking such a lenient position."

Laurie wished fervently that she were still with Sym in the beech tree.

Sir William said evenly, "Laura had not yet attained her fifth birthday when I married you, and she had recently lost her mother. Under such circumstances, my dearest, you can hardly blame me for thinking that your notions of discipline seemed overly harsh."

"She would not be as she is now," Blanche said with a sweeping gesture toward Laurie, "if you had left her to proper maternal discipline."

Remembering that her stepmother's notion of discipline had included a leather slipper and a switch, both of which had left bruises that lasted long after the initial punishment, Laurie could only be grateful that her father had intervened. She had not heard him discuss the matter with Blanche before, but she vividly remembered that the vicious punishments had abruptly stopped. After that, Sir William had disciplined her himself, albeit rarely.

She had an unhappy feeling that this might prove to be one more of those rare occasions. Certainly it would be if Blanche had her way.

"You may safely leave this matter to me, madam," Sir William said.

With a nod and a curtsy, Blanche replied, "One bows to your authority as always, dear husband. Pray do not forget, however, that her actions inevitably affect lives other than her own."

Rising from her curtsy, Blanche cast Laurie a look that from anyone less haughty would be called a triumphant smirk and then swept past her out of the hall.

Meeting Sir William's stern gaze at last, Laurie said, "I am sorry, Father."

"You should be," he retorted implacably. "I have never known a gently bred lass who could stir more trouble than you do. I shall not go so far as to say that you were responsible for the raid, of course—"

"No, sir."

"Do not interrupt," he said. "I own, I'm sorely tempted to take a switch to you, to teach you to behave. Did I not command you to cease your visits to Davy Elliot and that tribe of his unless and until your mother agreed to accompany you?"

Stifling the impulse to remind him that Blanche was not her mother, Laurie said only, "Yes, sir, but you said that only because she insisted that you say it. She will not set a foot anywhere near Tarras Wood."

"I did say it, however, and I expected you to obey me," he said, ignoring the rider. "I know that, having been acquainted with Davy Elliot and his Lucy since you were a babe in your mother's arms, you consider them to be great friends."

"Davy put me on my first pony," Laurie said. "Lucy was my nursemaid."

"Aye, but that is no reason to run free in their household, Laura. Davy is my tenant and nothing more. Your mother is quite right when she declares that your frequent visits to his cottage are unseemly."

Seeing nothing to gain by pointing out that Davy Elliot and his family had been far kinder to her than her own family had, Laurie remained silent.

Sir William's tone gentled as he said, "Were you hurt, child?"

"No, sir. Davy put Sym and me up a tree. It was Sym who warned us that the raiders were coming."

"You should have ridden straight home. You'd have been safer."

"I couldn't know that, sir. Moreover, they needed my pony for Lucy and the babe."

If such reasoning moved him, she saw no sign of it, but at least he did not castigate her for letting the Elliots use her pony. Instead, he gestured impatiently toward the documents on the table before him. "Do you see these?" he demanded.

"Aye, sir.

"Warden's business, they are, and I should be attending to them, not dealing with trivial domestic matters. Those documents are grievances, English grievances against our people. They are of great importance—far greater importance than anything you can have done—because if I do not manage them well, the result could be war between England and Scotland. Do you understand that?"

"Yes, sir," she said. "They have to do with your new position, then." King James had recently appointed Sir William to act in Buccleuch's place as warden of the Scottish middle march.

"Aye, they do," he said, "and if you think that I am grateful to Jamie for dumping this lot in my lap, you were never more mistaken. Scrope has agreed to a wardens' meeting next month at Lochmaben, but since that blasted raid on Carlisle, there has been naught but trouble. Moreover, since my deputy is apparently the man the raiders rescued from Carlisle, and since he has been too busy of late with Buccleuch's troubles, he won't be of much use to me against Scrope."

Sir William's deputy was Sir Quinton Scott of Broadhaugh, one of Buccleuch's numerous cousins and the man whom many thought Jamie ought to have appointed warden after he arrested Buccleuch and put him in ward at Blackness Castle. Other cousins included Scott of Harden and Sir Adam Scott of Hawkburne (whose chief claim to notoriety was that he descended directly from an erstwhile King of the Reivers). They had all expressed a strong interest in taking over the wardenship, but James had appointed Sir William of Aylewood, declaring that

Sir William was more likely to appease Elizabeth than any Scott was.

"But Scrope arrested Sir Quinton in violation of a truce, did he not?" Laurie asked, grateful for a change of subject.

"Scrope denies it," Sir William said. "He insists that outlaws captured a man in a raid on Bewcastle, that Musgraves in pursuit of those outlaws crossed the line quite legally to a house where they discovered Rabbie Redcloak. Scrope says Redcloak tried to raise the countryside against Francis Musgrave and his men, whereupon in self-defense they were forced to take Redcloak into custody. They all deny that Sir Quinton ever was a prisoner at Carlisle."

"But—"

"None of that matters now, Laura. Queen Elizabeth believes that Buccleuch led the raid against Carlisle and freed a prisoner, and although Buccleuch does not bother to deny it, James continues to ignore demands that he send him to London to answer to the English authorities. All he agreed to do was to house Buccleuch at Blackness for a time and to appoint a new warden for the middle march. As you know, Buccleuch has been acting warden here these two years past."

"Aye," Laurie said. Davy had told her as much, and Davy knew all about Buccleuch. According to Davy, Buccleuch was the most powerful of all the Border lords. Men on both sides of the line called him "God's Curse" and had excellent reason, Davy said, to do so. "Buccleuch is still Keeper of Liddesdale and Hermitage, though," Laurie said.

"Aye, he is and doubtless will remain so unless Elizabeth gets her way and James sends him to face the English authorities," Sir William said.

"Do you think he will?"

"Nay, and Scrope may have overstepped himself today. James did not like arresting Buccleuch and did so only because he feared that Elizabeth might change her mind about letting him succeed her if he thwarted her will too defiantly. I hold no great opinion of any Scott and especially Buccleuch," he added grimly. " 'Tis a hasty, hot-headed family, but today's invasion of Liddesdale will infuriate James when he learns of it. I'd certainly not advise him to release Buccleuch, if he were to ask for my advice on the matter, but he won't. Therefore I'll not be surprised to see Buccleuch back at Hermitage very soon."

"Well, I think it is a pity that Elizabeth blames him for Carlisle when he did not even go there," Laurie said. "Nearly everyone hereabouts knows that he was laid up with an injured leg at the time."

"You know nothing about such matters, nor should you," her father said testily. "In any event, I did not draw your attention to my duties as warden in order to discuss them with you but to remind you that I have far more important matters on my mind than dealing with the trouble you manage to stir up. I dislike punishing you, Laura . . ."

Laurie braced herself.

". . . but I fear that I must do so if I am ever to have peace in this house. I should send you out to cut a switch right now, but I won't do that."

Relieved, she said quietly, "Thank you."

"Faith, lass, don't thank me yet. I'm still likely to put you over my knee, but I won't do so now, because in your present state, I'd only soil my hand and my clothing. Go up and tidy yourself. Indeed, bathe yourself and wash your hair. You may go without your dinner to do so. Then you may keep to your bedchamber until suppertime, when you may beg my leave to sup with the family. By then I shall have decided what to do with you."

Grateful, even if the reprieve proved no more than temporary, Laurie made a hasty curtsy and fled to her bedchamber.

Four

Lances and halberds in splinters were torn . . .
Buckler and armlet in shivers were shorn.

The drizzle and mist had cleared, letting the sun's rays touch
the land again. Only carnage, smoking fields, and the charred
remains of cottages remained.

Sir Hugh Graham regarded the bleak sight with an expres-
sionless face, grateful that Martin Loder had taken himself off
to present the dead boar to Scrope. Loder was crude enough
to gloat over the misfortunes of others while claiming he was
only enjoying victory, and Hugh knew that his tolerance for
gloating just then would be small.

When his dun-colored gelding sidled nervously at the smell
of blood and smoke, he muttered, "Gently, lad. We'll be away
soon."

The gelding was well trained and had seen battle before,
and Hugh was a stern master, but he did not do anything more
to curb its unrest. He didn't like what he was seeing or smelling either. Naked women and children wandered among the
dead, seeking their menfolk. Some of Scrope's men clearly
thought the women were spoils of victory, and the comeliest
paid a heavy price for their beauty.

Hugh found himself thinking again of the girl in the tree.
She had seemed little more than a child, but her pale face
haunted him now. He knew that she would have delighted
many of the men who believed rape was a victor's right, and

any second thoughts he'd had about keeping silent vanished. He stared woodenly out at the landscape, watching for the return of his men.

A horseman rode up behind him to say, "Sir Hugh, me lord wants a word wi' ye. Yonder, on the hilltop."

Suppressing a sigh, Hugh turned the gelding and gave it a touch of spur. At the top of the hill, he drew up before Thomas, Lord Scrope.

"Your man said you wanted to speak with me, your lordship," Hugh said evenly, without doffing his helmet.

"Aye," Scrope said. "Nearly everyone else has returned, Graham. Where have your lads got to?"

"I sent them to watch the route from Hermitage," Hugh said.

Scrope sneered. "Buccleuch is safely caged in Edinburgh."

"Aye, but his men are not," Hugh said, "and I sent my lads to make sure they would not interfere with your raid. When they've heard it's over, they'll return."

"You did not accompany them." A clear note of disapproval underscored the statement.

"I had no need to do so," Hugh said. "My captain, Ned Rowan, has them in charge, and he's an excellent man. They all know their business, so I stayed hereabouts instead. Some of your other commanders are a bit green."

"Aye, that's true, but Loder told me you followed him, and he's not green."

Hugh shrugged. "It seemed odd, seeing him riding off alone as he did. Plain curiosity sent me after him, naught else."

"I trust Loder," Scrope said, giving him a direct look. "That this raid has gone smoothly is due in great part to his efforts. I trust you saw naught amiss."

"Nothing," Hugh admitted. "Loder knew of some cottages deep in the forest and hoped to catch the occupants off guard. They had fled, however."

"He tells me you forbade him to fire the cots."

"I did," Hugh said. "Had these lads seen smoke billowing from the forest, they'd have ridden in to see what pickings they could find. Tarras Wood is a maze of swampland, like the Moss hereabouts. We'd already lost men and horses to the mud," Hugh added. "But that was in the midst of fighting. Since we'd have lost more in the wood, I believed there was naught to gain and much to lose."

"Aye, well, Loder does not disagree, though he did want to teach those folks a lesson." Scrope frowned. "You should thank him for not saying otherwise, just as I should thank you for the boar meat he said you provided for my dinner. I'm surprised, though, that you found time for hunting."

Blandly, Hugh said, "Loder knew only one route through the forest. We dared not risk the boar attacking us."

Scrope regarded him silently for a long moment.

Although Hugh was the deputy warden, he knew that because he was also a Graham with a kinsman who had access to the Queen, Scrope had more often counted him enemy than friend even before the Carlisle raid. The knowledge did not trouble him overmuch. He waited.

"I am aware that you do not approve of this raid," Scrope said at last.

"I have not said that I do not approve."

"Nor have you said that you do."

Hugh shrugged. "Your quarrel is with Buccleuch and the men who raided Carlisle. Revenging yourself like this on women and bairns—"

"Don't babble to me of women and bairns! This is war, man, and I have a right to punish all Liddesdale for what they did at Carlisle. By rights, Buccleuch should have chased down the raiders and brought them to justice. It was his duty as march warden, and with him gone, it's now the new warden's duty. Thus, you might say that I'm just offering honorable and neighborlike assistance to a fellow march warden by coming here today. You Grahams—"

"I know that you blame certain Grahams," Hugh interjected. "You wrote as much to me after the raid. Moreover, you have already sent six Graham headsmen to London to see what the Privy Council will make of them."

"I hope they will hang them," Scrope said. "The only reason I did not was that you objected so fiercely."

"Nonetheless, to blame all Grahams because you believe some of them had a hand in that raid merely shows that you do not know much about us," Hugh said. "In any event, surely you do not blame the women or the children of Liddesdale. They are the ones who will starve first without food."

"Some say that a woman—a Graham woman—led that raid," Scrope said grimly. "I am not foolish enough to believe such puffery. Still, I suppose it is possible that a woman or even a child could have learned exactly where we were holding the reiver and then told Buccleuch where to find him."

Having no wish to pursue that subject, Hugh said, "You seem determined to blame the Grahams, my lord, even English Grahams. I might remind you that if they seem sometimes short of the loyalty you seek, it is because Grahams tend to think of themselves as having souls above nationality."

"Grahams have no souls, only an eye to the main chance," Scrope retorted. "They obey no master unless it suits them— just like the men of Liddesdale! If I do not know which side the ones involved in the raid hail from, it is no fault of mine. Likewise, it lends no credit to you."

"My men and I are the only ones who took up arms for England that night."

"Nevertheless, you, of all men, should know who amongst your own did what," Scrope said. "As I said when I wrote, you should thank heaven that I do not hold you personally accountable for the doings of every Graham."

Goaded, Hugh said, "I would remind you, sir—with respect—that not one man at Carlisle lifted a finger to defend it."

He resisted—albeit with considerable effort—the impulse to add that according to men on the scene Scrope had barricaded himself in the hall and refused to emerge until the raiders had gone.

Scrope snapped, "And I'll remind you that Buccleuch attacked my stronghold in the dead of night with five hundred heavily armed horsemen."

"It was not—"

Ignoring him, Scrope continued without pause, "They undermined the postern gate, broke into the chamber where Rabbie Redcloak was kept, carried him away, and left my watchmen for dead. They also hurt a servant of mine and killed one of Redcloak's keepers. Moreover, I do not believe that none of my men lifted a finger, but even if that is so, it is because the raiders escaped before anyone else had seen them and before any resistance could be made."

Seeing nothing to gain by telling him, yet again, that the force Hugh and his men had met that night had numbered less than a hundred men, Hugh said only, "Do you not mount a considerable watch at Carlisle, my lord?"

"Aye, certainly," Scrope retorted testily. "You know perfectly well, however, that a vicious storm struck that night. Since Buccleuch's attack came two hours before dawn, my guards were either asleep or had taken cover to defend themselves from the violent weather."

"I see," Hugh said. Giving way to his impulse, he added, "I wonder what became of Buccleuch and the five hundred. We saw less than a hundred men, as I've told you numerous times. If Buccleuch was leading them, I did not see him."

"Likely he hid amongst his men."

Hugh tried but failed to suppress a laugh. "That is the first time I've heard anyone accuse *Buccleuch* of cowardice," he said with gentle emphasis.

Scrope colored to the roots of his hair, certainly aware that many had accused him of that weakness—and not only with regard to the raid on Carlisle. His voice grew harsh. "Who knows why you did not see him? Likely he was with the rest of his men, elsewhere, and you met with only a group of Rabbie's Bairns."

"Aye, perhaps," Hugh said. He had better sense than to tell Scrope he had good reason to know that he had faced the entire rescue party.

If Scrope wanted to believe that Hugh's party had detected the presence of eighty men that night but had failed to detect four hundred and twenty others, so be it. At least his lordship was willing to acknowledge that Hugh and his men had attempted to prevent the return of the rescuers and their prize to Scotland.

" 'Tis a pity you were unable to recapture Rabbie Redcloak," Scrope said on a scornful note.

"Aye, it is," Hugh agreed. "The river was in full spate, though, due to the storm. It was well nigh a miracle that the Scots did not all drown in the crossing. In any event, I never saw any man whom I could identify as Rabbie Redcloak," he added truthfully.

"Still, you should have followed them," Scrope said, refraining as he had all along from asking Hugh if he had seen anyone whom he could have identified as Sir Quinton Scott.

The question would have been a perfectly logical one to ask. Sir Quinton had once served as Buccleuch's deputy at a wardens' meeting, opposite Hugh, who had acted for Scrope. However, political necessity dictated that Scrope continue to believe that his prisoner was a notorious reiver. To admit that that prisoner was cousin to the powerful Buccleuch and deputy warden of the Scottish middle march, mistakenly arrested under truce, would considerably damage Scrope's position with the Queen.

Testily, Scrope said, "You had every right as my deputy to declare a hot trod, go after them, and demand help from anyone you met on the Scottish side."

"Pursuing the Scots across that flooded river was too dangerous," Hugh said. "I could not be certain that my men, who were more heavily armored than the reivers, could make it across as safely."

Scrope's grimace made his feelings plain, but Hugh did not need to see the expression to know how much the man disliked and distrusted him. Nevertheless, he knew that Scrope would not dismiss him. He lacked just cause, and without it, he would not attempt to do so. Not only did Hugh's uncle still have the

Queen's ear in London, but finding another man who would take the position would be difficult.

Elizabeth feared putting too much power in her wardens' hands. Therefore, she gave them far too little power to do the job she demanded of them. She had also, with few exceptions, refused to name as warden any man born and bred in the Borders. The results were that few good men would accept the duty and those who did almost never understood the area or its people.

Scrope considered himself an exception to the standard, because his father had served as warden before him. But Scrope was a gambler who enjoyed little respect among his peers, let alone among those he served. Hugh knew that Thomas Scrope had gained little insight from Scrope senior, because Thomas had grown up in Nottinghamshire and married there. He still spent more time there and in London than he did in Carlisle. No matter what he thought, he was an outsider.

Scrope's chief land sergeant, Martin Loder, was also an outsider. Although Loder had married locally and well—twice, in fact—Borderers still regarded him as an interloper. Although Loder wanted to be Scrope's deputy, Elizabeth and even Scrope recognized that a warden needed a deputy who enjoyed the respect he lacked. Thus, although there could be little doubt that at least a few Grahams had taken part in the raid on Carlisle, Scrope would require more cause than that and his personal dislike to dismiss Hugh.

"Be these your lads coming now?" Scrope demanded.

"Aye, that's Rowan leading them," Hugh said.

"Then all the stragglers are here," Scrope said. "I've sent Loder and two other land sergeants on ahead with their men, so we'd best get this lot moving, too."

"Aye," Hugh agreed. "We cannot count on the men at Hermitage to dally there much longer."

Scrope shrugged. "I doubt they'll move without Buccleuch to lead them."

"You'd be wiser not to depend on that," Hugh warned. "You've killed a number of their kinsmen today and burned out untold numbers of others. My men forced Buccleuch's to keep their heads down till now, but with my lads away, they won't wait long to follow. Indeed, if we don't get moving, we're like to find ourselves in the midst of pitched battle, and our lads are tired. They lack the strength of purpose that the Liddesdale lot will have."

Scrope apparently saw wisdom in his words, for he signaled his lieutenants to gather their men. In minutes, the army of two thousand was riding for England.

Although war banners waved and the men seemed cheerful, Hugh thought their pace more that of retreat than victory. They took their tone from Scrope, who kept looking back, clearly fearing that the Scots could still mount an attack.

Hugh had counted on the Scots' fiery reputation to get Scrope moving toward home. But he knew, too, that the Liddesdale men were canny enough not to challenge so large an army. What they were more likely to do—and what he feared most—was attack some area in England as unsuspecting as Liddesdale had been. And they would leave just as much devastation in their path.

Buccleuch might be in ward, but everyone knew that James of Scotland had been reluctant to put him there, and if James was looking for an excuse to release him, Scrope's massive raid had provided it. In the time that it had taken Scrope to raise an army of two thousand, Buccleuch could raise three thousand.

Sir Hugh held no brief for Buccleuch. On the contrary, he had a score of his own to settle with the man, because it was Buccleuch who had arranged his sister Janet's marriage to Sir Quinton Scott of Broadhaugh.

Sir Hugh was well aware that his connection to Buccleuch was like a stone stuck in Scrope's craw, although Scrope himself had had more to do with arranging the marriage than Hugh had. They had requested Hugh's consent, of course, since he was Janet's nearest kinsman, but the two wardens had given him no choice. They had worked the details out between them after Sir Quinton had supposedly rescued Janet from a reiver, admired her beauty, and expressed a desire to marry her.

Elizabeth and James had supported the marriage, expressing the joint hope that it would help bring peace to the long-riotous Borders.

Hugh had not attended the wedding, but if he still harbored resentment over the connection, it was due mainly to his loss of an excellent housekeeper. There were certain details about the whole business, however, of which Scrope remained blissfully unaware, details that Hugh hoped would remain buried forever.

Although Scrope knew that Hugh and his men had met the Carlisle raiders and had tried unsuccessfully to prevent their return to Scotland, he clearly did not know that Hugh had fought single-handedly against the erstwhile prisoner. Nor did Scrope know that Hugh's sister Janet had been present at the time.

Even now, months after the raid, Hugh knew that Scrope wanted nothing more than to connect him to the Carlisle raiders and to punish him for it. If the scathing letter that he had written Hugh soon after the raid had not made it plain, the abandon with which he had ordered the arrest of suspect Grahams did. Although Hugh had done all that he could to prevent the raid's success, Scrope had only to learn that Janet had been among the rescuers to order his arrest.

In the meantime, Hugh was certain that the massive, murderous attack on Liddesdale could only escalate strife in the Borders. It was only a matter of time before Buccleuch would retaliate.

Five

There was an old man, and daughters he had three. . . .
"What are you doing, my fair lady?"

Shortly before five o'clock, freshly bathed, smelling of roses, and dressed in a modest gown that she knew became her, Laurie went in search of Sir William.

She found him in the hall, still at his table, still surrounded by documents. Servants bustled about, setting up trestle tables for supper, and she did not know how he could concentrate. But he seemed to be completely absorbed.

"Forgive me for interrupting your work, sir," she said when she stood in front of him. His scribe was no longer at his side.

Sir William had not so much as glanced up at her entrance, but he did so now with a frown, saying, "Is it time for supper already?"

"Aye, sir, nearly."

"I do not know where the afternoon went," he complained. Pushing away the document he had been reading, he sat straight and stretched his spine. Then, adjusting his cap, he looked at her more narrowly and added, "I like that dress."

"Thank you."

His lips twitched. "You know that I like it, lassie. I've told you so before, more than once. Hoping to soften me up, are you?"

"Aye, sir," she said frankly. "I'm hungry, and I would like to take supper with the family."

"You'd like to avoid a whipping, that's what you'd like."

"Aye, that too." She had not known what to expect, but now she relaxed. He might still punish her, but she knew from his light tone that he would not thrash her.

"I don't know what to do with you," he said, as if he had read her thoughts. "What were you thinking, lass, to slip off and go to the Elliots? You know how much your mother dislikes such visits."

"Davy and Lucy are my friends," she said simply. "I thought if I went early, before anyone here was up and about, I could see them and get back before anyone knew I'd gone. I did not know that the English would raid Liddesdale."

"It was that perfidious Scrope," Sir William said. "It was a foolish thing to do, too, because James will not like it. He may well release Buccleuch now, and Buccleuch will exact his revenge."

"Do you think the King really will release him?"

"Aye," Sir William said with a sigh. "He'll soon be on his way back from Edinburgh to Hermitage to begin plotting what he will do. But he should not. It will only make Elizabeth angrier than she is now."

"Aye, sir." Laurie did not think it wise to add that, whatever the cost, she hoped that Buccleuch would make the villainous English pay heavily for what they had done. She was in enough trouble already without stirring more.

Instead, she said, "Will you stop being warden if Buccleuch returns?"

He shook his head. "King James thinks me less warlike than Buccleuch and thus more likely to bring peace to the area."

Impressed, she said, "Can you?"

"God knows I prefer peace to war," Sir William said with a rueful smile, "but I'm no peacemaker. I'll be less so if Buccleuch comes back, too. I lack the power to fight him. If James wants peace, he should persuade Buccleuch to impose it. He could if he chose, but I doubt that any other man could."

A noisy group of men-at-arms entering the hall to take their supper drew his attention just then. He pushed back his arm-chair and stood up.

"You may come with me now, Laura," he said.

Laurie felt a prickle of fear. "Am I not to sup with the family then, sir?"

"Aye, you may, but your mother chooses to take supper in the ladies' parlor today. She's taken a notion into her mind that it is not suitable for your sisters to sup in company with my men."

"Not suitable? But why?"

" 'Tis acceptable at noon, she says, when everyone is in a hurry and no one talks much. But, at supper, she says, the men tend to become more boisterous and to say things that are not suited to young girls' ears."

Sir William extended a forearm as he spoke, and Laurie rested her right hand upon it as she considered his words.

Supper was certainly a more relaxed meal than dinner at Aylewood, just as it was in most households. Nonetheless, since Laurie and her two sisters had dined and supped with the men since childhood, she thought it more likely that Blanche had noticed May's recent inclination to flirt with any man who looked her way.

At fifteen, the elder of Laurie's half sisters was eager to marry. Thus, she tended to look upon any man she met as a potential mate. Moreover, despite Blanche's continued insis-tence that her daughters were perfect, Laurie was sure she had to know that May, at least, was nothing of the sort. May was flighty and headstrong. She was perhaps not as likely as Laurie was to slip out unattended, but she frequently managed to do as she pleased and count the cost later.

To her credit, Blanche did punish May for her misdeeds, albeit not so harshly as she demanded that Sir William punish Laurie. May's punishments were light, so light, in fact, that they rarely deterred her impulses. She knew that she enjoyed her mother's favor. That it had taken Blanche as long as it had to notice the flirting was rather remarkable, however. Laurie wondered if Blanche had said anything to May about it, and she decided to ask May as soon as a good opportunity arose.

As she and Sir William left the hall and crossed the gallery to the ladies' parlor, she gave his arm a squeeze, welcoming his escort. Blanche would be less likely to aim acid remarks at her in his presence.

She was not yet out of the briars, however.

"You must mend your ways, lass," Sir William said quietly.

"I will try, sir."

"You will do as I bid you," he said more sternly. "You set a poor example for your sisters when you disobey me. I won't allow anarchy in my household."

"But it is not fair to forbid me to visit my friends in the dale," she protested. "I do not have many friends elsewhere, after all."

"Your mother prefers that you behave in a more proper manner, Laura, and after seeing the state you were in this morning, I cannot disagree with her."

"But I had to hide in the tree!"

"Aye, perhaps, but you did not have to leave Aylewood—and certainly not without so much as putting shoes on your feet, lass. She did not like your coming home without your cloak, either."

"Well, she will not want me to return to Davy's to collect it," Laurie said. "She does not approve of anything I do, sir. You know that she does not."

He looked at her, and his grim expression told her that she had crossed the line of what he would accept.

Hastily, she said, "Pray, sir, forgive me. I should not have said that."

"No, you should not," he said. "You must learn to curb your tongue, daughter. I am in no mood to play the harsh parent, for I believe that you had some cause to act as you did this morning. But you must not count on my continued leniency. Should your mother have further cause for complaint, you will suffer whatever consequence she deems appropriate. Do you understand me?"

"Yes, sir," Laurie said dismally.

He said no more, and they entered the parlor to find the rest of the family ahead of them, gathered near the fireplace, talking quietly.

Blanche wore a gown of her customary, elegant, dove-gray silk. Decked as usual with an abundant array of expensive jewelry, she sat in a straight-backed chair with her feet on a blue velvet footstool. Even the French hood covering all but the smoothly combed forepart of her hair boasted fine pearled embroidery.

Ten-year-old Isabel stood beside her with one hand on the back of her chair. Isabel wore a modest milk-and-water gown similar in style to her mother's, with a stiff, smooth bodice and flaring skirts. Her light brown hair fell in a shiny curtain to her waist, held away from her face by a plain white coif, the strings of which tied neatly under her softly rounded chin.

Since May was talking and stood with her back to the doorway, when Laurie and Sir William entered, the other two saw them first.

Blanche nodded regally, and Isabel curtsied, whereupon May stopped talking and turned to face them, quickly making her curtsy to Sir William.

Her dress was the bluish-green color known as popinjay and was much less modest than those of her sister or mother. May's tightly laced corset pushed her plump bosom so high that when she curtsied, her breasts threatened to spill over the low-cut bodice. The narrow lace edging of her chemise peeped over the bodice edge but barely covered her nipples. A ruff around her neck matched the chemise lace, but it was so narrow that, in Laurie's opinion, it looked more like a necklace than a part of her gown. Laurie noticed, too, that May had reddened her lips and cheeks and had darkened her eyelashes.

Indeed, she thought, May looked almost as though she had expected to dine in company.

Even Sir William noticed, for he said heartily, "You are looking very fine tonight, May."

May blushed, and Blanche said, "She does look well, does

she not, sir? One can easily see that she will benefit from taking more care with her appearance."

"Aye, that she would," he agreed.

Blanche smiled archly. "I believe we should take her with us next month when we visit Fast Castle, for she is old enough now to show herself more in company."

"Well, as to that—"

"Faith, sir, she ought to have been doing so these two years past."

Sir William looked around the chamber as if to make certain that no servants had joined them before he said firmly, "I believe I understand you, madam. But we have discussed this matter before, and I do not intend to alter my decision."

May's lips pressed tightly together, for she knew better than to protest.

Laurie glanced at Blanche, wondering if her stepmother would dare at such a moment to speak her mind.

Blanche's expression remained firmly under control, however, and if Sir William could read her thoughts, Laurie could not.

Mildly Blanche said, "One would not wish to gainsay you, husband, but the present situation is most unfair to May. She is quite old enough for betrothing."

"You and I will discuss this anon," Sir William said. "It is no topic to bandy before the servants, and I warrant I hear them coming now with our supper."

The table was ready, and almost as an echo of Sir William's words, three menservants entered, carrying platters of food.

The members of the family took their places at the table.

Sir William glanced at the platters' contents and said to his carver, "We will tend to ourselves, I think. You may leave when you have served the soup and then return in half an hour to see if we require aught else."

"Aye, master."

While the carver ladled barley soup into bowls and a lackey set a bowl before each of them, Laurie became aware of Blanche's searching gaze. She returned the look steadily but said nothing, knowing that her stepmother was trying to determine what punishment, if any, Sir William had meted out. From experience, however, she knew Blanche would not ask, so she turned her attention to her food.

Much of the food was cold, left over from the noontime dinner, but the soup was hot and tasty to one who had had nothing to eat since before dawn. She might have shared a crust and some cheese with Davy's family when she and Sym rejoined them after the Englishmen had departed, but she never liked taking food from them. They had little to spare. Usually she took gifts to them from Aylewood's kitchens, but that morning she had been in a hurry. She had not seen them in days, and had thought—wrongly, as it turned out—that an early visit would be safe.

May said abruptly, the moment the servants had left the room, "May I go to Fast Castle when you go, sir?"

Isabel shot her a startled glance, then quickly turned back to her food.

"We'll see," Sir William said. "The King has asked me to attend a meeting of the Scottish wardens to discuss various things that we might do to encourage peace in the Borders. I had not thought of the meeting as a social occasion, but your mother has expressed a desire to go."

"I'll warrant that at least some of the other wardens' wives will be there," Blanche said, smiling at him.

Smiling back, he said, "Aye, perhaps. Do you want to go, too, Laurie?"

Conscious of May's hopeful gaze, and the sterner one of her stepmother, Laurie said, "It would be pleasant to visit Fast Castle, sir. I have never been there."

In an austere tone, Blanche said, "Is it not premature to promise such a treat to a daughter who disobeys us so easily, Sir William?"

Isabel gave May another quizzical look, and Laurie's curiosity stirred.

When May caught Laurie's eye and looked away quickly with a flush that was discernible despite her painted cheeks,

Laurie began to wonder what mischief she had been up to. She did nothing to draw attention to her, though, for she had no wish to harm May. In any event, if she expressed her thoughts aloud, she knew that Blanche's anger would fall on her no matter what May might have done.

Sir William and Blanche continued to talk of the forthcoming meeting at Fast Castle, but Laurie paid their discussion no heed. She did not care if she went with them or not. She liked music and dancing, and if the occasion proved a festive one, she would enjoy it. But she would not enjoy her stepmother's constant urging to encourage the attention of every marriageable gentleman who attended the gathering, regardless of age or appearance. Such occasions made her feel like the winning pony after a race, when all the men were looking it over and wondering if they could afford to buy it.

"Laura, you are not attending." Blanche's sharp voice drew her attention again. "Why do you stare so rudely at your sister?"

Realizing that she was still gazing blindly at May, Laurie collected herself and said, "I beg your pardon, May. I was not really looking at you. I was thinking about . . . about Fast Castle," she added hastily.

"You should have been attending to our conversation," Blanche said. "At polite gatherings, a young woman who finds her own thoughts more fascinating than the conversation around her is judged to be haughty or unbecomingly proud."

Sir William said, "No one who knows Laurie for long finds her overly proud, madam. For that matter, I have frequently heard you complain that she is not sufficiently aware of her worth."

"Pray, husband, do not encourage her to misbehave. It is her duty to pay heed when we discuss social occasions, for it is likewise her duty to marry. You agree with me on that head, as you have pointed out to her more than once."

"Aye, well, she should marry," he said.

"Indeed, she should," Blanche agreed. "Instead, however, she behaves like a lowborn hoyden. Should word of such behavior spread beyond Aylewood, no one will want her, and since you have commanded that your younger daughters may not marry until Laura has done so, she must do so at the first opportunity."

"Aye, well, there is no great rush about it."

"Perhaps there is not, but if she does not marry, you, my dear sir, will find yourself supporting three daughters until the day of your death." She crossed herself hastily, adding, "Although I certainly pray that the good Lord sees fit in His mercy to put off that dreaded day for many and many a year."

"Aye, there's no rush about that, either." Turning to Laurie, he added ruefully, "I cannot argue her point, you know."

Disliking the turn the conversation had taken, Laurie said quietly, "I have found no one with whom I can imagine spending the rest of my life."

"But I have introduced any number of excellent gentlemen to you, lass! They are the best Scotland has to offer, yet you have scorned them all."

"Had you simply commanded her to obey you and marry one of them, she must have done so," Blanche said.

"I am a man of law, madam," Sir William said testily. "I must not give an order that I lack the power to enforce. How would it look for a march warden to do such a thing?"

"You are her father," Blanche said, as if that were that.

"But Scottish laws are not secret, madam. Most men know the marriage laws well. Certainly the parson knows them. Would you have me command her to lie to him when he asks if she has agreed to the marriage she is about to enter?"

Blanche said grimly, "In my family, husband, daughters obey their fathers in everything."

"Aye, madam, but your father was fostered in an English household. Indeed, he was half English himself, but English ways are not my ways."

"If you would permit me to speak freely . . ."

When Blanche paused meaningfully, Sir William sighed and said, "Say what you will, madam. You generally do."

"Very well; then, I say 'tis folly to allow one daughter to

wind you round her thumb whilst you cast obstacles in the paths of your other daughters' happiness," Blanche said bluntly.

"Godamercy, Blanche, what—?"

"What if Laura should never marry? Have you thought about that?"

"Aye, every time you cast the prospect in my teeth, I think on it," he retorted.

"She is nearly twenty, sir. Girls normally marry as early as fourteen!"

"I'll admit that she's getting a bit old," he said. "If she's not married by the time she's one-and-twenty, I'll think on the matter again."

"But—"

"That is enough," he said sternly. "I've made my decision. Moreover, I'll remind you and your daughters that the same law that lets Laurie say aye or nay to a husband gives me full authority to forbid any daughter's marriage. Do not think you will get round me on that, madam, because you won't."

He scowled at Blanche and then at May.

May did not meet his gaze. She had finished eating and was sitting with her hands in her lap, looking down. Her demeanor appeared to be submissive, but Laurie saw Isabel give her yet another searching look.

Feeling guilty, Laurie wondered if May was simply trying to conceal irritation at Sir William's stubbornness, or hers.

She would have liked to tell May that she was sorry if her waywardness was causing difficulty. Had she been able to explain her aversion to marrying, she would have liked to do that, too. However, she could not explain it beyond saying she had never met a man she wanted to marry, so she sat quietly instead, saying nothing and hoping that no one would command her to speak.

A mental picture of the red-haired man in Tarras Wood suddenly filled her mind. So clear was it that she glanced hastily around to see if anyone had noted a change in her demeanor.

No one was looking at her. Blanche's gaze was drifting toward May, who was still looking down at her lap. Isabel was watching Blanche.

Turning to Sir William, Isabel said, "Sir, when will the English attack again? Will they murder us all, do you think?"

Sir William regarded his youngest daughter fondly and said, "They may attack again, lassie, but here at Aylewood we are as safe as mice in a mill. Our tower, sitting as it does on its rocky crag with only the one track approaching it and with someone always keeping watch, must be well nigh impregnable."

"But if the Laird of Buccleuch and Rabbie Redcloak go after those men who attacked today, Lord Scrope's men will attack Liddesdale again," Isabel said. "That frightens me, because dreadful things will happen and more people will die. And Bridget says that perhaps next time the raiders will come all the way to Aylewood."

Blanche said gently, "You must not listen to servants' gossip, Isabel."

"But Bridget kept crying all day. She said that she heard those horrid men had killed her brother and two of her uncles—even one of her brother's bairns!"

"Who the devil is Bridget?" Sir William demanded.

"Your daughters' maidservant, of course," Blanche said. "I will speak to her directly after we have finished here, I promise you. She may have received dreadful news, but she should not repeat such sordid tales to the child, nor should she speak of persons who do not exist, like that Rabbie Redcloak."

"Does he not exist, then?" Isabel demanded, wide-eyed. "Laurie said he does. She said that Sir Quinton Scott of Broadhaugh knows him. That is why Rabbie's Bairns helped Lady Scott rescue Sir Quinton from Carlisle, and that is why they call her 'Janet the Bold.' Also, Bridget says—"

"That will do, Isabel," Blanche said sternly. "If you cannot hold your tongue, you must retire to your bedchamber."

"I'm sorry, Mama," Isabel said in a small voice. "Must I go now?"

"The one who really should leave the table is Laura,"

Blanche said, giving her husband a look of irritation. "She should be ashamed of telling such untruths to the child, particularly tales like that utter nonsense about Janet Scott."

"That story is true," Laurie said quietly. "Everyone knows that she rode to Carlisle Castle. And that *is* why they call her 'Janet the Bold.' "

"You forget that I have become acquainted with Lady Scott," Blanche said. "There can be no doubt that she is a gentlewoman. Moreover, you seem to forget that she is English. Her brother is England's deputy warden for the western march."

"Still, she—"

"Be silent," Blanche commanded. "Doubtless people hereabouts tell foolish tales about her simply because she has the misfortune to be English and was raised in an odd way. Her mother and father died when she was small, and her brother, who they say is a harsh man, raised her himself. If she sometimes says or does odd things, 'tis doubtless because she had no mother to teach her how to go on."

Laurie had never met Janet Scott, but she had admired her bravery from the moment she first heard about it. Now she found herself envying Janet, as well.

"There will be no more such talk," Sir William said with a stern look at her. "Not of Janet the Bold or of Rabbie Redcloak. Do you hear me, lass?"

"Yes, sir," Laurie said meekly as she tried to imagine what it would be like to hear herself called Laurie the Bold.

Instead, however—and particularly if Blanche had anything to say about it—people were more likely to call her Laurie the Stubbornly Unwed.

Blanche seemed to have forgotten about Isabel's lapse, for she returned to the subject of Fast Castle, and the rest of the meal passed without incident.

As soon as Sir William excused Laurie and her sisters from the table, Laurie hurried to her bedchamber. She thought briefly of speaking to May. Then she remembered that Blanche had promised to have a talk with Bridget. At this hour, Bridget was likely to be in the bedchamber that May shared with Isabel, waiting to help them prepare to retire.

Having no wish to encounter Blanche again until time had done what it could to lessen that lady's displeasure with her, Laurie decided she would be wiser to wait until she and May could talk privately.

Six

There came an old lady
Running out of the wood . . .

"Ye've got company, Sir Hugh," Ned Rowan said over the noise of ponies' hooves clattering on cobblestones, as Hugh and his men rode into the inner bailey at Brackengill Castle a short time later.

Hugh grunted in response, for the unusual activity in the yard had already informed him that company had arrived. Unfamiliar lackeys tended unfamiliar horses, and some of his lads were dragging baggage through the main entrance. He had no idea who it could be, but unexpected company was common in the Borders. Frequently, passing travelers requested hospitality, and hosts rarely denied them.

"I'd better see who it is," he said to Rowan, adding in a louder voice, "Andrew, come and take charge of my lad here."

A thin, wiry little boy came running to take the dun's reins, saying cheerfully, "Aye, Sir Hugh, I'll look after him."

"See that you do, lad," Rowan said, dismounting and reaching out a hand to tousle the boy's dark, curly hair.

Andrew nodded without comment.

As the boy turned away toward the stable with the dun gelding, Hugh strode to the stone steps leading to the castle entrance. Taking them and the spiral stairs inside two at a time, he entered the great hall, where he found serving lads scurrying about in response to sharp commands issued by a frail-looking lady of indeterminate years who sat rigidly upright in his armchair at the high table.

Her elaborately dressed hair was such an improbable shade of red as to make him suspect that, like the Queen, she wore a wig. Her face was heavily made up to look fashionably pale with pink cheeks, red lips, and dark lashes and brows. Her clothing was rich looking and fashionable with beaded and jeweled trim.

She peered toward him myopically, frowned as if to reprove his hasty entrance. Then she smiled, saying in a high, bright, carefully cultured voice, "Why, you must be Sir Hugh!"

"I am Hugh Graham, madam," he affirmed with a nod, adding as he doffed his steel helmet and handed it, along with his steel-and-leather gauntlets and his sword belt, to a lackey, "May I inquire who escorted you here to Brackengill?"

"Why, I escorted myself, sir."

"Perhaps my people did not explain that this house lacks a proper hostess, madam. Indeed, there are no women here, barring the cook and her small daughter. I'll gladly provide you with an escort to Bewcastle, where I am persuaded that Lady Nixon will see to your every comfort."

"It is your lack of a hostess that brings me here," the lady replied.

Hugh stared at her, wondering if she was mad.

"But, there," she said, "I can see that you do not know who I am, and I warrant no one could blame you for that, since it must be fifteen years since you last clapped eyes on me."

She paused with birdlike expectancy, clearly assuming that she had provided sufficient information about her identity for him to deduce it.

Bewildered, he said, "I crave pardon, madam, but I have no idea who you are. It does not matter, in any event, since it is patently unsuitable for you to remain overnight. I will have my lads carry your things outside to your sumpter ponies, although perhaps I should provide fresh ones if you've traveled any distance today."

"Today I traveled from Carlisle, sir. I traveled there from

London in my coach, however, with a wagon to bear my baggage. A dreadful, rough journey it was, too. I feel obliged to inform you that your roads hereabouts are deplorable—where you have roads—but I have resolved not to complain about them."

"They are tracks rather than roads, I'm afraid," Hugh admitted.

"Yes, and because of them, although the distance I traveled today is not so great, I had to leave my coach in Carlisle and hire sumpters, saddle horses, and two men-at-arms to protect me and my tirewoman. Thus, I am worn to the bone from riding, and I am persuaded that you will not wish to turn your own aunt out again under such circumstances. Now, will you, sir?" She smiled sweetly.

Hugh had all he could do to conceal his shock. "My aunt? Lady Marjory? But how can that be, madam? Surely, my uncle Brampton—"

"Dead, I'm afraid," Lady Marjory Brampton said with a sigh.

"When?"

She pursed her lips thoughtfully. "I am afraid I have lost track of time during this dreadful trip, my dear sir. I believe it must be quite four months now, though."

Hugh stared at her, speechless. At last, he said, "If it has been as long as that, someone should have informed me. Do you not know the date of his death?"

"Why, yes, how clever of you to think of that! It was the fourth of April. Moreover, it was a Sunday. I remember the day distinctly, because I had just got home from services when they told me that your uncle had collapsed and died. So, you see, it has been more than four months. I did think that someone would have informed you by now, but of course, there always are complex matters to attend to in such cases, and being a man of law himself and so often with the Queen, Brampton was not accustomed to putting his own affairs in anyone else's hands."

"But I have written to him twice in that time," Hugh protested. "The second time was scarcely a month ago! I am surprised that you did not reply to my letters yourself, madam, if only to explain why my uncle was unable to do so."

"Oh, I could not. I would never presume to read his letters, you see, and I was quite utterly devastated. For a fortnight, I was unable even to see people. My daughters live with their husbands in places quite distant from London, and—"

"Surely, not so distant as Cumberland," Hugh muttered.

She had quick ears, for she said, "Oh, no, not so far as this! Still, they were unable to come to my support at once, you see, and although I did return to Southampton with my daughter Sarah, that situation did not prosper. I discovered that Brampton and I had been quite mistaken about her husband, who proved to be a frightfully quarrelsome man. I am not quarrelsome myself and simply cannot abide the quarreling of others, so I left and went to my younger daughter, Philadelphia. She lives in Cornwall."

"I see."

"Yes, but I did not find Cornwall appealing, either. So when I learned that your dear sister, Janet, had married a Scotsman— Really, my dear sir, I quite feel for you! For your sister to have married right out of her own country! But I shall say no more about that. I came to be a solace to you, so that is that."

Since it was clearly ineligible to tell her to go away again, Hugh said with an unfamiliar sense of creeping desperation, "But this household is bound to prove more distressing for you than any in Cornwall, madam. I would not have you sacrifice your comfort for my sake."

" 'Tis a measure of your character that you can say that, my dear sir, but you need not concern yourself one whit with my comfort. The boot is on the other foot, as my dear Brampton was used to say."

Again at a loss to guess her meaning, he said weakly, "Is it?"

"Yes, certainly, for I intend to concern myself solely with *your* comfort."

"Ah."

"As to maidservants, we need not consider them, for I have brought my own woman with me, of course, and Griselda will see to all that I require. You will find that I have no wish to turn everything upside down, either. Indeed, I shall be no trouble to you or your people, for I am quite accustomed to managing a large establishment."

"I believe you, madam, but truly—"

"I'll warrant that, by virtue of my many years of experience, I know a great deal more about it than our dear Janet did." She smiled hopefully. "Speak frankly now, sir. Do you not miss a woman's touch about the place?"

"In truth, madam, I have been going on admirably for some time now without a female to run things," Hugh said, forgetting how often he had cursed his sister's absence. He wondered what unforgivable sin he had committed to bring such a penance upon himself.

"I think that you will find you have not known comfort at all, sir. But where are my manners?" she exclaimed, springing up from the armchair and smoothing her wide skirts. "I promise you, I know my place, and it is not to be sitting in your chair when you are present. Do sit down, Sir Hugh. You have been in the saddle many hours today, for your people were kind enough to inform me that you had ridden out with Thomas Scrope's army. I know something about that, you see, for I was at Carlisle yesterday when they rode away. A most impressive array it was, too. How colorful and soul stirring it was to see all those handsome men-at-arms with their banners waving! I trust the outcome was as his lordship hoped it would be."

"We prevailed, madam. An army of two thousand could hardly have failed in such a mission against unsuspecting citizens fast asleep in their beds."

"Those dreadful Scots deserved to be trounced in their beds," Lady Marjory said. "Do not waste another moment's thought on them, my dear sir. Think instead about the delicious haunch of beef that your people have been roasting over the kitchen fire for your supper. Can you not smell it?"

He could, and he was hungry enough to eat the whole thing by himself.

He said politely, "Since you have your woman with you, I will offer no more objection, madam, but do not fear to offend me if you decide before long to leave Brackengill. I'll understand if you should prefer to return to one of your daughters."

"I shan't do that," she said. "You clearly need me far more than Sarah or Philadelphia. Here, you," she added more briskly, gesturing to one of the lackeys. "Bring Sir Hugh a cushion for his chair, and see what is keeping that fellow I sent to find herbs for the rushes in here."

Turning back to Sir Hugh, she added, "I find them rather malodorous, do not you? I believe some fresh herbs will help. But do sit down now, sir, and take your ease. Would you not like a mug of ale to slake the dust of travel from your throat?"

"Aye, I would," Hugh admitted, too tired to resist any longer and deciding that he would drink the ale and then go upstairs to change into something more suitable for eating his supper.

His sleeveless jack of plate was flexible enough to be comfortable while riding into battle, but worn over a shirt of chain mail, it felt damned cumbersome by day's end. He would be glad to exchange it for some comfortable clothing.

Shoving a hand through his thick hair, he moved to sit in the now cushioned chair, smiling politely when Lady Marjory asked him to sit just a little forward so that she could readjust the cushion.

"There, now," she said, giving it a final pat. "That will be more comfortable."

"Thank you, madam," he said. "Do not let me keep you, though. You must have things that you wish to attend to before you take your supper."

"Nothing that is more important than seeing to your needs, my dear sir."

"I require nothing presently save to drink my ale," Hugh insisted, hoping that he did not sound as desperate as he was beginning to feel. "Surely you want to tidy your hair, at least. My lads were still bringing in your baggage when I arrived."

"The sumpter ponies fell behind," she said. "I am quite tidy enough, I promise you. Shall I tell your kitchen people that you want your supper at once? Since you need not wait on my account, I believe you will be glad of it."

"No, thank you, for I want to take off this armor before I sup. My people know when to serve me. Moreover, madam, it is not necessary for you to eat here in the hall with me. Brackengill boasts no ladies' parlor, but Meggie, my cook, will be happy to serve you in your bedchamber. I am persuaded that you will enjoy a degree more comfort there than here in the hall with me and my men-at-arms."

Since he had begun to take her measure, her failure to take even so strong a hint did not surprise him.

"I shall begin as I mean to go on, sir," she said. "I can scarcely hide in my bedchamber whenever they serve a meal in this household. Is it really quite necessary that all your rough men sit at table with us? I can tell you, such a practice is quite out of keeping with our London ways."

"This is not London," Hugh said with more harshness than he had intended. Feeling instantly guilty in the face of her astonished expression, he said no more.

She bowed her head, saying ruefully, "I spoke out of turn, and I must apologize. I should not be telling you how to go on in your own residence. And to think that only a moment ago, I was saying that I would not change a thing! What you must think of me! But do not spare another thought for that. It will not happen again. You will find that I can adjust to anything. Faith, what are those men doing?"

Hugh had been staring blankly at the table before him, hoping he could thus keep a guard on tongue and temper. He straightened, saw the lads beginning to set up trestles, and said, "They are setting up the tables for supper, madam."

"Well, they must not make such a din. I will go and tell them so for you."

He opened his mouth to say that would not be necessary, then shut it again when he realized that at least for the too-brief time she spent harassing his men she would not be harassing him.

Drinking his ale in a few hasty gulps, he set down the pewter mug and got up, striding to the service stair near the kitchen in order to avoid passing Lady Marjory. Taking the spiral stone steps two at a time with a sense of being chased, he reached the next level and the safety of his own bedchamber. Shouting for his man, Thaddeus, he pushed open the door and entered, slamming it shut behind him with a sense of having escaped. Then he grimaced ruefully when he saw that Thaddeus was already in the room.

The plump, elderly man raised his eyebrows.

"I don't want to hear any of your gab," Hugh said.

"Nay, then, ye wouldn't," Thaddeus said. "So if ye'll oblige me by sitting on yon stool, I'll just pull off your boots and no say a word about naught. I'd a notion ye'd be along straightaway, so I've a clean shirt, doublet, and hosen ready for ye. Still, afore I shut me gob, will ye be wanting anything else besides them?"

"Clean netherstocks," Hugh said, sitting on the stool and extending his right leg. "The chains in these have rubbed my legs raw."

"Aye, well, they would," Thaddeus said, kneeling to release the spurs from Hugh's thigh-high leather riding boots. "But when it's wearing chains in your hose or getting your leg cut off, I warrant ye'll stand the chafing."

"I'm glad that you decided to hold your tongue," Hugh said sardonically. Then he grunted in pain when Thaddeus braced himself and gave the first boot a hefty jerk. "Easy! What made you so certain that I'd be along so quick?"

"Her ladyship being here," Thaddeus said, looking surprised. He set the boot aside and reached for the other one. "I knew ye'd no want to be sitting down to sup wi' her in all your dirt. 'Tis why I took the liberty o' choosing a doublet and clean shirt and all for ye. She seems a pleasant sort, does Lady Marjory." As he yanked off the second boot, he said, "Art sorry your uncle's dead?"

Hugh shrugged and stood up to doff his clothing. "I've scarcely laid eyes on him since I came of age," he said, "and I never felt close to him. He did his duty by me, certainly, and I expect that I've benefited from his influence with the Queen. I'm grateful that he was an honest man, but that's about all I can say of him."

"Seems a mite odd that Lady Marjory did not come with him in the old days when he stayed here," Thaddeus said, setting the boots aside for cleaning. "Our Mistress Janet should ha' had a lady here to show her how to go on."

"Aye, she should have, but Lady Marjory had daughters of her own to raise. I think, too, that she enjoyed life in London more than she would have here."

"Odd that she did not stay in London, then," Thaddeus said, taking Hugh's jack and breeches from him and handing him a clean shirt.

"Aye," Hugh agreed. He slipped the shirt on and reached for his hose. As he pulled them on, he said no more, not wanting to discuss his aunt further. Thaddeus had served him since boyhood and tended to take liberties in private. Although he had sense enough to show proper respect whenever anyone else was about, Hugh was not eager to make him a gift of his feelings about Lady Marjory.

Thaddeus had turned to the washstand, but as he poured water from the ewer into a basin, the little man shot a look at Hugh from under his bristling eyebrows.

"What?" Hugh said.

"I were just thinking, is all. Now Mistress Janet be away in Scotland, ye might be glad of a lady in the house again."

"She fusses," Hugh said.

"Aye, well, she's kind, is all, and while 'tis true enough that Mistress Janet were not one to fuss, I trow ye'll no dare to shout at Lady Marjory the way ye did at Mistress Janet."

"I did not shout at her."

"Aye, well, have it your way, but 'tis been sorely quiet since she left."

Hugh could not deny that. He remembered days not long

past when maidservants sang and laughed while they went about their work, when the castle had gleamed from the cellars to the ramparts. But the maidservants had departed soon after his sister had gone. Even the ones who only came in daily had stayed away, commanded to do so by husbands or fathers who believed it was unsuitable for them to work in what had perforce become an all-male household.

He had suffered from their departure for only a few weeks, however, before Jock's Meggie had arrived to take over the cooking and supervise the housekeeping.

Meggie, a widow with five small children, had moved her family into the kitchen quarters at Brackengill rather than go to her own people when Hugh had installed his captain, Ned Rowan, to look after her late husband's tenant farm. Rowan had a fond eye for Meggie, and Hugh had hoped they might marry, but Meggie had refused.

Hugh was under no illusions about Meggie's loyalty to him, either. He knew that, having refused to marry Rowan or to go to her parents, and with five children to rear, Meggie had chosen life at Brackengill as her least objectionable alternative. If she was loyal to anyone, it was to his sister, Janet. The only one at Brackengill more loyal to Janet than Meggie was Meggie's nine-year-old son, Andrew.

With her children underfoot all day, Meggie was not as efficient as Janet had been, but at least she knew her place, and Hugh did not miss his frequent battles with his sister. Growing up alongside him at Brackengill, Janet had shared his lessons simply by demanding of his mild-mannered tutor that she be allowed to do so. Despite the combined efforts of the tutor and Hugh's uncle Brampton, during his annual visits, to teach her to submit to Hugh's authority, neither they nor Hugh had succeeded to any extent that he could discern.

Because Janet had taken control of the household when she was little older than Meggie's Nancy was now, she had come in time to wield her authority as housekeeper as if it were equal to her brother's authority as master of Brackengill. Her

temper was certainly equal to Hugh's, and their battles had
been loud.

It occurred to him that Lady Marjory might well return
things to the more comfortable way they had been before, and
without the quarreling. She might even prove to be a better
housekeeper than Janet.

Perhaps Thaddeus was right and he was judging his aunt
too hastily. She was clearly a kind and considerate woman. He
could do worse than to let her have the run of Brackengill.

Logic told him that such a city-loving woman would not
long be content in Border country, but as long as she wanted
to stay, he would be churlish not to welcome her.

Having made this decision, he decided that what had first
seemed a penance would soon prove a boon. Then, in a much
better mood, he finished dressing and went downstairs, prepared to enjoy his supper and be polite to his new housekeeper.

Seven

False Sir John a wooing came
To a maid of beauty fair . . .

It was customary on evenings when Sir William's family dined without company, for his daughters to retire soon after supper, so that they could be up and about their duties early each morning. It was not dark yet, however, nor would it be for two more hours, and despite her busy day, Laurie was not the least bit sleepy.

The maidservant Bridget served all three daughters of the household. Since Blanche would keep her occupied for a short time, and since Bridget favored May over Sir William's other daughters, Laurie knew she might well have a full hour to herself before the maid would come to her.

There was no fire in her fireplace, because Blanche did not approve of wasting wood during the summer months when she believed that fires were not necessary to warm bedchambers other than her own. Laurie's bed curtains were plain blue damask, decorated only with simple embroidery that she had worked herself at the age of thirteen. The chamber was bleak, but she was used to it.

For a time, she busied herself by taking off her cap and brushing her hair while she gazed out her window and enjoyed the soft breeze that wafted gently in.

The tall, narrow window provided no barrier to the elements, other than the thickness of the wall surrounding it, unless she closed its shutter, and she did that only on those rare occasions when a storm raged outside with such ferocity that it blew rain into the room.

She liked to gaze at the view, which was far more interesting than her bedchamber even when the landscape began to turn golden brown toward the end of summer. The oak trees retained their dark green leaves into the autumn, and now the grass was still green and wildflowers spattered the land with vibrant colors.

Her window faced west, so she could rest her elbows on the stone sill and watch the sun go down, and she was high enough to ignore activity in the bailey below. She would have liked to have a larger window with a cushioned seat like the one in the ladies' parlor, but since that one faced south, the evening view from it was never as spectacular as hers could be.

Lingering clouds began to turn color before the sun touched the horizon, and soon vivid hues of orange, red, pink, and purple streaked the sky. Dusk would linger after the sun departed, but sunrise would come early, and the dawn's light always woke her. Therefore, when Bridget came at last to help her undress, Laurie did so quickly. And when Bridget had gone, she climbed into bed, leaving the bed curtains open as she always did, except in the dead of winter when leaving them open meant the risk of waking up to find oneself frozen into an icicle.

She was soon asleep and had been sleeping for some time when a small hand touched her bare arm and startled her awake. Moonlight through the window cast a faint halo around Isabel's slight figure and gilded her long hair where it fanned out from her little nightcap.

Laurie sat up. "Isabel, what is it?"

Bursting into tears, Isabel flung herself into Laurie's arms. "Oh, Laurie, I don't know what I should do!"

"Hush now," Laurie said, shifting a little and helping the child climb into her bed. Plumping pillows, she drew the coverlet over them both. "Here," she said, "snuggle close and tell me what's wrong. Did you have a bad dream?"

"Nay, I have not slept at all." Sniffling, she wiped her eyes with the sleeve of her bedgown. "Mama will be so angry!"

"She will not be angry with you, love," Laurie said, giving her a squeeze. "Come now, what can you have done that is so terrible?"

"May is gone, and I did not tell."

"What?" Laurie sat up straighter. "You must be mistaken. May would not go anywhere after dark. She would be too frightened."

"Nay, but she did, and Bridget went with her. Mama told Bridget she could not go to her family till her usual day out, and she was crying and crying. Then May told her she could go to them if she would help May go out, too."

"But, why? May has no reason to slip out. Not only is it dangerous, but she usually takes more care to avoid trouble with your mother. Why would she go?"

"Because she is in love," Isabel said, heaving a deep sigh.

"Don't be daft, Isabel. May does not know any gentlemen other than our father's friends and acquaintances. Where would she find one to fall in love with?"

"She found him in Tarras Wood," Isabel said. "His name is Sir John. I do not recall his surname, if she told me. She met him about a fortnight ago, and she has been able to think of nothing and no one else since."

"But how did she meet him?"

"She was trying to follow you one day, to see where you went. It was all my fault," Isabel added guiltily. "I told her that I thought you were brave to ride out alone as you do, and she said she was just as brave as you are. To prove it, she ordered her pony saddled and rode straight out the gate. No one stopped her. I think she must have done it other times, too."

"But did your mama not find out May left?"

"Nay, for the servants did not tell her, and that day she had ridden with our father to Broadhaugh. He wanted to talk to

Sir Quinton, and she went along to cultivate Lady Scott's acquaintance, she said."

"Godamercy, child, you hear a good deal, do you not?"

"Aye, for no one pays me much heed unless it is to correct my grammar or tell me that I should be minding my lessons. But Mama gives us our lessons, and she had explained to me why she would not be doing so that day. I told May, and that was when she decided to ride out."

"What else do you know?"

"Well, Sir John is a man of wealth, for he has two castles in England—"

"England!"

"Aye, and in England a man can marry a maid without her father's permission, May said. He need only persuade a parson to perform the ceremony. And if a maid has a proper dowry, Sir John said, the thing is arranged in a trice."

"But May has no dowry. At least, she will have none if she runs away to England," Laurie pointed out.

"But she said she is taking her dowry with her!"

"What can you mean, child? She has nothing to take."

"Nay, but our father has much in his coffers, does he not? And Mama has jewelry that she said she will give to May when she marries. So May is taking some jewelry and what gold Sir John said would be suitable from our father's coffers."

Stunned to speechless dismay by Isabel's artless revelation, Laurie sought for something sensible to say, and failed.

In a voice even smaller than before, Isabel said, "Are you dreadfully vexed, Laurie? I know that it was wrong not to tell Mama at once, but May made me promise that I would not tell her at all."

Weakly, and not expecting any answer, Laurie said, "What demon can have possessed her to do such a thing?"

"Well, May said it was all your fault."

"Mine?"

"Aye, for she said that she is ripe for marriage, that she has been old enough to marry for nearly two years. Since she can never marry till you do, and since you never will, she said that she had decided to take matters into her own hands."

"What makes her think that I never will marry?"

"She says that you hate men. Do you hate them, Laurie? I think that some men are rather nice."

Taking a deep breath, Laurie said, "I do not hate men, Isabel. I do not even dislike them. I just have never met one with whom I can imagine spending the rest of my life. If I ever do meet such a man—one to whom I can talk the way I talk to our father or to Davy Elliot—perhaps it will be different. But most of the marriageable men I have met behave as if they think they are grander than God."

"Laurie, that is blasphemy!"

"I know, but they do act so. I'll tell you a secret, though. I would like to meet Rabbie Redcloak. I believe I would like him very well."

"But he is a made-up man, Mama says."

"Aye, I know she does. Look, Isabel, are you certain that May has already left Aylewood?"

"She crept out of our bedchamber a long while ago. I do not know when, exactly, but I have been lying there so long that I thought the sun must be coming up soon. I was afraid to face Mama, so I came to find you."

"It is hard to tell the hour when the moon is bright, but let me look."

Laurie got out of bed and went to the window. "I don't believe it is as late as you think it is," she said, peering out. "The stars move during the night, you see, and although they move slowly, they seem scarcely to have moved at all since I went to bed. It may be close to midnight, but I doubt it is later than that. Are you truly certain that May and Bridget have left the castle?"

"I think so."

"Surely someone would stop them," Laurie said.

"All I know is that May said she had it all fixed. I think that she must have planned this carefully, Laurie. She told

Bridget that she would help her because it meant that she would have company at least as far as Tarras Moss."

"Godamercy, has she actually arranged to meet this man, then?"

"Aye, she has. He promised to wait for her tonight, and he told her not to fear our father because he would take her far beyond his reach—and beyond Mama's reach, too."

"Did May say where she is to meet him?"

"Nay, but she must have been planning to ride toward Tarras Moss. She said that Bridget could ride with her that far if only she would say—if anyone dared to challenge them—that May was her sister, come to fetch her home. I don't know who would believe that, though, because everyone here knows May."

"She must have disguised herself somehow," Laurie said. She thought swiftly. "Perhaps I can still find them before it's too late. If May meant to collect her dowry, surely she also took time to pack some clothing, and she will not be able to move fast. She is not an intrepid rider, and she will have Bridget up with her."

"Oh, Laurie, can you stop her? She ought not to go to England. I will miss her dreadfully, and Mama will be so angry there will be no peace for any of us."

"Let me see what I can do," Laurie said reassuringly. "You go back to bed, and go to sleep. That way, if May and I are not back here in the morning, you can claim that you were fast asleep the whole time and know nothing about it."

"But that would be a lie."

"It is too late to think about that now," Laurie said. "If you were going to succumb to moral principles, you should have done so before now."

"You *are* vexed."

"Oh, aye, but not at you, love. Go to bed now, so that I can . . . No, wait," she amended hastily. "You had better stay to help fasten me up."

Dressing as quickly as she could with the help of her un-skilled assistant, Laurie took an old, black, hooded cloak from the wardrobe with a fleeting wish that she had the newer, warmer one she had left at Davy's. Putting that thought aside, she snatched up her gloves and whip and slipped down the service stairs to the postern door as silently and quickly as she could, stopping on the way in the armory to take a pistol off the wall and slip it awkwardly into the pouch attached to her belt. The gun's handle stuck out, but she believed her cloak would cover it.

She did not bother looking for powder or bullets, because she did not know how to use either, but she felt safer, knowing that she had a weapon with her. If anyone dared to accost her along the way, she could at least point it at him. He would have no way to know if it were loaded or not.

Although the armory lay near the great hall, too many men slept in that chamber to risk trying to slip out the main door. The postern door near the kitchen was safer and, having frequently used that route, she knew the way of its bolts. From there, she felt sure she could slip across to the stables without drawing attention. The guards watching for trouble expected it to come from outside the wall, not from within.

She reached the stables without incident, and inside, she found Davy's cousin, a lad with the interesting to-name of Bangtail Willie. He was snoring peacefully, rolled up in a blanket on a pile of straw near her pony's stall.

Gently touching his shoulder, she said, "Willie, wake up. I need you."

The slim youth rolled over with barely a sound. In the ambient moonlight, she could see his eyes widen.

"Mistress Laurie?"

"Aye," she said. "Rub the sleep out of your eyes, and attend to me. May is gone, and I must go after her. Saddle my pony, and quietly. Do not wake a soul."

"I'll gang wi' ye, then, an ye're riding out, mistress. There may still be English soldiers about."

"Nay, Willie, they are all gone or we'd have heard differently, and there may be trouble over this. You must not suffer for May's sins or mine. I'll tell no one that you helped, but it may be wise for you to pretend that you were sick tonight—

vomiting or some such. Then you can say that you never even saw me."

"Aye, no one will wonder that I am sick after all that's happened in the dale today," he said. He was already throwing a cross-saddle over her pony's back. "The fact is that I never did see Mistress May leave. Are ye sure she's awa'?"

"I'm sure. She slipped out with Bridget, pretending to be Bridget's sister."

"Then I did see them," Willie acknowledged, looking surprised. "She were wearing a hood, and Nebless Sam—he's watching the postern gate—asked how did Bridget's sister get inside the wall without him seeing her. He's soft on Bridget, ye ken, so he *would* notice even did she come in through the main gate. Bridget said that she had come earlier, afore they changed the guards. Then she said that she—Bridget, that is— couldna leave till she got her lasses off to bed."

"Did they not take a horse, then?" Laurie asked.

"Aye, but they did," Willie said. "Now that I think on it, Sam said they was riding Mistress May's white palfrey. He thought it were right kind o' her to lend it."

Laurie sighed. "I just hope Bridget does not come to grief over this. I know that she is wild with grief over her brother and her uncles dying, but Lady Halliot will be very angry if she discovers that she left without permission."

"Then she didna ha' leave to go?"

"No."

"Aye, well, then the wicked lass best come home afore dawn."

"May must do so, too," Laurie said. "That gives them only a few hours, for it will begin to get light soon after four."

Willie shrugged as he gave a last tug to the saddle to be sure that it was secure. "Ye've your work ahead, it seems."

He moved to adjust the pony's bridle, and as Laurie stepped back out of his way, she felt the pistol move and clapped her hand against it to keep it from falling.

"There is one more thing, Willie," she said, trying to keep

her tone matter-of-fact. "I shall need a holster fixed to my saddle."

He looked at her in surprise. "A holster?"

"Aye, I've a pistol with me, and I've no proper way to carry it."

She could feel his disapproval, but he did not question her, merely moving away for a moment or two, then coming back. "That should do you," he said, adding bluntly, "D'ye ken how to shoot that pistol, mistress?"

Laurie hesitated.

"Is it loaded?" he asked.

"I don't know," she admitted. "I took it from the wall in the armory."

" 'Tis likely to be loaded, then. Let's ha' a look."

Reluctantly, she handed it to him.

Holding it toward what light there was from outside, he peered at it, then handed it back. "Dinna shoot yourself wi' this thing. Shall I put you up now?"

"Please," she said with relief "Then I must ask you to let me out through the postern gate. I dare not ride across the bailey and ask them to open the main gates."

"Nay, they wouldna do it at this hour," he said, making a stirrup with his hands for her to put her foot in. As he lifted her to her saddle, he said, "I'll let you out, but I'll have to shift Sam first. I'll just tell him that I canna sleep for the grippe and may as well be useful. I'll say he can nap for a bit if he likes."

"Good," Laurie said, gratefully transferring the pistol from pouch to holster. "You must watch for our return, too, if you can. The men will likely see us from the wall, but if we just ride round to the postern gate again, they'll think we are only women coming in for the day to work, and that we've just arrived a bit early."

"Do ye think ye can be back afore sunrise?"

"I hope so," Laurie said, wishing that she believed they would be. "First, though, I must find May."

Willie nodded, gazing up at her. "I'm thinking, mistress,

that 'tis most likely they be headed down the burn towards Tarras Moss. 'Tis the way Bridget would go home, and if they went another way, I'm like to have heard about it from one of the men. 'Twould be noted, ye ken, just as Mistress May's palfrey were noted."

She agreed. "Thank you, Willie. Now, go and shift that gate guard."

A moment later, she heard his low whistle.

Riding out of the stable, she crossed the narrow space between the stable end and the narrow postern gate in the outer wall. The gate opened as she approached, and a moment later, she was outside on the narrow dirt track that skirted the wall.

Hearing Willie's low-spoken "God speed, mistress," Laurie raised her hand in farewell and let her pony have its head.

Near the main gates, the little track joined the wider one leading down to the tumbling burn from the crag. She half expected to hear a shout from the ramparts, but the night remained silent. Doubtless, with the moonlight revealing only her dark, hooded figure on a bay horse, those above assumed that whoever had let her out knew who she was and where she was bound.

"Who dares meddle with me?" she muttered. Repeating that ancient motto of the Halliots and Elliots under her breath, Laurie the Bold rode into the night.

Eight

For it never became a gentleman
A naked woman to see.

The moon had moved nearer the horizon, and it cast long shadows over the land. Scudding clouds and a brisk wind made those shadows dance and stippled the landscape with an eerie light that looked as if ghosts had been set free to wander. The third time Laurie had jumped at a shadowy movement, a tiny voice in her mind muttered that she had been mad to keep quiet about May's plan and madder still to follow her alone. No longer feeling very bold, she pushed on nonetheless.

Her only plan had been to catch up with her sister and talk her into returning to Aylewood, but she had feared for the success of that plan from the moment she realized that May had slipped out of the castle without challenge.

May was too far ahead now, and in any event, she would not stop merely because Laurie shouted at her to do so, even if Laurie caught sight of her and were close enough to make May hear her.

In fact, Laurie realized belatedly, if May truly believed she was in love, she was unlikely to listen to anything that her older sister said, in any event. And Laurie did not feel confident that she could force May to return if May refused.

The terrain was rugged enough so that she had to pay close heed to where she was going, and for a time she could not see much of the way ahead. But when at last she reached the top of a rise and saw the dense blackness of Tarras Wood sprawled below her, a pale horse and lone rider stood out clearly against it.

Laurie saw no sign of Bridget, but she realized that if May looked back, she was likely to see her silhouetted against the sky unless the moon conveniently chose that moment to disappear behind a cloud. But she dared not slow down if she wanted to catch her.

Her horse would not show as easily as May's did, and Laurie's clothing was dark, too. Once she was below the ridge top, she felt confident that May would not see her even if she did look back.

May did not pause, however. Indeed, she had put her pony to what was, for her, a reckless pace. Clearly, she realized that the more quickly she put distance between herself and Aylewood, the more likely her mad scheme was to succeed.

Laurie urged the bay to a lope. The faster pace was risky, but she dared not let May get too far ahead. As it was, the chance that at any moment she might lose sight of her was all too great.

May skirted the eastern edge of Tarras Wood, moving away from Tarras Burn and heading toward the forest's southern end, where it met the Liddel. From there, she followed the river east. Passing through the elongated shadow of an abandoned peel tower called Corbies Nest—an old, deteriorating hilltop tower that many claimed was haunted—she rode on without pause toward Kershopefoot.

Laurie had hoped that May would not go so far. She knew that Kershopefoot provided the easiest access to England from the Scottish Borders. From the bridge at the little village to the point where the Liddel joined the Esk at Canonbie, Liddel Water formed the boundary between the two countries. However, even knowing that and anticipating that May might take that route if she somehow managed to meet her lover before Laurie caught up with her, Laurie had not suspected that May would have the courage, or reason, to ride so far alone.

Laurie realized that she had two choices. She could shout

at May and hope that her sister heard her, or she could simply keep riding and try to catch up without May catching sight of her. Fearing that May would simply give spur to her pony and ride at an even more reckless pace to get away, she opted for the latter.

She knew that May was less likely to catch sight of her while they followed the well-worn rocky path that ran close to the Liddel, because it wound through shrubbery. Thus, its twists and turns and ups and downs provided more concealment than the more open land of the Moss near the edge of the forest.

The clouds overhead helped, too, whenever they veiled the moon's bright light. That made it harder to see May, however, and at one point, where boulders blocked the direct route to the village of Kershopefoot and the path led away from the river for a time, she feared that she had lost sight of May altogether.

Drawing rein in the shadow of an immense boulder on a low rise, she scanned the landscape ahead where the hillside sloped down to the dark village. She could easily make out the village and the ribbon of glittering water beyond it, but foliage thickened near the Liddel. She saw no movement.

The white palfrey was nowhere in sight.

Surely, she thought, May would not ride into the village. To be sure, it provided the most direct route to the bridge spanning the Liddel, but she did not believe for one moment that May, riding unescorted, would go into the village.

Remembering another detail, Laurie grew doubly sure that May had not entered the village. Kershopefoot Bridge did not sit with a foot in each country. It actually led to the point of Dayholm, the triangular patch of land that lay in the fork where the river met Kershopefoot Burn.

Dayholm, on Scottish soil, was one of the favorite sites for grievance meetings between the two countries, because England lay just on the other side of the holm, separated from it only by narrow Kershopefoot Burn. In any event, there would be guards on the bridge, awake and alert.

With these thoughts in mind, Laurie decided that May would meet her lover somewhere nearby. She still found it hard to believe that her younger sister had ridden so far on her own; it was impossible to imagine that May would have the courage to cross the border by herself.

She had been staring southeast toward the village, but just then she remembered that Davy had once mentioned a reivers' ford that lay a half-mile or so west of Kershopefoot. Davy had said that the Liddel was more treacherous there but that the reivers were safer than they would be trying to cross the bridge.

As she turned her head to look west, movement flickered and she saw the palfrey at last. But May was no longer alone. A larger dark horse trotted beside hers, its rider a big, solid-looking man.

The moon eased from behind a cloud, and moonlight glittered on the man's torso, making it look as if he wore silver trappings.

For a moment, Laurie thought that perhaps May's knight really was as wealthy as May and Isabel believed he was. Then she realized that he was wearing chain mail. Such prudence was not unusual, though. Any Englishman of sense who crossed to the Scottish side of the line would wear protective gear. And good chain mail was expensive.

The two riders vanished into woodland near the river, and Laurie hastily urged her pony to a lope again. Neither May nor her knight had looked back while she watched them, and she could only hope that they had not ridden into the shelter of the trees simply to wait for anyone who might be following.

Her fear now was that they would cross the Liddel before she could get near enough to see where they crossed. She knew only that a ford existed and that it was somewhere west of Kershopefoot. She did not know its exact location, and lack of that information could doom her mission before it had properly begun.

Moments later, she rode into the woods, letting her pony pick its way through the undergrowth while her eyes adjusted to the increased darkness. She could hear swift moving water beyond, and soon she was able to discern a natural pathway through the trees. The sight reassured her that the ford would be nearby.

She reached the riverside margin of the trees moments later to see a rocky shore and roiling, tumbling water. Although she did not immediately spot the pair she followed, a murmur of voices to her right soon drew her attention to their shadowy figures. She saw with surprise that, rather than crossing, they had ridden some distance along the riverbank and stopped.

Since at that point the Liddel tumbled downhill and away, no doubt to behave even more energetically than the water in front of her, which flowed swiftly around and between huge boulders and over others, she was certain that they must have missed the ford. Her confusion increased when she saw May dismount.

"What *is* she doing?" she muttered to herself.

She dared not simply ride up to them and demand answers, because she knew nothing about May's lover other than what May had told Isabel. They would surely see her coming long before she could reach them, and the notion that Sir John would just let May return with her to Aylewood was patently absurd.

His face was in a shadow, so she could not make out his features, let alone read his expression, but a man who would encourage a girl to betray her parents the way he had could hardly be trusted to behave properly when caught at his mischief. At the very least, he would ride off with the gold and jewelry that May had stolen from Sir William's coffers. At the very worst—

To her shock, she saw him draw a pistol and point it at May.

Slowly, watching him the way a rabbit might watch a fox, May slipped off her cloak and let it fall to the ground beside her. Then, while Laurie watched helplessly and with increasing horror, May walked toward the rushing river, moving with a reluctance that was evident even at that distance and in that dim light until she stood right at the water's edge.

Fighting off her terror, Laurie pulled the pistol from its holster and slipped down from her saddle. Wrapping the reins around a branch of a nearby bush, she left the pony standing and moved as quickly as she dared through the shadows at the edge of the woodland.

Although terrified of what lay ahead, she did not think she risked discovery as long as she did not run into the open. The sounds of the river drowned those of her passage, and the shadows would conceal her movements.

A moment later, she heard May's tearful voice raised in protest. "But I don't understand, Sir John! I thought you loved me!"

Her companion spoke in a less audible tone, and Laurie could not make out his words, but she saw May reach to unfasten her belt and girdle. When she dropped them to the ground just beyond the water's reach, moonlight revealed the glint of tears on her cheeks.

Laurie pushed past branches that barred her way, moving faster. Shouting would do no good, nor could she try to fire her pistol. She still was not sure whether it was loaded, for one thing. In any event, she knew she would be wiser to get close enough for him to see it and hope that he would believe she could fire it.

She heard him speak again and froze, straining her ears to hear him, hoping that he had changed his mind about harming May. His words reached Laurie's ears this time, aided either by a breeze or by the fact that she was closer and he had raised his voice to be sure that May heard it over the noise of the river.

"Don't waste time now, lass. Take off the rest, as I bade you. Those garments be worth a tidy sum, and I don't want to lose them to the river. And save your tears. They will avail you naught, and they annoy me."

May bit her lip and reached for the lacing of her bodice with hands that Laurie was certain must be shaking with terror.

Laurie moved closer, trying to think. The man's English accent reminded her of the two men she had seen in Tarras Woods, but it was no time to be thinking of them.

"You said you loved me," May said.

"Be damned to your romantical nonsense. Take off your clothes!"

"I can't take them off by myself," May protested through a new burst of tears. "I have a maid! I cannot even reach the fastenings down the back."

Muttering angrily, the man dismounted and walked toward her.

He had his back to Laurie now, but he still held his gun pointed at May, and Laurie gritted her teeth in frustration. She did not dare shoot for fear of hitting May. Even if she could hit him without hitting May, if he fell against May, they both would go into the water. She would have to wait until he moved away again.

She wished she could see his face and try to read his intent. What if he just picked May up and threw her into the turbulent river?

Rapidly, she considered her options. She could not just step forward and demand that he unhand her sister. There was nothing to keep him from pushing May in then, because Laurie was not sure she could wound him even if she fired.

She had never fired a pistol in her life, and she was sure that there was some skill involved. What if it failed to go off when she pulled the trigger? It had a mechanism that one was supposed to wind at some point. She did know that much, but she had not asked Willie how to do it. She could only hope that someone had wound it before hanging it on the wall. Still, even if she had only to point it and squeeze the trigger, the man looked much smaller when one thought of him as a target rather than as an enemy who threatened one's safety.

If she could get close enough, he might believe her threat, but would he also be able to tell if the gun would not fire? Even if it did, if she missed him, he could just snatch it away from her. That would put her in as much jeopardy as May.

While these thoughts tumbled over each other in her mind,

she saw him move closer to May. For a terrifying moment, she feared he would push May in, but then she saw that he had tucked his pistol under one arm and was actually helping May unfasten her gown.

He was talking, too, for Laurie could hear the sound of his voice if not the words that he spoke. When he had released the hooks in the back, which he did with a speed that revealed some practice in the art, May suddenly turned to face him, shifting position slightly so that Laurie could see their profiles. May's gown gaped at the back and had slipped from her shoulders. Moonlight touched her breasts.

Laurie could not hear what she said, but she saw May's hand move to the man's face in a surprisingly gentle gesture. Then, to Laurie's shock, May tilted her face up, clearly inviting the villain to kiss her.

Obligingly, he bent his head down, and his lips touched May's. As he shifted the pistol from beneath his arm to his right hand, that arm went around her waist, pulling her nearer. The other hand moved to her cheek, stroking it and cupping her chin. Then briefly the hand grasped her throat before stroking downward toward those inviting breasts.

Laurie could not breathe. Was May trying even now to seduce him?

Suddenly, May's knee came up hard between the man's legs. As he doubled up toward her, she slipped from his grasp. Then, before he could recover, she turned back, put both hands against him, and shoved hard.

He tumbled into the water, and the current swept him away.

Nine

Lie there, lie there, you false-hearted man,
Lie there instead of me.

Gaping, Laurie fought to collect her wits. Then, lowering her pistol, she ran up behind May and grabbed her arm.

May jumped and cried out, bringing a hand up defensively as she turned.

"It's me, May! It's Laurie! Oh, my dearest dear, are you hurt? Whatever happened just now?"

"He tried to kill me, that's what," May snapped. "But I sent him to lie for eternity with his other wives, and now I suppose that you and everyone else will say that I got no more than what I deserved. What are you doing here, anyway?"

"I followed you, of course," Laurie said, understanding May's fury albeit little else. "But why would he try to harm you, May? I thought that he wanted to take you to England and marry you."

"You know a great deal about it," May said bitterly. "I suppose Isabel has been talking out of turn again. That child wants whipping."

"We will not speak of what anyone wants or deserves," Laurie said quietly.

Peering at the river, she saw no sign of the man. The current was swift, its power undeniable, as the river swept on down the hillside. Doubtless, it was the end of him. Although Laurie felt no sorrow, she silently offered a prayer for his soul before turning back to her sister to ask, "Where are the things you took?"

"So you know about that, too, do you," May said bitterly.

"Where are they, May?"

"Yonder," May said, pointing toward the palfrey and the black standing quietly beside it. "In two sacks tied to his saddle." She bent to pick up her cloak, clutching the front of her gown to her bosom with the other hand as she did.

"We should leave at once," Laurie said, moving to make sure that the sacks were still where May said they were. When she found them, she added, "We are too close to the village. Even at this hour someone may be up and about, and it would not do for anyone to see us."

"But what should we do with his horse?"

"I don't think we should leave it here, and I'd rather leave those sacks tied where they are than carry them." Laurie patted the black's neck. "It seems well trained and would make a fine addition to our stable. We can say we found it wandering free."

"Oh, indeed," May said sarcastically. "We'll ride into the yard in the middle of the night and say that whilst we were out, we happened upon a stray horse. We'll say it followed us home, just as Isabel said about the kitten she found last year."

Laurie grimaced. "It will not be as bad as that. Bangtail Willie let me out through the postern gate, and he is there now, awaiting our return. He will tell no one that he has seen us."

"How can you be certain of that?"

"Faith, I think he is more worried about Bridget getting back safely than he is about us. So, turn around and let me do up your gown. Then we'll go home."

When May's hooks were fastened again, Laurie left her to put on her cloak and led the black to where she had left her bay gelding.

May followed silently a moment later, leading the palfrey. She had not even protested Laurie's decision to leave the sacks of gold and jewelry where they were.

With her thoughts taken up by the recent events, and then on protecting the precious sacks and getting away from the village unseen, it was not until they were riding up the slope above Kershopefoot that Laurie remembered what May had said about sending her false knight to his other wives. She glanced at May now, riding silently beside her, hunched over the palfrey's neck as if it were too much effort to sit straight on her saddle.

"What did you mean back there when you spoke of his other wives?"

May shot her a look of resentment, but Laurie easily detected the hurt beneath it when May said bitterly, "He has been married before, Laurie. I don't know how many times, but more than once. He told me he married the others only for their dowries. Once he had their dowries safe, he killed them."

"Godamercy!"

"He is a wealthy man," May went on. "But a man cannot be too wealthy, he said, and it occurred to him that he did not need to marry me to get my dowry, since I had brought it with me and had told no one where I was going. I forgot how much I had told Isabel."

Laurie opened her mouth to say what she thought about May's behavior, but she shut it again. It was no time for recriminations.

May was quiet for a few moments. Then she said, "Why did he not tell me before that he had had other wives? Many men marry more than once. Wives die in childbed or from disease. . . . Why didn't he tell me, Laurie?"

"He did not think it important, I expect."

"Well, I think it was important!"

"Aye, but you did not ask him, nor do you seem to have heeded other matters of practicality," Laurie pointed out. She added more gently, "You thought you loved him, May."

"I did." With a sob, she added, "I was a fool, Laurie. He killed them and told their families they died in childbed. He wanted to kill me, too, but instead . . ." She hesitated, glancing back the way they had come. "How quickly does a dead man become a ghost, do you think? What if his ghost comes after us?"

"It will not," Laurie said calmly. "And if you fear that he might somehow have survived, May, recall that the river was very swift and he was wearing chain mail. I do not see how he could survive. Did you see him even try to swim?"

"No, he went under straightaway, and I never saw him again. He's dead. I'm sure of it, but I do fear his ghost."

She faced forward again, straightening her shoulders, as if to show Laurie how calm she felt. Then, suddenly, her face crumpled. "I killed him! Godamercy, Laurie, what if someone finds out? We cannot take his horse home with us. They'll know what we did!"

Laurie pressed her lips firmly together to keep from pointing out that *they* had not killed the false knight.

She heard another sob and saw that May had bent forward again. Her whole body was shaking.

Reaching to grasp her shoulder, Laurie said, "No one will know, May. Even if we take his horse to Aylewood, all anyone will know is that we found it. Willie will just put it with the others, and no one will think anything about it. Strange horses often show up in the stables. No one asks questions about them. And no one can possibly know what happened between you and Sir John, except me, and I won't tell a soul. I will protect you, May. I promise, I will."

"Oh, Laurie, can you?"

"Of course I can. Now, dry your tears. We'll have more immediate trouble to deal with if anyone has discovered our absence, so think about that instead."

May gulped and brushed a hand across her eyes. "What will become of me?"

"One day, whether I marry or not, you will find a man who is worthy of your love, my dear. Then, you will marry him and bear his children and live happily ever after," Laurie added, hoping she spoke the truth.

* * *

Bangtail Willie admitted them at the postern gate, and they slipped into the yard without incident.

"Bridget's back," Willie murmured the moment they were inside the gate.

"Good," Laurie said.

"Aye, her dad brung her straight back when she told him she didna have her ladyship's permission to go."

"Did anyone see her?" Laurie asked.

"Nay, then, I dinna think so. No one who would speak of it, any road."

He seemed surprised to see a third horse, but he accepted Laurie's glib explanation of finding it roaming free beside the burn. Folks living along Tarras Burn, like those in Liddesdale, often spoke of mysteriously acquired horses, and children learned from the cradle not to ask many questions about them.

May and Laurie each took one of the heavy sacks from the black. Hefting hers, Laurie knew that Bridget had to have helped May carry them.

No one challenged them in the yard before they reached the safety of the tower, however. And when they had succeeded in returning the gold and jewelry to Sir William's strongbox, Laurie felt confident that her father and stepmother would not learn that May had been outside the wall, let alone that she had run away in the hope of marrying a villainous Englishman.

Leaving May at her bedchamber door, Laurie went quietly to her own room. Pushing open the door, she walked in to find glowing coals on the hearth and her stepmother dozing on the bed with a coverlet pulled over her. Faint orange light from the coals colored her cheeks. Her ruffled cap had slipped to her eyebrows.

Moving cautiously, Laurie took off her cloak, gloves, and boots and put them in the wardrobe. Then, slipping her feet into lambskin slippers and drawing a deep breath, she tiptoed to the fireplace and bent to lay a fresh log gently atop the hot coals. Blowing on them, she waited until flames leapt merrily around the log before she went to the bed and gently touched Blanche's shoulder.

"Madam, wake up. Why are you sleeping in my bed? Were you looking for me? Is aught amiss with my father?"

Blanche started at her touch, then glowered at her. "Where have you been? If I learn that you have been consorting with one of the servants, I swear that I will order you soundly whipped, Laura."

"I have consorted with no one, madam," Laurie said. "I could not sleep, so I went outside for a short time. How long have you been here?"

Blanche looked around. "Not long, I expect. Something woke me, and I got up to see what it was that I'd heard. I had someone make a fire, so I must have dozed off quickly, for it has scarcely died down at all."

Laurie nodded but said nothing.

"If you must know," Blanche said, "I looked out a window and thought I saw someone riding down the hill. I . . . I came to see if you knew who it might be. When you were not here, I assumed that it must be you, and I waited to see if you would return."

Laurie suppressed a sigh, knowing despite her stepmother's matter-of-fact tone, that it was unfortunately more likely that Blanche had hoped she would not return. Had she really believed that the rider was Laurie, she would surely have roused the men to search for her.

She would at least have awakened Sir William. However, since it was far more likely that she had hoped Laurie was running away, Laurie knew that Blanche had doubtless intended to give her a good head start before alarming anyone. For that, May would be grateful if Laurie was not.

She said evenly, "I must apologize, madam, if I gave you concern by leaving my chamber."

"You had no business to leave it," Blanche said curtly, getting to her feet. "You would be well served should I order you to keep to your bedchamber tomorrow as punishment."

Laurie kept silent.

"I will speak to your father of this," Blanche said, moving

haughtily to the doorway. "It would behoove you to mind your manners, Laura."

"Yes, madam."

When she had gone, Laurie shut the door and leaned against it with a deep sigh, wondering what it would be like really to run away. Even Isabel would not miss her for long, she thought. Sir William would profess to miss her, but she doubted that he would try very hard to find her. His life, after all, would be more comfortable without her around to stir Blanche so frequently to anger.

These thoughts, although dismal, did not particularly distress her. She had thought the same thoughts before, many times, and had felt the same feelings.

She supposed that other people were happier in their lives than she was in hers. Indeed, she knew that many were, for she could see as much for herself whenever she visited Davy Elliot and his family. Davy's Sym, during the good times, was as merry a child as one could know and loved his family dearly.

Thinking of Sym turned her thoughts to Tarras Wood and an image flashed to her mind of the Englishman with the red curls. Would such a man be married, she wondered. Doubtless, he would. Would he have many children?

She tried to imagine herself married—not to him, of course, but to any man. There were times when she thought that, since marriage would take her away from Aylewood and Blanche, she ought to marry the first man who wanted her. But she had seen little to make marriage seem appealing.

How had her father come to marry Blanche? How did people so mismatched end up together? The answer, she knew, was that marriage had to do with property and with little else. Men married women who could provide them with more property than they had previously possessed. It was generally just that simple.

Sir William was a man of some wealth and would provide each of his daughters with a respectable dowry, but like most

Borderers, he preferred to display what he had by bedecking his wife in jewelry. He did not give anything away easily.

Had he owned vast acres of property, Laurie knew that men would be demanding her hand even without seeing her or knowing a thing about her. She was his eldest daughter. They would expect a great landowner to dower his eldest well.

Gentlemen were not beating down the doors at Aylewood, although over the past five years she had received numerous offers. No man had offered enough to make Sir William order her to marry, though, and she had not seen anything in any suitor that made her want to accept his offer. It occurred to her now that she might have felt differently about a man who had persisted despite her lack of interest. Surely, no woman leapt by choice into marriage with a man she scarcely knew.

Even as that thought flitted through her mind, though, she knew it was foolish. Her own sister had not only been willing to leap into marriage, she had gone through dark of night to meet a man she hardly knew and had intended to ride off with him to a foreign country. May would have married Sir John without a qualm and without the support or approval of her family.

Laurie sighed and went to find her bedgown. She did not understand May, but clearly she herself was at least partially responsible for May's flight and, thus, for the cost of that flight. She had promised to protect May from the consequences, and so far, she had managed to protect them both. She did not know how long she could do so, however, and just the thought of what might lie ahead made her feel dismal again. Altogether, she decided, it had been a dismal day.

Then she thought about the English raid and the people who had died. There were many, many people whose lives were much sadder just now than her own.

Mentally scolding herself for thinking too much about her own life and not enough about the lives of others, she undressed, said her prayers, and went to bed.

Morning would come soon, and the sun was bound to make everything look much more promising.

* * *

But when morning came, although the sun shone with August brightness, nothing seemed to have changed for the better. Many of the men and women who worked at Aylewood received word of deaths in their families, all at the hands of the hateful English.

Agreeing that such loss and sorrow demanded attention, Blanche did not question Sir William's decision to do everything they could do to help the people of Liddesdale and its environs recover from the devastation. She insisted, too, that their daughters do what they could to help.

Laurie and Isabel were perfectly willing, and when May realized that neither of her parents was aware of her escapade, she quickly recovered her customary good spirits and agreed to ride out with her mother and Laurie to visit tenants and see what could be done for them.

Sir William still had much to do to prepare for the forthcoming Truce Day, but he encouraged tenants to approach him with their needs, and he met those needs whenever he could do so. Many people insisted that he file a grievance against Scrope for the terrible invasion, but he soon had other things to think about.

Four days later, Sir Walter Scott of Buccleuch returned to Hermitage and declared his intent to "shake the bones out of that pestilential malt worm, Scrope."

Ten

Thou bold border ranger,
Beware of thy danger.

Brackengill Castle

"Shall I just inform any of your men who ask about you that you intend to return shortly, my dear Sir Hugh?" Lady Marjory asked ten days after the raid, as Hugh pushed the remains of his breakfast away and stood up.

An increasingly familiar tension tightened his jaw. He said evenly, "You need not concern yourself so with my comings and goings, madam. My men will not ask you about them."

"I suggested it only because I would be of service to you, my dear sir. You must make good use of me whilst I am here."

"I would be unwise to become too dependent upon you, madam, for I doubt that you will want to stay through the winter. Life at Brackengill cannot be what you are used to. You will soon miss your London comforts."

"Ah, but I cannot bemoan them when I see you living like this," she said with a sweeping gesture. "Brackengill needs a woman's touch, sir. Anyone can see as much. And if there is one thing at which I excel, it is in being a woman." She fluttered her eyelashes in a way that made him want to run from the room.

Suppressing the impulse, he said, "Your comment makes me wonder why you did not come to us after my father died, madam. You never accompanied your husband, for that matter. Nor did either of you see fit to remove my sister to London or to provide a gently reared female companion to look after her here."

"Oh, my dear sir, if only you knew how I longed to come to you then! But Brampton would not hear of it. Only recall, if you will, how volatile this region was! You were but twelve, and your sister, Janet, some years younger than that, so I did suggest that he bring you both to London, but he refused to do that."

"Perhaps because duty demanded that I stay here and look after Brackengill," Hugh said crisply. "My uncle made annual visits to us afterward until I came of age. Otherwise, he left me in the hands of my steward and tutor, and Janet in the hands of local women who would serve in a castle that lacked a proper chatelaine. It was no upbringing for her, or indeed, for any girl of her rank. If you were willing to care for her, surely my uncle would have taken her to you."

"He did suggest bringing Janet by herself," Lady Marjory admitted. "But I could not allow him to separate her from you, my dear sir. Only think how miserable she would have been, carried off to live with two cousins and an aunt whom she had never so much as clapped eyes on before!"

"Aye, well, she might not have liked it, but it would have done her good," Hugh said grimly. "Had she lived in London, 'tis unlikely that she would have married across the line as she did."

"You cannot know that, dear sir, and you should bethink yourself instead of her certain misery in London. She is practically Scottish, after all, living as close to them as you do here. And I must tell you, Londoners are not always as charitable as they might be. I try to rise above such common prejudice, of course, so you need not bother your head about me. Once we have improved Brackengill a trifle, I believe I shall be quite comfortable here."

"I have done much to modernize the place over the years," Hugh said stiffly.

"Oh, and indeed, my dear sir, anyone can see that. Pray, do not take offense! Why, that Meggie woman in the kitchen told me that she remembers when the castle wall was naught but an enclosure of timber posts! And when I tell you how ruthless I had to be with myself during my journey to keep from recalling things Brampton had told me about Brackengill—for I was determined to sacrifice all, if need be, to see to your comfort . . . But . . ."

She fell silent, clearly struggling to reclaim her train of thought. Then, brightly, she added, "You must tell me what foods you enjoy, Sir Hugh, so that I can see to it that your people serve them to you often."

"I care little what I eat, madam."

"Oh, that cannot be, for gentlemen, in my experience, care a great deal about such things. They just do not realize that they do if their people take proper care of them. And that is just what I mean to do for you."

"Thank you," he muttered, despising the apparent weakness that made it impossible for him to send her packing. Despite the strong interest she took in his household and his need for a good housekeeper, he did not like her. But that only made him feel guilty, since she clearly cared about his comfort.

"You need not thank me," Lady Marjory said earnestly. "And, indeed, sir, if you do not wish to make a list of your favorite foods just now, perhaps that Meggie can tell me what they are. I do not mean to plague you with questions. But where are you going?" she added on a note of surprise when he turned away. "We have only just begun our little chat."

"I have work to do," Hugh said curtly, feeling desperate again and wishing again that he could just tell her to take herself back to London. He knew perfectly well that generally he was capable of such ruthlessness. He even smiled a little when he realized that his sister, if she were to hear of his problem, would wonder at it. Nevertheless, to order the fragile-looking, well-meaning Lady Marjory back to London less than a fortnight after her arrival seemed heartlessly cruel.

Keeping these thoughts to himself, he left the hall, retiring instead to a small chamber between it and the stairs to the kitchen, where he hoped he could enjoy some privacy. The chamber was small and contained numerous coffers, where he stored his personal wines and other things away from his men and the maidservants—when Brackengill had maidservants.

The coffers also contained some of his personal arms, and others decked the walls. A small fireplace sat in the middle of the wall opposite the door. The room was a bit cramped for a man of Hugh's size, and there had never before been a need to put a lock on the door, but it contained a small table on which he could work. Even if Lady Marjory presumed to disturb him, surely she would see that the room was too small for two.

Had anyone asked him what she had done to stir him to such dislike, he could not have explained it. Indeed, he had seen blessedly little of her since her arrival, for not only had his prediction about Buccleuch returning soon from Blackness come true, but his own duties as deputy warden kept him busy.

The Laird of Buccleuch had wasted little time before exacting revenge for Scrope's Liddesdale raid. Within two days of returning to Hermitage, he and Scott of Hawkburne invaded Tynedale—in the English middle march—with a hastily gathered army. They left nearly as much death and destruction in their wake as Scrope had in Liddesdale.

Receiving word of the raid and knowing that Buccleuch's daring and disregard for the law were even more expansive than Scrope's, Hugh and his men had ridden at speed to offer Lord Eure, warden of the middle march, any help he might require. They soon learned, however, that Buccleuch and Hawkburne had invaded and gone again so swiftly that Eure had not lifted a finger against them.

"I felt utterly helpless, Hugh," Lord Eure said, venting his feelings as soon as the two were face-to-face. "I had not six able horses to follow the fray! I tell you, I wish I had never come to serve in such a place, where men obey neither Her Majesty nor her officers. I mean to submit my resignation to the Privy Council, and I shall plead with them to provide more support to my successor. If Her Majesty's forces do not assist us here, Buccleuch and his ilk will lay waste to the entire region."

Hugh sympathized, knowing that the Queen shamefully neglected her wardens. Lacking men, horses, and money enough for their purpose, they frequently were helpless against the Scots, which encouraged the raiders to greater boldness.

Although he doubted that either Eure's letter or resignation would achieve much, he knew they would have to provide a new warden for the middle march soon and wondered if that poor chap would fare any better than Eure had.

Hugh had been home only two days since meeting with Eure, only five days in all since his aunt's arrival. But his notion that he would enjoy having a competent housekeeper again had not survived his first supper with her.

The plain fact was that Lady Marjory was nice. She was thoughtful. She was one of the nicest, most thoughtful people it had ever been his misfortune to meet.

She hovered over him, leaping to her feet if he so much as glanced around, believing that he was searching for something she could fetch for him more quickly than he could fetch it himself.

If he told her that he was thinking, just gazing blindly into space, she would ask what he was thinking about. "For if you are mulling over a problem, my dear sir," she would say, "pray, remember that two heads are better than one."

If he went out, she asked whither he was going and when he would return, assuring him she would be sure that his people had food ready for him when he did so and would tell anyone seeking him where to find him. Her demeanor was always kindly, her attitude sweetly interested.

Although he wondered at his apparent incapability to deal with her, it did not require much thought to understand it. Lady Marjory was of a gender and age that his mentors had taught him must demand respect. Therefore, even when he yearned to bellow at her, he could not bring himself to do so. Thus it was that in the short time she had been at Brackengill he barely recognized the man he had become.

He had noted a change in his men's behavior, too. Hitherto, at mealtimes, they had surged into the great hall with noisy good cheer. But Lady Marjory had ended that by gliding like a wraith among them, gently explaining that the din they made disturbed their master. The result was that the men tended to glance curiously at him, clearly wondering if he was ill.

On the other hand, when the hall was quiet, she would chatter like a magpie, certain that he must be bored and required entertaining.

He missed his sister sorely, having persuaded himself that had Janet been there Lady Marjory would not have troubled him one whit.

It was not the first time since Janet's departure that he had missed her. Upon discovering that she had left Brackengill, he had ranted and raved—in a perfectly reasonable way, of course, considering the circumstances and the fact that Janet could fire his temper more easily than anyone else. Whenever he thought about their many battles, he realized that he and Janet probably were both happier with her living in Scotland, but it took no more than a kind word from his aunt to make him yearn anew for his sister's return.

He was too busy, for one thing, to play the gentle host. Since Scrope preferred trips to London and visiting friends at their great houses—where gambling and other favored activities took place—to his more mundane warden's duties, many of those duties fell upon his deputy. With the next wardens' meeting rapidly approaching, Hugh had much to do to prepare for it.

The march wardens enforced what little law existed in the Borders at periodic meetings, where an English warden met publicly with one or another of his Scottish counterparts to settle grievances that had arisen between their marches since their last meeting. On such occasions, known locally as Truce Days, everyone with an interest in the proceedings gathered at a previously agreed-upon site. There, each side aired its grievances against the other before a carefully selected jury.

The next Truce Day between the English west march and the Scottish middle march was soon to take place at Lochmaben. Scrope had already passed on several packets of grievances to his deputy that he had received from the Scottish warden, Sir William Halliot of Aylewood.

Hugh did not know Aylewood, but he was certain the man would be a vast improvement over his predecessor, Buccleuch. Buccleuch had had a reputation—according to Scrope, at least—of delaying meetings and then of wreaking havoc at them when they finally took place. Hugh had never dealt with Buccleuch, because he had acted in Scrope's place only once, when he had faced Buccleuch's deputy and his own brother-in-law, Sir Quinton Scott.

Much as Hugh disapproved of Janet's marriage across the line, he realized that some of his attitudes toward the Scots in general had altered slightly because of it. For one thing, he had enjoyed sitting at the wardens' table with Sir Quinton, who was his age and had displayed a sense of fair play that seemed to match his own.

It was helpful if one could deal dispassionately with one's opposite warden, since such meetings were always fraught with peril. Juries, claimants, and defendants were notoriously unpredictable.

Presently, Hugh's official duties included making a list of appropriate jurors. That posed several problems, not least among which was his legal obligation to seat only respectable men. Even on the English side, it was not always easy to find six Borderers who answered that description.

Since English jurors tried the Scottish bills of grievance against English defendants, and vice versa, in order to determine who the best men were, he first needed to understand exactly what grievances the Scots had filed. That meant that he had a great deal of reading and thinking to do.

Within days, the little chamber near the hall began to feel

uncomfortably claustrophobic, and Hugh decided that it was time for a change.

The following morning, an hour after he had broken his fast, knowing that Lady Marjory was engaged in rearranging her bedchamber with the help of her companion and Meggie's little daughter Nancy, he took his work to the hall again.

He had no sooner sat down and spread out his documents on the high table, however, than his aunt appeared, seeming almost to materialize out of thin air.

"My dear Sir Hugh, here you are," she said in a tone of great satisfaction, as if she had been searching for him for hours. She wore a gray silk gown, her thin torso stiffly erect above skirts that billowed over her wide farthingale, and wisps of her bright red wig fluttered like avian plumage with each graceful step.

She said, "You look busy, my dear sir."

"I *am* busy," he replied evenly. "Did you want to ask me something in particular, madam?"

"Oh, no, for I am quite content. I shall just run back up to my chamber and fetch my needlework, so that I can keep you company. Then, if you require anything, I shall be right here at hand to fetch it for you."

"I shall not require anything," he said, striving to keep his annoyance from his voice.

Evidently he succeeded, for she said brightly, "But you cannot know when you will, my dear sir. Why, Brampton was used to insist that he needed nothing and then find that two minutes later he required ink, or his spectacles, or had neglected to order his ale. There is always something. You will see."

He pressed his lips together to stop the harsh words that leapt to his tongue.

Without waiting for him to find more tactful ones, she turned toward the doorway to the main stairway.

"Wait, madam," he said, fairly hurling the words after her. She turned with a knowing smile and a look of expectant inquiry. "I told you how it would be, sir," she said. "Did you already think of something?"

"I need nothing but quiet," he said. "I have much to do and little time in which to do it. I know that you mean well, but if you want to sit here in the hall rather than in your bedchamber, I must go elsewhere to work."

"But I would not dream of putting you out of your own hall, sir! Think nothing about my comfort. I own that I do find it a trifle inconvenient that Brackengill does not possess a ladies' parlor or even a proper solar, but I shall do well enough without them. My chamber is nearly habitable now, I promise you. Brampton frequently required time to himself, too. He was a very busy man. He—"

"I know he was," Hugh said, cutting her off without compunction, well aware now that she would chatter until he stopped her. "I thank you for your understanding, madam. I would like to work undisturbed until dinnertime."

"Certainly, my dear sir. Just shout then when you need me." Her agreeable smile still firmly in place, she left the room.

Feeling as if he had just won an enormous victory, Hugh applied himself for the next half hour to drawing up a list of eligible jurors, trying to think of men who did not bear a grudge of some sort against any of the Englishmen against whom the Scots had filed grievances. Since more than one defendant was a Graham, the task was not easy.

Grahams spent as much time fighting among themselves as they did feuding with the Scots, and since many Grahams lived on the Scottish side of the line, he had to consider the unfortunate possibility that a feud between a juror and one of the defendants could lead to an international incident.

This Truce Day, being the first to follow the breaking of a truce and the raid on Carlisle, simply had to go well. If it did not, Hugh knew that Truce Days in general might soon cease to exist.

He had decided upon two men who seemed safe enough—at least, they did unless he received a new batch of grievances that proved otherwise—when the clicking of feminine heels on the main stairway warned him that his aunt was returning. He looked up in resignation as she entered the hall.

"I thought that perhaps I should just look in on you and see if you had thought of anything that you require," she said.

"Nothing, thank you," he said curtly and without bothering, this time, to conceal his irritation.

"Perhaps a mug of ale, or a crust of bread," she suggested, clearly oblivious of his tone. "Meggie baked some fresh bread this morning. Surely, that delicious odor has wafted up from the kitchen to tempt your appetite."

"I am not hungry, nor am I thirsty," Hugh said, goaded almost to snapping. "If I require anything, madam, I have only to shout for a lad to get it. Pray, do not disturb yourself again on my account."

"Oh, it does not disturb me," she said, her customary brightness unimpaired. "It is the sole reason I bide here, after all, my dear sir. Whether you will admit it or not, you need a woman to look after you, but I do see that you are still busy. That task is taking a tiresome amount of time, is it not? I'll leave you to it, though, and perhaps you will be finished soon."

She left, but this time he did not delude himself, merely wondering to himself how long she would stay away. When she returned less than twenty minutes later with a suggestion that it really was not good for him to stay so long indoors on such a splendid day, he snatched at the opportunity her words presented.

"You are right, madam," he said, standing and gathering up his papers. "I shall go out at once."

"Oh, but surely you would like me to help you tidy your table, sir. Or perhaps I should call a manservant to put those documents away for you."

"I'll take them with me," he snapped.

"Well, of course, if you think it is wise to do so," she said doubtfully. "I cannot imagine where you will take them, though."

He did not enlighten her but gathered up the documents with such speed that bits of red sealing wax went flying.

"Take care that you do not rip one of those," she said. "You would be quite vexed with yourself if you did. In any event, I do not see why you want to take them from this room if you have not finished with them. Would it not be more convenient if I were just to sit here and watch to be sure that no one disturbs them whilst you take a turn about the bailey?"

When he did not reply, she added with a laugh, "You can scarcely sit on a hillside and read them, my dear sir. Perhaps I was wrong, after all, in advising you to go outside."

Hugh pressed his lips together, determined to remain civil.

"You are looking a trifle feverish now," she declared. "Indeed, your cheeks are as red as if you had been sitting by a hot fire, or walking outside on a chilly day, but the fire has died to embers and the day is quite warm."

"I am quite well, madam. Now, if you will excuse me . . ."

Escaping at last, Hugh went to the stable and ruthlessly turned Meggie's Andrew and two grooms out of the tack room, where they were polishing some of the men's plating. Still angry, he shot his commands at them in near snarls.

"Andrew and Will," he said as the lads hurriedly put away their gear, "fetch me a table and a stool. I don't care where you find them; just find them at once."

"Be ye going to work on them papers out here?" Andrew asked, wide-eyed.

"I am, and warn the rest of the lads to let no one disturb me, or I swear . . ."

He fell silent, for Andrew had already fled to do his bidding.

When table and stool arrived, Hugh shut the door to the tack room and set to work, as certain as he could be that Lady Marjory would not seek him in the stables.

He worked diligently for an hour undisturbed and finished his preliminary list of potential jurors. That done, he began a report for Scrope detailing the means by which he intended to notify men named in the Scottish grievances that the law demanded their presence at Lochmaben. It was Scrope's responsibility—and thus his—to see that they attended the meeting to answer the charges laid against them.

A sudden commotion outside the closed door drew his attention halfway through a sentence. Recognizing Andrew's voice raised in objection and the deeper one responding sternly to it, he put down his quill and waited, knowing that he need not intervene.

The door opened, and Ned Rowan stepped in, his big body filling the doorway and what little space remained in the room. Andrew, only a shadowy form behind him, started to move away, but Rowan reached back and caught him by his baggy shirt.

"Don't leave," he said sternly. "I've been too busy to deal with ye yet, but we're going to have a talk, the two of us. We'll do it as soon as I've finished here."

Turning back to Hugh, he added, "The lad was gone all day yesterday and didna show himself till nearly nine this morning. 'Tis my belief he's been across the line again, but I'll deal wi' him. I come t' tell ye that your cousin Musgrave just rode in. D'ye want him here or in the hall? They be setting up now for dinner."

Surprised that so much time had passed, Hugh said nonetheless reluctantly, "I can scarcely send him off without feeding him. Has he brought many with him?"

"Five or six," Rowan said, still keeping a firm grip on Andrew.

Hugh's cousin Musgrave was no great favorite of his, but he could hardly talk to him in the tack room, and he would send no man away hungry at the dinner hour. "I'll see him in the hall," he said, adding, "Tell him that I'll expect him and his men to dine here."

"Aye, I'll tell him," Rowan replied, "and then I'll deal with this young varmint. Doubtless, he'll miss his dinner unless he wants to eat it standing up, but I'll see that he doesna cross into Scotland again till he's of age to go on a foray."

Watching them go, Hugh felt little sympathy for Andrew. He knew the lad had probably gone to visit Janet at Broadhaugh, because he had done so before, and they had to put an end to the habit before Andrew ran into trouble. Most likely, the Scots would leave him alone unless they came to fear that he was spying on them, but neither Hugh nor Ned Rowan wanted to think about what could happen then.

Hugh gathered his documents and carried them inside, using the postern door and stowing them in his little chamber near the hall. He entered the hall at the same moment that Sir Francis Musgrave strode in at the far end, having used the main entrance and its stairway.

Hugh waited, letting Musgrave come to him.

Musgrave was a burly, bearded man nearly twenty-five years Hugh's senior. As far as Hugh was concerned, his cousin was as responsible as anyone for the raid on Carlisle, since Musgrave was the one who had arrested the prisoner over whose cause all the fury erupted. He was also one of Scrope's captains, however, and Edgelair, his seat on the fells between Redesdale and Tynedale, was nearly as important strategically as Brackengill or Bewcastle. Located to guard one of the most popular reivers' routes into England, it served its purpose well.

As Musgrave drew nearer, wending his way among trestles and men, Hugh noted the leather satchel he carried and wondered what he wanted.

It was neither Musgrave's connection to the Carlisle raid nor his power that made Hugh wary, however, but the fact that for several years, his cousin had been pressing him to marry one of his daughters. Musgrave possessed three of them and, like any father, desired them all to marry well. Hugh had not met even one of them, but since rumor had it that they were three of the homeliest females in Christendom, he had little wish to do so. He had even less desire to marry one.

His uncle Brampton had attempted once to arrange a marriage for Hugh with a reputedly beautiful Percy of Alnwick. Although the mighty Percys were willing enough to negotiate, Hugh had turned that down, too. Having done so, he certainly would not marry a homely Musgrave. Still, he wanted no trouble with Francis.

Musgrave walked up to him and clapped him on the shoulder. "Good den to ye, Hugh!" he exclaimed heartily. " 'Tis glad I am to see ye looking so stout, lad."

"Thank you, sir," Hugh said, shaking hands with him. "You look well, too."

"Faith, but I'm nowt compared to a man like yourself. Ye should be setting up your nursery and begetting yourself a litter o' fine sons in your image!"

"What brings you to Brackengill, cousin?" Hugh asked evenly as he led the way to the high table and signed to a passing lad to bring them ale.

"Aye, well, I've come from Carlisle," the older man said, taking a seat on the long bench to the right of Hugh's chair. "Scrope no sooner returned from Tynedale than new grievances arrived from Aylewood. And, since he had one or two more himself that he wants delivered to Aylewood, I offered to carry them here t' ye."

"Indeed, sir," Hugh began, when an interruption occurred.

"My dear Sir Hugh, why did you not send to inform me that company had arrived?" Lady Marjory exclaimed, hurrying into the hall. "Indeed, you naughty man, you quite failed to inform me that anyone was coming. I just hope we have enough food!" Directing an arch smile at Musgrave, she waited expectantly.

As both men stood up again, Hugh said politely, "May I present my cousin, Sir Francis Musgrave, madam. Sir, Lady Marjory is my uncle Brampton's widow."

"My pleasure, my lady, and likewise my condolences," Musgrave said, making his bow to her. "I had no notion that Brampton had died or that Brackengill had acquired such a handsome hostess."

Fluttering her lashes and bobbing her wig, Lady Marjory thanked him, took her seat at Hugh's left, and gracefully gestured for the gentlemen to sit again.

"What pleasant good fortune brings you to us today, Sir Francis?" she added.

"As to that, my lady," Musgrave began with a twinkle in

his eyes, "I have a cause to which, mayhap, you will be kind enough to lend your support."

Knowing that Musgrave was not talking about Scrope or grievances, Hugh said hastily, "He brought me some documents, madam. I'm curious, though, sir. Why did Scrope not send a courier to Aylewood to deliver our added grievances? As warden, he can provide safe conduct for one, after all."

"Aye, and he sent a safe conduct along, too," Musgrave said, turning back to him with a smile. "His lordship wants you to deliver these grievances personally."

"I'm honored," Hugh said dryly. "To what purpose?"

"Well, you *should* be honored," Musgrave said with a chuckle. "Scrope said he'd like to do it himself just to see the look on Aylewood's face when he gets it."

Lady Marjory glanced quizzically from one man to the other, but although she appeared deeply interested, she did not comment.

"What sort of grievance would so greatly interest Aylewood?" Hugh asked.

" 'Tis one that Scrope himself has written against Aylewood's middle daughter, charging the lass with illicit seduction and murder, as well," Musgrave said solemnly. "Scrope says she murdered his chief land sergeant."

Astonished, Hugh said, "Martin Loder's dead?"

"Aye, I'm surprised ye hadn't heard. Surely, ye must ha' noted his absence when we tried to take Buccleuch in Tynedale."

"Everything was in disarray then," Hugh reminded him. "I might have noticed if one of my own captains had gone missing, but I paid heed to no one else."

Lady Marjory said, "Pray, Sir Francis, are you saying that a gently raised young woman murdered one of Lord Scrope's soldiers? Surely, that cannot be."

"Nonetheless, I vow that it is so, madam," Musgrave said, "although I cannot speak for the gentleness of her upbringing. She's a Scot, after all. Moreover, Scrope says the lass pushed

Loder into the Liddel and the current swept him away, so I'll wager that she caught him unaware."

"Ah, now, that is possible," Lady Marjory said, nodding.

"Aye, and Scrope means to hang her for it." Turning back to Hugh, Musgrave added, "He said to tell ye to remind Aylewood that since he cannot sit in judgment of her case, he must have his deputy with him at Lochmaben."

Lady Marjory's eyes opened wide. "But what occurs at Lochmaben, sir?"

Leaving Musgrave to explain the wardens' meeting to her, Hugh felt grateful for the first time for his aunt's presence. He was grateful, too, that Scrope had decided to represent England at the Lochmaben meeting.

Hugh did not want to have to sentence any young gentlewoman to hang.

Eleven

Thy foes are determined,
relentless, and nigh.

Aylewood Towers

The day was pale gray and overcast, the sun hidden behind a thin layer of flat-bottomed clouds. Seeking freedom and fresh air, Laurie had just walked down from the hall into the inner bailey when activity on the ramparts warned of visitors approaching. Curious, she moved to a vantage point from which she could watch the main entrance.

The gates swung wide, and a party of four men rode in. They wore chain mail and swords, but as a show of peace, they carried their helmets under their arms instead of wearing them. One carried a white banner bearing a device that she did not recognize.

Bangtail Willie came up beside her, muttering, "It be Sir Hugh Graham, deputy warden of England's western marches, mistress."

"How do you know?"

"I were on the wall and heard his man shout as much afore they opened the gates," Willie said. "Said he's here at Scroop's command to see Sir William."

Laurie had stopped listening, her attention fixed on the large man riding directly behind the one with the banner. She recognized his bronzed curls instantly. An icy thrill shot up her spine when his gaze collided with hers.

For nearly a fortnight, she had exerted herself to stay on good terms with her stepmother. Thus, for once, she had dressed in a manner befitting her station. She wore a becoming pale yellow silk gown, banded vertically down the front center and around the hem with gold-embroidered black velvet braid. Believing that she could bear no possible resemblance to the young woman who had taken shelter in the tree, she returned his piercing gaze without faltering and tried to ignore an unnatural tingling in her midsection. He had not seen her in the tree, she reassured herself, and even if he had, he could not possibly recognize her now.

He continued to watch her while he dismounted and held out the reins of his mount for one of his men to take. When he began to stride toward her, she realized that by standing like a post, she was behaving in a way that would surely earn her stepmother's censure, but she could not seem to move.

Only when one of her father's men-at-arms stepped forward to intercept the tall, red-haired man did she snap herself out of whatever spell had overcome her. Gesturing to the man-at-arms to stay where he was, she curtsied without breaking eye contact and said, "We bid you welcome to Aylewood, sir."

While continuing to hold her gaze, he bowed, sweeping his helmet beneath him. Then, straightening, he said, "I am Hugh Graham of Brackengill, mistress. Are you, perchance, Sir William's daughter?"

"I have that honor, sir," Laurie said, thinking that he looked much larger up close. His shoulders were the broadest she had ever seen. "You will find my father in the hall, I believe. These men will take you to him," she added, indicating two of Sir William's men-at-arms who had moved nearer.

Sir Hugh Graham nodded, but he was frowning slightly. "Forgive my uncivil curiosity, mistress, but are you May Halliot?"

"May is my younger sister," she said, wondering how he knew May's name and wondering even more why the knowledge that she was not May should erase the frown from his ruggedly handsome face. He had the lightest eyes she had ever seen. They were light gray, like the sky, with slightly darker rings around the irises. His voice was deep and melodic. The sound of it seemed to vibrate through her.

Tucking his helmet more securely under his left arm, he offered his right one to her invitingly. "Surely it is too chilly here in the yard for you, mistress. Pray, allow me to escort you inside."

"Thank you," she said, amazed that her voice sounded steady when her heart seemed to be thumping wildly in her chest. Catching up her skirts with one hand, she placed the other lightly on his forearm and let him escort her toward the steps. One of her father's men hastened ahead of them, and Sir Hugh's men fell in behind.

Feeling unnaturally small in the midst of such a group, she wondered what her father would think of her entrance in their company, but that thought was fleeting at best.

The arm beneath her ungloved hand felt hard and muscular, the material covering it roughly textured. As they went up the stairs, it was as if she had a solid block of wood to hold, so steadily did he support her. His large presence beside her seemed overwhelmingly nerve tingling one moment, reassuring the next.

Sir William was sitting in an armchair drawn up with its back to the fireplace to face the hall entry. Several men-at-arms stood near him, and from his expectant posture, Laurie knew he was aware of his visitor's identity. His surprised look when his gaze met hers made it plain that he had not expected her to escort Sir Hugh.

"You may leave us, daughter," Sir William said.

"There is no cause to send her away, sir," Hugh Graham said calmly. "I'll not impose on your hospitality longer than I must. I come in peace to bring documents that Lord Scrope thought it best not to entrust to a common courier."

"Documents?"

"Aye, sir, English grievances. One merits your personal attention."

"But why should one in particular stand out?" Sir William asked reasonably.

"Set the coffer on yon table," Sir Hugh said to one of his men.

Laurie watched curiously as the fellow carried a small wooden chest to the high table and put it down.

"Open it," Sir Hugh said, "and give Sir William the document that sits atop the others, the one with Scrope's personal seal."

Sir William's eyebrows shot upward. "Scrope has filed a grievance of his own? I have heard naught of this. Do you know who is named within, sir?"

"Aye, I do," Sir Hugh said gravely.

Laurie felt a muscle twitch in the forearm beneath her hand, and only then did she realize that she still rested her hand there. Hastily, she took it away, folding her hands demurely at her waist and hoping that her movement would not draw her father's attention to her just then. Something in Sir Hugh's tone warned her that Sir William was not going to like the news the Englishman had brought, and she did not want to be sent away before she learned what it was.

The room was still while Sir William untied the ribbon and carefully unrolled the parchment. He read slowly, his eyes narrowing as he did.

Laurie heard his sharply indrawn breath, and as she did, she remembered that Sir Hugh Graham had known her sister's name.

"Godamercy," Sir William muttered, "May? My May? This is utter folly, sir. What can Scrope be thinking? May can have murdered no one."

Laurie gasped and felt her knees give way.

Hugh heard the gasp and reached to steady her. He had been watching her closely from the moment of his arrival, continuously from the moment she had taken her hand from his arm—and not just because it was a pleasure to do so.

He had recognized her the moment his eyes met hers.

At first, he had not believed it could be the same girl. The one he had seen in the tree had seemed scarcely more than a child, and this self-possessed, elegantly garbed young woman clearly was nearer twenty than twelve. The girl had seemed to be just a pretty ragamuffin. The young woman was extraordinary.

She wore no cap or veil. Her glossy raven curls were piled atop her head in a knot from which curling strands wisped to form a frame around her heart-shaped face. He had been right about her eyes, too. They were blue, but of so dark a blue as to look either purple or black, depending on how the light struck them.

Her gown suited her. He knew enough about feminine fashion to realize that she had a sense of style and no fear of new colors. In his opinion, too many women still wore black and the other dark colors that had been fashionable for years. His sister liked the new lighter colors, too, but the pale yellow silk with its velvety black-and-gold trim would not suit Janet. It suited Mistress Halliot especially well.

Its close-fitting bodice emphasized her curvaceous figure rather than concealing it. Her sleeves puffed out at the shoulder but fit closely to her arms, ending just above the elbow. Broad stiff frills extended from there to her wrists, and when she moved, he caught glimpses of white lace-edged linen beneath them.

The waist of her gown plunged low to a vee at the center, and although her skirt was full, he could tell from the natural way she moved that she wore no hoops or corsets. Under the gown, he was certain, Mistress Halliot wore only a fine white linen, lace-edged smock. The lace edging was visible at the front, emphasizing the swell of her soft breasts above the low-cut square neckline of her bodice. A high lace ruff encircled her slender throat, dipping from just below her ears to frame the lower part of her face and her chin. The ruff's shape drew

Hugh's gaze—because of his height and vantage point—directly to her breasts.

He realized that he was still holding Mistress Halliot's arm and that silence had returned to the hall. Sir William of Aylewood was awaiting a response from him, apparently oblivious to his daughter's reaction.

Hoping that the Scotsman had not noted the exact direction of his gaze, Hugh released Mistress Halliot, looked at her father, and said calmly, "I cannot presume to tell you what Lord Scrope was thinking, sir. I know only that his lordship filed the grievance himself. I did take the liberty of reading it, however, and it seems straightforward enough."

"It is a tissue of lies, sir!"

"Doubtless, the lass will have her own tale to tell, and she will do so at the warden's meeting," Hugh said calmly. "As Scrope's deputy, I may have to sit if he cannot, and therefore I should not enter into a discussion about it with you now. Scrope did ask me to remind you that it would be inappropriate for you to sit in judgment of your daughter, which is why I brought the grievance to you as soon as I received it. You should take your deputy with you, sir."

"Aye, I'll take him along," Halliot said curtly, "but I do not understand what Scrope thinks he is about, to have made up such a tale about my daughter. I'll take my oath that she does not so much as know this Martin Loder. She certainly cannot have killed him. The lass has not been out beyond the wall without her mother or her sisters at her side. The accusation is absurd."

"Then you and your daughter will easily establish that impossibility before the jury, sir," Hugh said, glancing at Mistress Halliot again and noting how pale her cheeks had become. He turned back to Halliot and saw that his gaze, too, had shifted to Mistress Halliot.

"Laura," Halliot said, "do you know aught of this business?"

"I do not know anyone called Martin Loder," Mistress Halliot said, frowning. "I do not believe that May knows anyone by that name, either."

"Where is she?"

Before Mistress Halliot could reply, Hugh said, "If you will forgive me, Halliot, I'll take my leave of you now. You will prefer to deal with this in private, I know. As it is, darkness will fall before we cross back into England."

Halliot stood up. "I'll send a party of my men along to see to your safety." He gestured to a man-at-arms. "Attend to it, Edwin. Sir Hugh Graham and his men have done me a kindness at some risk to themselves, so I want them to have every consideration. See that they get food and drink and then escort them safely back to the line."

As the henchman nodded and left the room, Hugh said, "I thank you for your courtesy, sir. Good day to you. Good day to you, as well, mistress."

Leaving the hall, Hugh wondered if he was being a fool. It would be as easy for Halliot's men to attack them as for any raiding party to do so. Still, he believed that he had taken the man's measure accurately and could trust him to do as he promised. Halliot was crusty and bluff, but Hugh had never heard ill of him, and instinct told him that Halliot was a man of honor, that at most he wanted to assure that Hugh and his party left Scotland. His instinct also told him, however, that Mistress Halliot knew more than she had admitted to her father.

Hugh had heard her gasp before she swayed, and when he steadied her, he felt her stiffen. Shock at hearing her sister accused of murder might explain such a reaction, of course, but Hugh had experience in judging whether people were lying or telling the truth. His life frequently depended upon that skill, and a note in her voice when she answered her father's question had warned Hugh that she was taking unnatural care in choosing her words. He believed that, to the best of Mistress Halliot's knowledge, her sister did not know Martin Loder. He was not so certain, however, that Mistress Halliot did not know Loder.

After all, Hugh told himself, Loder had an eye for a pretty woman, and if Hugh had seen her in that tree, Loder might have, too.

If Loder did see her, the only reason he might have had for neglecting to mention it was that he knew exactly who she was. He clearly knew his way around Tarras Woods. Perhaps Mistress Halliot was the reason for his acquiring such knowledge in the first place.

When Sir Hugh Graham had gone, Laurie looked warily at her father, wondering how much of her dismay he had observed.

"Where is your sister?" he said.

"I do not know, sir, but I will gladly go and find her."

"Do so at once," Sir William said. "I cannot imagine that she knows aught of this tragedy, but I must be sure before I write to tell Scrope that he is mistaken."

Laurie turned toward the spiral stairway, grateful that he had not questioned her further and that he was letting her fetch May. Somehow, she would have to prepare her, and together they would decide what to tell him.

May had seemed to recover swiftly from her ordeal. Caught up in helping the people of Liddesdale and Tarrasdale recover from the raid, she had found little time to indulge her thoughts or fears, but once the crisis had passed, Laurie had seen a change. Lately, May had seemed nervous and frightened. There was no sign of the anger she had displayed immediately after the incident. She would not talk about it, either, and generally avoided talking with Laurie.

Therefore, Laurie did not hold out much hope that May would find it possible to evade Sir William's questions. In no time, she would confess the sordid details about Sir John, even about taking her supposed dowry. Nevertheless, Laurie had promised to protect May, so she would do all that she could.

She had taken only a few steps, however, when her stepmother entered the hall from the stairway with her usual brisk grace and a swirl of dove-gray skirts.

Stopping abruptly, Blanche looked around in puzzlement before she said, "I was told that we had visitors. Pray, husband, what have you done with them?"

"They have gone," Sir William said.

"Gone? But did you not invite them to spend the night? From whence came they, and whither do they go?"

"They came from England," Sir William said, his thoughts clearly elsewhere.

"England? But why, and who were they?"

He gave her a direct look. "It was Sir Hugh Graham, madam, deputy warden to Lord Scrope, and he came to present me with a grievance against my own daughter. Are you still vexed that I did not invite him to be our guest for the night?"

Blanche looked daggers at Laurie as she said, "Pray, sir, what is *your* daughter supposed to have done now?"

"Laura is not the one Scrope named in the bill of grievance, madam."

"Then who?" Blanche looked bewildered.

"Aye, well, it would hardly be Isabel, now, would it?"

Visibly distressed, she ignored his sarcasm. "But who could be so cruel as to accuse May of anything? It must be Laura and they have mistaken her identity."

"That will do, madam," Sir William said, his tone harsher than any Laurie had heard him use before, speaking to Blanche. "This has naught to do with Laura."

Blanche bowed her head. "Forgive me, husband." Looking up again, she added, "But how, sir, could anyone accuse our May of anything that could amount to an official grievance?"

"She stands accused of murder, madam."

Blanche stared at him, then shook her head. "Someone must be making a game of you, husband. No one could possibly believe May capable of murder."

"So I think, myself," Sir William said. "Much as I dislike it, though, I must question her about this. Laura, go up now and send her down to me, if you please."

"She is not feeling well," Blanche said doubtfully. "I told her to lie down on her bed until supper."

"Nevertheless," Sir William said firmly, nodding at Laurie.

Hastily, lest Blanche again ask what she knew about it, Laurie left and went upstairs to her sisters' bedchamber. Without ceremony, she pushed open the door.

Isabel sat on a stool beside May's bed, reading aloud to her.

"Leave us, Isabel," Laurie said.

Without question, Isabel set down the book and went out.

"What is it?" May asked, sitting up. "You look as if the sky had fallen."

"Perhaps it has," Laurie said. "Someone knows about Sir John's death. It's worse than that, May," she added when May gasped and clutched a hand to her breast. "His name was not Sir John. It was Martin Loder."

"Godamercy," May exclaimed. "But how can you know that? Even if someone found his body"—hastily she crossed herself—"h-how would they know that he called himself Sir John? How can you know that it is the same man?"

"I cannot answer those questions," Laurie said. "Nor can I guess how anyone came to associate us with his death. That is," she amended, "they seem to have associated you with it. You stand accused of his murder, May. You will have to answer to the accusation at the next Truce Day. Our father has the grievance in his hands even now, and he wants to question you."

May burst into tears, and for several moments Laurie had her hands full. She tried to calm her first by stroking her shoulder and speaking quietly. When that did not work, knowing that someone—most likely, Blanche—would soon be coming upstairs to discover what had delayed May, she grabbed her by the shoulders and gave her a shake.

"May, listen to me! Hysterics will avail you naught. You must calm yourself and help me think what to do."

"I cannot! I won't go before the wardens! I won't! All those people! They will hang me for murder!"

"No one is going to hang you," Laurie said. "I've never

heard of a girl your age being hanged, and no one is going to hang the Scottish warden's daughter."

"But I cannot stand up before all those people. I'd die of shame! And what will I tell our father when he asks me what happened? What will *you* tell him?"

That was a much larger, more imminent problem, but at least May seemed calm enough now to discuss the matter.

Quietly, Laurie said, "He does not believe that you can have done such a thing. Now, he thinks Scrope made a stupid mistake. I know of no reason why he should not continue to believe that until we can think of something credible to tell him—something that will not cast both of us straight into the suds."

"You promised to protect me," May whimpered.

"I know I did, but I cannot think how"—she broke off, then added thoughtfully—"the most urgent thing is to prevent our father from questioning you in this state. We have to decide exactly what you will say, and we must decide before you confront him. We need some time to think, May. Why are you in bed?"

"Because I cannot stop thinking about him going into the river," May replied with a sob. "I've scarcely talked to anyone but you or Bridget since it happened, Laurie. If you had not been so busy, you would have seen that much for yourself."

"I have been trying to keep out of your mother's way," Laurie said. "Recall that she was waiting for me when we got home that night. I fobbed her off then, but you know that she'd like nothing better than for Father to beat me soundly. Indeed, she nearly persuaded him to do it the day of Scrope's raid."

"I know," May said with a sigh. "I wish you would find a man you could bear to marry. That would resolve everything, for all of us."

"It would not bring Sir John back to life," Laurie said dryly. "Or Martin Loder, if that's who he was. In any event, he was English, and Scrope will scream till he gets some sort of justice."

"Until he manages to hang me for it, you mean," May said. Tears welled into her eyes and spilled down her cheeks.

Pulling a handkerchief from her own sleeve and handing it to her, Laurie said, "The reason I asked why you were in bed is that I think you are about to become sicker. Do you think you could manage to be sick at your stomach and manage to play the invalid at least until morning? It will mean missing meals."

"I don't care about that," May said, slumping back against her pillows and mopping her face with the kerchief. "If you can keep Father from quizzing me, I will do whatever you say. Bridget will do anything I ask of her, but Isabel might tell Mama that I am not as sick as I say. Still, I can stick a finger down my throat. It will not be the first time I have done that."

"I know," Laurie said, smiling at her. "You do it now and again to keep from going to kirk. Your mother always believes you are really sick, too."

May nodded, and Laurie stood up. "I'll go now and tell them. Perhaps you ought to do the finger thing straightaway, though. If Isabel sees you do it, our plan will fail. The child has a tendency to speak whatever words come into her head."

"Aye, she's a prattler," May said with a meaningful look. "I've not forgiven her yet for telling you about Sir John."

Gently, Laurie said, "Do you wish that I had not followed you that night?"

May flushed. "I don't know what I'd have done if you hadn't come along," she admitted. "The plain fact is that I might well have flung myself in after him rather than come home again to face everyone."

"That is blasphemous, May. You mustn't think such things! We got through that night, and we'll get through this and what follows, as well. I promise."

May sighed, but she got up and followed Laurie out of the bedchamber. When Laurie turned toward the stairway, May went toward the necessary-stool chamber shared by the three sisters and the maidservant who tended them.

In the hall, she faced Sir William and Blanche. "I'm sorry,

sir, but May became quite unwell when I told her. She cannot possibly talk to you now."

Sir William sighed and said, "I should have told you not to tell her why I wished to speak with her. I've no doubt that you did, did you not?"

"I did, sir, and I realize that I should not have done so. She already was feeling ill, and she flew into a panic. When I left, she had retired rather hastily to the necessary stool. I sent Bridget to her, but I'm afraid May has made herself sick."

"I'll go up to her at once," Blanche said. "I am very vexed with you for upsetting her, Laurie, and with you, sir, for allowing such an upset. Instead of accusing poor May, you should be writing an angry letter of protest to Lord Scrope. The very idea of that dreadful Englishman accusing my darling of such a dreadful act! He should be ashamed of himself!" She turned with what in any less haughty dame would be described as a flounce and went out of the hall.

Laurie was left to face her father. "I'm sorry, sir. I should have known it would upset her. She has not been feeling well for days now."

"It is probably no more than her time of the month," he said. "I will talk with her tomorrow when she is feeling better, but I do not want you discussing this with her further before then. Do you understand me?"

"Aye, sir, I do."

She understood him very well, but she intended to talk with May just as soon as she could be sure they would enjoy an hour's privacy.

Since Bridget slept in an alcove adjoining Isabel and May's room and Isabel was a very light sleeper, Laurie did not seek May out until early the next morning.

Then, knowing that Bridget would be up and about, helping the other maidservants, and intending to bring May to her own bedchamber to talk, Laurie crept silently in and went to May's bed.

It was empty.

May was not in her room, or anywhere else in the castle.

Recalling her sister's claim that, left to herself, she would have flung herself into the Liddel after Martin Loder, and terrified that May intended to kill herself rather than face a wardens' meeting, Laurie went at once to Sir William.

"May's gone, sir," she told him, "and something she said yesterday when she was so distraught gives me to fear that she might do herself an injury. She was terrified of having to answer to such a charge."

Rather distraught himself, Sir William sent for Blanche and told her the terrible news.

She paled but answered with her customary calm, "I am certain that she must be somewhere about, husband. She would not go outside the wall alone."

When they discovered that Bridget was missing, too, Blanche grew calmer still. "Depend upon it," she said, "they will both return soon."

Mistrusting her confidence, Sir William sent men out at once to search the dales, but they found no sign of Bridget or of May. One of the men said that Bridget's sister had come for her again, but when Laurie asked Bangtail Willie, he said he had seen no such person and that Nebless Sam had sworn no one had passed through the postern gate.

Blanche retired to her chamber and would speak to no one for days. When she emerged at last, she seemed as calm as usual, but she refused to discuss May.

The wardens' meeting loomed before them, only days away, and still there was no sign of May.

Twelve

Yett was our meeting meek enough,
Begun wi' merriement and mowes . . .

Truce Day, Lochmaben

From a grassy hillside above the site set for the wardens'
meeting, just as dawn was breaking, Hugh Graham surveyed
the landscape below with narrowing, speculative eyes. He and
fifty of his men awaited Thomas Scrope's arrival, but Hugh
was in no hurry. The activities would not begin without them,
and there was no sign yet of Sir William Halliot of Aylewood
with the Scottish party.

Horses shifted, pawed, and occasionally whinnied. Men
chatted quietly. At Hugh's right, his captain, Ned Rowan, sat
alertly on his black gelding, his restless gaze scanning the
countryside and the surrounding hills.

On Rowan's right, Meggie's Andrew sat proudly on his gray
pony. The lad's behavior having been unexceptionable since
his run-in with the captain, Rowan had suggested and Hugh
had agreed that he should accompany them to Lochmaben. At
least a few other children would attend the proceedings, and
Hugh thought it would be a good experience for the lad.

Borderers enjoyed few opportunities for recreation, and
Hugh knew from experience that folks from both sides of the
line had been looking forward to the occasion with lively anticipation. At least, those who had a comparatively clear con-

science and did not expect to find themselves too actively engaged in the proceedings looked forward to it. He realized cynically that despite evidence to the contrary—not least of which included the events succeeding the last meeting—most people believed that the truce guaranteed them safe passage until the next day's sunrise. They wondered only what today would present for their entertainment.

The appointed meeting place was a Scottish field about a mile east of the point where the Water of Sark flows into the Solway. Some three hundred yards from the water's edge stood a tall stone that was once—or so men said—part of a prehistoric circle. Nowadays, they called it simply the Lochmaben stone.

Already spectators from far and wide were converging upon the field, giving it the appearance of a holiday fair. A distant murmur of their voices drifted up to Hugh, punctuated occasionally by barks of laughter, as they picked their way over the moors and fells and along riverside tracks.

Some walked; others rode shaggy ponies.

Peddlers, tinkers, and other itinerant merchants already were setting up their stalls for business. Hugh knew that many of the men below would make wagers on the miscreants' chances, and particularly on the fate of the unfortunate young woman the Scots were bound to present for trial. Doubtless word of the complaint against her had traveled on the wind by now to every cot and tower in the Borders.

The field soon teemed with groups of men, a few of their women, and here and there, a child or two, all gossiping and perhaps bargaining over horses or sleuth hounds. Everyone wore his or her Sunday best, although Hugh was certain that every man carried arms.

Once or twice in the past, someone—usually an English warden—had suggested banning weapons on such occasions. But never had the suggestion gone beyond the wish. Few Borderers on either side felt fully dressed without their weapons, since danger was part of their everyday lives.

A stiff, sea-scented wind was blowing toward them from

Solway Firth, fluttering banners and causing more than one person to grab for cap or skirt. But winds usually blew through the Borders, even in summer, so although it meant the peddlers had to stake their tents firmly, no one else paid it much heed.

"Master, they come," Ned Rowan muttered beside him.

Andrew nudged his brown pony closer, leaning near to hear Rowan and to see what he had seen.

Hugh saw at once that the Scots had arrived. Against the northeastern horizon, their cavalcade lined a hillside. Sunlight glittered on arms and armor.

"Them be the bluidy Scots," Andrew said sagely. "Be they thinking they'll attack us, then?" He sounded as though he relished the possibility.

Hugh turned to him with a quelling frown. "You are here today so that you can observe what takes place on a Truce Day, my lad, not to stir trouble."

"I've seen Truce Days afore," Andrew said, his tone irritated but civil.

"Not with my permission, you haven't. If you want to continue to serve me when you grow up, then you must learn to follow orders and to pay attention now." With a straight look, he added, "I thought you had learned your lesson, lad."

"Aye, I have, and all," Andrew said in a smaller voice, shooting an oblique, resentful look at Ned Rowan.

Satisfied, Hugh turned his attention back to the Scots. He knew that Rowan had skelped the lad, but he knew, too, that the big man cared more about Andrew than other men might. Rowan was nearly as hard a man as Hugh was, but Hugh knew that Andrew would learn from him, and he hoped that those lessons would permit the lad to live long enough to enjoy at least a few adult years in the always treacherous Borders.

"*Will* they attack us?" Andrew asked curiously.

"That has been known to happen," Hugh admitted, "but they have little cause at present to stir trouble, and I do not believe that Halliot is an aggressive man. He certainly is not as belligerent as Buccleuch."

"What's 'belligerent' mean?"

"Likely to make war," Hugh said, still watching the Scots.

"Aye, well, I ken the Buccleuch," Andrew said wisely. "He and all his bluidy reivers need hanging, me da said, but Mistress Janet—"

"Likely your father was right," Hugh said, cutting in because he did not want to hear what his sister thought about Buccleuch. Another thought followed that one, and he wondered if Buccleuch would attend the proceedings. Dismissing the thought as it formed, he realized the Border leader was unlikely to attend just to watch others wield power. Hugh hoped he was right. A meeting between Buccleuch and Scrope just now, the truce notwithstanding, was likely to stir coals.

Curiously, Andrew said, "Who's Halliot, then, and what's he like?"

"He is acting warden of the Scottish middle march," Hugh said. "King James of Scotland appointed him to take Buccleuch's place in that role. I'll wager he'd have liked to make him Keeper of Liddesdale, too, but he dared not."

"The man would ha' been a fool to accept," Ned Rowan said grimly. "Few men ha' the strength or power to rule Liddesdale." A brief silence fell before he added, "They be waiting for us, master."

"Let them wait," Hugh retorted. "We don't move until Scrope arrives."

"What the devil are they waiting for?" Sir William Halliot growled testily.

" 'Tis likely they wait for Scrope," the tall, broad-shouldered rider on Sir William's left said. "Buccleuch says that Scrope enjoys making folks wait. You must have learned as much, just trying to get Scrope to agree to a date and a site for this meeting. He prefers delay over action, Buccleuch says."

"Aye, 'tis true," Sir William agreed.

Laurie, sitting quietly nearby on her horse, had been watching the two as curiously as she had watched the scene in the open field at the foot of the hill. Her father's companion was

Sir Quinton Scott of Broadhaugh, the very man the English had arrested during the previous truce and husband, besides, of Janet the Bold.

Sir Quinton had served as Buccleuch's deputy warden and now served Sir William in the same capacity.

When Blanche had refused to attend the proceedings, Laurie had been able to persuade her father to let her accompany him only because he had expected Janet to accompany her husband and thought Janet would enjoy her company. Not until the two parties joined did they learn that Lady Scott had been taken by sickness of late, and her husband had decreed that she should stay at home.

By then it was too late to send Laurie back to Aylewood without sending a considerable escort with her. Since Sir William wanted to make as grand an impression of power on the field as he could, he kept her with him.

Laurie observed that her father seemed nervous and decided that he had cause for concern. With two cavalcades of armed men facing each other across a field alive with interested spectators, the scene resembled battle lines drawn up on either side of a holiday fair.

Gaily colored tents dotted the field, and people wandered about, seeming to pay no heed to the heavily armed riders converging on them from two directions.

Laurie felt increasing excitement tempered only by her deep concern for her sister. No one had laid eyes on May since her disappearance, nor had they heard a word from her. She had vanished like a puff of smoke before the wind, and Bridget had vanished with her.

Sir William had questioned every man and woman at Aylewood, and every single one had insisted that he or she knew nothing about May's disappearance.

Knowing that May had escaped the castle's confines once before, Laurie nonetheless found it hard to believe that she had done so again, even with Bridget's assistance. She had spoken to Bangtail Willie again, but the only new thing she learned from him was that Nebless Sam, who had guarded the postern through the night, had gone off to visit kinsmen in Liddesdale and had not yet returned.

Recalling that Willie had also once told her that Nebless Sam had an avid interest in Bridget, Laurie wondered if Sam might have helped them. Willie said that the man had sworn to him that no one had passed through the postern gate all night, but she knew that May and Bridget had not flown from the ramparts.

Turning away from her father and Sir Quinton, Laurie observed movement on the far hillside. "There are more of them there now," she said.

Sir William nodded. "That will be Scrope," he said.

"Aye," Sir Quinton said. " 'Tis his banner flying beside Hugh Graham's."

"We will go to meet them, then," Sir William said.

Sir Quinton cleared his throat, then said quietly, "I'll not be telling you how to manage your business, sir, but 'tis ever Buccleuch's way to await the exchange of assurances. 'Tis safer so, he says."

"Aye, perhaps."

"One avoids fatal misunderstandings, Buccleuch says, by following strict procedure. If you will recall, an unfortunate riot occurred at Redeswire some years ago, and many died, due to confusion over the assurances."

"I'll be happy if this lot simply observes the truce," Sir William said bleakly. "I had hoped that I might be dealing with Hugh Graham. I've met the man, and you said he served honorably and well when you dealt with him."

"Aye, he did." Sir Quinton's eyebrows arched. "I wish I might say the others had been as fair-minded. I might just add, though, that Hugh Graham is not always to be trusted either, sir. You'd do well to guard your back whilst we're here."

"I will." Sir William looked narrowly at him. "Do not forget that you must serve in my place when they present the bill of complaint against my daughter."

Sir Quinton nodded, and Laurie looked away again, unable to face her father's wretched unhappiness over May's disappearance. He clearly believed that she had run away or killed herself rather than face her accusers and trust him to see her safe from them. His disappointment in her was nearly palpable.

He had not questioned Laurie at any length about her sister's disappearance, and for that she was deeply grateful.

Even Blanche had not questioned her beyond asking rather vaguely if she had any idea what had become of May. Laurie had feared that Blanche would recall the night that she had found her missing from her bedchamber, but by the time Sir Hugh Graham presented Scrope's grievance to Sir William, Blanche apparently had forgotten the incident.

For all that she tried to insist that someone had sneaked into the castle and stolen her elder daughter away in the night, it was clear enough to everyone that Blanche, like her husband, believed that May had run away. Laurie believed she was the only one who suspected that Blanche herself might have had a hand in May's departure.

The sight of four riders and one of the banners separating from the cavalcade across the way and galloping toward them diverted her from her thoughts just then. She watched their rapid approach with increasing tension.

Sir William and Sir Quinton remained where they were, flanked now by the captain of the guard at Aylewood and a huge man of Sir Quinton's who was known—absurdly, Laurie thought, considering his size—as Hob the Mouse.

She noticed that, below, the people in the field had seen the riders and were watching them. Although the brightly colored banners continued to wave in the breeze, she could see her tension reflected in the stiff way people stood, and she felt it emanating from the men who made up the rest of the Scottish party.

The hoofbeats of the riders' horses sounded clearly now. One rider led the others, and Laurie's interest heightened when she recognized him. Sir Hugh Graham rode very well, as if he were part of his horse.

When the riders drew near, Sir Hugh raised a hand, signaling the others to stop. They slowed their ponies to a walk, then drew rein.

Sir Hugh rode forward a few paces, saying clearly, "Greetings, Halliot. We come in the name of Thomas Lord Scrope to seek assurance that you and your people have come to this place for the sole purpose of seeking justice and agree to keep the peace until sunrise tomorrow. Do we have your promise, sir?"

"Aye, you have it," Sir William said.

Laurie, watching them, knew that it was vital that both sides agree to the truce, because that would enable everyone to reach home in safety before it expired. Suddenly encountering a direct look from Sir Hugh, she felt heat rush to her cheeks and to the core of her body. She could not tell what he was thinking.

He looked grim, and his eyes were as gray as hard steel, but he had looked that way while demanding the assurance. Perhaps he did not approve of women attending Truce Days. Many men did not approve, particularly since they knew that violence could break out at any moment.

She wanted to look away but found it impossible to do so. He broke the contact at last, turning his pony hard and riding away at a gallop, not seeming to care whether his men followed or not.

"Wait till they have passed the halfway point, then follow them, Quin," Sir William said. "You should go with our lads, since Scrope sent his deputy to me."

"Aye," Sir Quinton said. "He'll not embrace you afterward, though, sir. Do not expect it."

"I won't."

Sir Quinton grinned boyishly, and Laurie felt her tension ease. "When I acted for Buccleuch, Graham insisted on meeting in the middle of Kershopefoot Burn," he said. "Said he didn't want to look as if he'd entered Scotland as a supplicant. Scrope can't do that here, though. He will be content to meet where you will."

Sir William nodded. He was still watching the riders. "Go now, Quin."

Hob the Mouse, the captain from Aylewood, and one other man rode with him, and they repeated the ritual across the way.

Within moments of their meeting with Scrope, the other warden held up his hand and Sir William did likewise, signaling for the benefit of everyone watching their mutual agreement to the terms of the truce. Then, shouting at his men to keep the peace or answer to him and King James, Sir William gave the sign to ride forward. The entire Scottish party rode en masse to meet the English.

Hugh wondered what had possessed Sir William to allow Mistress Halliot to attend the day's proceedings. Was the man mad? Apparently Quinton Scott had forbidden Janet to attend, so Sir William could have no good reason. And where had he concealed his younger daughter, the one who was to answer to a charge of murder? Surely he had not consigned her to wait with the men he had brought to answer complaints laid against them.

Ruthlessly, Hugh forced himself to focus on the day's business. He still knew little about Sir William Halliot of Aylewood, but he did not trust the Scots on general principle. He knew that Scrope wanted no trouble, and he knew, too, that if any started, it had better begin with the Scots.

If it began with the English, Scrope was likely to blame the Grahams for it whether they were guilty or not. Hugh knew he could speak for his men, but he could not speak for all Grahams. No one spoke for all Grahams.

Scrope and Halliot greeted each other with nods, trumpets sounded the beginning of the meeting, and the two sides quickly mingled. The wardens' table was ready, and the clerk—a man from Canonbie agreed to by both sides—awaited them there. He took charge of the grievances, quickly sorting them with the most recent ones on top as the wardens and their deputies took places at the table and prepared to begin the business of the day.

Hugh noted that Mistress Halliot remained nearby, apparently guarded by the huge man who generally rode beside Quinton Scott. Hugh remembered the man's name only because it was the most inappropriate to-name he had ever heard. Doubtless somewhere in the past there had been reason to call him Hob the Mouse, but no mouse stood six feet four inches tall in its bare feet or wielded a Jedburgh ax as easily as if it were a jackstraw.

While the clerk rearranged inkwell and quills, and the two wardens settled in their chairs, Hugh found his gaze returning to Mistress Halliot. She was dressed as richly as her father was, and her father's attire was as rich as Scrope's.

Hugh remembered from his own experience as acting warden that it had seemed important that he not allow the other side to outshine him. Doubtless Halliot and Scrope felt the same way.

He watched Mistress Halliot, thinking again how beautiful she was. Her dark curls gleamed in the sunlight. With her dark eyes, pink cheeks, and red lips, she seemed to have more color than the other women. Most were older than she was, of course, but Hugh did not think it would matter if every one of them were young and beautiful. Mistress Halliot would still stand out.

She looked excited by the activity but worried, as well. No doubt, she was concerned for her sister's fate—as she ought to be if the lass had killed a man. Not that murder was always a hanging offense, for it wasn't, but the murder of Scrope's chief land sergeant would be, even if the accused murderer was a young woman.

Having known Loder, Hugh wondered if May Halliot had merely defended herself. Scrope had written the complaint, and although Hugh had read it, it said little about the circumstances surrounding Loder's death. Clearly, Scrope was keeping the details to himself until the time came to reveal them.

It would not be long, either, Hugh realized. The wardens would hear the most recent grievances first.

They selected their juries quickly, and it amused Hugh to watch the two of them pretend to consider their choices. Scrope had been quite willing to accept the list of Scots that Hugh had drawn up, and he was certain that Halliot had made his choices long before leaving home.

The English warden chose the six Scottish jurors, and the Scottish warden chose the six English. Any defendant who requested a jury trial would be tried before the jury of his countrymen, albeit one carefully chosen by his enemies.

The oaths given and taken, the clerk called the first case, a grievance against an Englishman, Steven Musgrave, and five of his cohorts.

The charge alleged that they had come over into Scotland and stolen fifty cattle and horses, and that on being pursued they had captured four of their pursuers and subsequently ransomed them for a total of twenty-five pounds. They had also ransomed their captives' horses—except for those that they had kept.

The case was over quickly, because Musgrave pleaded guilty, hoping for leniency. The two wardens, after a brief conference, agreed on the fine he and his friends would pay, and he agreed to return the livestock and the ransom money.

Hugh thought that Buccleuch would not have agreed to so tame a penalty, but his duties as deputy warden did not include giving advice to the Scottish warden or arguing with Scrope. Knowing Steven Musgrave, he knew there would be another grievance against him soon, probably for the same offense, even the same livestock. Justice would catch up with him.

Not long after that, the clerk called out, "Mistress May Halliot, step forth and answer to the grievances laid against you. The charge is seduction of an officer of the English Crown, and the willful murder of that same officer, one Martin Loder, chief land sergeant to Thomas Lord Scrope."

The steady murmur of conversation that had accompanied the proceedings to that point died away to silence. It lasted only seconds before a pony snorted and shook its head, rattling its bridle. Hugh saw that Halliot was looking down at the table. Deep color tinged the man's cheeks.

Scrope said testily, "I believe the accused is your daughter, sir. You were charged with guaranteeing her presence before this court."

"Aye, my lord, and well do I know it," Halliot said. He looked Scrope straight in the eye. "I regret to inform you that my daughter disappeared the very night the bill of complaint arrived. We have not seen her since."

"An unlikely tale," Scrope snarled. "I took you for a man of honor, and yet now we see the truth. You are as much a villain as any other damned Scotsman."

Angry muttering from members of the crowd reminded Hugh that the situation could take a violent turn at any moment. He said evenly, "With respect, my lord, we have no cause to doubt his word. Sir William Halliot's reputation is that of a man of honor. Moreover, my lord, you and every man here must know that women often act without consulting their menfolk."

"Aye, that's a fact," Scrope agreed, nodding.

It being well known that Lady Scrope was as great a game-ster as her husband and was as often as not the cause of his frequent financial woes, men amongst the audience quickly covered impulsive smiles, stifled laughter, and nodded with him.

Scrope's frown told Hugh that he had seen the smiles. He glanced at Mistress Halliot, trying to read her expression, as Scrope said sharply, "It matters not that the wench is absent. It only proves that she stands guilty of the charge."

"One moment," Sir Quinion Scott said, his deep voice car-rying easily over the murmuring crowd. "No one can wonder if a gently reared maiden fears to stand before such a tribunal as this. We can only hope that she is safe. We have not yet heard any evidence against Mistress May Halliot, and the bill of complaint clearly states that the other side intends to present such evidence. I suggest that we hear it before anyone makes rash declarations about punishment."

"Aye, let's hear the evidence—if ye've got any," shouted a skeptic from the audience. Others immediately echoed his cry.

Scrope nodded, and a man stepped forward.

He waited until the shouting died away, then said clearly, "I seen it."

"One moment," Scrope said. "You must tell your story to the Scottish jurors. I doubt there can be any other form of trial in such a case."

He glowered at Halliot, but it was a moment before Halliot became aware of it. Hob the Mouse, standing just behind the Scottish warden and his deputy, had briefly claimed his attention.

"What is it?" Halliot said, turning back when he realized that Scrope had spoken to him.

Scrope said with a sneer, "I trust that you will not expect us to accept your avowal or Sir Quinton's for your daughter's innocence."

"I do not know what your trust has to do with it," Halliot growled, showing hackle at last. "My word ought to be as good as yours or that so-called witness of yours. I am told that he is just another of your own men."

"Aye, and what of it? Who else was likely to see what happened in the dead of night but the man riding with Loder? Do you think he'd be serving anyone else?"

Hugh was watching Laura Halliot, and when he saw her frown, he was not surprised. She had seemed to be a woman of intelligence as well as beauty.

Halliot said, "Does this fellow of yours mean to testify that my daughter overpowered two grown men-at-arms and murdered one of them without the other doing aught to prevent it. Because, if he does, we certainly will declare the complaint invalid."

"That is not what I asked you," Scrope said, raising his voice to make himself heard above a growing rumble of mutters. "I asked you, sir, if you—or you, Sir Quinton, if you act in his behalf—can declare out of your own personal knowledge and on your honor, whether the complaint against May Halliot, a subject of your march, is valid or not. Will you then take responsibility for the offense yourself if we can prove that you are mistaken?"

Silence fell again, and Hugh felt a certain compassion for the Scottish warden and his deputy. He found it hard to believe, himself, that a lass could have murdered Martin Loder.

Sir Quinton said quietly, "We should hear the evidence against her first."

"You either have such knowledge or you do not," Scrope retorted.

"I feel certain that Mistress May Halliot is physically incapable . . ."

Halliot put a hand on his arm, silencing him. Then he said, "Her ability is not at question here, I'm afraid. Neither of us can speak honestly about what she was doing in the middle of the night when Loder died, my lord. You must hear the evidence, Quinton, and so must the jury unless some other man will step forward to speak for her. If May were here, she could speak for herself and we could judge her truthfulness, but since she is not . . ." He, too, fell silent, looking wretched.

Hugh saw that Mistress Halliot had tears trickling down her cheeks.

Scrope grunted with satisfaction and gestured to his witness. "Tell us who you are and what you saw, man."

"One moment," Sir Quinton said. To the clerk, he said, "Swear him."

The clerk administered the oath, whereupon the witness straightened and jutted his chin out, clearly feeling his importance. In a loud voice, he declared, "I be Cornus Grant, aid t' Martin Loder, who be chief land sergeant t' Lord Scrope. I saw the whole thing. That night, Loder were meeting wi' the lass for . . . for purposes o' mutual entertainment, as ye might say, the which she had suggested and agreed to."

Looking around, he leered at the now fascinated audience.

Sharply recalling his attention, Scrope snapped, "Where did they meet?"

"Near Liddel Water below Kershopefoot, your lordship."

Hugh saw that Mistress Halliot was watching Cornus Grant. Her eyes narrowed, and her forehead creased in a deep frown. Hugh felt sorry for her. Doubtless, she loved her sister, but if the lass had gone that far to meet a lover, she was not the innocent maid that Halliot would have them all believe her to be.

"What happened there?" Scrope demanded harshly.

"I were watching from below when Loder bent to kiss the lass. She pushed him into the water, and the current swept him away. When I caught up wi' the poor lad, he were dead, and it bein' summer and all, we had t' bury him soon as we got him home. That wicked lass killed him, my lord, as sure as if she'd shot him."

This time the muttering had a different sound. It was easier for them all to believe that the lass had just pushed Loder. Even a big man could be pushed.

Sir Quinton Scott said hastily, "That is a serious charge. Is there anyone here who will speak for May Halliot?"

No one stirred, although many continued to mutter comments.

"Is there no man amongst you willing to speak for May Halliot?" Sir Quinton repeated in a louder voice.

"I will speak for her."

Laura Halliot stepped forward, silencing everyone.

Thirteen

I myself will be the formost man
That shall come, lady, to feitch you home.

Laurie had not paused to think before speaking, and now, as she scanned the huge crowd, she could hardly breathe. Her face felt numb, and her knees threatened to collapse under her. She looked at her father but saw no offer of help there.

Sir William stared back at her, mouth open, clearly even more appalled by her declaration than everyone else was.

Scrope found his tongue first. "Women have no place before a jury. Stand back now, lass, and keep a still tongue in your head."

Sir Quinton said evenly, "In Scotland, women do have a voice, my lord. Although you or others from your side picked our jury, its members are Scottish, and I believe they will agree to hear her." He looked at the six men.

Each nodded solemnly in response.

Laurie noted that despite their nods, not one member of the jury looked at her or seemed particularly eager to hear what she would say.

Taking a deep breath to steady her nerves, she looked back at Sir Quinton. He, at least, seemed willing to support her right to speak.

He nodded encouragingly.

Feeling more terrified than she had ever felt facing Blanche, she exhaled, faced the Scottish jury, and said clearly, "I am

Laura Halliot of Aylewood. May Halliot is my sister. She did not murder anyone." Realizing that her hands were shaking, she clasped them firmly at her waist.

Over a new wave of commentary from the crowd, Scrope stood and pointed at her, shouting, "If she is the accused's sister, we should believe nothing she says! She is bound to declare her innocent. Women have no comprehension of honor."

Laurie stiffened, but as she opened her mouth to speak, he turned to her and added, "You know naught about such things, lass. Your sister condemns herself by her failure to appear before us to answer to the complaint. Now, stand back."

Stubbornly, Laurie said, "May is not here because such an unjust charge terrified her into running away, my lord, not because she committed murder."

Before Scrope could answer, Sir Quinton said, "Do you understand the taking of an oath, Mistress Halliot?"

"Certainly, I do, sir."

"Swear her as a witness," he said to the clerk.

The clerk stood. "Mistress Halliot, d'ye swear by heaven above ye, hell beneath ye, by your part of Paradise, by all that God made in six days and seven nights, and by God Himself, to tell the truth in this matter, so help ye God?"

"I swear," Laurie said. "My sister is not a murderess."

Sir Quinton said, "Understand me, mistress. You must declare this of your own knowledge and on your honor. You cannot simply claim to know your sister's character and therefore to believe that she could never have done such a thing."

"I do declare it of my own knowledge," Laurie said.

She gave him look for look and hoped he and the others staring at her could not tell that her knees quaked or that her stomach had knotted itself round her liver.

Scrope sneered again and declared loudly as he sat down, "Clearly, she does not understand the terms of her avowal. How can you declare anything of your own knowledge, mistress? To do so, you had to be there when the crime occurred."

"I was there," Laurie admitted, but she did not direct her words to Scrope.

Instead, her eyes shifted to meet the startled gaze of his deputy, Sir Hugh Graham. It was to him that she said, "It is true that a man fell into the river, but he called himself Sir John something. He was attempting to drown my sister when he fell, and he was certainly still alive then. It seems odd that your eyewitness did not mention that, since he claims to have seen all that happened," she added with a challenging look. "It is also odd that he did not mention my presence."

A cacophony of gasps and outcries greeted her words, but Scrope leapt to his feet again, quelling the worst of the noise with an angry gesture.

"I believe Cornus Grant," he bellowed. "Were the lass here a reliable witness and May Halliot *not* a murderess, I say she would *be* here!" Turning to Laurie, he went on, "The reason Cornus Grant did not mention your presence, mistress, is because you were not there, and I tell you to your face that if I had a daughter capable of lying like this to a wardens' court, I would beat better sense into her. The next thing we know, you will be claiming to have murdered Loder yourself!"

Outraged at being called a liar before such a gathering, Laurie snapped back angrily and without thinking, "And what if I did make such a claim, sir? That still would not alter the fact that your witness lies through his teeth. What if I did kill that man—whatever his name is? What if my sister was not even present? Could your witness declare otherwise? For that matter, how is he so certain that the woman he claims to have seen was my sister? Let him tell us what she looks like. What color is her hair?"

The witness looked dismayed, and pandemonium erupted.

When several men lunged toward Laurie, it was all she could do to stand still without cowering. In a twinkling, men with drawn swords surrounded her, but to her relief, they faced the multitude with their broad backs toward her.

To her astonishment, at least two were English and another a defenseless child. Sir Hugh Graham and the big man who had been at his side from the outset had moved as quickly as Quinton Scott and Hob the Mouse, and the Englishmen's swords, like the Scots', were drawn and pointed threateningly outward.

Between the two Englishmen stood a lad of perhaps ten summers. He carried no weapon, but his hands were fisted on his skinny hips, and he leaned forward belligerently, as if he dared any man to attack her.

Laurie began to breathe a little easier.

"Stand back," Sir Hugh shouted. "We'll have no violence here. We've heard Cornus Grant; now we'll hear the lass. The jury will decide who speaks the truth."

Sir Quinton waved the Scots back, and Laurie saw several of his men move among them, calming tempers.

The English were slower to respond, doubtless because Scrope's fury was plain to see. He stood with his hand on his sword hilt, color suffusing his face, as he glared at his deputy.

"This is an outrage," he snapped when he could make himself heard. "I'll tell you how Cornus Grant knows that he saw May Halliot. He knows it because Martin Loder told him what lass he was meeting and why. Grant saw them meet, saw them ride into the woods together, and he saw that lass kill Loder. It matters not whether he can describe her to her family's satisfaction. He can describe her horse. Tell them," he ordered.

" 'Twere a white palfrey," Cornus Grant replied instantly.

Caught off guard, Sir William's reaction to the words was plain for all to see.

"There now," Scrope announced triumphantly, "we have the truth of it. And I'll tell you what else we have. We have a second murderess, because if Mistress Halliot *was* there, she is as guilty as her sister. We should hang them both!"

Hugh had not moved. He gestured again to his men and saw with satisfaction that this time they obeyed him. He sheathed his sword and, ignoring Scrope, looked over his shoulder to see how Mistress Halliot fared.

She had lost the roses in her cheeks. Her face was stark white, but her dark eyes blazed anger and she had pressed her lips together tightly, as if she were doing all she could to keep from speaking her mind again.

Hugh's thoughts flitted to Janet, and he was glad that she was not present. In Laura's place, he doubted Janet would have had the sense to keep silent.

In a low voice that would not carry beyond her ears, he said, "Don't speak again, mistress. That was a near thing, and we do not want a battle to erupt here." Raising his voice a bit, he said to Sir Quinton, "If you are wise, you won't ask her to say any more. The jury has heard enough to make a decision. They have no more than Grant's word against hers, and surely your Scots will believe the lass."

Quinton grimaced. "Generally, that might be true," he said, "but you chose the jury, remember? I know them all, and more than one is unfriendly to Halliot and thus to his family."

The two men looked long at each other, and Hugh knew that Quinton Scott was right. He had selected the jury, knowing that at least two Elliots numbered among the Scottish defendants, men he suspected of being members of Rabbie's Bairns. He had therefore chosen jurors known to have feuds with the Elliots, hoping they would not automatically side with them or with Sir Quinton Scott if he should sit as acting warden, as he had in the past.

"I'll speak to Scrope," Hugh said, "but I cannot promise it will do any good."

"I'd be grateful, nonetheless," Quinton said.

They exchanged another long look, and Hugh found himself wondering what the other man was thinking. They had a certain respect for each other, and now that Quinton was Janet's husband, the man had become family, whether either of them liked it or not. Still, there was little love lost between them.

Hugh watched as Sir Quinton took Mistress Halliot aside and began to speak quietly to her. All around them, groups of men chatted energetically, each man making no secret of his personal viewpoint. Instead of a murmur of conversation, the noise had grown to an uproar. Hugh saw Scrope talking with several of his men and strode over to join them.

"A word with you, my lord, if you please," he said firmly. A sweeping, authoritative look told the others to take themselves elsewhere.

A moment later, despite the crowd, he was as good as alone with Scrope.

"What the devil do you want?" Scrope demanded. "I saw how you leapt to defend the wench. You are supposed to be my deputy, I'll remind you."

"Aye, and so I am," Hugh said evenly. "Your anger was like a spark to tinder, my lord, and the Scots are ever quick to flare up. You saw how our men swarmed forward. Their action threatened her, and the Scots were quick to defend her. Had I not moved to her side as well, we'd likely be in the midst of pitched battle now. I thought it was your fondest wish—as it is her majesty's—to avoid any hint of violence or foul play by our side this time. After last time—"

"Enough," Scrope snapped, cutting him off with an impatient gesture. "What would you have me do? Nay, do not answer that. I have seen how easily you bow to the damned Scots now that your sister has married one of them."

"If you will recall the details of that arrangement," Hugh said, controlling his temper, "you will recall that you and Buccleuch arranged that marriage without my leave and that you ordered me to consent to it."

"Aye, well, there was naught I could do about it once her majesty and James of Scotland decided to stick their royal noses into the business. We both know that the marriage was naught but a move in the game of politics, one they hoped would help lead to peace in the Borders. They expected us to support it, and since Buccleuch desired the match, they hoped he would be grateful. Instead, he attacked my stronghold and came damned near to murdering me and all my men."

Knowing that it would be futile to point out that Buccleuch, at least, had had good reason for his actions, Hugh said, "That

Scottish jury is unlikely to order the hanging of one young woman, my lord, let alone two."

"Well, they are not going to turn them both loose, either," Scrope said. "I don't care what they do, as long as those wicked wenches pay for killing Loder. I mean to see to that, my lad, I promise you."

With a sigh, Hugh turned his attention to helping restore a semblance of calm to the proceedings.

When the wardens and their deputies had taken their seats again, and the crowd had quieted, the clerk said formally to Scrope, "What will you, my lord?"

Without waiting for his answer, Hugh said, "His lordship is loath to accept the word of any single person in such an important matter. Is there not someone else who will step forward to speak for May Halliot?"

Silence fell again. Men and women in the crowd looked to their neighbors. No one stepped forward.

When one of the Scottish jurors made a gesture to draw attention to himself, Hugh feared briefly that the man would offer to speak for May Halliot. Since jurors were not supposed to support any defendant, that would create another crisis. Then he recognized the man as one he had hoped would side against the Elliots.

"Begging pardon for the presumption, m'lord," the man said to Scrope. "We believe the lassie be tellin' a wee fable, and nobbut standing up for her sister. Still and all, do we no ha' an established procedure to deal wi' a case like this? If May Halliot ha' taken leg bail, as it seems she has, can we no demand that some'un pledge hisself t' stand hostage in her stead till we can lay her by the heels?"

Halliot said on a note of profound relief, "Aye, sure, you can do that! I am persuaded that my daughter will not stay long away from her home and family. When she returns, I'll see to it that she makes everything clear to us at once."

" 'Tis a fine notion, that one," Scrope said sarcastically, "but who will offer to stand pledge for the lass when none would speak for her?"

Hugh scanned the crowd, looking for movement that would indicate someone's willingness to offer himself as pledge for May Halliot.

No one stirred.

The silence lengthened until Mistress Halliot said clearly, "I will stand for my sister until she can speak for herself or until some other event occurs to make her innocence plain."

When her words provoked a burst of laughter, color leapt to her cheeks, and her eyes sparkled angrily.

Hugh raised a hand and saw that Sir Quinton was doing the same. A semblance of quiet was soon restored.

"Your offer reveals a kind spirit, mistress," Quinton said gently.

"It's daft," Scrope snarled. "No one would accept a female hostage. Let Sir William Halliot stand hostage for both of his daughters."

Hugh's irritation with the man flared to anger. He said impulsively, "I'd accept a female hostage, my lord. Brackengill is well equipped to house one."

Every eye turned toward him.

Hearing the echo of his words, Hugh wondered what madness had possessed him. He met Scrope's angry gaze, however, and managing to instill a note of amusement into his voice, added, "I believe she would prove a less taxing guest than some prisoners I have housed."

Chuckles from some of his men died away when Halliot said curtly, "I will not hear of such a thing. Do you make a game of my daughter, sir?"

"That was not my intent, sir, I assure you," Hugh said.

Ignoring the reply, Halliot continued angrily, "Even if anyone here were mad enough to agree to such a thing, surely you must admit that for any unmarried man to hold a maiden hostage would be most unseemly."

Feeling heat in his cheeks and knowing that they must be flaming now as brightly as Mistress Halliot's were, Hugh said stiffly, "You are mistaken if you think Brackengill lacks a proper hostess, sir. My uncle's widow, Lady Marjory Graham of Brampton, presently makes her home with me."

Unimpressed, Halliot snapped, "Am I to believe that this Lady Marjory would stand between my daughter and the nephew on whom her ladyship depends for her home? Do I look like a simpleton, sir?"

"Take care, Halliot, lest you go beyond what I will tolerate," Hugh said, restraining his temper with difficulty. "If it will ease your mind, you may send another woman as companion to your daughter."

Doggedly, Sir William said, "Though it may further offend you, sir, I doubt that another woman would make much difference if you decided to take advantage of the situation. Nor can I think of any gentlewoman who would agree to dwell in England under such circumstances."

"Her mother, perhaps," Hugh suggested.

Mistress Halliot winced, but Halliot said only, "Even were I to allow it, Lady Halliot would not agree. The very suggestion is absurd."

"Aye," Scrope agreed. " 'Tis a foolish notion." Sarcastically, he said to Hugh, "If you're so damned hot to keep her at Brackengill, sir, perhaps we should arrange for you to marry the wench. Our esteemed sovereigns have already agreed to one match for your family across the line. Doubtless, two will delight them."

"No, thank you, my lord," Hugh snapped.

He heard Mistress Halliot echo his sentiments in exactly the same words.

Scrope said, "Then put Mistress Halliot to judgment with her sister, and let us have done with this. We've much still remaining to do today."

"Perhaps I can suggest an acceptable compromise," Halliot said hastily.

When all eyes turned toward him, he said, "If my daughter Laura truly wishes to stand as a pledge for her sister's honor, and if Hugh Graham agrees to honor that pledge, perhaps there is a way."

Take A Trip Into A Timeless World of Passion and Adventure with Kensington Choice Historical Romances!
—Absolutely FREE!

Let your spirits fly away and enjoy the passion and adventure of another time. Kensington Choice Historical Romances are the finest novels of their kind, written by today's best selling romance authors. Each Kensington Choice Historical Romance transports you to distant lands in a bygone age. Experience the adventure and share the delight as proud men and spirited women discover the wonder and passion of true love.

4 BOOKS WORTH UP TO $24.96— Absolutely FREE!

Take 4 FREE Books!

We created our convenient Home Subscription Service so you'll be sure to have the hottest new romances delivered each month right to your doorstep — usually before they are available in book stores. Just to show you how convenient Zebra Home Subscription Service is, we would like to send you 4 Kensington Choice Historical Romances as a FREE gift. You receive a gift worth up to $24.96 — absolutely FREE. There's no extra charge for shipping and handling. There's no obligation to buy anything - ever!

Save Up To 32% On Home Delivery!

Accept your FREE gift and each month we'll deliver 4 brand new titles as soon as they are published. They'll be yours to examine FREE for 10 days. Then if you decide to keep the books, you'll pay the preferred subscriber's price of just $4.20 per title. That's $16.80 for all 4 books for a savings of up to 32% off the cover price! Just add $1.50 to offset the cost of shipping and handling. Remember, you are under no obligation to buy any of these books at any time! If you are not delighted with them, simply return them and owe nothing. But if you enjoy Kensington Choice Historical Romances as much as we think you will, pay the special preferred subscriber rate of only $16.80 each month and save over $8.00 off the bookstore price!

We have 4 FREE BOOKS for you as your introduction to
KENSINGTON CHOICE!

To get your FREE BOOKS,
worth up to $24.96, mail the card below
or call TOLL-FREE 1-888-345-BOOK
Visit our website at www.kensingtonbooks.com.

Take 4 Kensington Choice Historical Romances FREE!

YES! Please send me my 4 FREE KENSINGTON CHOICE HISTORICAL ROMANCES (without obligation to purchase other books). Unless you hear from me after I receive my 4 FREE BOOKS, you may send me 4 new novels - as soon as they are published - to preview each month FREE for 10 days. If I am not satisfied, I may return them and owe nothing. Otherwise, I will pay the money-saving preferred subscriber's price of just $4.20 each... a total of $16.80 plus $1.50 for shipping and handling. That's a savings of over $8.00 each month. I may return any shipment within 10 days and owe nothing, and I may cancel any time I wish. In any case the 4 FREE books will be mine to keep.

Name _____

Address _____ Apt No _____

City _____ State _____ Zip _____

Telephone ( ) _____ Signature _____

(If under 18, parent or guardian must sign)

KN011A

4 FREE
Kensington
Choice
Historical
Romances
are waiting
for you to
claim them!

(worth up
to $24.96)

See details
inside....

IllIIluIlIIuIIllIIIuIIlIIuIlIIuIllIIuIIlIIuIlIIuI

KENSINGTON CHOICE
Zebra Home Subscription Service, Inc.
P.O. Box 5214
Clifton NJ 07015-5214

"What way?" Scrope demanded.

"I will agree to the arrangement if they will agree to be handfasted. He must also agree that if he beds her and then fails to marry her after the usual year and a day—assuming that the situation is not resolved long before then—he will pay a *tocher* equal to the amount of her present dowry. That is, after all, the customary way to arrange handfasting betwixt persons of the nobility and gentry. Moreover, doubling her dowry would give my daughter at least some small chance of finding another man willing to marry her if Sir Hugh does take advantage of her."

Rendered speechless by the outrageous suggestion, Hugh glanced at Laurie Halliot and saw that she looked equally stunned.

Scrope, however, clapped his hands together gleefully and shouted, "Done! We accept your terms, Halliot. The clerk will proclaim their handfasting at once, so we can move on to the rest of our business. When May Halliot returns, I expect you to inform me at once, Halliot, so that we can immediately arrange another meeting to decide her fate."

"Wait!" Hugh cried.

"Be silent, sir," Scrope ordered. "The wardens have agreed. It is finished."

"It is *not* finished!"

"It will be once the clerk proclaims the handfasting," Scrope said, adding curtly, "Proclaim it, man. We have much work yet to do before sundown."

Turning to Hugh, he said in a vicious undertone, "You brought this on yourself with your foolish ways, Graham, so sit down and accept the consequences or answer later to me and to her majesty. I have already written to inform her that, in my opinion, you have far too many connections in Scotland, and with your uncle dead—yes, I know about that, no thanks to you—your sun is setting, sir."

"Forgive me, my lord," the clerk interjected. "Sir Hugh and Mistress Halliot must stand before me and agree to the arrangement before I can inscribe the log."

Glaring at the interruption, Scrope growled, "Trust a Scottish clerk to throw a rub in the way. I should have insisted on an English one."

"Had he been English," Halliot said testily, "he would doubtless refuse to inscribe it at all. Recall that English law does not recognize handfasting."

Laurie Halliot said nothing. She had neither moved nor spoken.

"Forgive me, sir," Hugh said quietly, still watching her. "But how can you accept my word in this when you know the laws of my country will not support it?"

"I'll accept it, because Border law does support it," Halliot said, giving him a straight look. "Whatever we decide here today will legally bind you, my lad. Moreover, sir," he added on a softer note, "my deputy informs me that your sworn word is your bond. I will put my faith in that."

Hugh was silent for a long moment, still watching Laurie. She was like a statue, her gaze blank, unseeing. The murmuring of the crowd had died away until he could hear the wind blowing. A bird shrieked overhead, and the sound startled her. Her gaze sharpened, meeting his.

Only then did he speak. "Mistress Halliot can rely upon my sworn word, sir, if she is willing. Will you agree to a handfasting betwixt us, mistress?"

Her soft bosom swelled as she inhaled deeply. Still meeting his gaze, she said, "I have agreed to pledge myself for my sister, sir. What form that pledge takes does not matter. My sister will return soon, and she will explain everything to the jury's satisfaction. Then you will have to release me."

"There is a bit more—"

"She has agreed," Scrope interjected swiftly. "Sign the agreement and have done. Then, if May Halliot has not returned before the next wardens' meeting, her sister can stand trial in her place."

Hugh did not press the point, for he knew that to do so might well result in the violence they had so far avoided.

The clerk required only simple agreement from each, so the

words were quickly spoken. However, for the rest of the day, Hugh's thoughts kept returning to the huge responsibility he had so impulsively accepted.

Whether Laurie Halliot realized it or not—and he believed that she did not—she was now legally his wife and subject to his authority in all things.

"Are you truly resigned to this business, daughter?" Sir William demanded during the brief midday recess when the wardens took time to eat a hasty meal.

Laurie shrugged, thinking it was like him to ask her the question only after the agreement was made and the papers signed.

"May cannot stay away long," she said, "and the Englishman will not harm me in the meantime. Only think what everyone would say if he did and what dreadful consequences could result!"

"Nevertheless, handfasting is a serious business, lass."

"Oh, aye, in the normal way of things, it is. But this is hardly a normal handfasting, sir. When May returns, it will be over and I can return home. The handfasting was necessary only to impose some semblance of propriety into an otherwise prodigiously awkward arrangement."

"An otherwise impossible arrangement," he amended. "I have no faith in any aunt of Sir Hugh Graham's being able to keep you safe from him. Indeed, I am not at all sure that—"

"Sir William," Scrope said, approaching them and interrupting in his usual imperious way, "you should eat your dinner, sir, so that we can finish today's business. The matter of your daughter is done, and you cannot undo it."

"Aye, that's true enough, but 'tis a brave thing she does."

"Oh, aye, 'tis wondrous brave," Scrope agreed. Turning to Laurie, he added briskly, "You must come with me now, mistress. It is your duty to present yourself to Sir Hugh Graham and ask for his instruction. After all, Sir Hugh, not your father, is now your lord and master. Take yourself off to him at once, lass."

A shiver raced up Laurie's spine, but she could hardly debate the point with Scrope, and she saw Sir Hugh nearby, talking with some other men. Feeling conspicuous and certain that everyone on the field was watching her, she made her way toward him through the crowd.

He soon saw her and turned away from the man who was speaking to say, "Mistress, where is your maid?"

"I have none with me, sir," she said. "The one who generally serves me disappeared when my sister did."

"Then, surely, you must have a manservant!"

"Nay," Laurie said, keeping her eyes on him, but wishing he would simply welcome her and not make her feel like Blanche did whenever she neglected to wear shoes. "Lord Scrope told me that I should present myself to you, sir."

"Did he, indeed?" Sir Hugh looked past her, frowning and narrow-eyed, as if he were searching the crowd. But if his search was successful, he gave no sign. Still frowning, he looked back at Laurie, his grim look making her wish that she were safely back at Aylewood and had not stirred from her bedchamber that day.

At last, his countenance relaxed, but he said firmly, "You must not wander about unattended, mistress. This place is not safe for my men-at-arms, let alone for an unarmed lass like yourself."

"I'll wager that every man here knows who I am," Laurie said calmly. "Do you believe anyone would risk the consequences of harming me, sir?"

"Perhaps not," he said with what looked like the beginning of a smile. "Still, you must not stir from my side without one of my men to look after you."

"As you wish, Sir Hugh," Laurie said. "Have you other commands for me?"

The frown returned. "I expected you to return home with your father, then come to me after you had packed suitable clothing and so forth."

"Lord Scrope commanded me to come to you now, so I doubt that my father expects me to return to Aylewood with him, or that he would allow me to do so."

Sir Hugh was silent, his brow still creased. After a long moment, he said, "I see. In that event, I expect you to stay near me through the rest of the day's business, so that you can be ready to leave at once when they have finished. I won't want to dawdle. If we can get through the afternoon without anyone picking a fight, I will be surprised. Tension is running high today."

She nodded and made no objection when he turned away to speak briefly to one of his men, whom she recognized as the one who had stood with him in the ring of swords.

Sir Hugh turned back, saying, "This is Ned Rowan. He'll look after you whilst I attend to my duties. Obey him as you would me." With that, he turned and strode off to meet the wardens at their table.

Politely, Ned Rowan said, "Would you not prefer to sit in the shade of one of the tents, mistress?"

"No, thank you," Laurie replied. "I'd rather watch what is going on."

He nodded, and she was grateful. She had been afraid that he might take his master's words to mean he could simply order her to do as he thought best.

She had been standing for some time, watching as one man after another answered to the complaint laid against him, when she became aware of a lad standing nearby, staring at her as if he would memorize her features. He was the one who had stood with Sir Hugh and Ned Rowan to defend her.

She smiled at him.

Grinning, he approached at once.

Beside her, Ned Rowan said sternly, "Mind your manners, lad. Ye're approachin' a lady. Make a proper leg, and dinna speak till she gives ye leave."

Coloring, the boy made an awkward bow, then looked at her expectantly.

"What is your name?" Laurie asked.

"I be Meggie's Andrew, mistress. They say ye be wedded now to Sir Hugh."

"We have agreed to a handfasting," Laurie said. "That is a bit like a wedding, generally, but not at all the same thing in our case."

Andrew nodded. "Brackengill hasna had a mistress since our Mistress Janet went away," he said. "Me mother and me sister, Nancy—"

"Dinna chatter, lad," Ned Rowan said. "Ye've no cause to be plaguing Mistress Halliot."

"I don't mind," Laurie said. "Life at Brackengill will be more pleasant if I have a friend or two. Andrew can tell me as much as he likes about the place."

The big man frowned and glanced at Sir Hugh, but the two wardens and their deputies were busy discussing something with the jury, so there was no help there. With a sigh he looked at Laurie and said, "Ye must do as ye like, mistress, but the wee scamp is no the one I'd recommend to be telling ye about Brackengill."

"I do not believe he will tell me any untruths," Laurie said with a smile.

"I will not," Andrew declared, drawing himself to his full height. "Me and Mistress Janet are good friends," he confided to Laurie.

"Are you, indeed? You must miss her now that she is living in Scotland."

"Oh, aye, I miss her, but—" Glancing at Ned Rowan, who had stepped away to talk to another man, Andrew put a finger alongside his nose and winked at her.

Laurie smiled, wondering exactly what message he thought that should convey to her. She found him amusing, and while she waited for the day's business to end, she allowed him to tell her everything he thought she should know about the place that would be her home until May returned—if she returned.

Andrew's description of Brackengill relayed little useful information to one who was accustomed to Aylewood. Although he described the castle as immense, insisting that its wall was the second highest he had seen, she doubted that he had seen many castles in his young life. Still, she was glad of his company, for no one else seemed inclined to speak to her.

The day's business ended at last with the clerk's report, summing up the penalties imposed. Two men were summarily hanged for their offenses, and then people began to gather belongings, preparing to leave.

Laurie saw Sir Hugh glance around, his stern gaze searching until it came to rest on her. She met it calmly, determined not to let him see how he affected her.

She was not frightened of him—or so she had told herself frequently during the long afternoon. Still, when he turned back to speak with her father, she felt herself relax. When he turned and strode toward her, she tensed again.

"Fetch her pony," he said to Ned Rowan. "Halliot will show you where to find it. She will ride beside me."

When Rowan had gone to do his bidding, he added, "Your father agreed to send some of your belongings to Brackengill, lass. You will be glad to have more gowns to wear, at least. If there is aught you particularly desire him to remember to send, just tell me and I will see that he is informed of it at once."

"He did not even say good-bye to me," Laurie said, trying to speak matter-of-factly but aware of a certain wistfulness in her tone.

Sir Hugh said evenly, "He is apparently feeling some remorse about his part in the business, mistress, but do not judge him harshly. You presented him with a dilemma, and Scrope made it difficult for any of us to think clearly."

She did not like to hear him make excuses for her father, and so she said no more, waiting silently until his men brought their horses. When she moved toward hers, Sir Hugh came up behind her, catching her at the waist before she realized his intent and lifting her without apparent effort to her saddle.

No one had done such a thing since her childhood; so

clearly, he was a man who took liberties without thought. Just as soon as she could catch her breath again and think sensibly, she would have to do something about that.

Fourteen

So shalt thou do at my command . . .

Sir Hugh and Laurie rode ahead of his men, and until they had crossed into England, they rode without speaking. She did not know what to say to him, but her thoughts were busy.

She knew, as did anyone living in the Borders, that hand-fasting was a form of marriage, albeit an irregular one. Traditionally, the parties contracted to live together for a year and a day, and if no issue resulted within the period, they were at liberty to dissolve the contract. That tradition, like other irregular forms of Scottish marriage, had developed because frequently no parson or priest was available to perform a proper church wedding. Still, Laurie's union with Sir Hugh was not normal, even for handfasting.

She stole glances at him as they rode together, trying to decide what manner of man now controlled her life, and wondering, too, if he would try to take advantage of his authority. She did not know many gentlemen.

Those she did know were Scottish and wielded great power over their minions. Her father was unusual in preferring peace to war. Most were as unruly as Buccleuch, and lived for raiding and battle. A few, like Sir Quinton Scott of Broadhaugh, were said to be quieter but nonetheless merry, and were ruthless when they thought it was necessary. She had never met a man of power whose will it was safe to cross, and Sir Hugh did not seem as if he would be any exception.

He had scarcely looked at her since mounting a well-muscled bay with a white blaze on its face and long black stockings. The man's flinty gray eyes moved constantly, however, scanning the landscape, and she noted that his men were as watchful as he was. Despite the truce, which was supposed to last until the next day's sunrise, everyone with any sense kept an eye out for trouble.

As they prepared to ford the River Sark at Gretna village, she saw Sir Hugh look her way at last. His glance was brief, however. Apparently satisfied that she could manage without assistance, he returned to his study of the landscape.

When her pony's feet were on firm ground again, Laurie looked back at Scotland. Knowing that she had left one country for another, she would not have been surprised to find the grass in England a different color, the trees more plentiful, the road better cared for. But the landscape looked the same.

"We be in England now," Andrew said, urging his pony up beside hers, so that she rode between him and Sir Hugh. "Men call this the Debatable Land," he added cheerfully.

"Andrew," Ned Rowan called from behind them, "dinna plague the mistress, lad. Come back and ride wi' me."

With an audible sigh, Andrew turned his pony aside to wait for him.

"You have been very quiet, mistress."

Sir Hugh's voice startled her, but years of concealing her feelings from her stepmother allowed Laurie to reply calmly. "You did not appear to invite conversation, sir," she said. "Are we truly in England now?"

"Aye, we are. And once we pass through Longtown, it will not be far to Brackengill. We should arrive shortly before nightfall."

"I look forward to seeing your home," she said politely. "Meggie's Andrew was kind enough to tell me about it earlier."

"Did he?" Sir Hugh's eyes glinted, but whether with amusement or something else, she did not know. "I'll warrant the young scoundrel made it sound like a palace. It is no such thing, but you will be comfortable enough."

Laurie felt her stomach knot, and her hands gripped the reins so tightly that her fingernails dug into her palms. Staring straight ahead, avoiding Sir Hugh's all-too-penetrating gaze, she realized that she had put off thinking about how comfortable or uncomfortable her immediate future might be.

She had thought only of May and her distress after the false Sir John had fallen in the river and been swept away. But she did not want to think about that now, either. May was no murderess. If only she would come home and . . .

"Let us ride a little ahead of these others, mistress."

Again, his voice seemed to invade her thoughts, startling her back to the present, but she was willing enough to ride on ahead with him.

With a sign to his men to maintain their steady pace, Sir Hugh urged the bay to a canter, and Laurie's pony followed its lead. When they had established some distance between themselves and the others, Sir Hugh slowed his horse to a walk again, waiting for her to draw even before he said, "We must talk, I think."

"Aye," she agreed. "I own, sir, that I know nothing about being a hostage. Must I stay in your dungeon?"

"Nay, mistress. My dungeon is no place for a lady of gentle birth. You will have a proper bedchamber, and my people will treat you kindly. Indeed, if I have your promise to give me no cause for concern, I'll say naught to them about your true situation. They will treat you as my guest."

She smiled. " 'Tis kind of you, sir. Mayhap I shall enjoy my visit to Brackengill as much as the laird of Buccleuch is said to have enjoyed Blackness."

"I would not compare you with Buccleuch, mistress. Nor would I treat him to such luxury as he enjoyed there. But regardless of what your father might think about my aunt, she is a gentlewoman and will be glad to have your company. You have naught to fear as long as you obey"

"As to that," Laurie said, summoning courage, "I have no intention of disobeying, but I pray you will remember that our handfasting was not my doing."

"You agreed to it," he reminded her.

"Aye, but I had little choice. No one asked what I thought."

"You could have refused."

"Perhaps, but I could not allow them to pass a sentence of death against my sister without so much as granting her a proper trial, and you could not expect me to contradict my father's wishes publicly, or Lord Scrope's."

"In fact, mistress, you were the one who began it, by offering to stand hostage for your sister. I expect you to abide by your agreement."

"I did agree to stand hostage, but I did not and do not agree to share your bed, sir," she said flatly. "Perhaps I ought to have considered from the outset, as my father did, the likelihood that any English captor might take advantage of a female hostage, but I did not. I believed that you would treat me with the honor due to my name and lineage. Was I wrong about that?"

"I cannot imagine why you should think me so noble," he said, giving her a look so direct that it startled her. "After all, you saw me only that one time at Aylewood and can know little about me. Or is it possible that you were spying . . . that is, that you saw me on some other occasion?"

Every muscle in her body tensed sharply. He *had* seen her in Tarras Wood. She knew it as certainly as if he had said the words, and she could think of nothing to say in reply. Neither could she seem to look away from that stern gaze. It held hers as if the two were locked together.

Licking suddenly dry lips, she said, "I . . . I do not know what you mean."

"Tell me this, then. How well did you know Martin Loder?"

Surprised by the abrupt change of subject, she said without thinking, "I did not know him at all."

"I think you did," he declared. "I think you knew him very well."

"Then you are mistaken," she said. "I did not even know his real name. He told my sister that his name was Sir John, that he was a wealthy English knight."

She turned to look straight ahead, lifting her chin as she added, "To learn that he was not a knight, that he was in fact Lord Scrope's land sergeant, came as a shock to me—and to my sister, as well. I had never seen him before that night."

As she said the words, Laurie felt a twinge of conscience, recalling that something about the figure standing next to May in the moonlight had seemed familiar. She suppressed the feeling, telling herself that under such circumstances almost any man in chain mail might have looked like any other. The familiarity most likely sprang from his mode of dress and accent, nothing more.

She felt Sir Hugh's hard gaze upon her.

After a nerve-racking silence, he said with a dangerous edge to his voice, "We will get along better if you do not lie to me, mistress. I say that you did know him. Moreover, I believe that you knew him very well."

"But I didn't!"

"If you continue to prevaricate," he said, his tone now sending icicles through her veins, "I swear I will examine you the moment we reach Brackengill. And furthermore, I will do so in my aunt's presence, in order to have a reliable witness when I learn if you are truly the maiden you claim to be."

Dismayed, she cried, "You can't do that! You wouldn't!"

"Oh, but I can and I will," he retorted. "I have every legal right to do as I like with you. Moreover, if I must pay for any loss of innocence when I return you to your family, I certainly have the right to see if you are virgin now."

"Please, sir, I beg you, do not humiliate me so! I give you my word that I never knew that man in any way."

"But you lied a moment ago. I could see it in your face. I say that you did know him, just as I say that you had seen me before my brief visit to Aylewood."

"I realize that you must have seen me in the tree that day," she admitted.

"Aye, I did, and if you saw me, you saw Martin Loder, for he was riding at my side. But you knew that, lass. Loder knew

Tarras Wood far better than any Englishman should. Will you deny that you are the one who showed him its ways?"

"That was him—the same man that May . . . the . . . the one in the river?"

"You know it was," he said ruthlessly. "He rode into Tarras Wood alone, doubtless to meet you, since you were waiting for him. He did not know that I followed until I shouted. Do you deny that you shinned up that tree only because you heard me shout and knew that he was no longer alone?"

He paused, and the truth swept over her like a flood. Her body tensed as she struggled to avoid revealing her thoughts to him.

If the man with him that day had been Martin Loder, Loder did know the forest, and his knowledge of its secret ways had not come from her. Could May have helped the English raid Liddesdale?

She had not considered May's false knight before in connection with the riders in Tarras Wood the day of the raid. But now that the two incidents had crashed together in her mind and she knew the supposed Sir John was also the man with Sir Hugh, that knowledge explained the odd sense of familiarity when she had heard him speak by the river.

Certain that her cheeks must be as red as hellfire, she swallowed carefully, trying to think of something sensible to say. She could think of nothing, however, that would divert Sir Hugh's thoughts to a new topic.

He said impatiently, "I did not think you were a coward."

"I'm not!"

But she was. She still could not think, and his anger distressed her more than she had imagined it could. She knew it would be hard to convince him that she had not known Martin Loder, but for now, she would be content if she could just talk him out of examining her.

Remembering that she had heard him express surprise at how well Loder knew his way, she understood why Sir Hugh suspected what he did. But even if she could persuade him of his error, would he not instantly suspect what she now suspected about the source of Loder's knowledge?

May rarely, if ever, rode out alone, and Laurie doubted that she would have ridden into Tarras Wood without a companion. But that would not matter to a jury. Just the suspicion that May might have helped Loder would be another damning piece of evidence against her if . . . *when* she returned to stand her trial.

Drawing a deep breath, Laurie said earnestly, "I swear to you, sir, by all that is holy, until you told me, I did not know that the two men were one and the same. I only just guessed a few moments ago that you saw me that day in the forest."

"I thought you a child," he said grimly. "You still look innocent enough, but 'tis plain that you are more knowledgeable than you look."

"I am not what you think, but neither am I a child," she said, adding wistfully, "If I were, perhaps you would recognize my innocence more easily."

More to give herself a respite than for any other reason, she added curiously, "When you shot at the boar, did you intend to frighten it away or to kill it?"

"The first time to frighten it away, the second to kill."

"Then you did not want your companion to see us."

"Us? Godamercy, was your sister in that tree, too?"

"No, certainly not. I misspoke." She added hastily, "Why did you frighten off the boar? And why did you not tell Loder that you had seen me?"

He regarded her for a long moment, but she met his gaze steadily.

He shrugged and said, "I should have told him, of course. Scrope would demand my head if he were to learn that I knew you were there and did nothing about it. But I do not make war on women, mistress."

"You did that day," she said bitterly, "and on children, too. So did every Englishman with you."

"I won't debate that with you," he said shortly. "In battle, people get hurt. I was referring only to my failure to reveal your presence to Loder. How is it that you so easily recall having seen me and do not recall seeing him?"

Since she did not want to tell him that she had watched him and only him from the moment he took off his helmet and she saw the mop of reddish curls, she said instead, "I was terrified that you had seen me, of course. I dared not take my eyes from you after that, lest you tell him."

"Still, you must have—"

Impatiently, she said, "Have you listened to nothing I have said? I did not see him clearly then, and I never saw him after that until the night he fell into the river. Then it was dark except for the moon, and everything was in shadows. I was not near enough, in any event, to get a good look at him."

"Yet you would have had Scrope and those jurors believe that you and not your sister killed him," he reminded her flatly.

"My sister did not kill anyone," Laurie said, wishing almost the instant the words were out of her mouth that she had kept silent rather than let him hear the note of desperation in her voice.

"Then you did."

"No!"

"One of you must have done so," he said. "Cornus Grant saw you."

"Cornus Grant lied!"

Suddenly, believing she could discern a purpose in his insistence that she talk about the incident, she said, "Why do you pursue this now? Do you mean to use what I say to you against me at the next wardens' meeting? I should have realized your intent before now. I will say no more about it."

"Just answer me this," he said quietly. "*Did* you murder Martin Loder?"

"No!"

" 'No,' you will not answer the question or 'no,' you did not kill him?"

She hesitated, but she could not let him think her a murderess any more than she could think of May as one. "I swear before God that I did not kill him."

"Then just how far did you intend to press Scrope?" he demanded. "Suppose that he had insisted on carrying through to your sister's judgment. Would you have declared yourself the murderess before them all?"

"I certainly hope that I would have," she retorted, looking daggers at him.

When he shot them right back, she added defiantly, "I would do anything to protect May. If declaring myself the killer would have forced his lordship to delay her sentencing, I would have lied to him and to everyone else."

"It would be as well, mistress, if you never lie to me," he said, the dangerous note back in his voice.

She looked away.

Gently, he added, "Do you know what I do to liars?"

Her throat threatened to close, but she managed to say, "No, what?"

"I beat them," he said.

She believed him, because it was exactly what she had expected him to say.

Fifteen

Wide in, wide in, my lady fair,
No harm shall thee befall . . .

Laurie's first impression of Brackengill Castle, against a dusky sky, was one of bleakness. Accustomed to Aylewood, perched on its high, rocky outcropping, she thought Brackengill—surrounded by low-rolling, nearly barren grassland—both gloomy and vulnerable. From a distance, the gray stone wall looked no higher than the eight-foot one around Aylewood Tower. But at Aylewood, a steep, uphill approach served to augment the wall's height.

Not until they had forded the River Lyne did she realize that Brackengill, too, sat on a hill. The slope was gentle, but as they drew nearer, she saw that the castle was imposing. Its curtain wall was twice the height of the one at Aylewood and looked strong and forbidding.

She knew that Sir Hugh was watching her, waiting for a reaction, but she did not speak. Seeing the great walled castle brought home to her—as the handfasting and even his threat to examine her had not—just what she had agreed to. She was far from home, and the closer they got to Brackengill, the more vulnerable she felt. A thicket of trees stood halfway between the castle and the frothy river. Otherwise, only distantly scattered, wind-sculpted oaks dotted the undulating landscape. In the faint light of dusk, everything seemed gray, and Laurie's spirits sank further when movement on the ramparts revealed men-at-arms keeping watch. Her pony, sensing her unease, tossed its head and whinnied.

The gates remained shut until the riders drew near, then swung wide to admit them. Flaring torches already lit the courtyard, where more men-at-arms waited at the ready, stepping back only when Sir Hugh gestured to them to do so.

Stable lads ran forward then to take the horses, and she saw young Andrew slip down from his pony and hurry to help them.

When Sir Hugh dismounted and turned to help her, her tension increased until it felt as if every nerve in her body were taut and screaming.

His gloved hands firmly encompassed her waist. She felt the length of his fingers, the strength of his hands. Then, with no apparent effort, he lifted her and set her down in front of him. "Welcome to Brackengill, mistress," he said, still holding her. His voice was low and vibrant. He looked right into her eyes.

Standing so close, he seemed particularly large and intimidating, and she could not think of a reply. She could only think of his threat. She had not dared to ask him if he had changed his mind, lest he say no.

"I'll wager that you are hungry," he went on, releasing her and offering his arm. "Shall we go in and see what my people can offer for our supper?"

Still tingling where his hands had touched her, Laurie nodded and laid her hand on his arm. Her stomach growled, but her apprehension and curiosity were stronger than her desire for food. "I'll need the satchel that's tied to my saddle."

He nodded. "Someone will take it in for you," he said.

The warm glow of the torches lit the central area, revealing men's faces here and there but not the more shadowy corners. Ahead, light gleamed cheerfully from arched windows on the second level of the main tower.

As they approached the entrance, she became aware that men in the yard were still watching her, muttering and whispering to one another.

Knowing that those who had not been at Lochmaben must wonder who she was, and certain that the men who had been there were relating everything they knew, she gathered her dignity. She did not want to admit her fears even to herself. She would certainly not allow these men to see how she felt.

Lackeys sprang to open the door, and she saw that, like its Aylewood counterpart, it boasted heavy iron reinforcement and an iron yett, or gate, as well.

Following Sir Hugh up a spiral stairway, she entered a spacious hall with rushes on the floor. The aroma wafting from them told her that no one had changed them in some time but that someone had recently scattered herbs to cover the smell.

Lackeys were hastily setting up tables for the newcomers' supper, stepping over dogs that sprawled here and there, but one hurried to them to take Sir Hugh's cloak and gloves, and Laurie's as well.

The chamber occupied the entire floor of the tower, for she could see arrow slits along the rear wall, opposite the arched windows she had seen from the bailey. Candles and firelight set shadows dancing merrily on the high, vaulted ceiling.

A vividly colored arras cloth and turkey carpets draped the walls. At the far end, beyond a dais on which the laird's table stood, an enormous arched fireplace roared with a blazing, crackling fire. Sparks shot high and wide.

Hearing echoing cracks behind her and feeling heat, as well, she turned her head to see a second fire blazing in a second fireplace, a twin to the first. A portrait above the second one depicted a pale, pretty woman in a rose-pink gown. She stood with a hand resting on a carved wooden armchair, her eyes submissively downcast.

"That is my mother," Sir Hugh said. "My father had it painted shortly before she died."

"She was young," Laurie said.

"Aye, she was."

Silken rustling punctuated by the click of hard heels on stone drew Laurie's attention to a doorway at the left end of the hall. As she turned, a tall, frail-looking lady of indeterminate age bustled in, wearing a gown of black velvet over a swaying French farthingale. A lacy veil did little to conceal her elaborately dressed red hair.

"My dear Sir Hugh," the lady exclaimed when she saw them, "how glad I am that you have returned! Your entire household—as I need not tell you—is delighted to welcome you home." Blinking myopically at Laurie, she added, "But who is this lady, if you please?"

Sir Hugh replied, "In a manner of speaking, madam, some might say she is my wife. You need not consider her any such thing, however." Drawing Laurie forward, he added, "May I present Laura Halliot. She will be staying with us for a time." To Laurie, he added, "As I told you before, Lady Marjory is my uncle's widow and presently makes her home at Brackengill."

"I am happy to make your acquaintance, my lady," Laurie said with a curtsy.

"But I do not understand," Lady Marjory protested, making her curtsy but fixing a bewildered gaze on Sir Hugh. "Did you say you are married?"

Laurie looked at Sir Hugh. With an impatient gesture, he said, "Mistress Halliot can explain the details to you later, madam. Suffice it to say that there was a ceremony but only one of political necessity."

"But what ceremony?"

"Only a Scottish one. They call it a handfasting."

"But I know about handfasting," Lady Marjory said. "Brampton told me about it long ago. He said it is a form of marriage, one of the odder ways that Scots marry but a marriage nonetheless. Are you Scottish, Mistress Halliot?"

"Yes," Laurie said. "My father is warden of the Scottish middle march."

"Godamercy, but when did this extraordinary event take place?" Lady Marjory demanded. "I vow, sir, I was not aware that you had even formed an intention to marry. Indeed, I should have liked to attend your wedding, even to assist you in preparing for it."

"There was no need for you to do either, madam," Sir Hugh said. "It was not a true marriage, you see, only a rite performed to protect Mistress Halliot's good name. I should explain that she is a hostage consigned to my care and protection until the person for whom she has pledged herself returns to face justice. Her father insisted on the ritual, and Scrope agreed to it before I could refuse. That's all."

"Still, it was a form of marriage, was it not?"

"It was. Nevertheless—"

"Then I do not think it is either wise of you or kind to make a game of her position, sir," she said archly. "Hostage, indeed! I am persuaded that a handsome young man like you can have no need to drape a wife in chains to keep her. Moreover, you should use her proper title when you speak of her, even to me."

Sir Hugh, gaping at her, appeared to be at a loss for words.

With an understanding smile, Lady Marjory said, "I see just how it is, my dear sir. Brampton was exactly the same."

"Pray, madam, what *are* you talking about?"

"Why, for at least six months after our wedding, your uncle persisted in presenting me as Lady Marjory Hatherlea instead of Lady Marjory Graham."

Laurie looked to Sir Hugh for an explanation.

He was still staring slack-jawed at Lady Marjory, but he collected his wits enough to say, "I'm afraid that you still do not understand, madam."

"Oh, but I do, sir! I tell you, it was by turns both amusing and exasperating for me. Brampton generally corrected the surname when one drew his attention to the error, but he could never bring himself to call me plain Lady Graham."

"But why should he?"

"Well, I should have been just as happy had no one known that my father was an earl, but Brampton took pleasure in puffing off that noble connection. So Lady Marjory I remained. But in your case, for dear Lady Graham's sake, one hopes that you will quickly learn to employ her correct title."

Sir Hugh's mouth shut again, and his lips pressed together

so tightly they looked white at the edges. His hands clenched into fists at his sides.

Noting these ominous signs, Laurie said gently, "Indeed, my lady, there is no need to call me so. The ritual to which Sir Hugh referred took place, just as he said, for no reason other than to protect me. You see, my father feared that Sir Hugh might exploit the authority he now wields over me, that he might—"

"Oh, but my dear, husbands always take such advantage of their wives!"

"That will do, madam," Sir Hugh said sharply. "Pray, say no more about the matter now. We can discuss it later if you insist."

Lady Marjory, though silenced, still looked doubtful and unhappy.

"Truly, my lady," Laurie said, "I shall stay here no longer than I must. I assure you that I do not look upon him as my husband, and neither should you."

Lady Marjory's frown deepened. "But *a form* of marriage is still a marriage, is it not?" When neither Laurie nor Sir Hugh replied, she repeated, "Is it not?"

"One must suppose that, in some ways, it is," Laurie admitted reluctantly.

Sir Hugh did not offer an opinion.

"Well, if it *was* a marriage, then it follows that you are Lady Graham," Lady Marjory said with satisfaction. "Moreover, it now becomes most fortunate that Brampton insisted upon my remaining Lady Marjory. Otherwise, we should have two ladies Graham in this household. I think that is always confusing, do not you?"

Visibly giving himself a shake, Sir Hugh found his voice at last and said sternly to Laurie, "This household will refer to you as Mistress Halliot. That is how I wish it to be, and so that is how it *will* be."

Lady Marjory raised her hands in protest. "But, my dear Sir Hugh—"

"Madam," he interjected angrily, "unless you wish to incur

my strongest displeasure, you will not refer to her again as
Lady Graham."

"But I do not understand, my dear sir! Indeed, I have no
wish to displease you. Quite the contrary, I wish only to make
your life comfortable, but I think 'tis you and your lady who
do not understand. For how can it be—?"

"God's wounds, woman," Hugh roared, "hold your tongue
and do as I say!"

"Yes, of course," Lady Marjory said, bowing her head submissively.

Watching her, Laurie had a sudden, irrelevant thought that
it was a pity Blanche could not see her, for Lady Marjory's
deference was far more believable than Blanche's would ever
be. Glancing back at the portrait over the fireplace near the
main entrance, she wondered if Graham men purposely married meek women.

Lady Marjory recovered gracefully, saying, "We should not
keep dear Mistress Halliot standing after her long journey,
should we, sir?"

Sir Hugh did not deign to reply, and Laurie saw that it still
was only with strong effort that he controlled his temper.

His gaze met hers briefly and moved away again.

Unabashed by his silence, Lady Marjory said kindly, "If
you will permit me, my dear Mistress Halliot, I will show you
upstairs now, and—"

Breaking off with a comical look, she turned back to Sir
Hugh. "One must suppose under such circumstances, sir, that
you do not want her to sleep in your bedchamber. Therefore,
pray tell me where she *is* to sleep."

When he hesitated, she said, "If you *do* wish her to share
your chamber, you have only to say so. You are master here,
and your wish is—"

"I will not sleep with him," Laurie said hastily. "He—"

"Enough, mistress," Sir Hugh said with an audible sigh. "I
will try to explain matters more clearly to her ladyship whilst
you refresh yourself." Turning his head toward the door

through which Lady Marjory had entered, he shouted, "Nancy!"

Light, rapid footsteps preceded the entrance of a child of ten or eleven, who bore a strong resemblance to Meggie's Andrew. She wore an apron over a plain gray dress and a simple white cap tied under her chin. Long sable curls fanned nearly to her waist, and she carried an unlit torch. Skidding to a halt before them, she bobbed a one-handed curtsy and said, "Aye, master?"

"Take this lady upstairs to Mistress Janet's bedchamber. She will sleep there for the present."

"Aye, Sir Hugh. This way, m'lady, an it please ye. I'm Nancy."

"And I am Mistress Halliot," Laurie said, correcting her gently.

Wide-eyed, the child said, "But me mam said ye've married wi' Sir Hugh. She said I should say m'lady. The men in the yard be saying the same, and our Andrew did say—"

"Nancy," Sir Hugh snarled.

Flushing, the child bobbed another curtsy and said anxiously, "Aye, sir?"

"Stop chattering and take Mistress Halliot upstairs. And do as she bids you!"

"Aye, sir. This way, mistress." She bent to light her torch from the nearby fire, then glanced back as if to be sure that Laurie followed her.

Laurie had taken but one step when Lady Marjory said, "I shall be along shortly to help get you settled, my dear. In my experience, new places are always confusing. I believe that you will be glad of my help."

"Thank you, madam," Laurie said, not knowing what else to say and feeling bemused at the memory of the frail, kindly lady standing up to Sir Hugh. Avoiding his gimlet gaze, she hurried after Nancy without saying another word.

The service stairway, like the one from the main entrance to the hall, spiraled upward in a clockwise direction, as most such stairways did. Laurie knew the direction of the spiral

meant Brackengill men had historically been right-handed, for
it gave such men the wider part of the stairwell to accommo-
date the sweep of their swords when defending against an enemy attacking from below.

Ferniehurst in Scotland was the only castle she had seen
with a stair that twisted to the left. The stairways there all did,
because Kerr men were left-handed. Indeed, in the Borders,
"ker-handed" meant left-handed.

Nancy pushed open a door on the second landing to reveal
a gloomy chamber of shadows. With an apologetic smile, the
little girl darted in, and from the threshold, Laurie watched as
she tried to open shutters on a window wider than Laurie's
own at Aylewood, without putting down the burning torch.

Smiling for the first time since her arrival, she went to help.

"They be gey stuck, m'lady," Nancy said, stepping out of
the way and looking critically around the room.

"My shutter at home sticks, too," Laurie said, giving the
shutters a sharp thump with her fist. " 'Tis the nature of shutters, I believe, particularly after it rains."

"It's no rained for weeks," Nancy said as she put the torch
in a bracket provided for the purpose near the door. "But neither ha' the master ordered the ones opened, and I see now
that ye've nobbut a wee stub of a candle in yon dish. What
wi' all the other work me mam and me ha' to do, and no one
sleepin' here, we've no got round to cleaning this chamber yet
a while. We thought ye'd sleep wi' Sir Hugh. When he shouted,
I were just meanin' to go to his chamber wi' that torch, in
case ye needed me. They said in the yard that ye didna bring
a woman wi' ye."

"Godamercy, are you and your mother the only maidservants in the castle?"

"Aye," Nancy said. "Her ladyship brung a woman with her,
but she only does for Lady Marjory. She willna lift a finger
otherwise."

"Mercy," Laurie exclaimed, opening the shutters at last and
taking a deep breath of fresh evening air. It was dark out now.

"But why no more?" she asked. "Sir Hugh seems wealthy enough to afford any number of servants."

"Aye, but after Mistress Janet went, no woman would come here. Their men all said a household wi'out a mistress were no suited for 'em."

"Then you and your mam came because of Lady Marjory?"

"Nay, then," Nancy said as she moved to smooth the coverlet and plump pillows on the curtained bed. "Her ladyship ha' been here but a wee while," she added. "Me mam brought us here months ago, when the master sent Ned Rowan to look after our farm. Our da died, chasing reivers." Nibbling her lower lip, she cast Laurie an oblique, rueful look.

Matter-of-factly, Laurie said, "Scottish reivers, I expect."

"Aye," Nancy said, looking down at her hands.

" 'Tis ever the way," Laurie said quietly. "Women and children sit at home, wondering if the men will return again, no matter what side of the line they are on."

"Aye, that's what Mistress Janet did say," Nancy said with a nod. Then, with a sigh, she added, "Sir Hugh said our mam needs a new husband. But she didna want to take Ned Rowan."

"I can understand that, too," Laurie said with feeling.

"Sir Hugh were vexed at first when Mam refused Ned Rowan," Nancy said. "But then he said that if Mam would cook for 'im, at least we'd be safe here. Our Andrew, though, all he can think about is shooting reivers, just like our da."

"Is Andrew your only brother?"

"Nay, then, I'm cursed wi' three o' them," Nancy said as she stepped away from the bed and bent to wipe cobwebs off a stool with a handful of her skirt. "Our new bairn is a girl like me, though—only smaller, o' course."

"So your mother looks after five children and does the cooking and cleaning for the castle, as well."

"Aye, but I help her. Wee Susan's nobbut a babe yet." She glanced at the cold, bare hearth. "Shall I fetch ye some wood, my—?" Looking self-conscious, she broke off. "Can I call ye 'mistress' then, or must it always be Mistress Halliot?"

" 'Mistress' is enough, or perhaps you could call me 'Mistress Laura,' as our servants at home do," Laurie said. "I'd like that."

"Aye, sure. Shall I leave ye this torch, then?"

"Yes, please, unless you need it to light your way. As for wood, if you will tell a manservant to bring some up—and a tinderbox—I can light a fire after supper. Or perhaps the manservant might return then and light one for me."

"Likely, Mistress Janet left a tinderbox somewhere hereabouts," Nancy said. "Mam will tell our Andrew to bring up your wood." She did not question Laurie's suggestion that she could make her own fire.

That omission told Laurie much more about the household. Just the thought of one of the family at Aylewood building his or her fire would scandalize their servants. Laurie had learned to do so only because Lucy Elliot had been willing to teach her such things when she visited the cottage in Tarras Wood.

"Tell Andrew to bring a broom, too," Laurie said. "And some candles."

Nodding, Nancy gave the stool a last, hasty rub and hurried away.

A gentle breeze wafted through the open window, and finding herself alone for the first time since leaving Aylewood, Laurie walked over to look outside. There was no moon yet. She could make out dense shapes in the darkness, but little else.

The breeze was fresh and bore a slight chill. She would be glad of a fire.

Soon she heard the clatter of the boy's boots on the stairs, and a moment later he appeared on the threshold with a leather sling of wood hanging so heavily from his right hand that it dragged down his whole right side. He held a besom broom tucked under that arm and the satchel from her saddle in his left hand.

"This be Mistress Janet's room," he said with strong accusation in his voice.

"Yes," she said. "It is a very pleasant room."

"Aye, it is," he agreed, setting down the sling of wood and

reaching into his shirt to extract two candles. "I've brung wood and these candles. Someone brung the wee satchel and said ye'd want it, and Nan said ye wanted the broom."

"Thank you. Put the satchel on the bed. It contains only a few of my things. Will you come back later to light the fire for me, or have you other chores to do?"

"Me mam said I'm to do it now, but ye should close yon shutters first. Mistress Janet always said we should when she came to our cot. 'Cause when they're open they let out the warm, she said."

Amused by his knowledgeable air, she went to shut them while he lighted the two candles from the torch Nancy had left.

While he dripped hot tallow into a pewter dish to set the first candle in, Laurie tried to figure out how the shutters' latch worked. By the time she had done so and turned back, he had attended to the second candle and was kneeling on the hearth, dealing competently with the fire. Soon, it was crackling merrily.

Looking at her over his shoulder, he said, "I'll slip down the noo and bring ye some water. Me mam said ye'd likely be wanting a wash afore supper."

"Thank you," Laurie said. "You must be a big help to her."

He grimaced. "I stay in the stables, mostly, and Sir Hugh said if I'm good, I can help 'em put his mark on the new cattle over Haggbeck way. I dinna like bein' indoors, fetching and carrying. I'd rather be out helpin' the men wi' the beasts."

Since she felt much the same way, Laurie merely thanked him for all he had done and dismissed him. She passed the time until he returned with her hot water by exploring the bedchamber, then turned her attention to refreshing her appearance.

She had scrubbed her face and was washing her hands when, without ceremony, Lady Marjory entered and said with brisk good cheer, "Oh, good. I see they have managed to provide you with hot water. I must warn you, you will learn quickly that one must not rely too heavily upon the servants here."

"They seem pleasant folk to me," Laurie said.

"Oh, yes, indeed," Lady Marjory agreed. She smiled and added confidingly, "My woman complains unceasingly, but I warrant Griselda would complain in any house outside the gates of London. Indeed, I know she does, because she even complained in Southampton when we stayed with my daughter Sarah, and again in Cornwall, when we visited my daughter Philadelphia."

"So you are enjoying a round of visits with your family," Laurie said. "That must be pleasant for you—a regular royal progress."

"Oh, I am not visiting, my dear. I am surprised that our dear Sir Hugh did not explain. I have come to lend him the benefit of my experience in running a large household, because his sister, Janet, has married and gone to live in Scotland."

"How kind you are to have come so far to look after him!"

"Yes, it was a tiresome journey, but I am persuaded that he must be glad to have me here, for I found this household in a dreadful state. But I must confess to you that even my presence has not stirred the servants to a much higher standard."

"It seems a rather large place," Laurie said, reaching for the towel Andrew had provided with her water.

"Indeed, although it is not so large as my house in London."

"Surely, though, it is too large for one woman and a few small children to manage," Laurie added, hanging the towel on a hook by the washstand to dry.

"Doubtless, that is so," Lady Marjory agreed. She peered critically at the bed curtains without touching them. "Dear me," she said, "these curtains want shaking. I see cobwebs between the folds."

"It would help, perhaps, if there were more maidservants," Laurie suggested.

"Oh, I dare not hire more, my dear, and although Sir Hugh has a steward, the man says he deals only with the farms and such, not the household. In any event, I warrant that Sir Hugh would very much dislike seeing more women about the place when he is not used to them, and we must not plague him with trivial matters. In my experience, gentlemen dislike change," she went on. "It ruffles their feathers, as you might say, and I'm told that Sir Hugh has a fearsome temper. Indeed, just now, after you left the hall, he spoke rather disagreeably to me."

"He should not have done that," Laurie said, "not when you have been so kind to him. Whatever did he say?"

"Nothing to disturb me, I promise you," Lady Marjory said with an airy wave. "I know that he suffered a tiresome day, so I paid him no heed. Still, it just goes to show how careful we must be, does it not? A woman's duty is to see to a man's comfort, not to irritate him, and poor, dear Sir Hugh has so many duties that he is quite shamefully busy. As if his duties as warden were not enough to consume his time, they are marking all the livestock again in preparation for winter. But it was just the same with Brampton, I promise you," she added with a deep sigh.

Laurie said no more. She had finished her ablutions, so she did what she could to tidy her hair while Lady Marjory wandered around the bedchamber, peeping into the wardrobe, opening coffers, and maintaining a steady stream of commentary. The gist of it was that her ladyship had come to the sad conclusion that Janet Graham—"or Janet Scott as I fear we must call her now"—was not a very competent housekeeper.

"But I should not say such things when she is not here to defend herself," she said when she had run out of things to bemoan. "It is unfair, and I expect that she had much on her mind, poor dear. In any event, she is not here now, and we must do what we can. Are you ready to go downstairs, my dear? You look quite presentable, but I wonder that you do not choose to change your gown for supper."

Laurie said, "I thought Sir Hugh had explained how I came here, madam. When I left home this morning, I had no idea that I would be coming to Brackengill. As a result, I have no clothing other than what I stand in and the cloak that a man-servant took when I entered the hall."

"Mercy, but what will you wear?"

"I expect that my father will send some things to me soon."

"I could lend you something, I suppose," Lady Marjory said doubtfully.

"Not unless you would agree to letting me alter it considerably, madam. I must be six inches shorter than you are, and plumper, too."

"Well, we must think of something," Lady Marjory said.

Laurie believed she would simply have to resign herself to waiting for her things to arrive, but she soon discovered that she had not yet learned the extent of Lady Marjory's resilience to censure.

No sooner had they taken their places at the high table than the older woman said brightly to Sir Hugh, "One must suppose, my dear Sir Hugh, that you know exactly when our dear Laurie's things will arrive."

He blinked at her, clearly at sea. "What things?"

"Godamercy, sir, her clothing and other gear! I know that you are too kind to expect her to live here with nothing to wear but what she wears now."

Sir Hugh shot a rueful look at Laurie. "I forgot," he admitted. "Your father said something to the point, but I do not recall precisely what it was. Have you really nothing more than what you are wearing?"

"I was not expecting to be away longer than two days," Laurie said evenly. "I brought my bed gown but not much else."

He looked at her speculatively for a long moment, then said, "Since you are staying in my sister's room, and you are much the same size as she is, you may take what you like from her wardrobe and chests."

"I . . . I couldn't!"

"Of course you can. Janet has no need of those things any longer. She sent for what she wanted weeks ago, and I've left the rest wherever it lies. You need not fear to upset her. She would be more upset to hear that you were staying here with only the clothes on your back."

"But my father will send my things soon, sir. I'm sure he will."

"Perhaps, but until he does, make use of what you will. We need not discuss this again. Just do as I say."

He gave her a long look, as if he challenged her to defy him, but Laurie met the look silently. It was not her way to challenge authority—not directly, anyway.

Sixteen

The first step that she stepped in,
She stepped in to the knee . . .

At first, Laurie's time at Brackengill proved more pleasant than she had expected. In Janet Graham's wardrobe and coffers she found a number of items that fit her, although the colors that Janet had chosen were not ones that Laurie would have chosen for herself. Most were the newer pale shades that were becoming popular, and she preferred deeper shades. But one pale yellow gown, and another of gray velvet she liked very much.

She discovered that she was smaller in the bosom and hips than Janet was, but that did not matter with clothing that laced, only with items that hooked or buttoned. Their feet were the same size, and she found a pair of boots, and a pair of black satin slippers that fit her perfectly.

Sir Hugh was busy. For the first week, she scarcely laid eyes on him except at mealtimes, and not always then. When he was present, however, he seemed to fill any room he entered, and she did not have to watch for him to know when he was nearby. The very air seemed to vibrate with his presence.

He had said nothing more about examining her, and he had kept his word about behaving toward her as he would a guest. His people treated her with respect, and despite many having attended the proceedings at Lochmaben, most seemed to have no more understanding of her true position than Lady Marjory did. Her ladyship seemed to have put all notion of hostages out of her head. She treated Laurie like one of the family, which was exactly what she believed Laurie was.

Not only did she bring along her own Griselda the morning after Laurie's arrival to help choose clothing from Janet's wardrobe, but her ladyship insisted that Laurie make use of Griselda whenever she had need of her.

Some of Laurie's own clothing and a few trifles arrived from Aylewood at the end of that first week. A brief note from her father accompanied them, telling her to inform him if she wanted anything more than what he had sent. He said nothing about May, so she assumed that her sister still was missing.

Unaccustomed as Laurie was to kindness, she found Lady Marjory's outright devotion to her comfort an entirely new experience. Never before had anyone put so much effort into considering her needs and wishes.

If Laurie entered a room that Lady Marjory occupied, that lady set aside whatever she was doing to inquire if there was aught that Laurie wanted or desired of her. If Laurie sat down, Lady Marjory provided a cushion for her back or a footstool for her feet and offered numerous suggestions as to how she might pass the time. If Laurie yawned, Lady Marjory suggested that she might like to take a nap, and if Laurie's stomach rumbled, Lady Marjory sent instantly to the kitchen for something to stave off the hunger pangs.

If Laurie stayed too long in her bedchamber, she could be sure that Lady Marjory would soon appear, concerned that she might be ailing. And whenever Lady Marjory set foot in Laurie's bedchamber, she instantly examined it, peering at curtains, coffers, and washstand as if to check on the servants' work. Little did she know that Laurie looked after the bedchamber herself.

Indeed, the only thing that Lady Marjory did not attempt to provide for her was real activity, for her ladyship apparently had none to provide. She herself frequently took a tambour

frame in hand but rarely applied her needle, and she showed
no interest in common mending.

When, out of utter boredom, Laurie suggested that she
might help with the mending, Lady Marjory said that such
work was not suitable for a lady of gentle breeding and that
Griselda would do whatever mending she required. Although
Laurie had been thinking more of household mending, and
perhaps Sir Hugh's, she did not feel that such an explanation
would impress Lady Marjory.

So it was that, despite her ladyship's company and kindness,
by the end of Laurie's first week at Brackengill, she was thoroughly bored from lack of exercise and activity. After she had
dressed each morning and swept her room, she found herself
with little to do but converse with Lady Marjory.

For a time, that conversation at least provided entertainment,
because Lady Marjory was content to talk at length about London and London ways. However, Laurie soon realized that her
ladyship lacked an observing eye and had paid heed only to
her own comfort and that of family members in her household.
Since she was accustomed to having a steward and a houseful
of servants at her beck and bay, even that subject soon proved
a limited one.

The fact was that Lady Marjory preferred indolence to most
other ways of occupying her time. She exerted herself only to
question Sir Hugh's activities and to make suggestions as to
how she might aid him.

Sir Hugh, however, seemed receptive to few of those suggestions. Lady Marjory's entrance into a room, Laurie noted,
was frequently his signal to leave it.

Lady Marjory also occasionally looked over Meggie's shoulder in the kitchen and offered advice to her. Most of it was
either impractical or impossible, as far as Laurie could tell
from her ladyship's comments and observations afterward, but
she was sure that all of it was kindly meant.

Hitherto, her ladyship's notion of supervising a household
apparently had comprised little more than dropping a hint to
her steward. Since Sir Hugh's steward had paid no heed what-

soever to the household at Brackengill since Janet Graham had taken charge of it, Lady Marjory's hints fell on Laurie's ears or Meggie's.

"The rushes in this hall seem only to deteriorate," she said one morning some ten days after Laurie's arrival. "They were malodorous when I arrived and have now reached such a state that I doubt if anything can help them."

"Doubtless, they should be replaced, madam," Laurie replied.

"Yes, but who is to do it, my dear? Griselda will not, and from what I see of that Meggie, she has all she can do to put food on the tables each day."

"Perhaps if you were to mention it to Sir Hugh when he returns this evening from Bewcastle . . ."

"Now, my dear," Lady Marjory said, "I have told you before, gentlemen do not want to be burdened with such things."

"Well, now there are two of us, madam," Laurie said with a smile. "Let me see what I can do."

"Very well, my dear. I believe I shall just go up and confer with Griselda."

Feeling a sudden, welcome sense of purpose, Laurie went downstairs to the kitchen to seek Meggie's advice.

She liked Meggie. English or not, the woman reminded her of Lucy Elliot and Lucy's friends. She was comfortable, direct, and undemanding. Meggie did not look down her nose at one the way Blanche did, and Meggie smiled just as warmly at Laurie as she did at her own children.

Laurie had met them all. Nancy seemed like a miniature Meggie, Andrew reminded her strongly of Sym Elliot, and solemn Peter spent much of his time looking after merry little John, who was two. The baby, Susan, being no more than a few months old, slept away much of each day in a basket near the kitchen fire.

Laurie found Meggie shelling peas. A haunch of mutton roasted slowly over the kitchen fire, its aroma filling the large chamber. Voices and splashing sounds nearby suggested that two or three of her children were busy in the scullery.

"The rushes in the hall need replacing, Meggie," Laurie said when the two had exchanged greetings. "Who ought to attend to that for us? Do you know?"

"Nay, mistress, I've no time t' think about rushes. The master ordered 'em changed for the summer in June, but he's said naught about 'em since."

"They are in a wretched state," Laurie said. "The men let their dogs run free in there and the bones they toss them—and other, worse stuff—have got mixed in. Someone told me that Mistress Janet did not allow dogs in during mealtimes."

"Aye, she wouldna like it," Meggie said, frowning. "But Sir Hugh takes no notice o' such things."

"Men don't," Laurie said. "I know that you have no time to attend to it, but perhaps you can advise me what to do. I just need some lads to rake out the old rushes and strew new ones."

Turning her head toward the scullery, Meggie shouted, "Nan, Peter—where's our Andrew?"

"I'll find 'im for ye, Mam," Peter volunteered, darting out and around to the door that led to the yard, ignoring the shriek of protest that followed him from the scullery.

Appearing in the scullery doorway, Nancy muttered darkly, "Now, we'll likely lose him, too, for the day. And me wi' these pots and wee John t' watch."

"He'll come back," Meggie said placidly.

And Peter soon darted back in again to announce, "Our Andrew's gone off somewheres, mayhap to Bewcastle wi' Sir Hugh. But I brung ye Geordie, Mam."

"I dinna think Andrew went wi' Sir Hugh, mistress," the man at Peter's heels said as he entered, pulling off his cap and bobbing his head in Laurie's direction. "More likely, he went over Haggbeck way. He said they'd still be marking beasts there. I thought they'd finished, m'self, but the lad likes helpin' 'em, any road."

Laurie explained about the rushes, and Geordie agreed at once to have a couple of lads rake out the old ones that very afternoon.

When he left, Peter moved to follow him, but Meggie intercepted him and sent him back to the scullery. "When the pots are scrubbed, you can take Wee John outside to play for a time," she said when he protested.

Surprised by how easily she had resolved the matter of rushes, Laurie wondered why it had posed such difficulty for Lady Marjory.

"Has not her ladyship mentioned those rushes before now?" she asked.

With a rueful grimace, Meggie said, "Truth be, mistress, I dinna pay her much mind. Her ladyship never says just what she wants, and like as not, she doesna want nothing at all—only to natter on about this or that."

"I see," Laurie said, not altogether certain that she did.

"Aye, well, it's enough to make a woman daft," Meggie assured her. "She'll ask if I dinna think summat needs more salt in it or tell me her woman'd be glad to find a chore for our Nan if she's ever lookin' for summat to do. Nan doesna ha' to seek her chores. We've both more than we can manage."

Laurie felt a twinge of guilt, and it was not the first one she had felt since arriving at Brackengill. Having watched Meggie and Nancy scurry about, trying to do chores that required at least four women to do them properly, she had begun soon after her arrival to experience the same uneasiness that she had felt at first when visiting Lucy and Davy Elliot's cottage. It had not taken many such visits before she had demanded that Lucy let her help with chores. Nor did she hesitate now to make a similar suggestion, albeit not quite so bluntly.

"Meggie," she said, "it is absurd for you and Nancy to try to do everything without more help. Now that Lady Marjory and I are here, surely some of the other women who used to work here would come back."

"Aye, perhaps, did the master ask them to," Meggie said. "Perhaps ye could ask him, mistress."

"Lady Marjory said we should not," Laurie told her. "She

said that he does not like to be plagued about such things, but he is bound to realize sooner or later that Brackengill needs more maidservants. In the meantime, I can help you."

"Sir Hugh wouldna like that," Meggie said flatly.

"He need not even know," Laurie replied. "Please, Meggie, I have no needlework to occupy me, and even if I did, I'm not much good at it. But I can tend a fire, and I can scrub pots and sweep, and shake curtains, and help with laundry."

"Ye never did them things at Aylewood, mistress. Ye needna try telling me ye did."

Laurie grinned. "That's true. I did as little as possible. I don't get on with my stepmother, so I evaded the duties she set me whenever I could get away with it."

Meggie's eyes danced. She said, "Nae doubt, and I warrant my bairns would like t' ken how ye managed that."

"My stepmother would say that I ran away from them," Laurie said.

Meggie's humorous look faded. "I dinna hold wi' running awa' from chores," she said. "Ye'll no be teaching my lot such ways, Mistress Laura."

"Certainly not," Laurie said. "You'd demand my head on a platter."

"I would, that," Meggie agreed with a direct look. "Can ye turn a spit?"

"I can," Laurie said, stepping to the hearth to show her that she could.

"Ye're a strange one, right enough," Meggie said, watching her. "I'll say this for ye, though. Ye'll be a sight more helpful than her ladyship, for all that she came here to run the household."

"This household is not what she is used to," Laurie said gently.

"Aye, 'tis true, that," Meggie agreed. "Well, then, ye can do as ye please, mistress, but dinna say I didna warn ye. The master willna like it."

"The master will never even notice," Laurie said confidently. "He barely notices that I am living here."

* * *

Hugh had not expected to give much notice to his hostage. Having introduced her to Lady Marjory and explained that she could not leave the castle, he had believed that his dealings with her were, for the most part, at an end.

That had not proved to be the case, however. Not only did Lady Marjory seem incapable of comprehending that Laura Halliot was a hostage and not really his lawful wife but Hugh found himself unable to ignore Mistress Halliot's presence at Brackengill.

He had only to approach the great hall to know if she was inside or not. Some instinct gave warning of her presence and lifted his spirits, too. He told himself that it was merely that she provided a buffer between him and his aunt's incessant, intrusive conversation, but he knew it was more than that. He liked to look at her. He waited for her smile, and when it came, it warmed him to his toes.

Finding that his gaze came to rest on her with increasing frequency, he mentally chided himself, only to find his loins stirring in protest at the thought that he should pay her less heed. He realized that Halliot had been wiser than he knew in insisting on the handfasting—and on the *tocher,* as well.

As a result, Hugh had turned his thoughts more determinedly than ever toward his duties outside the castle walls, returning only to dine or sup, and to sleep. He soon found himself welcoming any duty or invitation that would take him away from Brackengill for even a few hours. Thus, he had accepted the invitation to dine at Bewcastle that day with Sir Edward Nixon and his lady, even though Sir Edward had warned him that he would be entertaining Lord Scrope at his table, too.

When Hugh presented himself to Sir Edward, Scrope stood beside his host.

"How goes it with your lovely hostage?" Scrope asked with uncharacteristic cheerfulness as they shook hands.

"Well enough," Hugh answered evenly.

Others were present, including Lord Eure, and Hugh glanced around, exchanging nods, before he realized that Scrope was waiting for him to say more. "Did you expect me to have trouble with her, my lord?"

"Not a bit," Scrope replied with a grin. "I just wondered how you are enjoying married life."

Hearing Eure gasp and Sir Edward stifle a cough, Hugh avoided their gazes, saying, "You are mistaken if you think that was a true wedding, your lordship. I agreed to the ritual only because the lass's father insisted. I'll have no cause to pay *tocher* at the end of the year and a day. Indeed, I doubt that I shall be burdened with her even half that long. Her sister will turn up soon."

" 'Tis you who mistake the matter," Scrope said, his good humor unimpaired. "Whilst we may not allow such marriages here in England, between an English man and woman, we do recognize all forms of Scottish marriage for Scotsmen, and the damned Scots believe that one took place at Lochmaben. I doubt that you will gain support on either side of the line by trying to pretend that you are not married to the wench. She is legally your wife, Hugh. Make the most of it."

"Would you have me take her about the countryside as my lady, paying bride visits?" Hugh demanded.

"If it suits you to do so, certainly," Scrope said. "Pray, do not forget, however, that you have guaranteed to produce her in her sister's stead at the next wardens' meeting. If the jury decides then that May Halliot is unlikely ever to return, then 'tis Lady Graham who must pay for her crime."

"Only if that same jury manages to find her guilty," Hugh said curtly.

"Oh, I'll wager anything you like that we can provide them with sufficient evidence," Scrope said. Looking sly, he added, "I should perhaps tell you that I took the liberty of informing her majesty and the Privy Council that you have married a hostage who may well hang for murder. Without your uncle Brampton at hand to whisper in her ear, I doubt that Her Majesty will express much sympathy for you. What do you think?"

"How dare you—!" Hugh began.

Sir Edward gripped his shoulder hard and said hastily, "Forgive me, gentlemen, but we have other important matters to discuss this afternoon."

Hugh glowered at Scrope but said grimly, "What matters?"

"That Liddesdale lot of Buccleuch's have raided north Tynedale again," Sir Edward said. "Six of our men died, and folks say they saw a red cloak leading the reivers. They want something done, but Eure insists that he has resigned as warden. Therefore, I suggest that we must decide what the devil we can do about it."

"I'll tell you the first thing we should do," Scrope said. "We should write to Sir William Halliot of Aylewood and demand that he arrest Buccleuch."

When the company greeted these words with stunned silence, he went on with a self-righteous air, "Word reached Her Majesty soon after that last raid, and she has renewed her demands to James that he deal with Buccleuch. This time, he had better do so promptly, or I cannot answer for Elizabeth's fury. James must order Buccleuch's arrest and turn him over to English authorities."

Visibly unimpressed, Lord Eure said, "Are you saying that we should tell the people of the middle march that they must await the Scottish King's decision?"

"I said naught of the sort," Scrope said testily. "Sir Hugh, here, will attend to the Liddesdale men and Rabbie Redcloak straightaway. If your men or the men of Tynedale want to accompany him, they are at liberty to do so."

Choosing his words carefully so as not to offend Eure, Hugh said, "I'd want to know who the men are before agreeing to lead them, my lord. In my experience, reckless raiding only leads to more violence. Neither side prevails for long."

Scrope shrugged. "I'll leave the details to you, Hugh. That's what deputy wardens are for, is it not? Just get the job done, and teach those Scotch ruffians to keep to themselves in the future."

"I wish you well in *that* endeavor," Lord Eure said with a bitter smile.

"Perhaps your pretty little hostage can help," Scrope said, grinning again.

Hugh did not bother to respond, and Sir Edward suggested that they all take places at the table to partake of the midday meal.

Scrope left as soon as he and his party had dined, but Hugh lingered to talk with Lord Eure and Sir Edward. It was Eure who told him that the six Graham headsmen whom Scrope had sent to answer to the Privy Council for the raid on Carlisle were on their way home again.

"Scrope received a message from London, relaying the news. He swears he will still find a way to hang them, but I think your lads are safe for a time, Hugh. As for going after Liddesdale again, you must do as you think best. I've little to offer by way of help, and you noted that Scrope did not offer to raise an army against them again, but perhaps you will think of something that will work."

"Perhaps," Hugh agreed. He had not thought of anything by the time the men separated and prepared to depart to their homes, however.

The news that the Privy Council had released the Graham men cheered Hugh, but he was not so cheerful when he thought about dealing with Liddesdale and Rabbie Redcloak again. He had suspected for some time that Redcloak was actually his brother-in-law, Sir Quinton Scott of Broadhaugh, because nothing had been heard from Rabbie since Quinton's marriage to Janet. If Rabbie had begun to stir again, though, something would have to be done about him.

Later that afternoon, Laurie stood at the hall threshold, gazing at the newly lain rushes with pleasure. She had found new ones drying in the long garret, and discovered, as well, that Janet Graham had hung bundles of fragrant herbs to dry with

them. The herbs mixed with the fresh rushes filled the hall
with their fragrance.

Lady Marjory, fresh from her afternoon nap, descended the
stairs behind her, saying cheerfully, " 'Tis an odd place to
stand, my dear. What are you doing?"

"Just smell them, my lady," Laurie said. " 'Tis rosemary
and some other herbs that I do not know as well. They smell
delightful, do they not?"

"Indeed, and it is time and more that someone replaced the
rushes in here," Lady Marjory said. "I have said so any number of times, for I knew that our dear Sir Hugh would prefer
it so, but I thought that Meggie woman would never get round
to it. Perhaps I have wronged her, though. I know that she is
busy."

"Indeed, she is," Laurie said, deciding not to tell her that
she had arranged for the change. "Will you excuse me for a
time before supper, madam? I have some things that I must
do before we eat."

"Oh, indeed, my dear, do as you please. This is your home
now, after all, and you should arrange everything just as you
like. If you need advice, do not hesitate to ask me. I quite
enjoy being useful, you know."

"Thank you," Laurie said. "I think you will be quite comfortable if you sit here now, but do not let them remove the
guards from the fires. There is a draft every time someone
enters from below, and these rushes are as dry as tinder. Oh,
and remind them all that the dogs must not come in whilst we
eat."

Lady Marjory nodded vaguely, whereupon Laurie hurried
off to the kitchen to find Meggie shaking sugar over crumbled
bread in a big wooden bowl.

"Ye'll no be supping till six the night, unless Sir Hugh returns afore then from Bewcastle," Meggie said when she saw
Laurie.

"That is unlikely, I think," Laurie said. "What are you making?"

" 'Tis nobbut bread and milk, cooked the way Sir Hugh

likes it," Meggie said. "He's a liking for sweets now and again. I'll do some mutton collops from that leg we roasted for the midday meal. My Andrew's not back yet, but I've put Peter and one of the other lads to plucking chickens for tomorrow, and Nan's in the scullery, shelling more peas."

"Do the collops only if Sir Hugh returns for supper," Laurie said. "Lady Marjory and I and the men can make do with cold, sliced mutton and peas. We can put out a cheese for those who want more."

"Aye, mistress," Meggie said, pouring milk over the sugared bread crumbs. Leaving it to stand, she began to count the old bread loaves they would use for trenchers, while Laurie hefted a kettle of hot water to the swey over the fire.

She helped with whatever Meggie would allow, thoroughly enjoying herself until Meggie said with a wry smile, "Ye've got grease from the spit on your gown, mistress. If ye're aiming t' change it afore supper, ye'd best do it soon. We've put it back an hour, as it is, waiting for the master to return. 'Tis a wonder her ladyship hasna been down here, demanding to ken when we'll sup."

"Godamercy," Laurie said, looking down at herself. "I must look a fright, and I'd lost all track of time. I'll go at once."

"Nancy," Meggie said as Laurie wiped her hands on a towel, "go and tell our Peter and Andrew to come in now, and to bring some others to help set up the tables. I'll give John his supper whilst they do, and you can ha' yours, as well."

"Thank you, Meggie," Laurie said with a smile. "I enjoyed helping you."

"Ye're daft, mistress, but ye're right welcome."

Laurie turned toward the service stair but stopped when a deep male voice said urgently, "Meggie, they've taken your Andrew!"

Turning sharply, she saw Geordie, his body filling the doorway to the yard. He paid her no heed, though. His attention was riveted on Meggie.

She stared back at him, speechless, her cheeks devoid of color.

"Who took him," Laurie demanded. "Where?"

"Scrope," Geordie said curtly. "Said he means to hang the wee lad."

A shout from the yard drew his attention.

Laurie saw Meggie's expression change to one of hope. "What is it?" Laurie said. "Do you think they've brought Andrew back?"

"Nay," Geordie said. "The master's home. He'll soon sort it out. I'll go and tell him straightaway."

"I'm going with you," Laurie said, tossing aside the towel she still held.

Seventeen

The next step that she stepped in,
She stepped to the middle . . .

It was growing dark when Hugh and his men rode into the bailey at Brackengill. He was hungry again and hoped they had something good for supper. Scrope had put him right off his appetite at Bewcastle.

He heard one of the men shout to Geordie that he was back, but he paid no heed, thinking only of going in, taking off his jack-of-plate, and eating his supper.

Dismounting, he handed the reins to a lad who ran up to take them. But as he turned toward the main tower, he saw Geordie hurrying toward him from the kitchen wing. Following, her skirts swirling around her slim legs, was his hostage.

Hugh noted that Mistress Halliot looked rather disheveled, as if she were in some agitation. Wisps of hair had escaped her cap, and her right cheek was smudged with soot or something similar. Her smock lay open above her low-cut bodice, and her soft white breasts heaved in her effort to keep up with Geordie.

Alarmed, Hugh strode to meet them.

Ned Rowan caught up with him as well.

"What's amiss, Geordie?" Hugh asked, forcing his gaze to his henchman.

"That bastard Scrope's arrested Meggie's Andrew," Geordie said.

Hugh glanced at Rowan and saw the man's fists clench.

His own jaw tightened, and a muscle twitched high in his cheek. He liked Andrew, and the lad was young, not yet ten years of age.

"Does Meggie know yet?" he asked Geordie.

Mistress Halliot answered, saying, "Aye, sir, she does. She is beside herself with terror for the lad. Geordie told us that Scrope means to hang Andrew, but surely he won't hang a laddie so young."

"He won't if I can stop him," Hugh said grimly. To Geordie, he said, "Have you given orders to the men yet?"

"Nay, master. I only just got back m'self, and when the men on the wall saw ye coming, I waited t' talk wi' ye first, but I did think I should tell Meggie."

"How the devil did they take him?" Hugh demanded.

Geordie flinched at the tone and shot a wary glance at Rowan before he said, "The lad were awa' nigh the whole day, master. I thought he'd gone over Haggbeck way to help 'em mark kine there. Howsomever, when one o' the men came here wi' a message, I learned the wee laddie'd no been there at all."

"Where was the young devil then?" Rowan snapped.

"By what I can make out, captain, he were in that thicket near Granny Fenicke's cottage," Geordie said, evading Rowan's sharp gaze. "It were one o' Scrope's land sergeants, Francis Potts, that grabbed the lad, master. But by what Granny Fenicke said to me, 'is lordship were there, too."

"It must have happened whilst they were on their way back to Carlisle from Bewcastle," Hugh said. "But why would they take Andrew?"

Geordie hesitated, shooting another wary glance at Rowan. When Hugh moved impatiently, however, the man said hastily, "Granny said Potts told her Andrew tried to murder 'im! Said he would ha' murdered Scrope, too. 'Cause he's a Graham, she said, Scrope means t' hang the lad straightway when they get back."

"But that must be nonsense," Laura exclaimed. "Andrew?

Murder? That charge is more absurd than the one against my sister."

"Aye, perhaps, mistress," Geordie agreed. "But they do say the wee rascal fired a pistol at them. Granny even showed me the one they say he fired. Said one o' Potts's men flung it into the thicket when they took it from the lad."

"When I get my hands on him," Rowan snarled, "I'll soon teach him about murder—and about firing pistols without any-one's leave to do so!"

"I just hope you *can* get your hands on him," Laura said. Turning to Hugh with a worried frown, she added, "But what could he have been thinking, sir?"

"I don't know," Hugh said gruffly, wishing he could give a better answer, one that would smooth the frown away. "Ned or Geordie might know."

Rowan said with a rueful sigh, "Doubtless, he thought Potts and his men were reivers, mistress. Andrew's fair got a bee in his head about shooting himself a Scots reiver. He's talked about it ever since the bluidy Scots killed his da last year. The bairn wants revenge for Jock's death."

Hugh said, "But where did he get the pistol?"

Rowan looked at Geordie.

"It were a wheel-lock," Geordie said. "I left it wi' Granny Fenicke."

"Likely it were Jock's wheel-lock, then," Rowan said. "Meggie left it at the cottage, but Andrew's always in and out o' the place and there'd be none to stop him from taking it." He added grimly, "Scrope willna waste time, master. Since the raid, he's been set on hanging as many Grahams as he can."

A vision of Janet flitted through Hugh's mind. If she were to learn of Andrew's predicament, she might well persuade Buccleuch to ride for Carlisle again. She might even go herself again if Quin were not at home to stop her, and Hugh could not let Scrope get his hands on anyone so close to him.

"Order fresh horses saddled," he told Rowan. "We'll take a score of the lads with us, but tell them not to dally. I want to leave within the hour. Come inside now, mistress," he added. "You should not be out here."

"Should I not?" She looked at him, her dark eyes wide.

He supposed he looked murderous. He certainly felt murderous. But he did his best to speak more gently to her.

"It is chilly," he said, offering her his arm. To his surprise, she wiped her hand on her skirt before placing it on his forearm.

When they entered the hall, he half expected to find Lady Marjory lying in wait, but the only ones there were two lads setting trenchers on the tables for supper. The thought of food reminded him that he should speak to Meggie.

"You go along upstairs now," he said to Laurie. "You'll want to tidy yourself before you have your supper, and I must go down to Meggie."

Instead of obeying, Mistress Halliot turned and put a gentle hand flat against his chest as she looked up into his eyes.

He felt his loins stir, and swallowed hard. "Aye, mistress?"

"You will save him, won't you, sir?" Her voice was low-pitched, throaty. Her gaze held his. He could hear the echo of Scrope's words in his head:

"She's your wife, Hugh. Make the most of it."

Resisting a strong impulse to put his arms around her and promise her whatever she asked of him, he said evenly instead, "I will do what I can. Carlisle is less than ten miles from here, so even in darkness, the journey will take only a couple of hours. I'll not try to get back tonight, though, so don't look for me. We'll return in the morning, come what may."

She nodded and turned away, and Hugh went reluctantly to the kitchen.

Jock's Meggie was stirring something in the big pot that hung on its swey over the kitchen fire, her gray overskirt and red-flannel underskirt kilted back to protect them from the flames. Strands of reddish-blond hair had escaped from her cap, and wisped around her face in much the same way that Laura's had. Nearby, her daughter Nancy cut vegetables at a small table. Her face was streaked with tears.

In an alcove near the fire, Meggie's baby slept peacefully in its wicker basket. The kitchen was warm and redolent with odors of roast mutton and baked bread. Hugh realized again how hungry he was.

Meggie raised her free hand to brush hair from her eyes and saw him. Straightening hastily, she bobbed a curtsy and said anxiously, "Master, what's to be done about my Andrew?"

"I'll get him back, Meggie."

From behind him, Nancy said angrily, "That Scrope's taken him, as if our Andrew was a Scotsman!"

Hugh turned to her and said gently, "Aye, lassie, but as I told your mam, I mean to bring him home again."

"Aye, ye will," Nancy said confidently, "and if ye canna do it, Mistress Janet will. There now, dinna cry, Mam. We'll get him back afore the cat can lick its ear."

Hugh realized with shock that the child had more faith in Janet's ability than his to retrieve Andrew. Exchanging a look with Meggie, he said, "Don't fret now. We'll get him back."

"Aye, master." Meggie's tone was subdued. "I'll pack food for ye to take wi' ye, shall I?"

"Thank you. Send someone to fetch a couple of lads to help you, and to carry it to the horses. I want to be away within the hour."

He did not linger, nor did she try to delay him.

Forty minutes later, having successfully eluded Lady Marjory, he rode out, followed by twenty of his men, all well armed and accoutered for battle. Not only did they usually dress so when they went outside the castle wall but with both Meggie and Laura depending on him to succeed, he would bring the walls of Carlisle down on Scrope's head, if necessary, to get Andrew back.

The moon had risen when they reached the great castle perched on its hilltop above the River Eden, giving light enough to let the guards at the gate recognize the banner of their master's deputy. After a slight delay, while they sum-

moned their captain to confirm Hugh's identity, the gates
swung wide, allowing the party from Brackengill to clatter
into the bailey.

Looking up at the massive walls around them, Ned Rowan
muttered, "They say Carlisle be the strongest castle in all Britain."

"Aye," Hugh said, "despite Scrope's cheese-paring mainte-
nance."

Carlisle was not a showy castle of towers and crenellated
battlements but a great square red keep that squatted like a
piece of living rock behind plain, massive walls that extended
to girdle the city. It was a castle built to keep enemies out and
prisoners in, and in general, it succeeded well at both tasks.

The only time in Hugh's memory that an enemy had
breeched its walls and a prisoner had escaped was the recent
raid, and the little band of raiders had succeeded with Scrope
himself on the premises. Fearing that a massive army had invaded his stronghold, the warden had barricaded himself in
his hall.

Dismounting in the inner bailey, Hugh entered the hall, accompanied only by Ned Rowan. The great chamber was filled
with men, laughter, and an air of celebration. The supper tables
were still up, and ale was flowing freely, for Scrope was entertaining company. The porter blew his horn to announce the
new arrivals.

"Sir Hugh Graham of Brackengill and his captain, your
lordship."

"In good time, Hugh," Scrope shouted, gesturing him forward. "I expected you sooner, but you come in excellent time,
nonetheless."

Relief surged through Hugh. Despite his confident words
to Laura and to Meggie, he had half expected to learn that
Scrope had already hanged the boy.

"I would have a word in private with you," he said when
he could make himself heard above the din. He recognized
captains from Brougham, Dalton, Muncaster, as well as his
cousin Musgrave from Edgelair.

Scrope grinned and raised his mug, saying, "So you've learned about my newest Graham captive, have you?"

"He is my kinsman," Hugh said, his voice carrying easily to the others in the great chamber. "I have come to plead his case to you, my lord."

"He tried to murder Francis Potts. He could have killed me, as well."

"I suppose I should be gratified that you credit him with so much skill," Hugh said sardonically. "Are you aware that he is only nine years old?"

"He fired upon my party," Scrope said stubbornly. "He deserves hanging."

"He deserves a skelping for taking the pistol without permission," Hugh said. "Had he actually shot anyone with it, my lord, you might have cause to punish him, but he thought he was shooting Scots reivers."

"He was shooting at my men," Scrope said indignantly. "Doubtless, he would have shot me, as well."

Noting Scrope's choice of words, and striving to retain his calm, Hugh said, "But you were not riding with your advance party, my lord. I'll warrant that you were some distance behind them, as usual. Moreover, you must admit that Francis Potts does not accouter his men well. They do look like thieves."

Laughter erupted in more than one corner of the hall, and several of the men sitting at the high table with Scrope grinned openly.

Sir Francis Musgrave said with a chuckle, "Cousin Hugh's right about that, my lord. I say let the young rascal go. His father should tend to him."

"Who is his father?" Scrope asked.

"A deceased tenant of mine, Jock Graham," Hugh said, adding, "He fell in a fray last year, against the Scots. The lad feels his loss sorely."

One of the others at the high table said, "Seems a pity to hang such a young lad, my lord. Sounds as if he need only learn to tell enemy from friend."

"The trouble with you, Graham, is that you're devilish soft,"

Scrope said, swallowing what remained in his mug and setting it down with a snap. "Very well, I'll give you the young rascal, for I've no doubt that you'll see him punished."

"Thank you, my lord,"

"Aye, well don't think I'm doing it to please you." Signing to one of his menservants, he sent the man to fetch Andrew, then said, "I'm doing it because I don't want anything to spoil my celebration. Would you not like to learn its cause?"

Hugh nodded. He could scarcely believe he had succeeded so easily and dared not trust himself to speak. Nothing he might say could improve the situation, but he could easily, and quite inadvertently, anger Scrope into changing his mind about the boy. Scrope was entirely capable of going back on his word out of spite.

He was grinning now, though. "I'd no sooner returned here this afternoon" he said, "than I received word from our ambassador in Edinburgh that Jamie has agreed to turn Buccleuch over to us."

"That surprises me," Hugh admitted.

"It was inevitable," Scrope said. "Not only did the villain raid Tynedale, killing and looting like a wild man, but after refusing to appear at the wardens' meeting to answer for his crimes, he dared to repeat them. He made it impossible for James to refuse a moment longer."

"I share your joy in the news, my lord," Hugh said. "Has King James actually agreed at last to send Buccleuch to London?"

"Not London yet, unfortunately," Scrope said. "Sir Robert Cary, warden of our eastern marches, is to hold him in ward at Berwick until Buccleuch can arrange pledges to guarantee that he will stand to answer for his crimes. In due time, he will answer for raiding Carlisle, I promise you."

"But Berwick's only a few miles from the border!" Hugh protested. "Moreover, Buccleuch can produce such pledges in a trice."

"Aye, and doubtless Cary will provide luxury on the same scale that Buccleuch enjoyed at Blackness," Scrope agreed bitterly. "Still, we can expect no more at this point, and at least it will get Buccleuch out of my hair again."

"You may come to rue his absence," Hugh said. "He is the only man in Scotland capable of keeping Liddesdale in order."

Scrope shrugged. "You worry too much, but without your uncle to speak for you in London, your days as my deputy might be numbered, in any event. 'Tis a pity Loder's no longer with us. He'd have liked to take your place. Still, if those villains set foot in England again, I'll deal with them if you and Eure cannot."

Hugh felt Rowan stir at his side and curbed his own temper with difficulty.

Scrope added, "I can see you don't like the sound of that, but that only proves what I've said before." Loudly enough for everyone to hear, he added, "You're soft, Hugh Graham, and you'll never be aught else. Here's your laddie now. Take him whilst I'm still in a pleasant frame of mind, and go home to that pretty little Scotch wife of yours."

"As you wish, my lord," Hugh said, bowing stiffly.

He left the hall, struggling so to contain his fury that he scarcely heeded whether Ned Rowan or Andrew followed him. Only when the men awaiting them raised a cheer at the sight of the boy did he collect his wits. Even then, he knew that Scrope's arrest of Andrew was not what infuriated him now. It was the man's disrespectful reference to Laura.

"I'll take the lad up with me, master," Ned Rowan said, as they reached the others. "I've some few things to say to him."

Hugh nodded, knowing he could safely leave Andrew to Ned. The big man cared for the lad as if he were his own son.

"Hugh Graham!"

Turning at the shout, he saw with annoyance that his cousin Musgrave was striding toward him from the hall entrance.

"Are you riding back to Brackengill tonight?" Musgrave said as soon as he was near enough to make himself heard.

Hugh had not given his schedule much thought since telling Laura that he would not return before morning. At that time, however, he had expected that he would have to endure protracted dealings with Scrope, but their meeting had taken little time at all. It was early yet, no more than half past nine or ten.

"Aye, we will," he said. "We can be there near about midnight. Why?"

"I brought only a small party of men with me," Musgrave said. "I arrived this afternoon, only to learn that his lordship was away. When he returned, I stayed to celebrate with him, because I had too few men with me to risk riding back after dark. Still, I'd as lief be on my way if we can ride with you and perchance spend the remainder of the night at Brackengill."

"Suit yourself, cousin," Hugh said. "You're welcome enough. I thank you for taking the lad's part in there."

"I'd my own reasons for that," Musgrave said with a chuckle. Turning his head, he shouted, "Tell the men to fetch out the horses! We'll be leaving at once."

He turned back to Hugh then and said, "You've been wroth wi' me these months past, saying I never should ha' arrested Quinton Scott against the truce. Oh, aye, I'll admit it, though I have not afore now. I did just break the truce, but 'twas a Scot dropped a word in my ear, saying he were Rabbie Redcloak."

"Even if he had been," Hugh said, "the truce on such days serves us all. When we break it, we not only give the Scots cause to distrust us on future Truce Days but we have no one to blame but ourselves when they break a truce."

"Aye, well, it's done, and there's an end to it," Musgrave said heartily. "We'll not speak of it again. I've heard yet another rumor, however."

"Indeed, sir, and what might that be?" Hugh said, knowing what was coming.

"Scrope tells me ye've got married, that's what. I said it were nowt o' the sort, but ye'll tell me plain, Hugh. Ha' ye been fool enough t' marry a Scot?"

Hugh hesitated, faced with a dilemma. Observing that the man with whom he had left his horse was holding out the reins to him, he took them and mounted. At the same time, he saw that Musgrave's men were already coming with his horse and their own. Realizing that his cousin must have sent word to have them make ready before Hugh had left the hall, he wondered what else the man had in mind.

Hugh knew that telling Musgrave that he and Laurie were married would end any hope his cousin might still harbor of marrying one of his ugly daughters to him. Nevertheless, he did not want to make more of his relationship with Laura than he should, lest she or her father come to hear of it. He did not need new problems.

Accordingly, he said bluntly, "We are handfasted, sir; that is all. Her father insisted on it to protect her reputation. She is a hostage, as you must know, pledged for her sister who may have committed murder and has disappeared."

Musgrave mounted his own horse and drew it in alongside Hugh's as he said, "Oh, aye, Scrope told me as much, but the ceremony was legal, was it not?"

"Yes, such as it was," Hugh said. "So long as we do not produce a child, however, we can end it when we choose, anytime short of a year and a day."

"But Scrope says ye'll ha' to pay an amount equal to the lass's dowry if ye touch her afore then and do not marry her. He's offered a wager, lad, that ye'll take the lass rather than pay the *tocher*. I've no doubt 'twould be a mort o' money."

"Scrope would offer a wager on which of two raindrops will first reach the ground," Hugh said. "There is another solution, however. I will not touch her."

"Ye might manage that if she were one o' my lasses," Musgrave said. "They be a mite plain, but Scrope says she's a little beauty."

"I suppose she's passable," Hugh said, aware that his body was stirring in protest of this understatement, and trying to ignore the discomfort.

"Aye, well, I'll see for myself now, won't I?" Musgrave said.

* * *

Laurie remained unaware of the men's return until morning. When Nancy came at her usual time, she discovered that Sir Hugh not only had recovered Andrew but had brought his cousin Musgrave home with him, as well. Dressing hurriedly, she went down to Meggie, finding her going about her work with a light step and a wide smile.

Hugging her, Laurie said, "I'm so glad, Meggie! Where is he?"

"In the scullery, scrubbing pots," Meggie said, still grinning. "Ned Rowan told him he's no to show his face in the yard again till he says he may."

"You must be glad to have him near," Laurie said.

"Aye, for all he's scowlin' over them pots."

"What can I do to help? Nancy told me that Sir Hugh's cousin returned with him late last night."

"Aye, but the master's up and about already, and Sir Francis be still abed. Likely, her ladyship will be down afore that man is. He's been here afore, and I ken him well. If he stirs afore noon, I'll be surprised. Still, his men and the others will want feeding, and we've fresh apples in the cellar for their dinner. Ye can fetch some if ye like, but then ye'd best go up and break your fast, mistress. Else we'll ha' her ladyship down here, looking for ye."

Laurie obeyed and took her seat at the high table beside Lady Marjory with a sense of accomplishment. Looking around the hall, she felt a thrill of real pleasure and was able to chat amiably with her ladyship for the duration of the meal and much of the morning. She rather hoped that Sir Hugh would return so that she could judge his reaction to the fresh rushes, for in his haste over Andrew, he had not noticed them the night before. He did not return to the hall, however, and she could think of no good reason to send for him, since his guest still had not got out of bed.

Her ladyship announced soon after eleven that she would go up to confer with Griselda. "For with such a fine gentleman joining us for dinner, my dear Laura, one wants to look one's best. Did Sir Hugh chance to mention whether Sir Francis is married?"

"No, madam, but since you yourself mentioned that he has three daughters, I must suppose that he is."

"Oh, but my dearest one, I've got two daughters and no husband," Lady Marjory pointed out. "It is possible that poor Sir Francis lost his wife in childbed or to some dreaded disease and is trying to raise his daughters by himself."

"Perhaps you should ask him."

Lady Marjory looked doubtful but bustled away, and Laurie went to the kitchen again to see if she could help Meggie prepare the noonday meal.

Meggie allowed her to count trenchers and to stir the barley soup on the swey. But Laurie had been there less than half an hour when Meggie said in much the same tone that she might have used in talking to one of her children, "Go and make yourself dainty now, mistress."

"I've done very little."

"Ye've company to dine wi' ye, so ye must go. I've fed the babe, and my lads can help with the serving. Moreover, Ned Rowan will send some of his men to help, as well, if I've need o' them. The food will get to the tables."

On the service stairway, Laurie met Sir Hugh's man, Thaddeus, coming down. He smiled at her and said, "I'm to tell the master that Sir Francis intends to dine with him. He'll no be gey surprised, I can tell ye that."

"Nor will Meggie," Laurie told him, smiling back.

In her own bedchamber, she took stock of her appearance. She had done nothing to soil the gown that Nancy had helped her put on earlier, so there was no reason to change it. It was the pale yellow one of Janet's that she fancied, and she knew that it became her.

She smoothed her hair from her face but left it unveiled. The one time she had tied a coif over it, Lady Marjory had protested that married ladies might wear French veils, but they did not wear common coifs. Having no French veil, Laurie had opted to leave her hair uncovered, which was the way she preferred it anyway.

She went back downstairs to find bustle in the hall, as men finished setting up the trestles and Andrew and Peter brought out baskets of trenchers to set upon them. She could still smell the delightful scent of the rosemary and other herbs mixed with the new rushes. She hoped Sir Hugh had noticed the change.

Even as she thought about him, he strode into the hall.

"Andrew," he said, his deep voice carrying easily the length of the chamber, "run tell your mam there will be other guests to dine. There is a party coming over the hill to the east, and the men on the wall say they carry Lord Eure's banner."

His gaze met Laurie's, and she felt her heartbeat quicken.

He smiled and said, "Forgive me, lass, but I must go up and let Thaddeus work his miracles. I've been helping Geordie and his lads repair a stall that one of the horses kicked to bits in the night, and I'm not fit for female company."

Lord Eure arrived before Sir Hugh or his overnight guest showed himself, and Lady Marjory entered the hall on his heels. Ned Rowan, having accompanied Lord Eure inside, presented him to her ladyship.

Lady Marjory made her curtsy. "It is a great pleasure and privilege to meet another of Her Majesty's march wardens, my lord." As she straightened, she gestured gracefully toward Laurie, adding, "I do not believe that you are yet acquainted with Lady Graham."

"No, madam," his lordship said, making his leg.

Laurie, rendered briefly speechless by her ladyship's casual reference to her, collected her wits sufficiently to say, "It is a pleasure, my lord."

His smile encompassed them both, but it was to Laurie that he said, "Her ladyship mistakes my position, I'm afraid. I am no longer Her Majesty's warden. I sent my resignation to the Privy Council immediately after Buccleuch's release from Blackness and his raid on Tynedale. I received word this morning that they have appointed a man to take my place."

"Indeed, sir," Lady Marjory said, "and who is the lucky gentleman?"

Eure chuckled. "Lucky? I don't count him so, my lady, but perhaps he will see the matter otherwise. We will learn that soon enough, though, for the gentleman in question is none other than your own Sir Hugh Graham."

Laurie heard an exclamation and turned to behold Sir Hugh standing at the threshold. He did not look particularly pleased by the news.

"There you are, Hugh," Eure said, striding to shake his hand. "I've brought the letter with me. It appears that Her Majesty, having learned that you not only gave your sister in marriage to an influential Scotsman but have married the daughter of another, believes you are unusually suited to serve as her warden of the middle marches, despite having been born and bred in the Borders. She says that if men with connections like yours cannot bring peace, no one can. What say you, sir?"

"I say that I shall never understand Her Majesty," Sir Hugh said sourly.

Eighteen

One kiss o your comely mouth,
I'm sure wad comfort me.

The discussion at the high table turned to the duties of a march warden and such difficulties as he might expect to encounter in the middle marches. Lady Marjory contributed her mite whenever she found an opening, but Laurie was content to listen. Despite Sir Hugh's obvious reluctance, she agreed with Lady Marjory in believing that he would make an excellent warden.

The gentlemen continued to talk after the trestle tables were cleared from the hall. When Lady Marjory excused herself to take her customary nap, Laurie returned to the kitchen, knowing there would be much work to do there before the time arrived to serve the next meal.

Despite Meggie's protests, it was not long before she tied a large apron over her gown and joined Nancy and Andrew in the scullery, helping them scrub the myriad pots and platters. When Meggie informed her sternly from the doorway that it was not suitable work for a gentlewoman, Laurie laughed.

Handing Nancy another platter to scrub, she said over her shoulder, "Would you let me cook, Meggie?"

"D'ye ken how t' do aught but turn the spit?"

"I know very little about cooking for so large a household."

"Well, then, what use could ye be till I could teach ye?"

"But that's just what I mean," Laurie said as she took a pot from Andrew and looked about to see where it should go. "At present, you must let me help you the best way I know."

"But the master—"

"I do not want to hear about the master," Laurie said. "I tell you, he would not care, nor need he ever know. Now, where in heaven's name do I hang this pot?"

"I'll hang it over the fire to dry first, so it willna rust," Meggie said, taking it from her and turning. "There be another hanging on the swey, waiting to go up on its hook, if ye'd like t' come and tak' it off for me."

Laurie followed her into the kitchen, picking up a towel to protect her hand from the hot iron pot. In order to hang it from the pothook, she pulled a stool over and climbed onto it. As she reached up with both hands to hang the pot from the hook, she heard Meggie give a sharp cry of dismay.

Looking over one shoulder to see what had startled the woman, Laurie gasped at the sight of Sir Hugh standing in the doorway, frowning. She missed the hook with the pot handle, and the hot pot swayed in her grasp, burning her forearm and startling her so that she lost her balance.

As the stool went out from under her, a strong arm caught her and a big hand knocked the pot out of her hand. The heavy iron vessel hit the floor with a crash.

Picking Laurie up in both arms, Sir Hugh said curtly, "Wet a towel with cold water, Meggie." Then, with a foot, he hooked the bench by the table where Nancy had chopped vegetables. Pulling it out, he sat on it, cradling Laurie in his arms.

"Hold out your arm," he ordered. "What the devil's keeping you, Meggie?"

"Here, master," Meggie said quietly, handing him a wet towel.

With his arms still around her, he ripped Laurie's sleeve, baring her reddened arm. Then he took the towel from Meggie and clapped it against the burn.

Laurie nearly protested his cavalier treatment of Janet's gown, but no man had ever held her so, and not being certain what he would do next, she kept silent. The cold water felt good against the burn.

She noted that Meggie was silent, too, and that the children in the scullery were as quiet as two mice.

When Sir Hugh took the towel away, Meggie said, "Will ye want herbs or such to put on it, master?"

"Nay, there is no blister. It will heal quickly. What the devil are you doing in here, mistress?" he demanded of Laurie.

A little frisson of fear shot up her spine when her gaze met his, and she remembered the many comments that she had heard about his temper in the time she had been at Brackengill. Wishing she didn't have damp blotches all down the front of her gown and that she could stand on her own two feet to face him, she said only, "I was helping Meggie."

"Dry your hands and come with me," he said grimly as he stood, still holding her, and then set her on her feet.

Fixing her gaze on the middle of his broad chest, she said, "What are you going to do?"

"Never mind that. Just do as I tell you."

Encountering a sympathetic look from Meggie, Laurie obeyed reluctantly. As she followed him up the spiral stone steps toward the hall, she told herself more than once that he could not eat her. Still, her stomach churned, and her hands felt damp even after she had rubbed them on her skirt.

Instead of going all the way into the hall, Sir Hugh entered a small chamber near it, waiting by the door until she had followed him in, then shutting it.

The room seemed small, too small to contain the two of them. It seemed to lack air, too, for Laurie could not seem to breathe. She could still feel where his hands had touched her, and she could feel the burn on her forearm throbbing.

Trying to compose herself, she avoided his gaze and looked about the room instead. It boasted a plastered ceiling and walls, oak wainscoting, and an arched fireplace that occupied nearly the entire wall opposite the door. Its furnishings comprised only a carved wooden chest against the wall to the left of the hearth and a writing table and chair against the wall on the right. Candles burned in a pair of sconces over the table. The only other light came from the small crackling fire.

Sir Hugh turned his back to the fire, clasped his hands behind him, and scowled at her. "From the look of you, you weren't just hanging pots. You were washing them as well. Why the devil were you working in the scullery?"

"Someone has to do it," Laurie said calmly.

"Not you!" A single stride closed the distance between them, and his hands gripped her upper arms tightly. "There are servants to do such things," he said, giving her a little shake. "I did not bring you here to be a servant, nor will I allow you to be used so. Meggie is going to hear what I think about this, I can tell you."

"That's not fair," Laurie said, looking up into his eyes. "I offered to help, sir. She did not ask."

He gave her another shake, and then with a groan he pulled her close and lowered his head, claiming her lips with his own.

Shocked, Laurie did not move. His lips were warm and moist against hers, but his body and arms felt hard and unyielding. She felt a part of him stir against her abdomen, and then she was conscious only of his lips and hands, and feelings they were awakening throughout her body.

Without a thought for consequence, she responded, kissing him back.

One of his hands moved to touch the bare skin of her breast above the edge of her bodice, and she heard him groan again. He sounded as if he were in pain, but he did not stop what he was doing. His tongue touched the opening of her lips, and his fingers dipped beneath the edge of her bodice. She felt a finger touch the nipple of one breast, and a burning far different from that on her arm swept through her. She gasped, and his tongue penetrated her mouth. No one had ever kissed her so, but she did not mind in the least. She pressed harder against him.

His fingers touched the lacing on her bodice, searching for the ties. Then they stopped moving. He put his hands at her waist and raised his head, glancing up at the ceiling as if he sought help from a higher source.

Quietly, he said, "That was unforgivable, lass. I did not mean to take advantage of you, but if I do not stop this, much more will happen. I could blame the fact that I have had little sleep in the past twenty-four hours, or the fact that much has happened in that time, but those things have naught to do with this. In truth, I have wanted to kiss you since the first day you came here."

She stared silently at him, thinking that God would probably strike her down if she admitted that she had wanted him to do so and wanted him to do so again, no matter what it led to. The thought was wanton and doubtless a betrayal of her family and her country. Encouraging him would be downright treasonous.

Doubtless he had similar feelings, for his voice sharpened as he said, "Stay out of the kitchen." He stepped away from her, adding, "You are never again to lower yourself to such menial tasks!"

"Don't be daft, sir," Laurie said, recovering her wits. "You cannot expect one woman and her children to go on doing the cooking and cleaning up for all the men here. It is cruel to expect such things of them."

"I don't expect such things," he said wearily. "There are any number of men and lads to help them. They have only to ask, and so I have told them."

"You cannot expect your men-at-arms to answer to Meggie or to allow the lackeys who serve them to do so unless your captain orders it," Laurie told him.

"Then he should order it."

"He does so but only on occasions like today's, when you entertain company. His men will not clean the rooms, and if any of them knows that you expect him to wash pots, none has admitted as much. They expect women to do those things. We can get Andrew, Peter, and other stable lads to pluck chickens and carry wood if they are not busy with their other chores, but it is nearly impossible for Meggie to issue a command to any of your men that they will obey. You should realize that for yourself. Have you ever given them direct orders to obey her? Who should do so when you and Ned Rowan are away from home?"

To her surprise, he looked rueful. Visibly collecting himself, he said, "I admit, lass, I had not noticed there even was a problem. My sister attended to such things, and my men obeyed her as they would obey me. I assumed that they did the same chores for Meggie, or if not for her, for my aunt. I will tell them that they must, but you are not to labor at such tasks again."

"Truly, I do not mind helping, sir," she said. "I have little else to do, and I am unaccustomed to being idle. Your aunt means well, but this household is not what she is accustomed to. In London, her steward commanded twelve menservants and as many maidservants. She had only to hint at a wish to see it fulfilled—or so she tells me, at all events."

"No doubt she is speaking the truth," he said with a sigh. "But if the pair of you want more maidservants, you have only to tell Meggie to hire them."

Surprised, Laurie said, "Can she do so? I am sure she does not know it."

"Then you must tell her," he said. "I have no time for such stuff, and if my aunt has had any complaints, she certainly has not spoken of them to me. I assumed she thought everything was fine as it is."

"She has her own maid, and she does not like to trouble you," Laurie said.

"Well, I don't deny that it would be a nuisance to look for maidservants," he said. "Indeed, I hope Meggie will attend to whatever you require, because I have no time for such stuff. I don't mean to linger here, as it is."

"You must leave again?" Unexpected disappointment washed over her.

"Aye," he said. "Your Liddesdale men been raiding again, and not only has Scrope ordered me to deal with them as his deputy but now I am warden for the middle march. James has agreed to turn Buccleuch over to Sir Robert Cary at Berwick, which means the Liddesdale men will be wild again."

Laurie tensed but forced herself to say calmly, "What are you going to do?"

"I intend to teach them another lesson," he said grimly. "This time, I'll make it clear that I will not tolerate their thieving in Redesdale or Tynedale."

"When must you go?"

"It will take my lads a day to gather the men, but I expect to be away by dawn's light on Thursday."

A day! Laurie knew she could not dissuade him, and she could think of nothing to say that would not infuriate him, but her thoughts tumbled over one another. He was going to raid Liddesdale again, and the toll would be terrible unless she could do something about it.

"I hope that we understand each other now with regard to your position here," he said, looking straight into her eyes.

"Aye, sir," she replied, letting his gaze hold hers and hoping that he would see no sign of the turmoil in her mind.

He nodded and opened the door for her, and she hurried past him to the stairway. Somehow, she would have to get outside the castle walls and make her way to Liddesdale to warn them of the coming raid. As warden of the middle marches, he would have even more authority to wreak havoc there, and she could not allow any more of her people to die at the hands of the English.

Upstairs in her bedchamber, as Laurie struggled to take off the torn dress without help, she realized that she could not escape Brackengill at once or on her own. She had walked often enough in the bailey to know where the postern gate lay, but she did not know how well guarded it was, and she did not have Bangtail Willie to help her.

She would need help, but whose? For that matter, did she dare involve anyone else? Her only real friend in the castle was Meggie.

She would need a horse, too, she realized. Her pony was in the stable, but she did not think any of the men would agree to saddle it for her without Sir Hugh's permission. She certainly could not walk to Scotland in what little time she had.

Setting aside the yellow dress to be mended, she found one of her own dresses in the wardrobe. It had most of its fastenings in the front, and as she put it on, she contemplated her problem. Plainly, what was possible for a daughter of the house at Aylewood simply was not possible for a hostage at Brackengill.

Whatever she might try to do, she could not do it while Sir Hugh was still at home, or at night when the gates and ramparts remained heavily guarded. Indeed, before she could do anything to warn Liddesdale, she would need a reason to step beyond Brackengill's walls, a plausible reason that Sir Hugh's men would accept.

She was still struggling to think of one when her door opened without ceremony and Lady Marjory entered, saying, "My dear, are you ailing? When Sir Hugh said that you had come upstairs, I did not at first believe him, for I know that you rarely change your gown for supper. Oh, but I see that you *have* changed it. Still, he said you came up here over an hour ago! Did you spill something on the other one? I did not notice, but you should have sent for Griselda to help you."

"I tore my sleeve, so I changed, madam," Laurie said glibly. "Perhaps Griselda will not mind mending the yellow one for me if it is not beyond repair."

"Oh, Griselda is a genius at mending things," her ladyship said. "I will tell her to come and fetch it whilst we sup. Faith, but this room is like an icehouse," she added with an exaggerated shiver. "You will catch your death, my dear Laurie. Do let me fetch someone to light your fire. It is nearly time for supper, of course, but in my experience, it will take hours to warm this chamber."

Laurie smiled, brushing a stray curl back where it belonged. "Thank you for your concern, madam, but I am quite accustomed to the temperature here. I think that perhaps it bothers you more than it does me, coming from London as you do."

"Oh, my dear, do not trouble your head about me. Although," she added with a little sigh, "I did wonder where you had got to. I was hoping for a comfortable chat, and Sir Hugh does not seem to be in a conversational mood. He barely spoke ten words to me before going out into the bailey."

"I'll warrant you are bored, madam," Laurie said with a smile. An idea stirred, and she added, "I wonder, would you enjoy a ride with me outside the castle walls tomorrow? We could ride down to the river and perhaps alongside it for a short distance. Neither of us has seen much of the countryside hereabouts yet."

"Dear me," Lady Marjory said, looking startled. "Would you really enjoy such an outing, my dear? I own, I am not one for physical exercise, but I have taken your measure, you know, and 'tis plain that you are not a sedentary young woman."

"No, madam, I am not, and I have been fretting for exercise," Laurie said, thinking that that much, at least, was perfectly true. She held her breath, hoping she was right in thinking that Lady Marjory still had small comprehension of her true position at Brackengill.

Her ladyship said thoughtfully, "Well, I know that Sir Hugh would say you ought not to ride out by yourself, and since there is no one else to ride with you, I expect that I must."

"Pray, madam, do not put yourself out so for me. If you do not like the notion, I can ask Meggie. Or perhaps your Griselda would like to accompany me."

"Godamercy, not Griselda," Lady Marjory said. "She has too much to do. In any event, she takes horses in the greatest aversion. I tell you, it was all I could do to make her ride one here from Carlisle. I will go with you, my dear."

"Thank you, madam. We should perhaps go down to take supper now. Oh, there is one other thing, though," she added, smiling. "Sir Hugh has agreed to hire more maidservants, so I shall tell Meggie that she can send for some. Perhaps we can visit one or two tomorrow to see if we find them to our liking."

"Whatever you wish, dear," Lady Marjory said, clearly resigned to her fate.

The evening proved uneventful. Sir Hugh ate his supper with a haste that suggested he had much on his mind, and since he still seemed disinclined toward conversation, the meal passed without reference to the following day's plan. The two women talked amiably for an hour after he left the table, and both retired early.

Laurie could only hope that her ladyship would not change her mind before morning and that she would not say something then to Sir Hugh about their planned venture. Since he usually got up, broke his fast, and left the castle before his aunt arose, Laurie told herself firmly that he would do so again on the morrow.

To her great relief, the next morning when she descended to the hall, there was no sign of him. Unfortunately, there also was no sign of Lady Marjory.

When Nancy came in to ask what she would like to eat, Laurie said, "I'll go down to the kitchen myself, Nan. Do you run upstairs and tell Lady Marjory's Griselda that I'd be obliged if her ladyship would join me as soon as she is dressed. Remind her, too, that we mean to ride out for a little exercise this morning."

"Aye, mistress, I'll tell her, but that Griselda, she dinna pay me much mind."

"She will do as I ask, however," Laurie said with a smile.

When the child had run upstairs, Laurie went to the kitchen to confer with Meggie. She believed that she was safe enough in telling the woman that she was going beyond the wall. She knew Meggie well enough to be nearly certain that she would not reveal the plan to Sir Hugh unless he asked her a direct question.

Therefore, having ascertained that he had broken his fast and left the castle, she said, "I'm going to ride out for a bit with Lady Marjory, Meggie, but I wanted to tell you before we go that Sir Hugh has agreed to hire more maidservants."

"Mercy," Meggie said, her eyes lighting. "That'll be a blessing, that will."

"Aye, it will," Laurie agreed. "He did not say how many, so I shall leave that to you to decide."

"There was two kitchen women here afore me, Matty and Sheila. They had some lassies, as well, to do the cleaning and such."

"Choose as many as you like and ask them to come straightaway," Laurie said. "I told Lady Marjory that we might visit one or two of them on our ramble this morning, so if any live close by, perhaps your Andrew can ride with us to show us the way," she added.

"Faith, mistress, if ye can persuade Matty and Sheila to come back, I'll thank ye for it, but I warrant that Lady Marjory will want armed men to escort ye, not a bit lad like my Andrew."

"Surely, we will be safe so long as we stay near the castle," Laurie said.

"Aye, well, but if Ned Rowan be in the yard, he might ha' summat t' say about my Andrew going. He said he's t' stay wi' the pots, and even if he's gone wi' the master, he might ha' told that Geordie t' keep Andrew inside."

Laurie had thought of that. "I'll tell them we do not mean to go far and that I'd like Andrew to accompany us. I know he is eager to get out of the kitchen, and I think even Ned Rowan would allow it in such a case as this. They can send a couple of men with us, too, but I do not want to look like some sort of raiding party."

"Aye, perhaps they'll agree." Meggie gave her a straight look, but Laurie met it blandly, turning away a moment later to take a hot roll from a rack by the oven. Breaking bits from it, she ate it standing, and then picked some fresh berries from a bowl nearby.

Watching her, Meggie said, "Will ye no want more than that?"

"Nay, 'tis enough." She was too tense to eat. "I'll find Lady Marjory and see what she would like."

"My Nan will look after her, mistress. Ye'll gang softly the day, d'ye hear?"

Laurie grinned. "Never fear, Meggie. Whatever you are thinking, I'll soon be right back here underfoot again."

"As if I'd want ye gone," Meggie exclaimed. "Dinna talk so daft! The place hasna been the same since ye came, mistress. 'Tis livelier now, and nae mistake."

Her words warmed Laurie's heart but at the same time filled her with guilt.

Surely, Sir Hugh would lay the blame where it belonged when he learned what she had done—as she was certain he would. He would not blame Meggie.

Lingering only long enough to learn where she would find Matty and Sheila, Laurie informed a delighted Andrew of his good fortune, then went to find Lady Marjory and urge her to some semblance of haste.

Despite these efforts, however, it was nearly two more hours before her ladyship, their horses, and the two men-at-arms who would escort them were ready to depart.

Nineteen

The next step that she stepped in,
She stepped to the chin . . .

Despite the fact that Hugh's morning had gone quickly and well, his mood at best was precarious. He had had only to tell his middle-march land sergeants that he meant to put an end to Liddesdale's mischief to stir them to action. By the time he had spoken to the first lot of their followers, promising them horses and supplies from Brackengill, he knew that Ned Rowan and his sergeants would easily collect an impressive army by the next day's sunrise.

He had met Lord Eure shortly after sunrise at Kielder, and Eure accompanied him for an hour or so, but since the ex-warden had done little to impress the citizens of his march, Hugh soon saw that he might as easily have sent Ned Rowan alone to rouse them to arms. The men were ripe for adventure. Many already were aware that raiders were on the move again and believed they were Liddesdale reivers. The men insisted, and Hugh agreed, that when King James surrendered Buccleuch to the English at Berwick, his submission would only stir more trouble in the region.

Hugh also knew, however, that Scrope and his lot had been busy spreading rumors about Grahams in general and himself in particular. Many of his new constituents had congratulated him on his recent nuptials, and although he began by trying to explain his relationship with Laura Halliot, he had given up that tactic before reaching the second hamlet.

His own men and many others, as well, understood hand-fasting. They also understood the concept of holding a hostage. Thus, logically, he thought, they ought to understand his position with regard to his present hostage. But he had already come to realize that since the hostage was female, many understood only the handfasting. The reason for it mattered not one whit.

They, like Scrope and Lady Marjory, saw only a ritual that anticipated cohabitation. In their eyes, that equaled marriage. Although some strongly disapproved of marrying across the line, they had heard the lass was bonny and seemed to think that Sir Hugh would sort out any legal difficulty with ease.

He had risen before dawn and spent half of a long morning with Eure, Ned Rowan, and one of his sergeants. However, after meeting the same eager reception even after Eure had returned home, Hugh left Ned and the others to their task and turned back toward Brackengill alone.

The warm sun shone brightly on the landscape, turning the browning hills to gold punctuated here and there with patches of still-green grass or spreading branches of an oak or a beech. The air smelled fresh and redolent of warm earth, wildflowers, and drying grass. Narrow, tumbling burns sparkled in the sunlight. Birds chirped merrily above the soft thuds of his pony's hoofbeats, and the hushing of wind in shrubbery as he passed sounded like ladies whispering to each other.

His thoughts were busy, for there was still much to be done before he rode into Scotland. Meggie would have plenty of food to bundle up, but the lads would see to all that. That thought took him straight to thinking about Laura, however, rather than to the next step in his own plans.

In his mind's eye, he could see his curvaceous, wide-eyed little hostage standing before him, calmly telling him that he had failed to look after his people properly. She looked so small and vulnerable, so childlike. Yet she had not hesitated to tell him that he had failed to take care of things as he should. The telling was something his sister Janet might have done, but the odd thing was that he had not resented Laura's interference as he would have resented Janet's.

He and Janet had rarely got on well together, though. He had never troubled himself to think much about that before, but now, looking back, he decided that the trouble had started early. She had been but a bairn when their parents died, when he had inherited Brackengill and responsibility for the welfare of all of its inhabitants and tenants. That included, of course, the welfare of his little sister. Though he could scarcely complain about it to anyone else at this late date, he knew now that at twelve he had been far too young to bear such heavy responsibility.

Then, of course, he had seen only his duty. Moreover, his uncle Brampton had encouraged him to shoulder that duty manfully rather than ask anyone else to step in. Both his uncle and his resident tutor had been stern, humorless men, and Hugh had taken his tone from them. He had treated Janet much as they treated him, and she had defied him as often as not, giving back as good as she got. In the end, she had been as defiant as ever and had betrayed him as easily as if it had been nothing, to follow her lover across the line into Scotland.

He still resented what she had done. It was no wonder, then, that he had resented her constant interference in the way he chose to run Brackengill. The wonder was that he had not resented Laura Halliot's opinion in a similar instance.

It occurred to him then that if he had come upon his sister scrubbing pots in the scullery, he would not have flown into a temper, as he had with Laura. In truth, he would have been glad to see Janet doing such things. After considering that thought for a moment, he pushed it away, knowing it was false but still rather enjoying the mental picture of his sister scrubbing pots.

The moment of humor was short-lived. He reached a hilltop from which he could see Brackengill again, and although sight of the castle stirred the usual sense of pride, movement caught his eye near the river a mile to the north. A small party of horsemen rode there. They were halfway between the castle and himself.

Frowning, he looked more carefully and saw two females with them. He told himself that they were undoubtedly from a place other than Brackengill, that even if they were from Brackengill, they could be only his aunt and her woman. Even as the thought crossed his mind, however, the instinct that warned him when Laura Halliot was in the hall or the bailey told him now that she was one of them.

Certain that she was attempting to escape, he put spurs to his pony, urging it to the reckless pace that he generally reserved for battle or raiding.

When Laurie saw the lone rider galloping downhill toward them, she knew instantly who it was. Her companions did not see him as soon as she did, but even when one of the two men-at-arms acting as their escort shouted warning that an unknown rider approached, she did not doubt his identity.

"That is Sir Hugh," she said flatly.

"Alone?" demanded the other man doubtfully.

"Aye," said Andrew, squinting in the bright sunlight. "That be his pony, right enough." He glanced uncertainly at Laurie.

She had been trying unsuccessfully for the past half hour to separate herself and Andrew from Lady Marjory and the two men-at-arms. When Lady Marjory complained that she was tired before they reached the riverbank, Laurie had suggested that her ladyship return with their escort and leave herself and Andrew to ride on to see Matty and Sheila.

"We can tell them they are wanted again at the castle, madam," she had said only moments before spying Sir Hugh.

"No, no, my dear! You must not ride about with only the boy for escort. 'Twould not suit your status as lady of the castle, don't you see."

"Then I will take one of the men, as well," Laurie said.

"Oh, but my dear, that would leave me with only one to protect me, and you would have only the one and the boy.

That will not do. I told you when I first saw them that two would provide insufficient protection for us, but you insisted and I did not like to deny you. It is nearly dinnertime, though, so we must go back. I had not realized how very tired I would become. Doubtless, it is this dreadful heat."

The day was mild, but Laurie had seen nothing to gain by pointing that out. Now, watching Sir Hugh's approach, she felt a distinct chill.

He was upon them in what seemed to be only moments, and she could read his expression easily. He was furious.

He reined in so abruptly that his horse reared, but he controlled it with practiced ease. For a moment, he seemed to look only at Laurie, but then his sweeping gaze took in the others. He nodded at Lady Marjory.

"Good morning, madam."

"Good morning, my dear Sir Hugh. It is a good thing, is it not, that our beasts are of such a placid nature. Your mad dash might otherwise have disturbed them. I do enjoy seeing an expert in control of a spirited steed, however. Your uncle was just such another in his youth. Sadly, I fear he grew less intrepid with age."

"I own, I am surprised to see you outside the castle walls, madam. I believe it is the first such excursion you have made since your arrival at Brackengill."

"Our dearest Laura desired to take some exercise," Lady Marjory said.

"Did she, indeed?"

Laurie felt his keen glance but kept her eyes fixed on her pony's left ear.

"Oh, yes," Lady Marjory said brightly. "I was happy to accompany her, of course, but I fear that I sadly underestimated my stamina, which has just presented us with a slight dilemma. Here we are with but two men-at-arms to escort us, and me so weary as to wish to return."

Sir Hugh said with deceptive mildness, "And how did that present a dilemma, madam?"

"Why, dearest Laura gallantly suggested that I return to the castle and let her continue with Andrew. I could not agree, though, for one must have a suitable escort, and although Andrew seems to be a nice child, he could not protect her."

"How wise you were to see that," Hugh said.

Though his tone was still mild, Laurie felt a shiver shoot up her spine.

Lady Marjory, clearly oblivious to his temper, assured him with a merry laugh that she only wanted to do what was best for Laura.

It was all that Laurie could do to sit quietly listening to them. She could feel his anger in every breath he took and every word that left his tongue. She dared not imagine what the men-at-arms were thinking, but surely they knew their master's moods well. Neither had said a word.

Sir Hugh said, "Since you are tired, Aunt, and doubtless hungry for your dinner, we will all return to the castle. Gibbs," he said to the larger of the two men, "I will take the mistress with me. You lead her horse and ride on with the others."

"Aye, master," the larger of the two men-at-arms said. He immediately drew his horse nearer to Laurie, holding his hand out for her reins.

Gripping them tightly, she glowered at him, about to protest, but before she could do so, Sir Hugh lifted her from her saddle and plunked her down sideways in front of him on his. Her mouth shut with a snap, but although she was furious, when her astonished gaze collided with his grim one, she decided not to speak just yet.

Sir Hugh took the reins from her and handed them to Gibbs.

Andrew looked from Laurie to Hugh and said matter-of-factly, "Mistress Laurie were going t' look in on Sheila and Matty to ask 'em if they'll come back to Brackengill. Me mam said they might."

"Then you go and tell them," Sir Hugh said curtly. "Go now," he added when the boy hesitated. "Tell them you've come from me and that her ladyship desires to have more women working at the castle."

"Should I say 'her ladyship,' then?" Andrew's eyes widened.

"Mam said we was t' call 'er Mistress Laura, but I like Mistress Laurie, which is what Nan says."

"Get along with you, lad," Sir Hugh said. "You're to say 'her ladyship.' "

Laurie straightened, giving Sir Hugh a speaking look. "I'm not—"

"You will be silent if you know what's good for you," he snapped.

Scarcely waiting for Andrew to urge his pony on, Sir Hugh reined his toward the castle. Lady Marjory and her escort had already ridden ahead.

"Just what the devil do you think you are doing out here?" he demanded.

Laurie looked down at her hands, wishing she were still on her own pony. Although she was still angry, it was hard to think what to say to him when her shoulder rested against his broad chest and she could feel the hardness of chain mail beneath his padded jack. She could feel each breath he took.

She remembered the feeling of his lips against hers and his hand touching her breast, and her body suddenly felt so warm that she decided Lady Marjory had been right about the hot day. Every movement of his horse jostled her against him, and her thoughts remained elusive, tangled, and unreachable.

He waited.

The tension increased until she knew he did not mean to speak until she did.

At last, she said, "I do not suppose you could bring yourself to believe that I was merely taking exercise with her ladyship."

"No."

Not encouraging. She swallowed, licked dry lips, and muttered, "I had to do something. I could not sit quietly at Brackengill and just let you attack Liddesdale again. Those are my people."

"And you are my hostage. Or did you chance to forget that?"

"You know I did not. I am not your wife, however. Not Lady Graham, and not 'her ladyship.' "

"As to that, by Scottish law and, thanks to Scrope's agreement, even by English law, you are all three of those things."

She turned toward him then, feeling a surge of her earlier fury. "I'm not! That ceremony was only a practical arrangement to protect me."

"We will not discuss that just now," he said.

His tone remained calm, but his anger was nearly palpable. "You are not to leave the castle again, Laura," he added sternly. "I accepted your word that you would remain at Brackengill as pledge for your sister's honor. That means—as I should not have to remind you—that you *must* remain in her stead, as a promise that she will appear to answer for the death of Martin Loder."

"I was not running away," Laurie protested, but she looked away again.

"Were you not?" he said. "I don't know what else to call it."

"I meant to warn them, that's all. I would have come back."

"Do you think you need stay only at your convenience?" he demanded.

When she did not reply, he gripped her right shoulder and forced her to turn toward him.

"Look at me," he said.

Reluctantly, she did.

"Now, tell me that you understand you cannot leave Brackengill just because some impulse stirs you to do so. You are my prisoner, Laura, not my guest."

Her stomach knotted. She did not want to speak the words. No other hostage that she had heard of seemed so strictly confined. The fact that the only other hostage that she had heard much about was Buccleuch did not occur to her.

He gave her a shake. "Answer me. Do you understand your position?"

"Aye, I understand it," she muttered.

"Good."

"I also understand that I am *not* your wife. Do not think you can bed me!"

She heard him sigh, but if he was exasperated with her, he did not say so.

He did not speak again, in fact, until they had ridden through the main gates into the bailey at Brackengill.

Lady Marjory, apparently, had already gone inside.

Laurie sat stiffly until Sir Hugh dismounted, and she did not relax when his hands grasped her waist and he lifted her from the saddle. Nor did she let her gaze meet his, keeping it fixed on a point beyond his shoulder, waiting for him to put her down. When he had held her for several moments with her feet still off the ground, she pressed her lips together. Knowing that somehow he was baiting her, she was determined not to leap to his bait.

His patience—or stubbornness—proved greater than hers, however.

Meeting his gaze at last, she said, "Do you mean to hold me like this forever? It must be well past noon by now. Meggie will be wondering if any of us intends to eat dinner today."

"I am wondering what to do with you," he said.

"You can begin by putting me down."

"I don't think so," he said, and to her shock, he hoisted her over his shoulder instead. The position was not only uncomfortable but mortifying, as well.

"What are you doing?" she demanded.

"I am going to teach you certain consequences of being a hostage, my lady."

"You have no right," she muttered between gritted teeth.

"I have every right, both as your jailer and as your husband. I have the right to do whatever I please with you, my lass. I can do it right here, if you insist, or I can do it in the privacy of your bedchamber. You may choose which."

He did not bother to lower his voice, and Laurie heard one of the men laugh. Although the man hastily stifled his laughter, it added to her mortification.

When Sir Hugh began to stride across the cobblestones, she could scarcely breathe, because the plating on his shoulder dug

into her ribs. She would have bruises, but she feared that he
meant to do more, much more, than that.

"Put me down!"

"Hush. You'll gain little by sputtering at me."

She pounded his back with her fists. "Do your worst, Hugh
Graham, but if you kill anyone I know, I swear I'll make you
sorry! Now, put me—"

She broke off with a shriek when he smacked her backside.

"I told you to hush," he reminded her. "Don't fight me so,
either. You'll hit your head or one of your fists on the wall if
you don't take care."

In her struggles, she had not paid heed to where he was
going. Now, she realized that he had passed through the main
entrance and had reached the twisting stairway. As he mounted
the steps, she saw Lady Marjory below, peering up at her.

Her ladyship's mouth hung open, and her eyes were wide
with shock. For once, she did not say a word.

Laurie shut her eyes.

She opened them again, however, when Sir Hugh sent a
door crashing back on its hinges. Just as she realized that he
had carried her into her bedchamber, he grasped her with both
hands by the waist and set her on her feet. He did not let go.

When she tried to step away from him, he held her with
one hand at her waist while he used the other to hold her chin
and tilt her head up.

Knowing what he meant to do, she stood still, frozen in
place by myriad feelings and thoughts that rushed through her.
She knew that he meant to punish her, even to frighten her,
to remind her of his power over her, which made her reaction
seem almost perverse.

A part of her knew that she ought to be frightened. But she
did not feel frightened. She felt only anticipation. If anything
frightened her, it was the knowledge that she wanted him to
kiss her again.

When his lips touched hers, her body leapt in response, and
she shut her eyes. He kissed her thoroughly, and although his
left hand remained firmly at her waist, holding her tight against

him, the other moved away from her chin and began to caress her body even more possessively than he had the previous time. Cupping a breast, he used his thumb to flick gently against her nipple.

Laurie gasped, opening her eyes.

His lips left hers and his hands moved back to grasp her waist again.

"You see how easily a husband can control a wife," he said.

"How dare you!"

"Easily," he said. "As I told you before, it is my right, just as it is my right as your jailer to lock you up. If a jailer were to beat you, however, some folks might object. But if your husband does so, no one will say a word."

"You wouldn't!"

"Wouldn't I?" He lifted her again, holding her close to him but with her feet off the floor. With his lips close to hers, he repeated gently, "Wouldn't I, lass?"

When without a thought she raised a hand to strike him, he dumped her unceremoniously onto the bed.

Realizing what she had nearly dared, she scrambled away from him as far as she could, only to get tangled in her skirts and bump hard against the wall.

He stood where he was, just watching her, and she realized that she could not escape. He could reach her easily by stretching out an arm. Her heart pounded.

"I see that you recognize your peril," he said, his voice deceptively gentle.

Seeing her eyes widen warily, Hugh felt a twinge of unfamiliar guilt at having frightened her. He had meant to do so, to teach her that she had to obey his orders, so he tried to suppress the guilt, but the feeling lingered.

It was hard to keep his hands off her. He wanted to behave well, but she was too tempting. He hoped with all his being that they laid hands on May Halliot soon.

When Laura did not speak, he said evenly, "What did you hope to accomplish, exactly, by venturing outside the wall?"

She licked her lips, and he felt a new stirring of desire.

Fighting it, he repeated, "What did you expect, Laura?"

"I knew her ladyship would get tired, and I was going to send the men back with her when she did. I'd have kept Andrew with me."

"My men would not have left you with just the boy."

"They seem to obey me easily enough. Perhaps you have not noticed."

"I know that they have orders to treat you with the respect due to your station, but they still know better than to let you ride off by yourself."

She sighed, and for the first time he saw defeat in her expression.

Hugh found that he did not like the look. He said, "There will be no unnecessary killing, lass. I shall declare a 'hot trod.' The most recent raid was only days ago, and that means that your father will be obliged to help me arrest the raiders. That is what Scrope should have done, and he knows it. He knew, too, unfortunately, that your father was new to his job."

She stayed where she was, but he had stirred her curiosity. "What had that to do with anything?"

"Only that Scrope's position, as he explained it to me—and I believe he wrote as much to the Queen—was that experience told him he'd get no help from the warden. Redress for the outrage against Carlisle being unobtainable, he said, he offered Liddesdale no more than honorable and neighborlike assistance by punishing the felons."

Bitterly, Laurie retorted, "The women and bairns led away in leashes like so many dogs were no doubt grateful to my lord Scrope and his minions for such kindly assistance."

"I do not intend to wreak more havoc on Liddesdale," Hugh said gently.

"I do not believe you."

"I must do my duty, because many suspect that Rabbie Redcloak is on the prowl again," he explained. "But whether he is or not, I am not Scrope, nor do I employ his methods."

"Do you not? You were in Liddesdale with him. Recall that I saw you there."

"Aye, that's true, but I have more than once risked my reputation and position by refusing to carry out the worst of his orders."

"You dare to refuse him'?"

"I do, but it's not as you might think," he said. "Scrope is a good soldier, but he is also a risk-taker with poor judgment who values his position. Hitherto, he has left me alone because he feared my uncle's influence with the Queen."

"But your uncle is dead," she said.

"Aye, and I am now a warden myself. One does not try to read the Queen's mind," he added, thinking it was probably just as well that he could not.

She had relaxed. Now she curled her legs beneath her, straightening her skirts as she said, "Then how does Scrope keep *his* position?"

"By sending plausible lies about his accomplishments to Elizabeth," Hugh said. "Also, by catering to certain members of the gentry and nobility who want him to keep the thankless job rather than saddle any of them with it."

"Truly?" She wrinkled her nose, thinking. "That seems odd."

"Does it?"

"Aye, for at home, men frequently fight over who gets to be warden. My father did not want the job, though, because he said others might try to take it, might even murder him for it. But when the King begged him to take over for Buccleuch, Buccleuch swore that no one would interfere with him, so he accepted. I thought it would be the same here."

"It is not." He paused, watching her smooth a stray curl from her brow.

Her every movement was seductive, and her innocence just made her more tempting. The gentle curve of her waist invited him to put his arms around her. He wanted to explore every curve of her body, to let his hands and lips roam free. The thought that, legally, she was his to do with as he pleased stirred temptation like he had never felt before. His body ached for her.

He reminded himself that although he seemed able to stir a response in her, she did not return his lust. A voice in the back of his head reminded him, as well, just how much it would cost him to give into his lust.

He stepped away from the bed toward the window as he said, "In Scotland, wardens wield great power, lass. It is not the same here in England."

"No?"

"No. Elizabeth rarely appoints anyone who was born and bred in the Borders. Worse, she keeps most of her wardens in debt and dependent upon her goodwill. I cannot expect much support from her or from the Privy Council."

"But why?"

"Because she does not want any warden to build a power base that might cause her the same sort of trouble that your Jamie's Border lords cause him."

She nodded. "It is true that Buccleuch and some others are very powerful."

"Buccleuch *was*," Hugh agreed with gentle emphasis. "Elizabeth will keep him on a tighter rein once she has him in ward at Berwick."

"But even your men say that Sir Robert Cary, who will be his jailer, is likely to give him as much comfort and freedom as James gave him at Blackness."

"Aye, that's true. No one wants to treat a powerful prisoner too harshly, lest he find himself captured by that same prisoner later. And Buccleuch has the right to offer pledges, too. He need only guarantee that he will appear for trial, and then Elizabeth will free him again. But he will be less quick to defy her then."

She nodded, as if she understood it all.

He doubted that she did understand, though. Few people understood the complexities of world politics. He rarely felt certain about them, himself, although as warden he would doubtless be embroiled in them.

He said, "In the meantime, lass, I still intend to leave in the morning."

The wary look returned, but this time he steeled himself against it. He had to make her understand both his power over her and her position as his hostage.

"You are to remain here until my men and I are gone," he said. "You may use the time to reflect upon your duty as pledge for your sister's honor. Since I must send my request for assistance to your father once I cross into Scotland, I will relay any message that you would like to send to him, but you are not to leave the castle again. Do you understand me?"

"Aye," she said with a sigh. "I understand."

"Good." He left without another word, shutting the door with a snap.

Watching him go, Laurie sighed again. She had heard of people being rendered witless by passion or lust, even by love. She could not for one minute imagine that she had fallen in love with Sir Hugh Graham, for not only was he her enemy but he was nothing like the man she had once envisioned herself marrying.

That man was a dashing courtier, handsome and debonair, with a keen wit and an appreciation for women who were not fond of household duties. That man would be rich enough to afford a house steward like Lady Marjory's to see to such things. To be sure, Sir Hugh had not liked seeing her in the kitchen, but that hardly counted for anything.

He just wanted to control her, she decided, grateful that she had made him no promises. Only then did she realize that he had not made her any, either.

Twenty

He turned his back towards her
And viewed the leaves so green . . .

Before Sir Hugh, Ned Rowan, and their men departed early the following morning, Sir Hugh sent Nancy to wake Laurie and ask if she had messages for her family. He even provided her with paper, ink, and a quill, but although she slipped the bit of paper into her bodice in case she thought of anything she wanted to write later, she set the other items aside and told Nancy she had nothing just then to write.

"Tell Sir Hugh I'd be grateful if he would relay my dutiful respects to my father and stepmother. He might also ask if they have had news of my sister, but that is all." She assumed that she would hear, in any event, if May returned home.

For the next few days, awaiting news, Laurie felt as jumpy as a hen on a hot griddle, but no word arrived from Sir Hugh or his men, or from Aylewood. Surely, she thought, her father must know May's whereabouts by now. If she had thrown herself into a river, someone would have found her body. Had Blanche succeeded in persuading Sir William to protect her favorite daughter from the authorities by assuring him that Laurie would be happier in England? Were they hiding May?

Surely not, she told herself. Even Blanche would not expect her to give her life for May, and even if Sir Hugh were in a mood to protect her, if she had to stand trial in her sister's place, that was what would happen. Scrope wanted vengeance for Martin Loder's death, and without May to corroborate her version of what had happened, it would be her word against Cornus Grant's. No one would believe her, and Scrope would insist on hanging her. The thought made her shiver.

Lady Marjory had no such worries. She continued in her usual blithe fashion, hovering over Laurie and behaving as if nothing mattered more to her than Laurie's comfort—except, perhaps, Sir Hugh's. Laurie had taken her measure, however, and although she was invariably friendly to the older woman, she had ceased to expect real support from her. Indeed, Lady Marjory's impractical suggestions frequently proved more nuisance than help, but fortunately, real help soon arrived.

Late the first morning, after Sir Hugh and his men had gone, Meggie made a rare appearance in the hall not long after Laurie and Lady Marjory sat down at the high table to break their fast. Two women followed in her wake.

"This be Matty," she said, gesturing to the older one. "And this be Sheila."

The two bobbed curtsies. They regarded Laurie curiously but seemed ready to accept her as the castle's mistress, and for once she had no wish to contradict that perception. The two had worked at Brackengill before Janet Graham's departure for Scotland, and it was clear from the start that they felt perfectly at home and had every intention of setting the castle to rights as quickly as they could.

By the end of the week, three younger maidservants had joined them, including one who would serve Laurie in Nan's stead. The very walls vibrated with their energy as they set to work under Matty's direction, turning out bedchambers, shaking curtains and wall hangings, and scrubbing everything in sight.

A week to the day after Sir Hugh left, as Laurie was discussing the day's schedule with Meggie and Matty, Andrew ran into the kitchen puffed with news.

"We've had word from the master," he exclaimed.

Nancy and Sheila bustled in from the scullery, wiping their hands on their aprons as they came. Peter turned on the bench by the little table, where he had been trying to teach John to play noughts and crosses with charcoal and a bit of slate.

Laurie tensed, waiting for Andrew to announce that Sir Hugh's men had burned more cottages and killed more citizens of Liddesdale.

"Well, tell us your news, then, laddie," Meggie said.

"Aye, I'll tell ye," he said. "All them bluidy—" Looking guilty, he cleared his throat and began again. "All them wicked Scots reivers left their homes and fled into the woods in Tarras Moss afore the master could catch 'em—went to ground like foxes, they said. The devil hisself guards them woods!"

"You guard your tongue, my wee laddie," Meggie said.

"Aye, sure, but they do say as much, Mam," Andrew said. "Men what go in get swallowed up by bogs and such, they say, as if old Clooty hisself reaches right up through the mud to snatch them to Hell. D'ye ken them woods, mistress?"

"Aye, I do," Laurie said. "They are treacherous, right enough. The forest floor is more bog than dirt. Only those who live there ken the safe ways to go."

"D'ye ken their secret ways?"

"Some of them I do," she said, remembering when she and Sym had hidden in the tree.

"Then ye could tell the master how to catch them bluidy reivers!"

Laurie said evenly, "I cannot do that, Andrew."

"But—"

"Haud your whist, ye fashious bairn," Nancy snapped at him. "D'ye no ken that them reivers be her ain folk? She's no going to split on them any more than ye would split on us!"

"I just might split on you, Nancy Tattle-Mouth!"

"Hush now," Meggie commanded.

"Did they say what your master means to do?" Laurie asked.

Andrew looked at her but hesitated. "Happen I shouldna tell ye," he said at last. "I plumb forgot ye be ain o' the enemy, and all."

"That will be enough of that kind of talk," Meggie said sharply.

To change the subject, Laurie said, "Are the men of Brackengill all safe?"

"Aye," Andrew replied. "Master be setting up for a siege, is all. He says he'll wait 'em out, that within a sennight they'll come begging to 'im, 'cause they canna ha' enough food to last them long, as many as what they be."

Laurie nodded, although she did not agree with Sir Hugh's assessment. She knew that Davy Elliot kept stores of food for just such crises, and most Borderers could get by on surprisingly little when they had to. Moreover, she was certain that no siege would succeed in keeping everyone in the woods.

Besieging Tarras Wood wasn't like besieging a castle, where doors and windows were easy to see. The forest sprawled for miles. She was confident that if she were in any position to visit the Elliots, she could slip into the woods, make her way to the cottage, and slip away without Sir Hugh or his men being any the wiser.

She kept these thoughts to herself but decided that Sir Hugh was less likely to succeed in his siege than to fail. Nevertheless, as the days passed, she found her thoughts often returning to Sir Hugh and the people of Tarras Wood.

The castle hummed with activity. Matty and Sheila had taken up residence in a room near Meggie's, and although the other maids went home at night, by day the sounds of their chatter and singing as they attended to their work enlivened life at Brackengill considerably. Even men who had been unhappy that Sir Hugh had left them behind to guard the castle grew more cheerful as each day passed.

For a time, Laurie was content with her role as chatelaine. Her days were so busy that she even looked forward to relaxing evening conversations with Lady Marjory. However, once things settled into a routine, her contentment vanished. She knew the maidservants liked her and that none resented her supervision, but she was not accustomed to the role and Meggie no longer needed her assistance.

Although Blanche had complained that she shirked her duties at Aylewood, she had not evaded them so much as she had evaded Blanche. Nonetheless, the result was the same. Without obvious work to do and with maids who knew their business better than she did, she soon found herself at a loss.

Had Brackengill been as much her home as most of the servants seemed to think it was, she might have sought advice from Meggie, Matty, or even Sheila. As it was, still uncertain of her right to take charge, she did not make the attempt.

The weather outside remained warm and beautiful, and she chafed more than ever at her imprisonment. She had expected Sir Hugh to return after a few days, either having succeeded or failed in his undertaking, and she missed him.

The longer he stayed away the more Lady Marjory's incessant, inquisitive kindness grated on her nerves.

"You must miss our dear Sir Hugh dreadfully," Lady Marjory said as the two of them lingered at the dinner table one afternoon when he had been gone nearly a fortnight.

Laurie stared at her in astonishment, for although the older woman seemed to have read her thoughts, she was determined not to let her know that. Since she could think of nothing to say, it was just as well that Lady Marjory required no assistance in maintaining a flow of conversation.

"This sort of thing—when men insist on going off to do battle or whatever it is that they choose to do—is always hard on women," she went on. "Brampton used to spend his time talking politics with friends in London when he was not waiting upon the Queen or traveling to outlandish places to look after business affairs."

"You must have been lonely, madam," Laurie said courteously, hoping to keep her talking about Brampton. "I imagine that when your husband came here to attend to Brackengill's affairs, he must have been gone for weeks at a time."

"Faith, he frequently was away half the year," Lady Marjory said. "Not that he spent all that time here, of course. He was used to say that Sir Hugh's tutor was so reliable that he needn't do more than look over the accounts once a year."

Smothering a yawn, Laurie apologized. "Forgive me, madam. I should not be sleepy so early in the day."

"What you want is fresh air, my dear," Lady Marjory said. "Perhaps you would like me to walk with you in the bailey. I know that you enjoy exercise, and I believe it would not harm me to accompany you."

Knowing that she would maintain a snail's pace, Laurie smiled and said, "I expect you would prefer to take your usual nap, madam. Still, I thank you for your kindness. What I really want is to get on a horse and ride for an hour on the fells."

"Then do so, by all means, child. The exercise will cheer your spirits."

Having already begun to suspect that Sir Hugh had said nothing to her or to his men about ordering her to remain inside the castle wall, Laurie hesitated on the brink of explaining, yet again, that she was not really mistress of Brackengill but its master's hostage.

Lady Marjory had never understood the situation, and Laurie's private opinion was that she did not want to understand it. Prisoners, in her ladyship's mind, were loathsome creatures—never females, and certainly never persons with whom one could enjoy an absorbing conversation.

Less than a moment's reflection persuaded Laurie that she was capable of keeping her word to remain Sir Hugh's hostage and still allow herself to enjoy occasional, much needed physical activity. Her pony was in the stable, after all, eating oats and getting fat.

Ignoring her conscience, which accused her of evading the truth, she said, "What an excellent notion, madam! I believe I will go for a ride if I can persuade one of the men to saddle a horse for me."

"You have merely to command it, my dear, but you should not go alone, you know. Take two men with you, and be certain they properly arm themselves."

"Aye, madam," Laurie said, but her spirits fell. Most of the men were friendly, but she doubted that any would provide her with a horse. Since she did not want to suffer the humiliation of having her order ignored or, worse, denied, she sought out Meggie, finding her in the kitchen nursing wee Susan.

"I'd like to explore the countryside a bit," Laurie told her after a few moments of desultory conversation.

"Aye, ye should do that," Meggie said, nodding. "It being Wednesday, Matty and I baked this morning. Mistress Janet were used to tak' fresh loaves to them that couldna bake their own. Likely ye'd enjoy meeting some o' Sir Hugh's tenants, and since Ned Rowan's made no objection to our Andrew goin' about his business again, he could gae wi' ye, to show ye who should get the loaves."

"I'd like that," Laurie said, surprised to discern no hint of disapproval in Meggie's expression. Was it possible Sir Hugh had said nothing to anyone except her? She said with a sigh, "Lady Marjory said I must take two of the men along."

"Find my Andrew, then, and tell him ye want your pony saddled. He'll ken who amongst the men-at-arms should gae wi' ye. Or ye can ask that Geordie. He be acting captain o' Brackengill, ye ken, whilst Sir Hugh and Ned Rowan be awa'.'"

Laurie nodded, still unable to believe that her plan might succeed. She liked Geordie, but if Sir Hugh had given him orders to keep her inside the wall, he would do so. Deciding to put it to the test, she went into the bailey and soon found him in the stable, overseeing yet another repair of a stall.

"Godamercy," Laurie exclaimed when she saw the splintered wall, "what happened here?"

Geordie grinned. " 'Twas that lad yonder," he said, pointing toward a large black in a neighboring stall who chose that moment to toss its regal head and snort. "He kicked out the boards and fair frighted the wee gelding in the next stall to death. We'll ha' it fixed in a twink though, mistress."

"I'm sure you will," Laurie said with a smile. "Will you have someone saddle my pony, please, Geordie, and one for Meggie's Andrew. I'd like to explore some of the countryside hereabouts and Meggie has loaves she said I should take to some tenants if you can spare Andrew to show me where they live."

Geordie nodded. "Aye, that's a good notion, that is, for they've missed their bread since Mistress Janet went awa' into Scotland. I can send Small Neck Tailor wi' ye, as well. We'll no miss him this afternoon. 'Tis been quiet as a grave hereabouts." He frowned, and Laurie tensed. "Ye'll no go far, mistress," he said. "The master wouldna like it an ye went north o' the Lyne."

"Then you must tell Andrew and your man," Laurie said calmly, "because I have been outside the wall only the one time since I came, and I am not certain that I would know the River Lyne from the Black Lyne if I walked into it."

Chuckling, Geordie said, "I'll see they keep ye dry, mistress." Then, cupping a hand alongside his mouth, he shouted for Andrew.

The boy came running, and when Geordie explained the task ahead of him, he grinned widely and agreed at once.

"Run to the kitchen and fetch the loaves whilst they saddle our ponies," Laurie said. "Your mam will tell you where we should go."

She stayed in the yard, not wanting to take time even to change her dress, lest Geordie change his mind and decide that he should not let her go.

Ten minutes later, when Andrew returned with a sack of loaves, the horses and Laurie were ready. Mounting astride, she kilted up her skirts and tucked them around her legs for propriety's sake. As she, Andrew, and the man-at-arms called Small Neck Tailor passed through the main entrance, the tall gates swung shut behind them.

Laurie drew a deep, satisfying breath of fresh air.

The afternoon was warm and sunny. Puffy white clouds floated in an azure sky, and a light breeze stirred grass and heather on surrounding hillsides. For a time, she was content to follow Andrew with Small Neck Tailor plodding behind, but after they had visited two cottages, she began to find the sedate pace tiresome.

"I am going to ride ahead to that thicket of trees in the distance," she called over her shoulder to the man-at-arms. "If you want to accompany me, you may do so. Andrew, do not drop the bread!"

With that, she dug her heels into the pony's flanks, and it leapt forward, clearly as eager as she was to go faster. A trail of sorts stretched ahead, and she followed it, knowing that if she did the pony would be less likely to step into a rabbit hole. Her spirits soared, and when she drew rein at the edge of the thicket, she felt more like her old self than she had since her arrival at Brackengill.

"Oh, that felt good," she said when Tailor and Andrew joined her. "I'd like to ride like that every day. Indeed, I believe I will begin taking a horse out regularly unless we receive news of danger in the neighborhood."

No one at Brackengill expressed objection to her plan, and so, reassuring herself that as long as she returned to the castle no one could object, she continued to ride out each day. Some days Geordie would assign a second man-at-arms, and she would know that he had received slightly disturbing news, but he never shared that news with her. Nor did he refuse to let her ride outside the wall.

Laurie began to feel perfectly safe in her outings, and sure than no one could object to them. It was no more, after all, than the freedom other hostages enjoyed.

A successful siege requires the patience of a saint, and Hugh Graham was no saint. Neither was Corbies Nest, the abandoned peel tower that he had taken over as his headquarters, a place that offered much comfort; however, the tower overlooked the Moss and Tarras Wood, which made it strategically ideal. Having reinforced its timber walls, he remained, determined to flush out the reivers.

Had the men now hidden in Tarras Wood been sensible, they would, he believed, have yielded at first sight of his small but powerful army. The law gave him the right, as deputy warden, to pursue back to their dens in Scotland any raiders who attacked English villages. That same law gave him the right to demand support from the opposing warden, and that he also had done, sending messages both to the warden at Aylewood and to his deputy at Broadhaugh. By rights, Hugh's mission should have succeeded. That it had not he blamed on a number of factors.

Halliot, although protesting that Hugh had provided evidence against no man in particular, merely an accusation against a legendary outlaw whom no one had yet proved really existed, nevertheless agreed to send men to assist him as soon as he had any to spare. Quinton Scott of Broadhaugh, Halliot's deputy, had likewise agreed to lend what support he could, but not until the past week had Hugh seen any sign of the promised help from either one. Then Halliot had sent four men to report that they had found no indication that men of Liddesdale or Teviotdale had taken part in any raid across the line since Buccleuch's legal pursuit of villains into North Tynedale after his release from Blackness.

Hugh received the report and the offered assistance of a mere four men with barely concealed scorn. He had expected no more, however, and his position with regard to Halliot was particularly delicate, since he was presently holding the man's daughter hostage.

Halliot had also included in his message a bleak statement that his daughter May's maidservant had been found dead on a Liddel riverbank, information that Hugh decided not to relay to Laura until he learned more. Even Halliot had not suggested that the maidservant's death meant that her mistress had died with her, and Hugh did not want to upset Laura unnecessarily. Halliot had not mentioned Laura, even to reply to the message Hugh had relayed for her.

He contented himself, therefore, with sending terse thanks to Halliot and nothing more.

He also sent a report of his activities to Scrope, but the only reply was a message informing him that his lordship was away from Carlisle, the guest of an indecipherably named lord. Knowing the likelihood was that Scrope was engaged in his favorite form of entertainment and that his reaction to the siege would depend on how much he won or lost did not improve Hugh's mood.

He spent his days overseeing his men, strengthening the wall round his tower in case the siege continued through the autumn, and practicing his swordsmanship. He had not been pleased with the showing he had made the night of the raid on Carlisle Castle and was determined never to lose such a match again.

He did not visit Brackengill. His body's reaction to the mere thought of Laura Halliot sleeping in his sister's bedchamber was enough to warn him that he should not seek her out. Even when he believed his mind was focused on his duties, a stray memory would catch him unaware. He would wonder idly if the skin under her clothing would be even softer to touch than the swell of her breasts above her bodice had been. He wondered if she would yield to his desire if he made it known to her. The wondering way her eyes widened when he caught her gaze and held it made him yearn to try her passions.

He dared not reveal his feelings, however, for he doubted that she shared them. Even if by some miracle of a benevolent God, she should come to do so, he knew it would only complicate matters. As her jailer, he could afford her some protection. If others suspected his feelings for her, it would become more difficult.

That did not keep him from thinking about her, however, or constantly wondering how she was spending her time. It did not occur to him that she might defy him. He had given an order, and his orders generally were obeyed.

At first, daily exercise was enough to satisfy Laurie's need to escape the confines of Brackengill, but when Sir Hugh sent word that his siege still had failed to bring the men in Tarras Woods to their knees and would continue indefinitely, even the daily rides began to seem restrictive.

Days when Andrew rode with her were not so bad, for she could ask him questions about the countryside and about his erstwhile mistress. It was in the course of such a conversation that she came to believe that she was closer to Tarras Wood than she had suspected.

The journey from Aylewood to Lochmaben had been long, requiring an overnight stay with friends. Because the trip from Lochmaben to Brackengill had been shorter, and because Sir Hugh had not returned from his siege even for brief visits, she had assumed that the castle was a long way from Tarras Wood.

To learn that Brackengill lay nearer than she had thought to the Moss presented undeniable temptation, particularly since she strongly suspected that Andrew frequently crossed the line to visit Janet Scott.

Laurie could not pretend even to herself that Sir Hugh would permit her to ride into Scotland. But the more she told herself she must not the more she wanted to do so, and Sir Hugh was, after all, in Tarras Moss, creating difficulties for her friends and family.

Her opportunity came at last, at the start of the third week of the siege, when Small Neck Tailor did not appear as usual to saddle her pony and ride out with her.

Only Andrew was there when she walked into the stable.

"Where is everyone?" she asked him.

He shrugged. "Geordie took Small Neck and some others to Bewcastle, because Sir Edward Nixon sent word o' yet another raid into Redesdale. They think it must be Rabbie Redcloak, that he's leadin' all these raids, but the men watching along the line ha' seen naught o' him or his Bairns. Geordie were a bit worried, like, 'cause he's got all them cattle Sir Hugh marked afore he left, pasturin' over Haggbeck way. He's set a guard on 'em o' course, but still . . ."

"Who is in charge here, then?"

"Asa Gibbs," the boy said.

Laurie nodded. She knew Gibbs. "I have bread to take round," she said.

The boy nodded. "Aye, then, I'll bring out our ponies."

Laurie smiled. "You will have to serve as my man-at-arms today, then."

Andrew squared his shoulders. "Aye, I'll look after ye."

Hoping that she was not about to get him into serious trouble, Laurie watched him run into the stable to get their horses. Then, realizing that if she sent him for the loaves he would brag to Meggie that he was to serve as her sole escort, she hurried to the kitchen to fetch them herself.

"We've just these four today," Meggie said grimly. "That feckless Sheila were t' watch them, but she got t' nattering wi' one o' the lads and forgot to shift 'em. The others be black—useless even as trenchers. I'll ha' to mix 'em with the hog slop." She sighed. "At least them hogs'll eat anything and be glad of it."

"We'll take these, then, and the other folks will just have to wait until next week," Laurie said, taking the cloth sack that Meggie held out to her.

She had not decided what to do about the bread if she succeeded in her plan, so it was just as well that she did not have eight or ten loaves. No one in the Borders looked kindly on wasting good food.

" 'Tis a fine, fresh day," Meggie said. "Ye'll ha' a good ride."

"I will," Laurie agreed.

Hurrying back outside, she found Andrew ready with the horses. Handing him the sack to tie to his saddle, she let one of the older lads give her a leg up, but she did not breathe easily until they were alone outside the gates.

Then, when Andrew skirted the wall and headed toward the low, sloping hillside that edged the area she had come to know as Bewcastle Waste, she said casually, "When you ride into Scotland, how do you go?"

He glanced at her, measuring her, as if he wondered whether talking to her about his adventures would get him into trouble.

She smiled. "I know you must do so. You talk so much about your Mistress Janet that I realized some time ago that you must ride over the line frequently to visit her. Does Sir Hugh not know about your visits?"

"Nay, and ye mustna tell him—nor Ned Rowan, neither.

Ned skelped me good the once for staying away all night and worrying me mam, and he promised he'd do it again, too, but he's no caught me since."

"But you've been to Broadhaugh since then, have you not?"

Glancing at her obliquely, his expression answered her question, but she waited to hear what he would say.

At last, reluctantly, he said, "Ye'll no split on me, will ye?"

"Never," Laurie said. "I've secrets enough of my own, laddie."

He relaxed visibly. "We'll ride through yon thicket to reach Granny Fenicke's cot," he said. "Then we go to Job Withrington's widow woman."

"Is not Granny Fenicke the one whose granddaughter lives with her—a lass about your age?"

"Aye," Andrew said, rolling his eyes. "She's that daft, Clara is."

Recalling the way the girl had followed him about during a previous visit, Laurie had no trouble translating this declaration. Smiling, she said, "I was thinking that perhaps Clara would not mind delivering the other loaves. They go to Job's widow, to Mistress Dunne, and to Mistress Hedley, do they not?"

"Aye, Mistress Hedley's ailing a bit, me mam said, so she would get the last one," Andrew said wisely. "But why would we give them to that daft Clara?"

"Because," Laurie said, lowering her tone confidingly, "I want you to take me a short way across the line today."

"I canna do that! Sir Hugh would . . . he would . . ." He fell silent, his eyes wide, clearly at a loss for words to express his dismay.

"Sir Hugh will not know," Laurie said. "I want only to ride on Scottish soil for a bit. Think how you would feel if someone kept you at Broadhaugh and you could not get back here to your own land and family."

His brow creased as he thought about that. "I wouldna like it," he said at last. "But still . . ."

Laurie said, "Just how far is Tarras Moss from here?"

The boy shrugged. "I dinna ken the miles," he said.

"How long does it take you to ride to Broadhaugh, then?"

"A good part o' the day. Wi' Ned Rowan awa', I can tak' supper there and slip back across the line afore sun-up. I tell me mam I'm awa' to Haggbeck, and if I'm in the kitchen when she wakens, she doesna ken I've been awa' the nicht."

"Do you not pass through Tarras Moss? Do you know how to ride there?"

"Oh, aye, I ken the way. 'Tis nobbut an hour and a bit if ye ride hard and if ye ford Liddel Water at Caulside, or so Ned Rowan says. I dinna go that way, though. I stay well east o' that plaguey forest where Sir Hugh's tower be."

Laurie did not even try to conceal her amazement. "They are really as close as that? I thought Tarras Moss must be miles from Brackengill, especially since we have not seen anything of Sir Hugh since this siege began."

"It's no so far as all that," Andrew said. "He sends messages, ye ken."

"What do you hear about the siege?" she asked.

With another casual shrug, he said, "The men dinna say so much, but Mistress Janet says it doesna prosper. She says folk in Tarras Wood ken its ways cleverly, so they go and come as they choose. But I canna tell Sir Hugh or his lads the things she says." He nibbled his lower lip.

"Aye, for they'd be bound to guess you had been to Broadhaugh, and then Ned Rowan would find out," Laurie said. "Now, tell me, which way do you go?"

"By Kershopefoot, where the wee burn runs. 'Tis the easiest way, and no one pays me any mind. I ride toward Hermitage and across the fells to Broadhaugh."

Laurie knew that route, and it would never do, for it led through the heart of Liddesdale. "Do you know the crossing west of Rowanburn, near the castle there?"

"Aye, I've been that road a time or two."

"Well, suppose we ride there? I know that countryside better than I know Liddesdale, and it's safer, I think. I do not suppose that anyone will heed a lone woman and a bairn thereabouts, do you?"

"I'm no bairn," he said indignantly.

"No, of course you are not. You are my man-at-arms."

"Aye, that I am. Just look here." To her shock, he reached down beneath his baggy netherstocks, struggled a moment with something attached to his saddle, and then pulled out a large wheel-lock pistol similar to the one she had taken with her the night she had followed May. He waved it triumphantly in the air.

"Godamercy, Andrew, how came you by that?"

" 'Twas me da's," the boy said. "Them villains o' Scrope's flung it into the thicket by Granny Fenicke's, but Clara found it and give it back t' me. If we meet any Scots reivers the day, I mean to shoot them. Lady Marjory said I couldna protect ye on me own, but I can, mistress. They'll no harm ye whilst I'm about!"

"They would not harm me, in any event," Laurie said gently. "You forget, laddie, they are my people." Repressing the thought of deadly feuds that reared their heads from year to year, feuds that could make her people as dangerous to her as any English Borderer, Laurie held his gaze. "You must not shoot anyone unless I say that you may. Promise me that you will not."

"Oh, aye, then. Mistress Janet said I was no to shoot it till I'm growed, but I'm nearly growed now, I think."

"So you are," she agreed, hoping that he understood the workings of the wicked looking weapon better than she did. "Perhaps one day you could show me how to shoot that thing."

"Aye, sure, perhaps," he said. "Where will we ride when we cross the line?"

"To the west side of Tarras Wood," she said. "If folks are slipping in and out at will, we may meet someone I know. I'd like to hear news of my family."

"News o' that sister o' yours, I'd wager," Andrew said with a grimace.

She looked at him. "Andrew, do you understand why I stay at Brackengill?"

"Aye, sure," he said, clearly surprised by the question. "Ye're Sir Hugh's lady, 'cause ye pledged yourself in your sister's stead. She killed a land sergeant, but the master didna like him, any road, so he's nae too wroth wi' ye, I think."

"That's what you think?" When he nodded, she said, "You seem to know a great deal for a"—he looked accusingly at her—"for a man-at-arms."

He grinned. "I ha' big ears, Ned Rowan says. They do say that no one kens where she is, but Mistress Janet says, like as not, she threw herself into a river like that maid o' hers, or your family be hiding her."

Laurie's heart lurched. "They found Bridget—my sister's maidservant?"

"Did ye no ken? Some men found her dead, lying in some muck on the Scotch side o' the Liddel."

Twenty-one

The lady fair being void of fear,
Her steed being swift and free . . .

Laurie struggled to keep from revealing the extent of her dismay. Surely, if they had found May's body, along with Bridget's, Sir Hugh would have learned of it and set her free. Even Scrope would not demand two lives for that of his land sergeant, not with so little evidence to present a jury comprised of Scots.

That she had not heard more from her father seemed increasingly odd. She was finding it increasingly easy to believe, as Janet Scott did, in a conspiracy to keep May safe at her expense. Forcing calm, she said, "What else do you know?"

"I ken that the laird o' Buccleuch did get free o' Blackness Castle, where your Jamie treated him like a prince and no like a prisoner. But then our Queen made your Jamie send the laird to Berwick where he's in prison again. I ken that Sir Quinton Scott—Mistress Janet's husband, ye ken—be acting Keeper o' Liddesdale whilst Buccleuch be awa', and deputy warden to somebody else, as well."

"Sir William Halliot of Aylewood," she said, adding gently, "my father."

"Aye, sure, I kenned that fine, too."

He did not look at her, though, and she could tell that he was feeling unsure of her motives again.

"I'm not trying to run away, Andrew, I promise you. When you return to Brackengill later today, I will be with you."

He looked at her then, and she met his gaze easily. If she felt guilt, it was not because she intended to harm Andrew. She would not let him suffer for her deeds any more than she would have let Bangtail Willie or Sym do so.

After a long moment, he said, "They do say that Rabbie Redcloak be leading all them raids against Tynedale and Redesdale. They say that he leads his Bairns against England at Buccleuch's command."

"Did your Mistress Janet say that?"

"Nay, then, she says that Rabbie's nae more than a . . . a . . ." He frowned, then said, "What d'ye call it when he's no a ghost but summat that's only a story and doesna exist at all?"

"A legend?"

"Aye, that's it. Rabbie's a legend, she says. I dinna think she can be right, though, 'cause Ned Rowan and the master say he's real. They ken it fine, for they caught 'im once and locked 'im in our dungeon at Brackengill. Still, he must be old Clooty hisself, 'cause he slipped out wi' the cell door and the dungeon door locked tight and Geordie a-guarding 'im wi' the keys in his pocket."

He looked around as if he expected the devil to pop out of the shrubbery, making Laurie smile again.

They rode on, talking desultorily until they had forded the Liddel. As she had hoped, they looked harmless and no one paid them any mind. It was not unusual for people to cross over, after all. Even armed men rode back and forth across the line almost at will, as likely to take a drop of ale in an English tavern as in a Scottish one. Since folks from both sides intermingled at markets, race meetings, football matches, and days of truce, no one looked twice at a young woman riding astride with a child on his pony beside her.

A short time later, the forest loomed ahead to their right.

"You're certain that Sir Hugh's fortress is not on this side," she said.

"Aye, I'm sure. It be a place called Corbies Nest."

"I know Corbies Nest," she said. "Some say it is haunted."

"He willna mind a ghost, ye ken, but he'll be gey wroth wi' us if he sees us."

"He will," Laurie said, feeling a chill shoot up her spine at the thought.

They saw no other rider as they skirted the trees, but she knew that anyone watching the forest would be doing so from one of the surrounding hilltops. With luck, no watcher would question her or Andrew unless he saw them ride into the woods, and she did not mean to do that.

She scanned the hillsides until she saw what she was seeking. "Yonder," she said. "We'll ride toward that flock of sheep. If the shepherd is who I think he is, he may have news for me."

She knew that Sym saw them long before they were near enough to speak to him, but if he recognized her he gave no sign. The two dogs also watched, clearly wondering if she and Andrew posed a threat to their woolly charges.

"Good day to you, Sym," Laurie said when at last they were near enough for him to hear her. "How do you fare?"

"Well enow," Sym said, casting a suspicious glance at Andrew. "Who's he?"

"This is Andrew," Laurie said. "He is a friend of mine."

"Aye, sure, and welcome to ye," Sym said, still eyeing Andrew warily.

"I've come for news of Aylewood," Laurie said. "What can you tell me?"

"Nobbut that Bridget be dead and Mistress May ha' no come back yet," Sym said. "Me dad's wi' Hob the Mouse this day. Likely, Hob can tell ye more."

"I ken Hob the Mouse," Andrew said, his tone indicating surprise that Sym also knew him. "He's gey big, like a giant."

"Aye, he is," Sym said, relaxing.

"Where are they, then?" Laurie said. "Hob and your father."

"Hob's."

"But that's quite near here! Is it safe for them? We know about the siege," she added when he looked surprised.

Sym sneered. "Them English. They watch over the wee trails outside the forest. They think no one treads elsewhere."

Glancing at Andrew, Laurie said, "They have been clever enough to keep people from going about their usual business, have they not?"

"Oh, aye," Sym said.

Andrew's eyes had narrowed at Sym's opinion of the English, and Laurie realized that she faced a slight dilemma. She could hardly ride right to Hob the Mouse's cottage with Andrew beside her, but she could not leave him with Sym, either. Even if Andrew would agree to such a plan, the two small warriors would be at each other's throats before she was out of sight.

"Yonder, they come," Sym said, shooting a sidelong, speculative look at Andrew as he spoke. "Down the wee dale."

Swiftly scanning the area he indicated, she saw the two figures—one unnaturally tall and broad, the other standing no higher than the first man's armpit and more slightly built. She made a hasty decision.

"Andrew, you come with me but no farther than the bottom of this slope. I want to talk to those men, but they will not like your being English and overhearing what they say. You can watch me, though, so that you will know I mean to keep my word to you. Will that satisfy you?"

"Aye, it will," he replied, looking curiously at the approaching pair.

A few moments later, Laurie was talking eagerly with Davy Elliot and Hob. Neither could tell her more about May than Andrew or Sym had.

"Doubtless the feckless lass ha' taken leg-bail and be bidin' safe wi' Lady Halliot's English kinsmen," Davy said glumly. "What they'll do to ye when Mistress May doesna show for the next wardens' meetin' I canna bear t' think on."

Not wanting to think about that herself, Laurie said lightly,

"If May has truly disappeared, you will just have to gather Rabbie's Bairns and rescue me."

"Nay, we dare not," Hob said. "Himself ha' given orders that the Bairns are no to stir till he's managed t' smooth Elizabeth's ruffled feathers."

Since "Himself" could refer only to Buccleuch, Laurie was surprised. "Then why have the Bairns organized so many raids?"

Davy said, "Faith, lass, the Bairns ha' done no raiding since Buccleuch led the raid on North Tynedale—which were a perfectly legal trod. We chased reivers right to their own den, and Himself hanged a few o' them."

"Are you sure, Davy?"

"Aye. Did they no clap Buccleuch up in Berwick, and did Sir Hugh Graham no fix himself at Corbies Nest? A man ha' to feed his family, but I trow, we've lain so doucely of late that we've no tasted beef in the forest for nigh onto a fortnight. Mind now, did I ken where I could lay hand to a herd close by wi'out stirring a ruckus, I'd whisk it home afore the cat could lick its ear."

"Despite the siege?"

Davy sneered. "Bless ye, lassie, we couldna drive a herd into the woods wi'out taking a wee precaution or two, but we'd easily drive a few beasts near enow t' butcher. And, butchered, we'd carry it in wi'out them English bein' the wiser."

"As it happens, a herd lies not far from here," Laurie said with a grin.

"Does it now?"

"Aye, near Haggbeck. It belongs to Sir Hugh. He marked the beasts not three weeks ago, but they are well guarded, Davy."

"Sir Hugh's own beef?"

"Aye," she said, "but you must not steal them all, for he's been kind to me. Take only what you need to feed folks in the forest, and then . . ." She paused with an impish look. "Davy, I've got a bit of paper. Can you carve me a quill?"

"Aye, sure, and Hob's got a brace o' pigeons in yon sack. Why?"

"I want to write a note to Sir Hugh."

"To him! Are ye daft?"

"Not at all, I am merely being polite. If you cross the line to steal his beef, I think you should leave one outside his fortress for him and his men," Laurie said as she removed the paper Sir Hugh had given her from her bodice. "I want you to put my note with it."

His open-mouthed expression told her he thought she was mad, but he did not argue. When he had provided her with a sharp quill and Hob had produced some pigeon's blood for ink, she wrote as swiftly as the primitive implements allowed.

On the way back to Brackengill, Laurie did not say anything to Andrew about the plan she had made with Hob and Davy. She had come to trust the boy during their daily rides and was certain that he would not willingly betray her, but she knew that only innocence would protect him if anyone came to suspect that he had had a part in it. In any event, Andrew spent the greater portion of their return journey alternately asking questions about Scotland and expressing his opinion of their folly in crossing the line.

When he noted that clouds were gathering overhead and that they would be lucky to get home before it began raining, she said only, "I warrant it may spit a little, but those clouds hold no great storm."

Still enjoying her pleasure in the little surprise she had planned for Sir Hugh, she answered Andrew's questions patiently and responded to his muttering about folly with silence or by tactfully changing the subject.

"Ye're plumb daft, that's what it is," he said at last. "First ye cross the line like it were naught, and now ye sit smiling when there's gey little t' smile about."

The temptation to tell him that the besieged men intended to steal Sir Hugh's cattle was nearly overwhelming, but she held her peace. "Doubtless you are right," was all she said in reply.

"Aye, sure, o' course I'm right," Andrew retorted indignantly. " 'Tis a good thing them villains didna try to keep ye there. I'd my pistol, and all, but I dinna mind tellin' ye, I didna like the notion o' shootin' Hob the Mouse when he's been a good friend to Mistress Janet. Like as no, she'd ha' been wroth wi' me."

"Indeed, she would," Laurie said. "You must not think of doing such a thing. Instead, I want you to teach me how to shoot that pistol of yours. You can begin giving me lessons tomorrow when we ride out again."

"Aye, sure, if it doesna rain," he agreed sourly without looking at her. A moment later, he muttered, "But we'll no go to Scotland again, though."

"No," she said, thinking that he did not seem very eager to show her how to shoot his pistol and wondering if he really knew how it worked.

Their conversation after that was desultory until they reached Brackengill, where, despite the length of time they had been gone, no one questioned their absence. The men had grown accustomed to her daily outings, and Geordie merely seemed glad to see Andrew.

"Dinna put your pony awa', laddie," he said, waving a lackey over to take Laurie's horse. "I've a message for them at Haggbeck, and if ye run tell your mam, ye can take it and ha' your supper wi' the men there. Ye'll like that, I'm thinking'."

"Aye, I will," Andrew said enthusiastically.

Watching his chest puff with the importance of his mission, Laurie felt doubly glad that she had not confided in him, and glad, too, that he would return before nightfall. She did not think the men of Tarras Wood could plan and execute even a small raid so quickly, but she would have worried to think that Andrew might be present when they did. Violence could break out quickly, and she would not like knowing that she had unwittingly placed the boy in danger.

The rain held off, and she spent the rest of the afternoon and evening with Lady Marjory, who had enjoyed visitors during the day and commiserated at length with Laurie for having missed them.

"It was Lady Nixon from Bewcastle, my dear, and I know she would have enjoyed making your acquaintance. She heard about you from Francis Musgrave, who is still quite put out that Sir Hugh has entered into marriage with you."

She chuckled, adding, "Sir Francis believed he would one day arrange a match between Sir Hugh and one of his daughters, you see. Lady Nixon told me that everyone for miles—even their parson—was taking wagers on whether Sir Francis would succeed. I could have set them right, had I but known. Hugh has always had an eye for a pretty lass, so by what they tell me, Sir Francis's daughters would *not* suit him." She went on to explain that she had tried to persuade her guest to remain for supper but that Lady Nixon, fearing a downpour, had declined.

Laurie listened with half an ear, her thoughts more often with Davy, Hob, and the others than with Lady Marjory. Nonetheless, she found the thought of Sir Hugh married to one of Musgrave's daughters or anyone else rather distasteful.

The clouds opened up just before sundown, and a light but steady rain fell for an hour or two—just enough to settle the dust, the men said.

Early the next morning, Laurie went in search of Andrew, hoping to persuade him to teach her to shoot his pistol. When she learned that the boy had not returned from Haggbeck but had apparently spent the night there, her first thought was that something had happened to him.

Geordie dispelled that fear quickly when she voiced her worry to him. "Like as not, the lad used that wee drizzle as his excuse to stay wi' the men," he said.

Laurie knew that answer was the most likely one, but her fear did not ease until Andrew returned later in the day.

"Aye, I wanted to stay," he told her, "but I'd no ha' done

it did I ken four o' them kine would wander off in the night. They had me lookin' for 'em all day!"

"Did you find them?" she asked, knowing the answer.

He shook his head. "Them silly beasts vanished as if they'd been cursed. I canna tak' ye out the day, neither. Geordie says I must muck out the stable."

"Indeed, you must not shirk your duties on my account," Laurie said. "You can show me how to shoot tomorrow instead."

The boy grimaced. "As to that, mistress, I should tell ye that I ha' five bullets for me pistol but no powder. Mayhap, if I tell Geordie ye're wishful to learn—"

"Let me see what I can find first," Laurie said, striving to sound matter-of-fact. She could not imagine that Geordie would look kindly on a female—let alone a hostage—learning to shoot a gun. "If I find no powder, perhaps you can just show me how the mechanism is supposed to work when one does have powder."

Looking more cheerful, Andrew hurried off to attend to his chores. His mistress watched him go, feeling rather smug at the thought that Sir Hugh and the English were not as smart as they thought they were.

At the end of the first fortnight, Hugh had sent another courier to Broadhaugh, reminding Sir Quinton of his promise to help lay the Tarras Wood reivers by the heels. The reply had come from his sister, Janet, however, expressing the hope that he was well and telling him that her husband had been called to Edinburgh and then on to Berwick but would doubtless write to Hugh on his return.

Instead, and to Hugh's surprise, Sir Quinton arrived in person, leading an entourage consisting of a score of his men and including his wife and a cousin whom he introduced as Gilbert Scott of Hawkburne.

Hugh's delight in their unexpected arrival surprised him even more than it did his guests.

Sir Quinton's eyes twinkled as the two shook hands. "I hope you don't expect me to express regret that your siege does not prosper," he said.

"It might prosper better did I receive the aid I'm due from you or Halliot," Hugh said.

He was annoyed, but only slightly. His relationship with Sir Quinton Scott had grown complicated with that gentleman's marriage to Janet. Moreover, his dealings with Quinton both at the wardens' table and on fighting ground had colored his natural enmity with strong respect for the Scotsman's humor and sense of fair play. Try though he had, Hugh found it difficult to dislike the man.

"We believe the men taking shelter in Tarras Wood are innocent of the raids you accuse them of perpetrating," Quinton said blandly.

"Then why did they flee their homes?"

"Doubtless because experience warned them that you would not believe in their innocence."

"I do not," Hugh said flatly. "Will you honor your obligation to me?"

Sir Quinton nodded, but at the same moment Gilbert Scott demanded, "Why should we help you capture good Scotsmen?"

"Perhaps because Border law requires it," Hugh said evenly. He had seen Quinton's nod and put more faith in that than in the younger man's brash attitude. Turning to greet his sister, he said on a lighter note, "You look fit, lass."

Janet ignored his outstretched hand and gave him a hug instead. "I am fit," she said. "How fares your hostage, Hugh? Quinton tells me she is quite lovely."

"She fares well enough," Hugh said, knowing that Janet was trying to change the subject to one less likely to lead to strife but wishing that she had not mentioned Laura. He tried to repress images of Laura's loveliness that instantly leapt to his mind's eye; however, the shrewd look his sister gave him told him that he had not succeeded. Quickly turning away, he shouted for ale for his guests, then said to no one in particular, "What do you hear of May Halliot?"

Janet and Quinton exchanged a look before Quinton said, "Nothing to the purpose. You've doubtless heard that they found her maid's body near the Liddel, but there was evidently no sign of May herself. From their silence, I'd say her own people have hidden her away somewhere."

"Would they dare sacrifice their older daughter to save the younger?"

Quinton shrugged, but Janet said, "They say that Lady Halliot favors May, because May is her own daughter. She is Sir William's second wife, you know."

"Aye, Mistress Halliot said there is no love lost between her and her stepmother, but they both are his daughters. Has he no say in the matter?"

"I have heard it said that he lives under the cat's paw and, moreover, that he believes his wife spirited the girl away to kinsmen of hers in England," Janet said. "Lady Halliot's mother was born in Northumberland, I believe."

"The plain fact is that Sir William is not a man of action," Quinton Scott said, accepting a mug of ale from one of Hugh's men. "He prefers solitude to soldiering. Buccleuch says Jamie chose him to replace Buccleuch for that very reason. The King fancies that Halliot is a man of peace. Buccleuch told him that he was wrong about that, that Halliot just likes peace at home—and at any price—but Jamie was in no mood to listen."

"The whole business is errant nonsense," Gilbert Scott declared with a challenging look at Hugh. "The notion that May Halliot or any woman murdered one of Scrope's land sergeants is laughable—as laughable as this siege of yours."

Sir Quinton put a hand on the younger man's shoulder, saying with deceptive gentleness, "Put away your arrogance for a few hours, Gil, and drink your ale. You forget that we are presently enjoying Sir Hugh's hospitality."

Grinning at Hugh, he added, "Forgive him. His father is Hawkburne, who was one of the leaders identified with Buccleuch in the North Tynedale raid. Thus, he accompanied him to Berwick, but he has not found it as easy as Buccleuch has to arrange for pledges, so I offered to help Gil here arrange them. The lad has courage but sometimes lacks common sense. I have been encouraging him to restrain his warlike impulses."

"By your good example, I suppose," Hugh said with an edge to his voice.

"Aye, exactly," Sir Quinton agreed. "How fares your sword arm?"

"Better than ever," Hugh said firmly. "If you mean to linger a day or so, I'll let you try your worst."

Sir Quinton's eyebrows shot upward. "I'd like that, for I've not had an opportunity to test my skill since our last match, but I can stay only till morning. I've arranged for Buccleuch's pledges, so he should persuade Her Majesty to release him soon. Then he will doubtless summon me to Berwick to ride back with him, and I have matters to attend at Broadhaugh before I go away again."

"In truth, Jamie ought to have sent him straight to London and not just to Berwick," Hugh said provocatively.

Sir Quinton smiled. "Considering the outrageous nature of Scrope's raid on Liddesdale, I think you English should consider yourselves fortunate that Buccleuch did nothing worse than hang a few North Tynedale raiders."

"Aye," Gil Scott agreed testily. "And that was a legal trod, what's more."

"Oh, aye, indeed," Hugh said. "Buccleuch carried off thirty-six prisoners, I'll remind you, whom he afterwards put to death. And that was only the first raid. Other expeditions have followed with unabated fury. Some even claim that raiders have burned innocent people in their cottages."

"That was Scrope in Liddesdale, not Buccleuch in Tynedale," Gil Scott snapped. "Buccleuch denies having committed slaughter, except of thieves taken red-handed, and Buccleuch does not lie. You cannot say the same of Scrope."

"As to that, you young hothead," Hugh retorted, "let me tell you—"

"Never mind that," Janet interjected swiftly. "It would be

hard to say which side is most to blame, Hugh. It is just as I always said it would be. One side incites the other, and the killing and destruction go on and on. Someone must stop it."

"Then let Buccleuch do so, or your precious Rabbie Redcloak," Hugh snapped, looking pointedly at Sir Quinton. "Buccleuch may not have led all the raids. In fact, he cannot have done so since he has been Her Majesty's guest at Berwick, but his share in them, added to the original outrage against Carlisle, have made the English indictment against him a heavy one. Scrope will not forget it. Indeed, the man can think of little else. And even if Buccleuch has been rendered idle, I'll wager that Redcloak has been damned busy."

"That's not true," Gil Scott declared angrily. "Buccleuch gave orders, devilish unfair orders, I think, and even—"

"Silence, you young cockerel," Quinton said.

He chuckled, but something in the look he gave Gil silenced the younger man at last. Giving Hugh a look as direct as the one Hugh had given him, Quinton said, "Rabbie Redcloak has not led any of the recent raids against the English."

"I should believe that, should I?" Hugh said. "You and your wretched Buccleuch refuse to admit even that such a reiver exists. Why should I believe anything else you say about him?"

"Because I say you may," Sir Quinton said. "Do you have food here, man? My lady is hungry, and although you may think she is growing rather stout and should practice economy in her dining, I should tell you that it is no such thing."

Hugh had already turned to look for someone he could send for food, but a note in Quinton's voice made him turn back. "What the devil are you talking about?" When Quinton grinned at him, he looked at Janet to find that she was smiling, too. "What?" As the answer dawned on him, he forgot his enmity toward Quinton and thought only of his sister and her evident delight. "You look quite smug," he said, his tone gentling. "So Janet the Bold is to become a mother, is she?"

"Aye, she is," Janet said happily.

"She wanted to tell you herself, in person," Quinton said. "And since I was bound to respond to your request for help,

I agreed to bring her. I want her to return first thing in the morning, however, and I dare not entrust her safety to only a small party of my men—not with English soldiers encamped on our side of the line."

Recognizing return provocation, Hugh smiled at Janet again. "Is that why you did not accompany him to Lochmaben?"

"Aye, I wanted to go, but he would have none of it." She smiled lovingly at her husband. "He treats me like a bairn."

Gil Scott said warningly, "Not like a Bairn, madam, surely!"

Quinton's gaze did not flicker. He continued to return his wife's look as he said easily, "Gil, you talk too much. Leave be, or I'll send you to Berwick to see what you can do to ease Buccleuch's temper whilst he awaits word from Elizabeth."

Quinton said, "He expects word to come soon, then?"

"Oh, aye, he is ever optimistic, and to be fair, he is rarely wrong about things that affect him so personally. It will doubtless annoy you to learn that I returned from Berwick some nights ago, but I dared not come to you until I had seen Hermitage made ready to receive him."

"I believe you wasted your time there," Hugh said. "Elizabeth is as unlikely to forgive him as Scrope is."

"Don't count on that," Quinton said. "The fame of his exploits evidently has been noised about all over England, and his Berwick jailors treat him more like a distinguished guest than a captive brought to answer for his offenses against the government. They say he has made a very favorable impression on the Queen, for although she insisted that he should yield himself her prisoner, once he did, she was satisfied. She has treated him with marked kindness."

"He has pledged to bring peace to the Borders if she will release him," Gil Scott said with visible disgust.

"And Elizabeth knows that he can do it," Quinton said. "Moreover, since I did not hide my disbelief in his ability to work his charm on her, it will not surprise me if he fails to warn me of his return and simply shows up one day to astonish me. Indeed, I think I should send Gil here to Berwick if only to give us fair warning."

Gil looked as if he intended to protest, but before he could do so, Ned Rowan approached Hugh, looking uncharacteristically wary.

"What is it?" Hugh demanded.

"Begging your pardon, master, but we've received word from Haggbeck that someone stole four kine from your herd there overnight."

"Four?"

"Aye, they raided by stealth this time, sir, not in numbers." He looked down at his feet, then up again. Glancing at Hugh's guests, he said, "Perhaps I might ha' a word wi' ye alone, master."

"There is no point in that," Hugh said, irritated. "Sir Quinton has been telling me that there are no Scottish reivers in this area."

"Well as to that, there be at least one, and we ha' captured him," Rowan said. "He walked up to the gate, leading a cow that bears your mark."

"Fetch him to me," Hugh ordered. "Perhaps Sir Quinton can identify him."

When Rowan returned, he brought a boy about the age of Meggie's Andrew.

Hugh's eyebrows shot upward. "This is the reiver you captured?"

"They didna capture me," the lad said scornfully. "I brung ye a message."

"Another message?" Hugh said. With a wry grimace, he said to Quinton and Janet, "They've sent several. In one, they said I was like the puffs of a haggis, hot only at first. They bade me stay here as long as the weather would give me leave."

"Very cordial," Quinton said. "I believe I have met your messenger before. How are you, Sym Elliot?"

Tugging his forelock, Sym replied warily, "I be well enow, sir."

"Let's hear your message," Hugh commanded.

To his surprise, instead of repeating an oral message as the reivers' messenger had done before, the boy reached under his ragged shirt, pulled out a folded bit of parchment, and offered it to him. "Ye're to read it," he said.

Glancing at the others, Hugh saw that they were as surprised as he was. He unfolded the parchment and read the crudely scrawled note, feeling first a rush of anger at its impudence, then momentary bewilderment. What common reiver could write such a thing?

"Are you going to show us the note?" Janet demanded. "What does it say?"

Silently, he handed it to her, and scanning it swiftly, she stifled a laugh and handed it to Sir Quinton, who read it and laughed much more heartily.

"Such impudence," Janet said. "How did they dare?"

"There is something damned odd about that note," Quinton said.

"There is, indeed," Hugh agreed, retrieving it and stuffing it under his jack. "But I'll deal with it. Take the boy away now, Ned. I'll talk with him later."

"Hugh, no," Janet protested. "He's only a bairn. Let him go!"

"He was in possession of stolen property, Janet. It is my right to question him. Even Quin will agree. Now, if you want to eat, I'll have my lads bring food."

She did not argue, and if the boy, Sym, looked frightened as Rowan led him away, Hugh decided it was no more than he deserved.

He had recognized both the parchment and the hand that wrote the note, and he was having all he could do to keep from shouting for his horse. He did not know how she had managed it, but he would find out, and when he did, she would quickly recognize the error she had made in taunting him.

The moment he was alone, he took out the note and read

it again. The message was no more humorous to him the second time than the first:

Greetings, Sir Hugh Graham! Fearing that you were short of provisions, we thought you might be hungering for good English beef.

so that at least the little belfry now concealed beneath her

Twenty-two

Then first she called the stable groom,
He was her waiting man . . .

Laurie spent the evening letting Lady Marjory teach her how to play Tables, using Sir Hugh's game board. Since Lady Marjory's skill at the game was limited, the effort was no great success, but it did pass the time until her ladyship announced that she would go to bed. Parting with her outside her bedchamber, Laurie went back downstairs to the little chamber near the hall where Sir Hugh had first kissed her. She had learned since then that he kept a number of interesting things there.

Keeping an ear cocked for noise from the hall where men had already begun to bed down for the night, and using a single candle for light, she rummaged quietly through chests and coffers until she found a leather strap with several small wooden bottles of powder attached to it. There was a pistol, too, but she did not take that. Not only was it of a more modern style than Andrew's, but it had a long stock and would be difficult to conceal. Taking the powder seemed a small crime, and she did not think anyone would miss it. A pistol was another matter. At least, she now knew where he kept such things, which might prove useful in future.

She slept with the powder bottles tucked safely under her quilt, and the next morning, before she went downstairs to break her fast, she attached the strap to her belt, arranging it so that it and the little bottles lay concealed beneath her skirts. After eating, she found Andrew ready and waiting in the bailey with their ponies.

"The bluidy Scots took them fiendish kine," he told her. "Small Neck's gone to Haggbeck, taking more men to guard the rest, so I'm your man-at-arms again."

She was sure that he had not told Geordie as much, but Geordie was nowhere in sight, and since it would not suit her plans to have one of the older men along, she said nothing until they were safely outside the castle wall. Then she asked only if Andrew had brought his pistol.

"Aye, I did, and the wee bullets, too. Did ye find powder?"

"I did. We can ride to the thicket near Granny Fenicke's cottage. No one will pay heed to any noise we make there."

They had ridden only over the first hill, however, before she became aware of a rider following them. They were beyond sight of the castle ramparts, and she felt suddenly vulnerable.

"Look back, Andrew, and see if you know who that rider is."

He obeyed, squinting. "I think 'tis that Scotsman," he said. "The one who was wi' Hob the Mouse t'other day when we crossed the line."

"Davy?" Looking back again, she saw the rider wave, realized that Andrew was right, and quickly drew rein to wait for Davy Elliot to catch up with them.

"They've taken Sym," he said as he pulled his pony to a stop beside them.

Shocked, Laurie said, "Who took him?"

"Sir Hugh Graham and them."

"How?"

"Delivering your good English beef, that's how," Davy said bitterly.

"What beef?" Andrew asked.

Appalled at Davy's news, Laurie ignored Andrew, saying, "But no one was supposed to get close enough to Corbies Nest to be caught. Certainly not Sym!"

"Aye, well, we wanted to be certain no one else got the

beef ye meant for Sir Hugh," Davy said. "It seemed safe enough to let the lad tie a lead to one kye and stake it near the gate. If they questioned him, he were t' tell 'em that he'd found it and give 'em the note ye wrote. I dinna ken what went amiss."

"What note?" Andrew demanded.

"They'll let him go, Davy," Laurie said at the same time, feeling a surge of guilt. "They must. Godamercy, what have I done?"

Andrew was frowning. "Them kine o' the master's that went missing," he muttered. "Them thievish reivers o' yours took 'em, didn't they? They been raiding right out o' that plaguey forest all along!"

"Nay, then, we have not," Davy said indignantly.

"Ye have, and all, and so I'll tell them back at the castle! What's more, ye're my prisoner," the boy announced, yanking his pistol from its place beneath his baggy netherstocks and pointing it at Davy.

Laurie said fiercely, "Andrew, put that down. It isn't even loaded, Davy. Pay him no heed. He only brought that out here to show me how to shoot a pistol. I've got the powder for it under my skirt."

"Do ye now, lass?" Davy said. Despite his distress, his eyes twinkled. "I'm that glad to hear it. I dinna ken what ye can do about our Sym, but I knew ye'd want to hear about it. I rode over in the night and waited till I saw ye ride out, but I'll be going on back now. Hob's talking wi' the lads. Ally the Bastard and some others be for looking for whoever's been raiding, but Hob's of a mind that we should wait for Himself. They'll free him soon, Hob said, and he'll get the lad back."

"Surely Sir Hugh will not harm Sym," Laurie said.

Davy frowned. "I doubt they'll hang him for stealing the one kye, but Sir Hugh's been known to hang men out o' sheer temper afore. Recall that he wanted to hang our Rabbie when he caught him that once, and Border law will be on his side this time if he claims Sym were caught red-handed wi' stolen goods."

"You must go and tell Sir Quinton," Laurie said. "You should have done that at once, Davy, before coming to me."

"There'd be naught to gain by that," Davy said. "Sir Quinton were there when they caught the lad. He told Hob that Sir Hugh willna harm him."

"Then he will not," Laurie said. "Doubtless he merely wants to question him, to find out how he got the cow. Sym will be frightened, though. Will he tell?"

"Nay then, he won't split on you or on us, but Sir Hugh's bound to think what this laddie does, that we've been raiding Tynedale and all. And we've not, lass. I give ye my word."

"What about Rabbie Redcloak then? Is he in Tarras Wood with the others?"

"Nay, but he's no leading raiders neither," Davy said.

Andrew said scornfully, "And how d'ye ken that?"

"Because if he were, I'd be ridin' with him, that's how," Davy retorted.

"Andrew," Laurie said, "have you heard any man at Brackengill or Haggbeck say that he has seen the raiders? Have Sir Hugh's men recognized anyone or followed any raiders back to Tarras Wood?"

"Nay, but them that raid leave no ponies behind, so the villagers canna follow 'em anywhere," Andrew said, still keeping a close eye on Davy. "Geordie says the reivers ken where our watchers lie and never ride near 'em."

"Well, I believe Davy, Andrew. Perhaps if you were to ride to Broadhaugh and speak to Lady Scott, she could persuade Sir Quinton . . . No, wait."

Laurie shook her head, realizing that although the boy looked eager to go, she could not send him to Broadhaugh. Even if he could persuade Janet Scott of something that he did not believe himself and Janet agreed to speak to her husband, Sir Quinton might not be home. And even if he was at home, by the time Sym persuaded Janet and Janet persuaded Sir Quinton, it might still be too late for Sym. Sir Hugh would not harm him if he had promised Quinton Scott that he would not. But if Sir Hugh had to hand Sym over to Scrope . . . That possibility terrified her.

"I'll have to go to Sir Hugh myself," she said.

Her stomach knotted at the thought, but she could tell by the relieved look on Davy's face that he had hoped she would go.

He said gently, "Can ye do it, lass? I ken fine that ye've crossed the line afore, but surely ye did it wi'out Sir Hugh's leave."

"I did," she admitted. "He will be furious with me, but that cannot be helped, Davy. This is my doing. I must do what I can to help."

"I'll ride wi' ye," Davy said.

"No, you must not. I'll ride with Andrew, as I did before. No one heeds a woman and a lad, riding alone. I'll be safer that way."

"Unless the lad splits on ye," Davy said, shooting a stern look at Andrew.

Laurie said calmly, "He won't, will you, Andrew?"

Instead of reassuring her, Andrew looked thoughtful. At last, he said, "I'll carry me gun, then, and we'll load it proper."

Davy started to protest, but Laurie said, "In truth, Davy, I'll feel safer with it loaded. If the raiders are not Liddesdale men, then we do not know who they are or where we might meet with them. I want to know how to load that pistol, in any event. Can you show us how—and quickly?"

"Aye, I can do that," Davy said. "Give it to me, ye wee villain."

Andrew obeyed, watching closely as Davy examined the wheel-lock mechanism. In the meantime, Laurie unhooked the strap with the little powder bottles and slipped it from beneath her skirts, showing it to Davy.

He nodded approvingly.

"Each o' them bottles ha' powder for one charge," he said. " 'Tis good, that is, because ye canna overload the pistol. Here's what ye do, then."

He showed them as he talked. "Ye wind the wheel wi' this

wee spanner clipped t' the stock until it locks the wheel . . .
so. Then ye pour the powder into the wee pan here by the hole
in the barrel. Then ye close the pan cover, so. The fine thing
about this gun is ye can load it and then put it back in yon
holster. The cover protects the powder, and the gun willna fire
till ye pull the trigger. But dinna touch the trigger till ye're
wantin' to shoot summat with it. It'll fire only the one time,
and 'tis likely ye'll no ha' time to wind it and load again."

"I want to shoot it now," Andrew said.

"Nay, then, ye'll have them at the castle down on us if ye
do," Davy warned. Looking at Laurie, he added, "I doubt this
be a good notion, lass."

"It's the only notion I have at present," Laurie said. "Sir
Hugh will not listen to you, and I do not see how you can
persuade Sir Quinton to speak for Sym if he did not do so at
once. But if I tell Sir Hugh that I believe Sym is innocent . . ."

She fell silent in the face of Davy's visible skepticism, then
rallied, saying firmly, "It's the only thing I can do, Davy. He
will be angry, but I think I can persuade him to listen to me.
In any event, for Sym's sake, I must try."

"Aye, lass, and I'm that grateful. I'll follow ye at a distance,
though. I dinna trust the young scamp there to guard ye, and
if ye ha' need o' that pistol, I'm no sure I trust it either. Wheel-
locks ha' a habit o' failing when ye need 'em most."

Laurie nodded. She would be glad to know that he was
nearby, although she did not believe she would be in any danger while crossing into Scotland. The danger she faced lay on
the other side, at Corbies Nest, when she confronted Sir Hugh
Graham. Just the thought of that confrontation tied a knot in
her stomach.

It was not generally her way to deal with problems directly,
but in her time at Brackengill, she had come to realize some
things about herself, and not all of them pleased her. She could
see that in the past, when impulse led her astray, she had usually managed to wheedle her way out of trouble. She saw, too,
that when she first offered herself as a pledge for May, she

had expected to manage Hugh as easily as she had managed her father.

Sir Hugh, however, had not proved to be as predictable as Sir William was. He had seemed determined to make her stay at Brackengill as comfortable as possible, and he had allowed her to do as she pleased about hiring maidservants, but recalling his anger when he found her doing work that he considered inappropriate for a woman of her rank, she felt the knot in her stomach tighten. Recalling that he had once threatened to beat her if she ever lied to him, she could not help but think that he might view her decision to ride to Scotland—no matter how righteous her purpose—in much the same way that he would view lying.

It was not until the tower and rough timber walls of Corbies Nest loomed ahead that it occurred to her that Sir Hugh had seen her handwriting and might have recognized it. Until that point, she had not been able to decide what she would say to him, but if he knew that she'd had a hand in the prank that resulted in Sym's arrest, she would have to tell him the truth and just hope for the best.

Hugh attempted only once to question Sym, but recognizing that the surge of anger that overcame him when Sym stood before him had little to do with the boy, he had sent him away again. He had no wish to vent his temper on one so young.

The temptation to ride to Brackengill and confront Laurie was nearly overwhelming, but he resisted that, too. Common sense told him that if she was involved with the so-called gift Sym had delivered, she was likely to be involved in a grander plot, as well. Since his temptation was to ride at speed to Brackengill, it was possible that the raiders had counted on his recognizing her hand and doing just that. Therefore, without first learning more, he could not afford to leave. His place was with his men, seeing to it that his siege succeeded in routing the reivers.

He had sent two men to Haggbeck early that morning, and

they had returned already to say that only four kine were missing from the herd but that Geordie had sent men from Brackengill to help guard the others, fearing that the reivers intended to return and seize the rest later.

He was tempted to send his messengers to Brackengill with an order that Geordie lock Mistress Halliot in her bedchamber until he could deal with her, but since the message would have had to be delivered orally, he did not. He did not yet know how the reivers had made contact with Laura, but it was possible that they had suborned one of his men to get to her. Exactly what they had done he would learn from her just as soon as he was certain that all was secure at Tarras Wood.

Since it had not occurred to him that Laura might have left Brackengill, he was able to attend to his duties in the serene belief that dealing with her could await his pleasure. He basked in this belief until early afternoon when Ned Rowan interrupted him by striding into the hall, his face grim.

"What is it?" Hugh demanded. His first thought was for Laura's safety, and thus it was that he did not immediately comprehend Rowan's meaning when the man spoke her name.

"What is it? What the devil's happened? Have they attacked Brackengill?"

"She's here, master."

"Here? What do you mean? Damnation, man, can you not speak plainly?"

"Lady Graham—Mistress Halliot—she's here!"

Comprehending at last, Hugh jumped to his feet. "Where?"

"Outside this hall. I'd ha' brung her in, but I didna ken . . ." He gestured toward the few men who were in the hall, beginning to set up for dinner while they waited to take their turns on the wall.

"Fetch her." Hugh got to his feet, glowering at Rowan.

"The lad's wi' her—Meggie's Andrew. D'ye want him, too?"

"You can deal with him and with whoever else she cozened into escorting her," Hugh snarled. "Just fetch her in here! The rest of you, leave."

His men left hurriedly, but when Laurie entered, Andrew was at her side.

She walked in briskly, saying, "I won't allow you to bully Andrew the way you've bullied Sym, Sir Hugh. I countermanded your order and told him that he could stay with me, because he is afraid to go with Ned Rowan. He's afraid that Ned will punish him."

"Ned *should* punish him," Hugh growled, 'just as I should punish you. I should hang every man jack that came with you, for aiding and abetting the escape of a prisoner. What the devil are you doing here?"

"I had to come," she said earnestly. "I cannot let you make war on children. Where is Sym Elliot? I know you've got him locked up here. They told me so."

"I want to know who's been talking out of turn," Hugh said. What he really wanted to do was grab her and shake her, but with Andrew standing white-faced at her side, his eyes wide with fear, he could not allow himself to touch her.

"No one talked out of turn," Laurie said. "Sym's father came to find me, to tell me what had happened. I know I should not have come here, but—"

"You should not have set foot outside the gates of Brackengill!"

She made an impatient gesture, as if she were dismissing something trivial. "Why are you holding Sym?"

"Because he walked right up to the gate with a cow he'd stolen from my herd. Tell me what you know about that, my lass, before we go any further."

When color flooded her cheeks and she pressed her lips tightly together, he felt a surge of satisfaction, believing that he had effectively silenced her.

The glint in Sir Hugh's eyes confirmed Laurie's fear that he had recognized her scrawl in the note he had received.

"Pray, sir, do not glower at me," she said at last, keeping her gaze fixed on a point in the middle of his chest. That way, she did not have to confront the anger in his eyes. To keep her courage, she knew she would have to remain calm, but it was not easy when she knew he was furious. "This is hard for me," she said. "I know I am pledged to remain at Brackengill until May returns, but I also knew that I had to come to you myself when I learned that you were holding Sym. You are wrong about the raiders, sir."

"Wrong? What can you know about it? And how the devil did you escape? By Heaven, I'll have answers to that, and my men will rue the day that—"

Meeting his gaze at last, she said, "Do not blame your men, sir. They took their cue from you. You never told them to treat me like a prisoner, and you have rarely done so yourself. You trusted my word, and I promise, you can still do so. I am as much your hostage today as I ever was."

"A proper hostage does not cross back into Scotland when she is pledged to remain in England, lass. I told you that you were to stay inside the castle, and you promised to do so."

"Not really," she said, looking down again. "You asked if I understood you, and I said that I did, but I never promised to stay inside the walls. Even so," she added hastily, "I pledged to remain your hostage, and I have. Surely, you know that you can trust me as much as your Queen trusts the Laird of Buccleuch when she allows him to hunt and gamble with his Berwick jailers."

His jaw tightened. "We are not discussing Buccleuch," he said. "I want to know how the men who stole my cattle came by a note in your hand—a most impertinent note, I might add."

She nibbled her lower lip. Speaking the truth was harder than she had thought it would be. "Well," she said at last, exchanging a quick look with Andrew, "the truth is that I rode into Scotland once before today."

Sir Hugh also looked at Andrew. After a momentary silence, during which Laurie noted with admiration that Andrew did not attempt to avoid that stern gaze, Hugh said, "What have you to say about this, lad?"

Andrew licked his lips nervously, but his voice was steady

when he said, "I do nobbut what the mistress asks of me, master. I did think she were daft when she said she believed them what told her the reivers are no men o' Liddesdale, but she be right about our lads no seeing 'em."

"You go and find Ned Rowan and do as he bids you."

"Rowan must not punish him," Laurie interjected hastily.

"Tell him that I'll talk to you about all this later," Hugh added.

"And what about Sym?" Laurie demanded as Andrew turned slowly away. "You must let him go back to his people, sir. He did no more than . . . than what I asked him to do," she added with a gulp.

"I see," Hugh said, shooting a look at her from under his brows that boded no good. "Tell Ned I want him," he told Andrew.

The boy left, and a moment later, Rowan returned. "Aye, master?"

"Send that boy Sym home to his people," Hugh said. "It seems that he was no more than the messenger he said he was, and regardless of what *some* might think, I do *not* make war on children."

"Aye, sir," Rowan said. "D'ye want me to tend to young Andrew now?"

"Nay, he did only as he was commanded. I'll deal with the true culprit myself." Dismissing Rowan with a gesture, Hugh said nothing for a long moment, and Laurie felt her knees weaken.

When he still said nothing, she blurted, "I never did run away. You must see that much, and you cannot have any notion how hard it was for me to come to you like this today. If you had any heart at all, you would surely—"

"Be silent," he snapped. "You behave as though you think you have done something noble in coming here. I see only a hostage who ran off without my permission, and I promise you, Scrope would see it my way."

"But I came because you had taken Sym, because you insist

on believing that the raiders are Rabbie's Bairns or the people
of Tarras Wood, and they are not!"

"I told you to be silent. You can know nothing about Rabbie
Redcloak or his activities. You know only what his men tell
you, and they are probably lying to protect themselves. Furthermore, you persist in refusing to see your own danger,
Laura. Do you not know that I would merely be complying
with Border law if I were to hang you for escaping and Andrew
for assisting you? Scrope will insist on both if he learns about
this."

"But—"

He closed the distance between them and grabbed her by
the shoulders, giving her a shake as he said, "Listen to me! I
cannot protect you from Scrope and his like if you continue
to defy me."

She stared up at him, hardly aware of his words, conscious
only of his hands grasping her, of his body so near. Vaguely,
in the back of her mind, she knew that she ought to be afraid,
but she felt no fear. She saw the harsh look in his eyes soften
and felt a tremor in the hands holding her.

Putting one hand gently against his chest, the way she might
have tried to soothe a nervous horse, she was surprised to feel
the rough cloth of his jacket. At some point, she had taken off
her gloves, but she did not remember when or where.

He ignored her hand, tightening his grip as he said, "Do
you not realize that he would blame me, too, lass? He would
point out, just as you did, that I failed to make it plain to my
people that you are a hostage."

She knew that he was not concerned for himself. "If I have
learned anything," she said, "I have learned that the notion of
a hostage depends on what men wish it to mean. For example,
when it pleased Scrope to call me your wife, he cannot have
expected you to keep me locked up. A man does not lock up
his wife—at least, in Scotland, he generally does not."

"The fact that Scrope himself insists on calling you my
wife hardly helps matters, but he would not care about that.
Indeed, I cannot doubt that he meant to muddy the water when

he did that, hoping I would treat you differently from the way I would treat a male hostage, just so that he could accuse me of being soft."

"Well, I do not know what you mean, exactly, inasmuch as one knows how James and Elizabeth both treated Buccleuch," Laurie said thoughtfully. "You could hardly have kept me locked in a dungeon all this time."

"*I* couldn't," Hugh said with emphasis. "But if Scrope learns that you have been riding out and about the countryside, even into Scotland, he will say that I gave you a free rein, and I could not deny it. You also have put Andrew and the others in grave danger, Laura. If Scrope insists that I hang you, he will also insist that I hang Andrew. Recall that the lad had already drawn his lordship's ire. As to Geordie and the others—"

"Now you are being nonsensical," Laurie said. It was hard to think with him holding her, but if she had learned anything about Sir Hugh Graham it was that he would protect his own and that he was capable of doing so. He might not want her as his wife, but he had taken her under his protection when he agreed to hold her as a hostage for May. She did not believe that he would let Scrope or anyone else hang her if he could help it. "What are you going to do?" she asked.

"I am going to send you straight back to Brackengill and order you locked in your bedchamber," he said. His hands tensed as he spoke, and for a moment, she thought he would shake her again.

She was a little disappointed when he didn't. Instead, he released her, doing so slowly, as if he were concentrating on the movement, being sure that he let go.

"Who rode here with you?" he growled, taking a step back.

When she did not reply at once, his eyes narrowed.

"I thought they told you," she said then. "I came with Andrew."

Color surged into his face, and she saw his hands clench and knew that he wanted to grab her again. This time, she was just as glad that he did not.

"Andrew? No one else? Are you mad, Laura?"

She nearly told him that Davy Elliot had followed her, that he had shown her how to load Andrew's pistol, and that the boy was armed, but she knew that none of those things would cool his hot temper. She did not want to land the boy in even more trouble, nor did she want Hugh to take his precious pistol away.

Forcing calm that she did not feel, she said, "I am not mad, sir. If you will but think, you must realize that alone with a lad like Andrew I was far safer than I'd have been had I somehow persuaded Geordie to send an armed escort with me."

She saw that he did not agree with her, but before he could explain how wrong she was, she added, "I never could have persuaded Geordie, in any event. My people are important to me, sir, just as yours are important to you. Once I knew that you had Sym, I had to come. He was with me that day in the tree. I care deeply about his welfare."

Hugh straightened, and she could tell that he had made his decision and would not easily be swayed from it. A chill touched her.

He said, "I will take you back to Brackengill myself. Henceforth, until the matter is settled before a jury, you will remain there. I should have made matters plain to my people from the outset. I will not make that error again."

He did not look at her, but she had already seen the new expression in his eyes, and the thought that she had given him pain tore at her. She admired his sense of honor and the compassion that she had seen him display, but presently those two traits were causing his pain, and she could blame only herself for that.

The least she could do now was to conceal her distress from him. He was doing what he thought was right, and knowing that he did not want to do it troubled her, but it also gave her the strength not to fight him anymore.

He gathered what men he could spare from Corbies Nest, leaving Ned Rowan in charge of those he left behind. Andrew rode with them, just behind Hugh and Laurie, and they rode southeast toward the crossing at Kershopefoot, the safest and easiest place to cross into England. They were riding alongside Liddel Water, quite near the place where Martin Loder had gone into the Liddel, and Sir Hugh had just asked Laurie to fall behind a bit because he wanted a few private words with Andrew, when a shout from behind drew their attention.

To Laurie's surprise, the rider was Sym, and he galloped his pony up to them as boldly as if he had not been Sir Hugh's prisoner just a few hours before.

As Sym drew rein, Hugh frowned, saying curtly, "What do you want?"

"Please, sir, me dad said I was to tell Mistress Laurie that there be raiders on the move on the English side. Ye'd all gone from Corbies Nest, but your man Rowan said he'd heard there might be raiders after your herd. He said he'd already sent a man after ye but that I should ride after ye, too, and tell ye so, although I dinna think he believed a word I tellt him," Sym added with a grimace.

Hugh looked from Laurie to the boy and back again, saying, "More of your tricks, lass? Because, by Heaven, if this is another of them, I'll take a strap to that pretty backside of yours as soon as we reach Brackengill. I don't doubt I should have done so long since."

She shook her head. "I know naught of this, sir. Who are the raiders, Sym?"

"I dinna ken, Mistress Laurie, but Davy did say 'twas Ally the Bastard wha' saw them, and Ally said they be English, not Scot—out o' Tynedale, most like."

Sardonically, Hugh said, "Just what would this Ally the Bastard be doing to see raiders on the English side? And where is the messenger Ned Rowan sent after us. Answer me that, lad."

Sym shrugged. "I dinna ken, but Ally didna say nothing about your herd, sir. Only Rowan did. Ally said only that he'd seen raiders and that Mistress Laurie should know about 'em afore she rode back to Brackengill."

"Why did he send you?"

" 'Cause me dad said ye'd be more like to believe it were true if I was the one to tell ye. He said ye'd ken that I'd no be putting me head in the lion's den twice in a day were I no telling the truth."

"I do not doubt that they want me to believe you," Hugh said. He looked around at the little party. "I dare not ignore the warning," he said to the nearest of his men. "The lad will stay with us. Four of you can ride on ahead to see if aught is amiss at Haggbeck and to warn them to keep a sharp eye out for raiders. The rest of us will stay out of the open by riding through Kershopefoot Forest to Bewcastle. We'll seek beds there and ride on to Brackengill in the morning."

Accordingly, he selected the four men to ride on, told Sym to ride beside Laurie because he still wanted to have a talk with Andrew, then led what remained of his little party through the village of Kershope, across the little burn that marked the line, and into the shelter of the forest on the English side.

The attack came twenty minutes later without warning, as men dropped from trees and riders surged out of the shrubbery to surround them, lashing out with clubs and swords. Gunshots rang out, several of Sir Hugh's men fell, and Laurie lost sight of both Hugh and Andrew when a number of attackers cut her off from them.

Finding herself still next to Sym, she quickly bent near him to say, "Get clear of this if you can, laddie. Take shelter in a tree as we did before, and then get to Davy and go with him to Sir Quinton at Broadhaugh. Tell them that I know not who these villains are but that they are none of ours, and we need help!"

Seeing him tumble from his pony moments later, she feared that he had been wounded but stifled her cry when she saw him roll into thick undergrowth and disappear. A moment later, she saw a man strike Sir Hugh from behind with a club, just as a man grabbed her reins from her hand and another wrapped a strong arm around her waist and held her. Although she kicked and fought, they held her so easily that one or the other of them even dared to fondle her breasts.

Within moments, they had tied her hands and bound a cloth sack over her head. Thus, although she was still on her own saddle, she could not see what direction they rode. Nor, although she strained her ears to hear just one familiar voice, could she hear any that she recognized. Terrified that Sir Hugh and Andrew were both dead, she did not try to stem the tears that streamed down her cheeks. After a time, exhausted, she slumped forward over her pony's neck and slept.

Twenty-three

The cat she came to my cage-door,
The thief I could not see . . .

Laurie's captors spoke little, their pace was leisurely, and she slept until they stopped riding. Someone lifted her from her saddle and slung her over his shoulder, still tied and blind-folded, but she could tell that he went indoors and began descending stairs. The sounds of boots on the steps told her that the steps were made of stone and that others followed them, but she knew no more than that until the man carrying her set her on her feet.

He still did not speak, but she heard a soft thud nearby as he untied her hands. Then he and whoever had been with him left, and there was only silence.

It took her a moment to find the strings tying the cloth over her head, and minutes more for her numbed fingers to untie the knots. When she pulled the cloth off, she saw through a narrow slit high in the wall that it was nearly dark outside, but sufficient light still penetrated the otherwise empty cell to let her see Sir Hugh's body lying nearby on a skimpy pile of straw.

Laurie saw almost at once that Sir Hugh was still breathing, but although she quickly untied his hands and feet, he remained unconscious and she could not wake him. She sat beside him, dozing off and on and listening unsuccessfully for sounds to reveal something of their surroundings. The cell grew black and then dimly light again before Hugh stirred at last.

Thanking God for His mercy, Laurie touched Hugh's arm gently and said, "Oh, do wake up!"

She saw one flinty gray eye slowly open, as if he meant to test each part of himself before deciding that he might survive.

He opened the other eye, moved his head slightly, then winced and groaned.

"One of the brutes struck you with a club," she said sympathetically.

"He struck hard." Hugh's voice sounded as if his vocal cords were mired in sand. "Where are we?"

"I don't know," she admitted. "They put something over my head. I don't know which direction we rode, so I do not know if we are in Scotland or England, and I'm afraid I fell asleep, so I cannot even say how long it took us to get here."

His eyes narrowed, then focused directly on her. "Did any of those bastards touch you?"

"Just to bind my hands and to secure the cloth over my head," she said, seeing nothing to gain by telling him about the lout who had dared to touch her breast. It would serve only to anger him, and he could do nothing about it now.

He sighed. "There is some light, at least, so I doubt we are in a dungeon."

"Well, the walls are stone, but there is a wooden door and that narrow window high up in the wall looks like some I saw at Corbies Nest," she said, gesturing toward it. "I think we must be in some sort of a peel tower like that one."

"Then, unless this one is in a similar state of disrepair, our captor may be a man of substance," Hugh said. "Did you not hear familiar voices?"

"None, but they spoke very little," she said. "There is one good thing, though, that I should tell you. I think Sym was able to conceal himself from them. If he did, he will ride for Broadhaugh as soon as he can to seek help."

"Excellent," he said, but she detected a slight twinkle in his eyes.

Ruffling, she said, "Do you dare to laugh, sir? I know he is only a lad—"

"Nay, lassie," he protested, "I cry innocence. He is no younger than Meggie's Andrew, and if I do feel some amusement, it is because I sent Andrew on the same mission. The young rascal had a pistol half drawn when I saw it, and fearing they would shoot him if any of them saw it, I grabbed his arm and ordered him to go for help. I think that must be when the man struck me, because I don't remember anything more. I only hope that the villains did not catch both lads."

"I think we would know if they had," she said. "Nothing I saw or heard suggested other than that they believed they had captured our entire party."

"Well, do not set your hopes too high," he advised.

"But if Andrew rode for Brackengill and Sym for Broadhaugh—"

"I did not send Andrew to Brackengill," he said. "With my men split between the castle and Haggbeck, there are too few in either place to do us much good. I sent Andrew to Broadhaugh, too. That is what seemed amusing."

"But why did you not send for Scrope?"

"Even if I could trust him, I do not know exactly where he is at present. Moreover, swift action is needed, and sending all the way to Carlisle would take too long. However, I do trust Janet. She may have married across the line, but she is a woman of integrity, and I am her brother. If there is aught that she can do to help us, she will. There may be one small problem, however."

She knew at once what it was. "If both Andrew and Sym rushed off to seek help, they will not know where to find us," she said with a sigh. "I told Sym to tell Davy, though, and . . ." She paused, wondering if she should say more, and deciding that she must. "Davy can get word to Rabbie Redcloak, sir, and some of Rabbie's men are excellent hunters and trackers. If they get word of our trouble, they may be still be able to follow us. There has been no rain to destroy our tracks."

He chuckled, winced again, then gathered himself, clearly intending to rise.

Laurie reached swiftly to stop him. "Don't! You may be more seriously hurt than you know. You may even do yourself further injury."

"Calm yourself, lass. I've naught amiss with me save a lump on my head. It aches like the devil and will doubtless continue to do so, but I do not mean to die yet, if that is what's troubling you."

"I never thought you would die; I just think you should move slowly," she said with careful dignity. She did not want him to know how terrified she had been, first when she had thought him dead and then again when he had failed to regain consciousness quickly.

He did not reply at once, clearly focusing his energy instead on raising himself to a sitting position. As he leaned back gently against the wall, he said, "I suppose it is too much to hope that they left us water."

"None," she said. "Does your head ache worse now that you are sitting?"

"Not noticeably. You lied to me, Laura."

A prickling sensation shot up her spine. "Did I?"

"Aye, when you said you did not fear that I would die."

"I never . . ." Her words trailed to silence when he grinned at her. He looked much more like his usual self.

"Lassie, give it up," he said. "Your thoughts are written plain on your face for anyone to see. They always are. You are safe enough, though. I doubt that I have strength enough to beat you."

"You wouldn't! Not for being worried about you—that would be daft."

"More than daft," he agreed. "Come here, lass. I feel a chill, and it is your duty to warm me, so that I do not sicken in this gruesome place."

Warily, she obeyed, uncertain of him in this odd humor. But when she sat beside him and he put an arm around her, drawing her close, she leaned her head against his shoulder with a grateful sigh.

"If you must know the truth," she muttered, "it frightened me nearly to death, seeing you so."

"I'll warrant it did," he said quietly. "It would have frightened the wits out of me had our positions been reversed. You are a remarkable woman, you know."

"Pray, sir, do not talk nonsense to me. I am naught of the sort."

"You should not contradict me. It is most unbecoming. I know of only one other woman who would greet our present circumstances with anything remotely akin to your equanimity, and she would be striding tiresomely back and forth, demanding that I get up and do something about it."

"Your sister?"

"Aye. Janet would not allow such a situation to terrify her, but she would not greet it calmly either. Did they ever tell you what she said when she found Quin in that cell at Carlisle?"

"No, what?"

"She taunted him. Told him that she'd disobeyed him again and that there was naught he could do about it since he was too weak even to stand up. She even swore at him and told him to get up and walk since she couldn't carry him. She told me about it herself, even boasted of her impudence, the cheeky wench."

Laurie tried and failed to suppress an unexpected bubble of laughter at the picture his words painted in her mind. "She didn't!"

"She did. She said she did it to stir him to action, because they had too little time for coaxing. I think she did it just because she knew she could get away with it and could say exactly what she wanted to say for once."

"Aye, well, I warrant she said it then, but I do not believe that Janet the Bold would have left him there even if she had not had others with her to help," Laurie said. "Nor would she demand that you get up now and do something when there is clearly nothing that either of us can do. You must regain your strength, and we must learn more about our situation. It would be foolhardy to waste our energy."

"My sister is overbold, however, and she rarely shows proper respect to the men in her family. I tell you, she would insist that I do something."

"Perhaps, but if she spoke to her husband the way you describe, I think she must have believed it was necessary," Laurie said. "They say she loves him dearly."

"I reckon she does, at that, so you may have the right of it. For a Scot, he's tolerable enough. It does annoy me, however, that I find myself presently dependent upon his goodwill and his ability to follow a trail."

"I doubt that Sir Quinton has as much skill as Rabbie's Bairns have," Laurie said with a smile. "We would be wiser to depend on Sym's going to Davy first. They will tell Lady Scott and Sir Quinton what occurred, but Davy will get word to Rabbie Redcloak."

"I suppose that means that Davy Elliot is one of Rabbie's Bairns," Hugh said with a wry grimace. "Oh, do not fear; I suspect that most of those men in Tarras Wood are his followers, but that does not matter a whit to me now. We must just hope that someone finds us soon and sets us free."

"Until they do, perhaps you would do better to sleep if you can," Laurie suggested. "If you would like to use my lap as a pillow, you may."

"I'll not turn down such a generous offer, lass."

That he did not argue told her his head ached more than he would admit. He eased himself back down again, and when he laid his head in her lap, she stroked his brow, trying to smooth the frown away. She was glad to find that, although his skin felt warm, he was not feverish.

"Your hand is cool," he said, "and your lap makes a soft pillow."

"Go to sleep," she said, not wanting to discuss what it felt like to have his head in her lap. The horrid cell was no place to think about the feelings and emotions that just touching him stirred within her.

He shifted to his side, trying to get more comfortable, and one large hand rested briefly on her knee and slid upward, stirring more tension in her body.

Restlessly, he turned again to his back and gazed up at her. "Are you sure that my head is not too heavy for you?"

"Just sleep," she muttered.

He shut his eyes, and she felt him relax. His head was heavy on her thigh, but she did not mind. Leaning her head against the stone wall, she closed her eyes and tried to think of something—anything—other than their present dilemma.

His hands on her breasts felt surprisingly smooth this time, not as rough as they had felt the first time. They were naked, and they lay beside each other on a soft bed of lush grass in Tarras Wood. Slanting rays of pale sunlight penetrated the green canopy overhead. Birds sang, and a brook babbled nearby, but conscious only of his touch, she barely heard those sounds.

Maybe Tarras Wood was heaven, she thought. A chuckle stirred in her mind at the sacrilege, and then he touched her again, and the chuckle turned to a gasp of pleasure. She forgot the woods, the birds, the brook, everything but the magic of his touch. His hands stroked lightly up and down her body, and wherever they touched her, sparks leapt to flame until her whole body was burning for him.

He kissed her shoulder, then her breasts and belly, his hands still moving gently, cupping a breast when he kissed it, then stroking her belly and moving lower as his lips moved lower. He touched her in places she was sure no other man had ever touched a woman. Surely, her father had never done such things to Blanche. Still, the things he did did not shock her. They seemed right and wonderful.

He did not speak, not a word, but she did not care. Had he spoken, she would not have known what to reply. Her thoughts were focused on the movements of his hands and lips. They moved over her body like warmth from the sun.

That he was hungry for her was evident from the increasing urgency of his touch. He would take her soon. She knew that, and she welcomed the taking. She would belong to him as she had to no other man, and he would be hers. The thought no longer dismayed her. It, too, seemed right, and she silently urged him on.

His body shifted, looming above her, but his weight seemed oddly centered on her right thigh, even though he had not lowered himself yet to claim her. He seemed to hover, stretched long and large above her, smiling down at her, his smile warm and inviting, teasing her; but the weight on her thigh was heavier, making the muscles cramp. It hurt, and that was not fair. The thought of that unfairness brought the woods crashing down and set the flames of Hell dancing all around her.

Startling at the sound of wood crashing against stone, Laurie jumped, and the fierce cramp in her thigh forced a cry from her lips before full awareness set in. Hugh's hand was resting between her legs, where it ought not to have been, but that was the least of her worries. The orange glow flickering on the walls around her came not from the flames of Hell, as she had feared, but from the flame of a torch held high by the burly man who had flung open the door to the cell.

"What the devil?" Hugh sat up, and evidently did so too quickly, because he shut his eyes tight and put a hand to his forehead.

"Ye're to come with us now, the pair o' ye," the man with the torch said gruffly. "And dinna be thinking ye can play off any o' your tricks, Sir Hugh Graham, for we've orders to bind your hands again. If ye dinna cooperate, we'll take the lass first and let the lads above play wi' her a bit whilst we teach ye manners. Then we'll take ye along up to play with, as well."

"I've no wish for trouble," Hugh said quietly. "My head aches, and I want only to know who is responsible for this outrage."

"Turn and face yon wall then," the man with the torch said.

"Put your hands behind ye wi' your wrists together. Lass, ye come to me, and be quick about it."

Getting stiffly to her feet, Laurie repressed a cry when a sharp pain shot through her thigh. She had no idea how long she had slept, but it was dark outside, and her stomach was growling with hunger. Striving to retain a semblance of her normal dignity, she said quietly, "I had begun to think you meant to starve us."

"We're no taking ye to a feast," the torchbearer said with a laugh as he grabbed her arm and pulled her nearer. "Ye'll no be needing food, either, unless I mistake the matter. Take him now, lads."

Two men who had been waiting outside the cell stepped in and moved warily toward Hugh. One was as large as he was, the other only a bit smaller. Laurie hoped that Hugh would not try to fight them.

He did not. He stood quietly while they bound his wrists with cording. When he turned, his face was set and pale, and she could see that he was in pain, but the look he shot Laurie told her he was more concerned for her welfare than for his.

The man holding the torch pulled her into the corridor, saying as he did, "Ye'll go ahead of us, Sir Hugh. If ye try anything foolish, know that I'll burn the lass wi' my torch. I'd not enjoy spoiling such a little beauty, but it'll no matter in the end, and I'd do it just to prove that I keep my word."

"I believe you," Hugh said. "I won't try to escape."

"Good. Go on, then."

The men did not bother to bind Laurie, and her emotions wavered between gratitude and indignation that they did not think her worth restraining. Their accents were English, but although she was glad they were not fellow Scots, she did not think the information would prove useful.

As the little group passed along the narrow corridor, she saw other torches in brackets and wondered if one might serve her as a weapon. The brackets were high on the wall, though, and logic told her that she could not reach one quickly enough or wield it deftly enough to make it practical.

When she slowed, the man with the torch jerked her arm and shoved her ahead of him.

"Move along, lass. Ye'll gain nowt by dawdling."

The short corridor ended in stone steps spiraling upward. One of the men guarding Hugh went ahead to the top and pushed open the door there. Hugh followed with his second guard close behind.

Laurie's escort pushed her again, urging her to follow. Reluctantly, she obeyed, filled with dread at what must lie ahead of them.

Hugh realized that the second man was close enough to him that a well-aimed kick would send him toppling back down the stairs, and the temptation to do it was nearly overwhelming. He dared not turn, lest he somehow give them warning of his intent, but he was nearly certain from the sounds below that Laurie was far enough behind the fellow that she would not be harmed by his fall. If the stunt succeeded, he would have only two men left to deal with.

As he hesitated, testing the bindings on his wrists, he became aware of new sounds ahead—muffled masculine laughter, the murmur of numerous voices, the shuffling of feet, and the clanking and clinking of metal and crockery. More villains were at hand than he had realized, and they were well within shouting distance. He would have to bide his time.

Stepping over the threshold, he emerged into a small anteroom lit only by an ambient glow through a low, narrow archway to his left.

"Go on," the first man said, standing aside to give him a push. "You lead the way now."

Taking a deep breath, wishing he were in possession of all his strength and that his head did not ache, Hugh ducked through the archway into a narrow stone corridor and eventually found himself entering a hall larger than the one at Corbies Nest but less than half the size of the great hall at Brackengill.

A score of men sat at two long tables set side by side down

the center, their attention and that of the numerous dogs with them fixed on the laden platters and trenchers of food on the tables.

Hugh's gaze shifted to a high table set perpendicular to the other two, where, flanked by two henchmen with places set for several others, the master of the castle sat at his ease. He held a pewter goblet, but at their entrance, he paused in the act of raising it to his lips and watched Hugh intently over the goblet's rim.

Stiffening, feeling his mouth fall open, Hugh knew that his reaction must have been everything the villain had hoped for.

Behind him, he heard Laurie gasp.

Their host said, "I'm told that you believed me dead, Hugh Graham. Doubtless you are relieved and delighted to discover your error."

Grimly, Hugh said, "So it is you, Martin Loder, and your death naught but a hoax connived by you and Cornus Grant. Does Scrope know you're alive?"

Loder smirked. "His lordship knows, and he approves. His debts are nearly paid now, you see, and his coffers soon will be straining their hinges."

"The recent raids," Hugh said. "You're the one who's been leading them."

With a shrug, Loder said, "I carried out orders, as usual; that's all. Once we realized that no one was likely to blame a dead man for raiding, especially since the raiders' leader wore a familiar red cloak—"

"But why take us?" Hugh demanded. "What can you hope to accomplish?"

"That were my own notion," Loder said with a sneer. "You're in my way, Hugh Graham. Scrope should have dismissed you and named me in your place long ago, when he learned how soft you were, but he were feared o' your uncle in London. Then your uncle died, and you and Eure were helpless against the raids, but Scrope could not manage to dismiss you even then, though he swears that he wrote Her Majesty and told her that you were inept. But what did she do? She appointed you warden in Eure's stead! Well, I know how to end the nonsense. You'll plague me no more. I mean to see to it once and for all."

"That's despicable," Laurie snapped.

"You shut your mouth, woman," Loder snapped back. "No woman speaks out of turn here. I don't want to hear your voice again."

Hugh glanced at Laurie and saw that her mouth was already open to reply. He caught her eye and frowned warningly.

Though she glowered at him, she held her tongue.

"That's right," Loder said. "You keep silent, lass. Women soon come to know their place in my household. Not that you'll grace it much longer."

"You mean to kill us then," Hugh said matter-of-factly, wanting to draw Loder's attention from Laurie.

He succeeded, but Loder said, "You'll agree that killing you would be wiser than setting you free. What would I do with you if I kept you? I doubt that Scrope wants you, and he certainly won't want you running amok, prattling to everyone about what he's been doing."

"He's been stealing from his own people."

"Aye, if you want to put it that way. He prefers to think of it as providing a service, finding their property and then charging a small fee to restore it."

"By finding their livestock on *their* land and then selling it back to them?"

"Aye, well, you never did display much of a sense of humor or imagination. Scrope, now, he's a man of vision."

"He's a liar, a gambler, and a damned villain. It won't be long before the entire world knows it, too," Hugh said. "Regardless of what you've done for him or what you do to us, he'll soon gamble the proceeds away again. His wife will help him. Then what will the pair of you do?"

Loder shrugged again. "You'd do better to worry about yourself."

"What exactly do you plan to do with us?"

"Me?" Loder sounded surprised. "I'm not going to do a

thing. I'm a peaceful man, I am. I mean to turn you over to Rabbie Redcloak."

"You'd not dare," Laurie said. "Rabbie would never deal with the likes of you, especially since you've been pretending to *be* him and have been doing dreadful things in his name."

Loder gestured to the man standing beside Laurie, and the man slapped her hard enough to send her staggering.

Without a thought for himself, Hugh lunged toward them, but his two captors grabbed his arms, yanking him back and holding him despite his struggles. His head began to pound.

In a quiet but deadly voice, Loder said, "I warned you to hold your tongue, woman. Don't speak again, or before God, I'll have it cut out. As for you, Hugh, my lad, stand easy, or I'll let each of my men taste the lass's charms in front of you before Rabbie Redcloak murders you both out on the fells somewhere."

"So that's your game," Hugh muttered. "You'll kill us and blame the reiver."

"Aye, and Buccleuch. He's to be freed again, you know, and Scrope has a score to settle with him. We know that Buccleuch is the power behind the reivers, and his lordship wants to make him pay for his crimes. This time he wants to make sure that neither Elizabeth nor Jamie can turn a blind eye."

Hugh didn't doubt that they could make things look bad for Buccleuch, but he wondered if either Loder or Scrope understood the man's true power. He was not responsible for every raid on English soil, of course, but he was responsible for most of the great ones. And since the reivers were not choosy about victims, he was doubtless responsible even for a few that had taken place in Scotland.

In any event, it was no great secret that Buccleuch afforded his protection to Rabbie Redcloak and others of his ilk. Buccleuch's greatest strength lay in the fact that his enemies, even knowing what he had done, generally lacked sufficient evidence to convict him.

"Have ye lost your tongue, Hugh Graham?"

"You are mad, Loder," Hugh said. "You and Scrope both."

"Aye, perhaps, but calling me names will not help. You'll die tonight, and your lass with you, unless I decide to keep her here to amuse my men."

"No!"

At first, Hugh thought the feminine shriek of horror had come from Laurie. It made sense that such a threat would terrify her. Moreover, the shriek was so loud that it reverberated from the walls of the chamber, making it difficult to tell where it had begun. But even as he turned toward Laurie and saw the stark amazement on her face, he realized that it had not been her voice.

She was staring beyond him.

Turning back, he saw a young woman in a very low-cut blue gown striding from the main entrance of the hall along the narrow pathway between the two long tables. As she strode angrily toward the dais, her blue skirts swirled and her plump bosom heaved with emotion.

She paid no heed to the other men in the room, having eyes only for Loder. Coming to an abrupt halt at the foot of the dais, she shouted at him, "You cannot kill them! I won't let you!"

Hugh had never seen her before, but Laurie's amazed expression revealed the woman's identity even before she told him.

"It's May," she said, her hand still touching her reddened cheek, but lightly, as if she had forgotten that she put it there when the man slapped her. "May heaven help us all! That's my sister, May."

Twenty-four

O lie you there, you traitor false
Where you thought to lay me . . .

Laurie could not believe her eyes. While the English had held her hostage, May had been living with Loder, the very man everyone believed she had killed.

When Loder stood up, May paled and took a step backward.

The men in the hall fell silent, but it was a silence filled with anticipation.

In the lengthening hush, Laurie saw some of Loder's men exchange smirks, and she wished she could see May's face. The angle was wrong, though. She could see only her sister's profile and not enough of that to guess what she was thinking.

Then May stiffened and Laurie saw that Loder had leaned forward and put both big hands flat on the table. His expression was murderous.

"You dare," he growled. "You burst into my hall, snapping like a fractious bitch at its master, but I'll soon school you, my lass. Come here to me."

The little color left in May's face vanished, and one slim hand moved to her throat as if to protect it. "Please, sir, she is my sister," she said in a voice that carried only because the room was silent. "You must not harm her."

"Fetch me a riding whip, one of you," Loder said without taking his eyes off May. "You'll take your lesson here, sweetheart, and if I have to come and fetch you for it, you'll strip off every stitch of clothing for their entertainment—just as you do for mine—before I take my whip to you."

May's body swayed, and Laurie could stand no more. The man-at-arms standing beside her, fascinated like the others with what was taking place in the center of the room, was paying no heed to her. So, without a thought for fear or consequence, she ran to May and put a protective arm around her shoulders.

"Now, that's touching, that is," Loder said sarcastically. "You may share her punishment if you like, lass. I've no objection. Indeed, I warrant we'd all enjoy it."

"Is it not enough that she betrayed her people to bide here with you?" Laurie asked. "You should be ashamed to repay such devotion and loyalty with brutality."

One of his lads ran up to him with the whip he had demanded, and Loder gripped it without comment. Then, seeming only to shift his weight to the hand still on the table, he leapt over it. One long stride put him directly in front of them.

Laurie felt May tremble.

Loder snarled, "Devotion? Loyalty?" Fury burned in his eyes. "Is that what you believe your sister offered me? You think she came here with me willingly?"

"Did she not?" Laurie asked.

Beside her, May moaned and buried her face in Laurie's shoulder.

"Clinging to your sister will not save you, my lass," Loder said to her. "Tell her how devoted you are. Tell her how much you love me."

A wracking sob shook May, and Laurie held her tighter. "Stop torturing her!" she exclaimed. "She cannot help what she feels. If you killed her love when you tried to drown her—"

"Aye, now you're thinking," Loder said with an abrupt nod. "She does hold that little incident against me. 'Twas why she forced me to seek her out, to take her out of her bedchamber with the help of that fool maid of hers, then to bring her here with me and teach her to mind me."

"Bridget helped you?"

"Aye, of course, she did."

"He killed her," May wailed. "He throttled her and threw her in the river!"

Loder slapped her. "I should have flung you in, to pay you out for tumbling *me* into that river. But I wanted more, did I not, sweetheart?"

May put her face against Laurie's shoulder again.

"She had been doing rather well, too, until this unfortunate incident," Loder went on tauntingly, "She was foolish to take your part, though, because now we shall have to begin her lessons all over again. Do you hear me, May, my love?"

May's trembling increased. She could not seem to stop, nor did she look up. Her voice shook as she muttered to Laurie, "He abducted me so that I could not appear at the Truce Day and tell them he murdered his wives. He is horrid!"

Loder snapped, "Move away from her, May Halliot, and look at me!"

"Leave her alone," Laurie said.

"You're very fierce for one who is about to die, lass."

"And you are very brave for one who threatens defenseless women," she replied. Looking around at the gape-jawed men, she said, "I suppose that all these brave lads will cheer you on. Just look at them. A pretty set you make, all of you."

She heard grumbling, but she was too numb now to fear them. She wanted only to help May, and she hoped that if Loder's louts could see themselves as they really were, they would at least feel some shame. Then, perhaps, they would not be too quick to support their brutal master.

He still held the whip, and when he reached out with it, putting its point under her chin, she stood still. Her gaze locked with his.

"You've more spirit than our May," he said with a leer. "I thought she was the one with spirit, but she don't hold a candle to you, lass. I threatened to keep you here just to stir coals with our Hugh here, but perhaps I'll keep you, after all. You

and May can take turns amusing me whilst I school the pair
of you to my ways."

"Stand away from her, you bastard!"

Startled by the sound of Hugh's voice, Laurie saw him surge
away from his captors and stride toward her, although his
hands still were tied behind him.

"Leave him," Loder ordered curtly when the two guards
leapt forward to grab Hugh again. "If he is so anxious to meet
his death, let him."

With dismay, Laurie saw that Loder had drawn his sword
and had tucked the whip handle into the sword's scabbard.

"May," she muttered, "collect yourself. He is going to kill
Sir Hugh."

Looking up, May said in a quavering voice, "Please, sir,
punish me if you must, but do not kill them like this. 'Tis
murder, clear and plain."

"Hold your tongue, damn you," he snapped. "I'll tend to
you after I deal with him. Come ahead, Hugh Graham. I'll spit
you here and now."

"Put a sword in my hand, and we'll see who spits what,"
Hugh said.

"Aye, you'd like that, would you not? But I wonder how
well you will enjoy dying like the traitor cur you are. You
betrayed England when you gave your sister to Buccleuch's
cousin. You gave aid to our enemies at Carlisle, and you continued to aid them when you joined in handfast with this bra-
zen Scotswoman."

"None of that is true," Hugh said steadily. "I had little to
say in my sister's marriage, because Jamie and Elizabeth arranged it between them through the offices of Scrope and Buccleuch. My blessing was naught but a formality. As to our
handfasting, your so-called death had more to do with that
than I did."

"Aye, well, perhaps I did have summat to do with that, since
you took the wench as hostage first and wife second. But she'll
not be counted your wife when she's dead, only as the sister
of a murderess, murdered herself by her own people. After

I've spitted you, my men will take you out onto the fells and someone—perhaps Cornus Grant—will claim to have seen Rabbie Redcloak kill you in cold blood. No one will be able to prove otherwise, either, since the bloody Scots still refuse to admit that the damned reiver even exists."

"You'll be quite a hero then, won't you?" Hugh said. Raising his voice so that everyone in the hall could hear, he added, "My lass is right, Loder, and your lads all know it. You're naught but a coward who makes war on defenseless women and bound men. God's wounds, man, you don't even have the courage to do your thieving in the open. You had to pretend to be dead before you dared go a-reiving. Even then, you borrowed another man's name and reputation to conceal your deeds. We all should have known Rabbie Redcloak wasn't the villain. He always shows himself and shouts his name for all to hear. Now, there's a man with courage!"

Loder's face reddened with rage, and he lunged, his sword pointed directly at Hugh, who had little room to move, let alone to defend himself.

Before Laurie could do more than gasp in shock, May leapt between the two men, arms extended to push Loder away, and his blade pierced her just below her right breast. She collapsed without a word, and so shocked was Loder that he snatched his hand away from his sword and stood gaping down at her as the color drained from his face.

"May?" he murmured. "Oh, my foolish lass, what have you done?"

Laurie flung herself to the floor beside May, trying to stanch the blood flowing from her wound. "May, dearest one, don't die! May, speak to me!"

May's eyelids fluttered, and one hand clutched weakly at Laurie's arm.

Bending to put her ear near May's lips, Laurie said, "What is it, love?"

"Take . . . take the dagger," May gasped, the words barely audible. "In . . . in my girdle. I was going to kill him, but . . .

I did not get the chance. St-stop him, or he'll make you take my . . ."

"May?" Turning her head to see why there was no answer, Laurie felt suddenly as if she and her sister were alone. She could scarcely breathe.

May's eyelids fluttered one last time.

Still hunched over her, Laurie did not move. Tears welled into her eyes, but she squeezed them tightly shut, trying to stem the flow. She knew that May was gone, but she could not react. She had to think.

The sword, Loder's sword, was still stuck in May's body, leaning crazily with blood still oozing around its point from the wound. Even if she could have forced herself to yank it free, she knew that she could not do so without Loder and everyone else seeing her.

The hall was deadly still and time seemed to have stopped, but she knew that she had scant seconds left to do anything. Loder meant to kill Hugh and to do unconscionable things to her. His men would not lift a finger to stop him.

Her fingers were already moving at May's waist, touching the items on her belt. She wondered how on earth May had come by a dagger. For a moment, she feared that her sister had made it up. Then she found it and could have wept, for it was small with a jeweled handle, no more than a woman's eating knife. Nevertheless, she swiftly concealed it in her sleeve and sat back on her heels, looking up at the men who had gathered around her.

"She's gone," she said sadly. "You killed her, Martin Loder, and whatever happens next, you will answer to God for it. He will see you punished."

"Aye, perhaps," he said, looking strangely deflated, "but God should know, if anyone does, that it was her fault. She ran in front of my sword, the witless wench. She should have known better."

He straightened, drawing a deep breath and visibly shrugging off whatever feelings he had for May, like a dog shaking water from its back. "Now, lads," he said briskly, "as to the matter at hand, it will be better, I think, if we just take them out onto the fells and kill them there. It will be more convincing with their blood spattered all about."

Laurie had gotten slowly to her feet as Loder spoke, and now she edged closer to Hugh, as if to take shelter behind him.

He stood straight, looking Loder in the eye, and Loder seemed to take pleasure from glowering back at him.

Certain that the men's attention was diverted from her, she slid the little dagger into her hand and began to saw at the cords binding Hugh's wrists. The knife was surprisingly sharp, but the cords were taut and tough.

Hearing a shout from the rear of the hall, she sawed faster, fearing that someone had seen what she was doing. With her attention so firmly riveted to her task, it was a moment before any words penetrated. Then, as men leapt to their feet and snatched up arms, she realized that several were shouting, "Raiders!"

Hugh wrenched his wrists apart and yanked the sword from May's body just as Loder lunged to do the same.

Loder froze, hands spread, staring at him.

"Find another sword," Hugh said. "We'll finish this here and now."

The hall was clearing swiftly, but several of Loder's men paused when they realized what had happened.

"One of you, throw me a sword," Loder snapped. "Then get outside and take care of those damned raiders, whoever they be!"

One of the men stepped forward to hand Loder a sword, keeping a watchful eye on Hugh. "Mayhap a few of us should stay, master," the man said.

"Do you think I cannot best this cur?" Loder demanded.

"I dinna doubt it," the man said. "I just thought 'twould be safer all round if ye had a man or two at your side to make sure."

"He's learned your ways well," Hugh said gently, "but it will make no difference to you in the end, Loder. Choose how!"

Two other men drew their swords.

From behind him, Hugh heard Laurie say quietly, "I swear I will shoot anyone who tries to interfere. This will be a fair fight."

Hugh kept his eyes on Loder, but he saw the others look toward her, their shock as plain as if a flagstone from the floor had risen to bite one of them.

"Where the devil did you get that pistol?" Loder demanded.

"I found it on the bench yonder," she said. "One of your men must have left it behind in his rush to get outside."

"If someone left it behind, it is not loaded."

"Oh, yes, it is. I looked, and I know how to tell. It is a wheel-lock, and the mechanism is wound. If you are wondering whether I know how to fire it—"

"I've no doubt that you do," he said. "You and your sister are both damned unnatural women. Get out now, you lot," he added with a glance at his two men. "They need you outside more than I do here, although they're likely facing no more than the few Hugh left at Brackengill whilst he kept watch over Tarras Wood. If you're going to shoot me with that thing, lass, you'd best make your shot count."

"I'd like to shoot you," Laurie replied, and Hugh nearly grinned at her wistful tone. She paused as if she were considering her options.

They were not safe yet, and he had yet to learn if he could hold his own against Loder. He was hardly at his best, but he would soon have support if the raiders outside the walls could breach them, and he knew that he was a better swordsman now than he had been the last time he had engaged in such a fight.

"Keep the pistol aimed at him, lass," he said. "We'll play by his rules, though. If he should happen to win this fight, then you can shoot him."

"I will," she said, her voice admirably steady.

"Very pretty behavior," Loder said with a sneer. "I should have known that your principles would prove no stronger than any other man's. A typical Graham, that's what you are."

"Thank you, but don't waste wit or energy on talk," Hugh told him. "Use them for fighting. You've naught to fear if you leave her alone, but she will keep the weapon to defend herself if your men win the battle outside. She'll take at least one down before the rest can grab her, and if that one chances to be you, so be it."

"We'll see about that," Loder said, lunging suddenly.

Hugh had expected the move and was prepared for it. In moments, he was sending silent thanks to Sir Quinton Scott for stirring him to practice more with his weapons. Despite his sore head and a certain amount of weakness from not having eaten since leaving Corbies Nest, his earlier dizziness was gone.

His arms and legs felt strong, and his feet moved nimbly. Catching Loder's blade on his, he deftly parried the first stroke, and then went on the attack, forcing Loder back and away from the narrow opening between the tables. There was barely enough room to fight cleanly, but he did not expect Loder to do that. He would just have to watch his step, conserve his energy, and hope for the best.

Laurie realized that she had been holding her breath and forced herself to exhale. She could not bear to watch, and she could not bear to look away.

Realizing that she still held the pistol and fearing that she might set it off with an involuntary twitch of a finger, she lowered it and held it loosely by the grip. Despite her bold words to Loder, she was not certain that it was loaded or that the mechanism had been wound all the way. She hoped that she had only to pull the trigger, but she did not want to find out by shooting it accidentally and startling Hugh. He would need all his concentration to win this fight.

She could hear clanging of weapons outside in the yard

now, and she knew that the wall had been breached and the fighting was in full sway. She hoped Rabbie's Bairns were out there, because she could be confident that they would win, but she did not know who it was. Raiders could come from anywhere.

She was grateful to them if only for drawing Loder's men out of the hall to fight. She had not even tried to keep the two who had lingered from joining the others, fearing that she would either betray her lack of confidence in her weapon or that one of them would succeed in snatching it from her. She had no illusions about what would have happened then.

But for Hugh's taunting, she believed that Loder would have demanded a pistol instead of a sword and that he would have shot Hugh dead on the spot. Even now, she could not be certain that Hugh would survive the sword fight.

Every time Loder's blade darted near him, she flinched, and she had to exert the strongest control over herself to keep from crying out when once it flashed between Hugh's arm and his side, narrowly missing his chest.

At first, Hugh seemed to attack, forcing Loder back toward the high table; but once they reached the open space that separated the dais from the two long tables, he eased up, letting Loder lunge back toward him.

Their pace increased.

When Loder grabbed a pewter pitcher from the high table and flung it at Hugh, she clapped her free hand over her mouth. She wanted to shut her eyes, but she couldn't. The pitcher clattered to the stone floor, spilling a river of golden ale.

Sword clashed against sword, flashing high and then low, in and out, slipping, gnashing, and twanging as the two men leapt agilely back and forth. Loder began dancing backward again, and Laurie thought that perhaps Hugh had taken the upper hand at last. Then she realized that Loder had maneuvered Hugh into turning his back on the spilled ale.

"Look out, Hugh!" she cried.

At the same moment, Loder lunged and Hugh leapt back as he parried. His rear foot slipped when it touched the wet stones, and as he struggled to retain his balance, Loder darted in for the kill.

Laurie screamed and raised the pistol, pulling the trigger. The explosion was louder than she had expected, and with amazing force, the pistol flew up, twisted out of her hand, and crashed to the floor. It all happened quickly but diverted her attention from the men. She looked back to see both of them lying on the floor.

As she stepped forward with a cry, terrified that both were dead, she saw that both were still breathing.

Hugh sat up, sword in hand. He touched its point against Loder's throat.

"We're done, Loder," he said. "You've committed enough crimes to assure your hanging, and I've a mind to see you swing from the gallows. Get up now, and do it slowly. Lass, are you all right? I feared that you had shot yourself."

"I meant to shoot *him*," Laurie said. "Are you not going to kill him?"

"We'll hang him instead," Hugh said, adding when Loder twisted to get his legs under him again, "Move slowly, Loder. Don't do anything foolhardy."

Hearing only silence outside, Laurie said, "Listen."

Automatically, he glanced toward the two high windows that apparently overlooked the yard. "The fighting's stopped," he said.

She nodded, and just then, Loder moved.

"Hugh, look out!"

Loder had uncoiled, and now he sprang at Hugh with a dagger murderously outstretched, which his clothing had concealed.

Hugh reacted instantly, parrying the dagger thrust with a deft upward arc of his sword and then whipping his point back to center.

Loder launched himself at Hugh. As though he knew that he had lost, he did not even try to avoid the sword and, to Laurie's shock, impaled himself upon it.

Hugh snatched it free as the man fell, then knelt swiftly at his side.

Loder was still breathing, but his breath came in ragged gasps, and he did not try to speak. Blood trickled from his mouth, and the harsh gasping ceased.

Laurie said quietly, "Is he dead?"

"Aye, lass, and 'tis sorry I am for it, too. I wanted to see the bastard hang for all he's done. I wanted him to see the gallows and the hangman, and to make his penance before God. He got off too easily."

"It is just as well," said a voice from the doorway.

They turned, and Laurie saw a slim man of ordinary height standing at the threshold with a number of men looking over his shoulder.

Meggie's Andrew slipped under his arm, his pistol at the ready, his eyes wide and worried until his gaze found Laurie and Hugh. He lowered the pistol and glanced up at the man beside him.

"They're safe, laird."

"Aye, so it seems," the man said.

Hugh got to his feet with a wry grimace. "I never thought I'd be so glad to see you, Buccleuch. You've won the day, I trust."

"Faith, did you think I would not, against such scrofulous vermin?"

"You must forgive me. I did not know that you had returned from Berwick."

"Then I'll excuse your lack of faith this time," the Laird of Buccleuch said magnanimously. "Quin's outside with Hob the Mouse and young Gil Scott, clearing away the mess. Unfortunately, we've had to take a few prisoners. Always a damned nuisance, prisoners are."

"At this point, I'm inclined to sympathize with the prisoners," Hugh said, reaching to heft a pitcher that sat on the nearest long table. Apparently finding its weight satisfactory, he raised it to his lips and drank thirstily.

"We are very grateful to see you, sir," Laurie said solemnly to Buccleuch, "but the news is not good, I'm afraid. My sister, May, lies dead on the floor between those tables yonder. She was killed saving Sir Hugh."

"Then she is a heroine, my lady," Buccleuch said. "I will see that she is well tended, and that her body is safely escorted to Aylewood for proper burial."

"Thank you."

The words seemed sadly inadequate when Buccleuch's timely arrival had undoubtedly saved their lives, but she could think of nothing more to say. Her emotions seemed to have frozen, and she hoped that they would remain so and not overcome her before such an audience. Fearing that movement or words would stir them to life, she dared not look at May's body or at anyone else. She did not want to cry in front of so many men. Janet the Bold would not cry.

She stared at the floor, holding herself in, waiting for the men to do whatever needed doing before they could leave. In an oddly distant way, she heard Buccleuch issuing orders, heard others respond to his commands, and heard the shuffle of feet and distant shouts from the yard. She was not aware of movement close to her, and so it was a shock when a large, warm hand grasped one shoulder.

"You come with me now, lassie," Sir Hugh said with unusual gentleness. "You need food and drink."

"I . . . I couldn't."

With more firmness, he said, "You can and you will unless you want to ride before me all the way back to Brackengill."

Even that did not seem so terrible, except for one thing. "I must go to Aylewood. I must go home with May."

"No, lass. You're in no shape to ride all the way to Aylewood tonight. I'll take you there myself after you've rested. Buccleuch has already promised me safe passage to do that. Now, do you want beef or just some bread and ale? I'll slice the beef myself, although it won't be as good as what you last offered to me."

She recognized the comment as an attempt at humor, but she could not seem to make herself smile. When she dared let herself try to think, her treacherous mind showed her only the image of May's soft body with a sword stuck in it.

Hugh gave her shoulder a shake, startling her. "It is useless to dwell on it, Laura," he said sternly. "She's gone, and letting yourself drift into a world of dark clouds and mist will not bring her back. You will grieve for her. 'Tis right and proper that you do. She was your sister, and you loved each other. But this is not the moment for it, lass. We must get you home first."

Tears welled into her eyes, and she said the first words that came to mind. "You're as bad as the rest! She gave her life to save yours, and all you can do is get angry because I fail to act the way you want me to."

In answer, he pulled her hard against him and wrapped his strong arms around her, and when he did, she gave way to her tears, no longer caring if every man with Buccleuch came inside to gape at her. She was conscious only of the man who held her.

His hard embrace warmed and comforted her, as all the tension, fears, and grief of the past thirty hours unleashed themselves. He did not say a word, not so much as "there, there," but he was with her, and she believed he understood what she was feeling. When the storm of weeping passed, he continued to hold her until she stirred to free herself.

"Now you will eat," he said matter-of-factly.

She surprised herself by smiling.

"That's better," he said.

"I still don't think I can eat," she said, wiping a sleeve across her eyes.

"Loder's tables don't run to finger bowls," he said, "but one of these pitchers is bound to hold water. You can wash your face whilst I get us some food."

She looked hastily around then, certain that she would see any number of silent men staring at her.

The hall was empty. Both Loder's body and May's were gone.

"Where did everyone go?"

"They are outside, dealing with prisoners and such. Here."
He handed her a wet towel. "Use this. You don't want to show
that face to them."

"Thank you." She did as he bade her, then blew her nose.
She still felt limp and wrung out, but the mists had receded,
and she was able to think again.

"I really should go with them to Aylewood," she said.

"No."

She sighed, knowing from his tone that she could say nothing that would change his mind. She knew, too, that if he
forbade her going, not even Buccleuch would attempt to over-
rule him.

When Hugh handed her bread and ale, she ate obediently,
deciding that the quickest way to get to Aylewood in time to
attend May's funeral would be to rest and regain her strength.
The bread was dry and tasteless, but she got it down, and by
the time Buccleuch and Sir Quinton joined them, she felt much
better.

Twenty-five

So Graeme is back to the wood o' Tore,
And he's killd the giant, as he killd the boar.

As they rode away from Loder's tower, Buccleuch said to Laurie, "We'll see that your sister goes gently home, lass. I'm thinking your father will be relieved to have certain questions laid to rest."

Laurie said quietly, "Had he questions, sir? He did not confide in me."

"I wrote him when I learned what happened at the wardens' meeting," Buccleuch said. "I was curious to know what had become of the daughter he had guaranteed to present there. I was perhaps a little forceful in my phrasing."

No one commented, but Laurie glanced at him and saw a twinkle. It made her wonder why anyone ever compared him to Thomas Scrope. Even fresh out of prison, Buccleuch's power was undeniable. It charged the air around him in a way that made Scrope seem insignificant. The twinkle helped her understand why even his enemies treated him well.

"What did my father reply?" she asked.

"That he did not know where May was but suspected that she might have run away to her English kinsmen. He said they were her mother's people, and I suspect that he believed Lady Halliot might have helped spirit the lass away."

"I suspected the same," Laurie admitted.

"Aye, well, you know the woman. Perhaps she is capable

of such things, but we now know that Loder bribed the maid-servant and mayhap one of the castle guards as well. Then he snatched the poor lass right out of her bed."

A silence fell, and they rode without speaking for a time before Hugh said, "I've heard a rumor, sir, that you pledged to impose peace in the Borders. Is it too much to hope that the rumor is true?"

"You probably had that from Gil Scott of Hawkburne," Buccleuch said with a grin. "His father approves, but Gil's dead set against it. Thinks the area's whole economy depends on raiding. But I think it's time, and so I informed your queen."

"Doubtless, Her Majesty will be grateful," Hugh said.

Laurie detected no sarcasm in his tone, but she suspected that he did not believe Buccleuch would do as he said. "If you say that you will do it, you will, sir," she said, "but will Queen Elizabeth not think that she forced you to it?"

"She can think what she likes," Buccleuch said. "That woman still wants me to go to London to answer for what she chooses to call my outrageous crimes, and I'll have to go, I expect. Jamie will insist on it if she plagues him enough, so I mean to show her first that I can wield my power to her benefit and to that of all Britain."

"I'm willing to help by lifting my siege, since it's clear that most of the damage was Loder's and not the doing of Liddesdale men," Hugh said. "But I should warn you, sir, Scrope will do all he can to undermine your efforts."

"That pestilential malt worm! I'll shake his bones right out of his garments if he gets in my way. He is a disease that should be cut away."

"He ought to hang," Laurie said flatly. "He is as much to blame as Loder for May's death. He must have known that Loder had her."

"Aye, perhaps," Buccleuch said, "but I'll not demand his arrest, lass, for we cannot control who will succeed him. We'll render him powerless instead."

"But how?"

"Ah, well, I've a fair relationship with the other two English wardens now," he replied, shooting a grin at Hugh. "With Jamie's help, I think we can persuade Elizabeth to urge that scrofulous want-wit to turn most of his authority over to his deputies and to the other wardens."

"Scrope would never agree," Hugh said.

"I think we can persuade him," Buccleuch said, twinkling.

It was nearly dark by the time Hugh and Laurie returned to Brackengill, and when it loomed before her, much as it had the first time she saw it, Laurie realized how much she had come to love the castle. Every stick and stone of it seemed to welcome her. She even looked forward to seeing Lady Marjory.

Hugh left her in the inner bailey, murmuring that he would see to the horses. His face was drawn and his jaw clenched. She thought he looked tired.

She went inside alone to find the great hall unoccupied. Small fires crackled cheerfully in both fireplaces.

Wondering where Lady Marjory was, Laurie went in search of her, running her to earth in her bedchamber, dozing with a tambour frame in hand.

"Oh, thank heaven, my child," Lady Marjory exclaimed, casting aside the embroidery. "I have not known what to think. Where, oh, where have you been all this time? That Geordie told me someone told him that you were with Sir Hugh, but I knew that could not be so."

"But I have been, madam. We have been captives."

"Captives!" Lady Marjory clutched her breast.

"Yes, a henchman of Thomas Scrope's captured us whilst we were returning from Scotland to Brackengill."

"May God have mercy on all our souls! Scotland! Captured! But all this time? Surely, someone should have sent word to Brackengill, demanding a ransom or whatever it is that they do under such circumstances."

Laurie bit her lower lip, realizing that Lady Marjory had not known where she was for two full days. "It is a long story," she said at last. "I went in search of Hugh, you see, and—"

"Sir Hugh, my dear, even with me," Lady Marjory interjected.

"I went looking for him, and when I found him, he decided to bring me back to Brackengill himself. We had only just reached the English side of the line, though, when we were set upon and taken prisoner."

Lady Marjory clutched her bosom again. "Mercy!" she exclaimed. "And you believe that was the doing of Thomas Scrope? But that cannot be, for he is loyal to the Queen and serves as her warden here, which makes him nearly as powerful as the Queen, himself, so why would he capture one of his own loyal henchmen?"

"It was not Scrope who captured us, madam. It was Martin Loder."

"Martin Loder! But is that not the man your sister killed?" The look on Lady Marjory's face altered slightly. Her eyes narrowed suspiciously.

"I cannot blame you for doubting my sanity, madam, for 'tis surely a wild tale, but I assure you, Loder is alive. That is," she amended, "he was alive before Hugh killed . . . that is, before Loder died."

She went on to explain matters as well as she could. When she had finished, she could not be sure that Lady Marjory understood it all, but her ladyship clearly had grasped at least one important detail.

Clapping her hands together with childish delight, she exclaimed, "Then if Martin Loder confessed to the raids, not to mention if he was alive all that time and not murdered, and if your sister has been found, no one will continue to insist any longer that you are Sir Hugh's hostage and not his proper wife. How very much more comfortable *that* will be for all of us!"

"Yes . . . yes, I expect it will," Laurie said, wondering why the light seemed to have gone out of the day. "I need no longer be his hostage."

"Yes, dear, that is what I just said, and it is such a relief, is it not? But you look chilled. Shall I send someone to fetch you some hot-spiced ale or claret, or perhaps some nourishing soup? Or are you hungry enough to drink some soup? But, of course, you must be hungry if you have not eaten in all this time," she went on, paying no heed to Laurie's silence. "And Sir Hugh will be ravenous. Gentlemen are always starving after a good set-to with an enemy. What have I been thinking just to be sitting here like a block?"

Leaping to her feet, she shook out her skirts, adding, "I shall soon stir them to action in the kitchen, I promise you. Not that Meggie and her Nan won't have kept something warm from the household supper, for I warrant they have, because I told them to do so yesterday when I thought you had merely stayed out late, riding with Meggie's Andrew.

"I will just go along and tell them that everything must be prepared to Sir Hugh's most exacting taste," she went on. "I know that they will be glad to learn that he is at home again. When I have spoken to them, I shall come to your room to be sure you have all you require to dress for supper. You will be wanting to change out of those dreadful clothes, and whilst I am sure that Rose girl you hired to attend you means well enough, I am not by any means certain that . . ."

Laurie let the flow of words pass over her until Lady Marjory had run out of things to say and had hurried off to the kitchen. Then, alone at last, she stood for a long moment, contemplating the unwelcome fact that her days as a hostage were over. She could now leave Brackengill forever. She was still handfasted to Hugh, of course, but since the handfasting had been no more than a way of making it acceptable for her to stand hostage for May, no one would expect her to remain with him for the full year and a day, and thanks to Providence, she was still a maiden. If she agreed to endure an examination, he would not even have to pay the *tocher*. He could just take her home to Aylewood, and he had already promised to do that.

Her feet felt heavy as she made her way to her bedchamber.

She would change out of her filthy clothes and ask Rose to begin packing her things.

Tears pricked her eyes, and she brushed them away, but her throat ached, too, and she could not brush the ache away with a gesture.

Surely, she told herself, her depression was just an emotional reaction to all that had happened in the past two days and was perfectly normal. It stemmed from finding May safe, then seeing her fall dead, and learning that Martin Loder was still alive. It grew from looking death in the face and then making it through the ordeal unscathed after seeing others die, and from hearing Buccleuch so casually declare that he had decided to impose peace in the Borders at last.

It had nothing to do with the thought of leaving Brackengill—and Hugh.

Tears trickled down her cheeks, and this time she did not brush them away. She had reached her bedchamber and, pushing open the door, found it dark and blessedly empty. Closing the door behind her, she went to the window and looked out toward Bewcastle Waste.

Stars twinkled overhead and reflected faintly in the sparkling, foamy water of two nearby burns, but otherwise she could see little besides the dark, curving line of the distant fells. Cool air touched her cheeks, and to keep other thoughts at bay, she tried to visualize the hills at her favorite time of day, when the sun was low, shooting golden rays straight at the fells, turning them and the Cheviots beyond them to burnished gold.

Though she resisted, her thoughts refused to comply with her wishes. She seemed able to think only that she was free to go home, and knowing that, she felt as if she had been suddenly trapped into leaving Brackengill. Hugh would be glad to be rid of her, though. Doubtless, he would want to dance with the joy of it. The trickle of tears grew to a flood when she found it easy to imagine him dancing.

"What's wrong with me?" she muttered to the ambient air. Realizing that Rose would come in at any moment, she struggled to control her emotions, to think of anything but the fact that she was now free to leave. Taking a deep breath, she scolded herself. Then, finding cold water in the ewer on the washstand, she splashed some on her face. She was being a fool.

The plain fact was that she did not want to leave, and this time it would do no good simply to wait and see what would happen. What would happen was that Hugh would take her back to Aylewood, to her family. If she wanted to stay, she would have to tell him herself and face the consequences. Just hoping that he would be sad to see her go, or that he would ask her to stay, would get her nowhere.

Accordingly, she dried her face with the towel, found flint and tinder to light a small fire and candles, then hurried to the clothes press to decide what to wear. When Rose arrived, if she noted signs of her mistress's tears, she did not speak of them, moving quickly instead to obey Laurie's commands.

An order to the kitchens brought hot water for the tub, and while they waited, Rose brushed the tangles and doubtless a few other oddments from Laurie's hair.

"It looks better, mistress, but it sadly wants a washing," the maidservant said quietly when she had finished.

"Not now," Laurie said. "It would take too long to dry. Just pin it up under a lace cap, Rose, whilst I bathe. You can dress it more carefully afterward."

Bathing quickly, she dressed quickly, too, but when she was ready, she hesitated, turning back at the door to say quietly, "Thank you, Rose."

Rose smiled. "Ye look gey beautiful, mistress. That blue gown becomes ye. None could guess that ye'd been a prisoner in a dungeon these past days."

Laurie thanked her again and told herself that the compliment should make her feel more confident. It failed dismally, however, and the weight of her steps made it seem as if she wore shoes made of lead.

She did not want to face Hugh, yet she wanted to know if he felt as she did. The fact was, however, that she feared he did not. It would be easier, in that case, simply to disappear from Brackengill without seeing him. A fleeting image stirred of Hugh on horseback, galloping after her, determined to bring her back. Gratifying though the image was, she knew she could not count on it. Even if he wanted her, he was as likely to respect her decision and say nothing to talk her out of it. If she wanted to know the truth, she would have to confront him again and ask him to speak his feelings aloud. But she had confronted him before, and she had confronted Martin Loder. Why, then, did this seem so difficult?

Just the thought of it chilled her blood. Much as she wished she were Laurie the Bold, she knew now that she never would be. Laurie the Timid—no, that wasn't right either. She had done some brave things. She had even done some good things, although she had not thought of them as brave or good at the time. They had just been things that needed doing. That was all.

"Well," she murmured as she entered the hall, "this needs doing also."

To her consternation, the only ones there were servants preparing tables for supper. Stopping one, she said, "Where shall I find Sir Hugh?"

"He be out in the yard, mistress."

"Thank you." Hurrying outside, she scanned the busy yard for his tall figure, hoping fervently that he had not ridden off again on some errand or other. Now that she had made up her mind to speak to him, she wanted to do so at once.

"Laura, my dear, there you are." Lady Marjory's voice sounded from the steps behind her. "I have been looking for you!"

Laurie turned impatiently. "What is it, madam?"

"Why, I went to your bedchamber to assist you with your dressing, as I said I would, but I found only that Rose girl within. She said you had come down to supper, and here you are."

"As you see," Laurie said.

"But you should not have come outside, my dear, for it is dark. Moreover, the yard is dusty and the wind is blowing.

"The wind always blows here," Laurie said. "As you can see, I do not require assistance. I came outside because I wish to speak with Hugh."

"*Sir* Hugh, my dear," Lady Marjory said with an arch look.

Laurie pressed her lips together, trapping words that begged to be spoken. Her hands clenched at her sides.

When a large, warm hand grasped her shoulder, she realized that the arch look on Lady Marjory's face was not directed at her but at Hugh. She relaxed when he said, "My wife surely is entitled to name me as she chooses, Aunt."

Lady Marjory made a graceful curtsy. "It must be as you wish, of course, my dear sir. Pray, do take her indoors, though. One cannot doubt that she needs rest after her ordeal and should not be tiring herself in this way."

"I will attend to her," Hugh said quietly.

"Shall we all go back inside, then? I warrant the servants will have our supper laid very quickly now."

"Please, sir, I want to talk to you," Laurie said in an undertone.

"And I, to you," he said, adding in a louder voice, "Tell them we will be along directly, madam. I know that you must be hungry, so they may serve you when they are ready. If we have not returned, you must begin without us."

"But I took my supper at the usual time," Lady Marjory protested. She added with an indulgent smile, "I shall send a lad to fetch you when they put the food out, if you will but tell me where he is likely to find you."

"Tell him to look in the little chamber near the kitchen that I use as an office," Hugh advised her.

She nodded cheerfully and bustled back inside.

As soon as she had disappeared, Hugh said, "This way, lass."

"But this is not the way to the wee chamber," Laurie protested when he led her through the postern door, past Meggie and the children, and up the spiral stair.

"No, this is the way to my bedchamber," he said with a mischievous grin. "I was just coming to look for you. Why were you looking for me?"

With a nervous smile, she hedged, saying, "I . . . I expect that you must have begun to make the arrangements for taking me back to Aylewood."

"I know that you want to return straightaway," he said.

Wanting to kick herself, Laurie said nothing more as she preceded him up the stairway to his bedchamber. She had already said more than enough, babbling like an idiot, and now he thought that she wanted to return to her family for good.

When he reached past her to open the bedchamber door, his arm brushed her shoulder, and she gasped at the jolt of yearning that shot through her. More than anything, she wished that she had the courage to turn and fling her arms around him. Instead, she walked into the tidy bedchamber, still silent but with her whole body tingling its awareness of his presence behind her.

She heard the snap of the bolt as it shot home.

After a momentary silence, he said gently, "Laurie, look at me. I cannot talk to your back."

Turning slowly, forcing her gaze to meet his, she said, "I suppose you will be glad to take me back to my father."

"Is that what you wanted to say, that you want to return to your father?"

She swallowed. His tone was so even, his countenance unreadable. Surely, if he wanted her to stay, she would see it in his eyes, in his expression.

Quietly, she said, "The sooner I return, the better, I suppose. If I submit to an examination, you will not even have to pay the *tocher.*"

"If I pay it, you will not have to submit to an examination."

"I . . . I do not mind," she said, knowing she was lying and that he probably knew it as well as she did. Remembering his warning about lies, she added hastily, "It is not fair that you should have to pay for something that you did not get."

"It is not right for you to have to submit to an examination."

Amanda Scott

"Naught else would satisfy my stepmother. Nor would it satisfy my father, for that matter, or any potential husband."

He frowned. "The money would satisfy them all, lass. Is that why you were looking for me, to discuss the arrangements?"

"Is that not why you were looking for me?"

He did not reply. He simply looked at her.

Suddenly furious with herself, she blurted, "I don't want to go back to them, Hugh . . . that is, I do but only for May's funeral. Can you possibly . . . That is, would you consider . . . ?"

When she could not continue, he said gently, "I'll not only consider it, lassie, I was going to insist on it. Come here to me, sweetheart."

When he held his arms wide, she flung herself into them, sighing with relief when they closed around her.

He pulled off her cap and she felt his warm breath stirring her hair when he murmured, "I was in the yard because I was sending lads to Bewcastle. Nixon's got his own parson, and I want the fellow to marry us properly at once."

"Really?"

"Aye, I told them that if he's away, they must ride after him and bring him back. I don't care if they find him in Carlisle or Berwick, Edinburgh or London, just so they find him and fetch him here to me before we leave for Aylewood. Does that sound like I want to leave you with your family, lass?"

"But you said—"

"You'll not fling my own words back in my teeth every time we have an argument, will you?"

She looked up into his face. "Will we have arguments?"

"Aye, I'm an argumentative man. Best you accept that from the start."

She cocked her head. "It takes two to argue, and I do not like it."

"Nay, lass, but you'll learn. I have already detected a grievous potential."

"Have you, indeed, sir?"

"Aye." He grinned at her. "I won't let you run away from it, either. You'll have to stay and fight."

"Do you really want me to stay?"

In answer, he put one hand under her chin, tilting her head up. Then he kissed her on the lips. He was gentle at first, then demanding, and her body leapt in response. When his hand moved from her chin to her breast, stroking lightly, she melted against him with a little moan of pleasure.

A moment later, still kissing her, he scooped her up into his arms. Only when she realized where he was headed did she protest.

"What are you doing?"

"Claiming my rights as your husband," he said gently. "If you're going to object, you'd best do so quickly, so we can argue about it first if we must."

"You sound as if you are certain that you will win such an argument."

"Will I not? Don't forget that I am legally your husband. I have the law on my side, sweetheart."

Overwhelmed by a wave of desire, she could not think clearly. Grasping at straws, she said, "But it's suppertime!"

"The lads will get theirs and nobody else will miss us. I'm hungry for you, lassie. I've wanted to taste your treasures these several weeks past. I'll not force you, but 'tis my right, and if you mean to stay, we have no reason to delay."

"You need not persuade me," Laurie said. "If you are certain that no one will disturb us, I have no objection."

He needed no further encouragement, pausing only long enough to help her remove her clothing and to remove his own. Any shyness she felt vanished in the face of his visible approval of her body, and his caresses soon stirred a passion in her to match his own.

"Your skin is so soft that I want to kiss every inch of you," he said moments later, suiting action to words.

She had thought that his caresses had already taken her into realms of passion as great as any woman could ever want to know, but she soon realized her error. Even her dream had not come close. She realized, too, that she could stimulate him, too, and she delighted in his sighs and groans of pleasure.

A sharp pounding on the door turned passion to consternation.

Hugh's man, Thaddeus, shouted, "Master, be ye in there? We canna find the mistress, and Lady Marjory be sore afeard that summat ha' become o' her. Be ye sick, Sir Hugh?"

Lady Marjory's anxious voice came next. "I knew you might catch a chill, my dear sir, out as late as you both were. Perhaps you will allow me to stir up a tisane as a preventative, before you fall ill from a catarrh or worse."

Hugh threw off the covers and got out of bed.

Seeing him stride toward the door, Laurie snatched the covers back up to her chin, stifling an urge to cover her head as well.

Realizing that he had given no thought to his appearance and was reaching to open the door, she said between tears and laughter, "Hugh, you're stark naked!"

Ignoring her, Hugh shot back the bolt and yanked open the door. "What the devil do you mean, pounding on my door like that?" he roared.

An eldritch shriek echoed through the stairway, followed by the sound of heels retreating rapidly down the stone steps.

Thaddeus said apologetically, "I expect I ought to have warned her ladyship that ye might answer the door wi'out thinking o' your appearance, sir."

Without bothering to reply, Hugh shut the door in his face and turned, his eyes twinkling with unholy glee. "That'll teach her," he said. "Now, where was I?"

When he found his place again, Laurie's laughter turned to gasps of pleasure.

Dear Reader,

I hope you enjoyed *Border Storm*. Once again, inspiration for the story came partially from reading Border ballads and partially from my interest in my family's genealogy. The plot is based on the following three ballads: "The False Sir John," also called "The Elf King," and "Isaac-a-Bell & Hugh the Graeme," both in *The English & Scottish Popular Ballads*, edited by Francis James Child (New York, 1965), and *Lock the Door, Larriston* by James Hogg, 1797, from the version in *Scottish Border Battles & Ballads*, edited by Michael Brander (New York, 1976).

The wheel-lock pistol was common in the Borders as early as the first half of the sixteenth century. Interestingly, it is thought to have been invented by Leonardo da Vinci, the great Italian artist and engineer. The wheel-lock worked on the principle of a modern cigarette lighter. A wheel with a rough edge revolving very fast against a piece of stone created the spark to light the powder. Instead of flint, however, a softer stone, iron pyrites, was used. For more information on the wheel-lock and other weapons of this period, see *English Weapons and Warfare, 449–1660*, by A.V. B. Norman and Don Pottinger (London, 1966).

Sincerely,

Amanda Scott

The Queen of Romance
Cassie Edwards